The
Adversaries

DAVID HAIR
The Adversaries

THE RETURN OF RAVANA
Book I I

Jo Fletcher
BOOKS

A version of this novel was first published as The Ghost Bride in India in 2011 by Penguin India
First published in Great Britain in 2016 by

Jo Fletcher Books
an imprint of
Quercus Editions Ltd
Carmelite House
50 Victoria Embankment
London EC4Y 0DZ

An Hachette UK company

A CIP catalogue record for this book is available
from the British Library

PB ISBN 978 0 85705 361 9
EBOOK ISBN 978 1 78429 081 8

10 9 8 7 6 5 4 3 2 1

Typeset by Jouve (UK), Milton Keynes
Printed and bound in Great Britain by Clays Ltd, St Ives plc

This book is dedicated to:
Sudeshna Shome Ghosh, for all her work in
bringing the original version of this series to life.

Contents

PART TWO: THE HEART OF BATTLE

PROLOGUE

Fallen King

Jodhpur, Rajasthan, April 2010

Fire, burning underwater, consuming flesh that is neither immortal nor wholly mortal.

Ravindra jerked back to consciousness to find the body he inhabited being consumed by a slow, intense tongue of flame, even though he was immersed in the underground stream. The water, frigid and slow, couldn't numb the agony nor quench the fire smouldering in his flesh. In the pitch-black tunnel of water that tumbled him deeper into the darkness, the only visible thing was that growing ring of crimson.

He wrenched the arrow from his flesh, howling soundlessly, and as the last bubble of air left his lungs, they filled with water, a suffocating flood. At last the shaft burned out and was washed from his hand, but the fires in his flesh continued to burn, the pain so excruciating that he almost allowed himself to sink to the bottom and lie there until the disintegrating flesh shook his soul free. Then he remembered this body was just a cloak, one of dozens he'd worn over the centuries.

But to lose it meant weeks or months, maybe even years as a disembodied spirit, before he could find the right body and insinuate himself into his unwitting new host, and time was suddenly precious.

My Enemy is alive! Our thousand-year-old war has begun again and there can be no rest! He kicked out until his flailing feet found purchase on the stony riverbed and he pushed off, half swimming, half walking, tugged along by the currents of the underground stream. Finally, his head broke the surface. His clothing was burned away and his skin was seared black, this body charred past usefulness. His sword was gone and his five queens dissipated; they wouldn't be able to re-form for months. He was utterly alone, and not even sure if there was any way out of this hidden warren beneath the Mehrangarh Fortress in Jodhpur.

But I am not dead yet . . . and what is death to me, anyway?

However deep his physical pain went, humiliation burned him deeper. Never before had his Enemy defeated him: Ravindra had *always* watched Aram Dhoop die, and not just the poet, but those others so intimately part of their centuries-old tale. *Shastri! Darya!* How many times had he killed them? How many more times would he have to destroy the three of them before he finally reincarnated as a god?

'Aram Dhoop: I am not finished!' he screamed at the blackness, the echoes mocking him, throbbing in the confined space. No one heard. Unbelievably, his enemies had got the better of him – *this* time. In all their many encounters, more than a dozen previous incarnations through the centuries, only once had the souls of Aram Dhoop and Madan Shastri come even close to defeating him. But this new encounter felt different: the girl Darya was here too, but this time, even the ghost of Padma was lurking. Everything was aligning: so many old faces returning, souls he had all but forgotten.

This life is to be the one! he told himself. *This is the final life, the one that will unravel all the tangled skeins of those desperate days in ancient Mandore.*

That thought goaded him, lending him energy and purpose, and he swam forward until the tunnel of water opened into a chamber of stone with a pocket of air below the surface – in the darkness he could just make out a small rocky bank ahead. In past lives he'd explored these caverns, but intriguingly, this was not a place he'd ever been before. Then his foot brushed against something that wasn't stone. He reached down and gripped a stick . . . no, not a stick, a *bone*.

His head emerged from the water and he held up the bone, whispering a word to kindle in his other hand a faint purple-blue light that lit the chamber, making the roof a few feet above glisten. Even using this sliver of power threatened to rip his consciousness away – he quickly examined the bone, then looked around; more were scattered all about the chamber, washed up amidst other debris. There were cracks in the walls here, and the air was moving. In a surge of hope he rose from the stream.

As soon as it left the water, his shoulder burst into flame and he howled in agony and fury. Rage filled him, and shame, that Aram Dhoop could have lit this fire in his sacred flesh. He felt the touch of fear too: in this life, Aram had mastered the Agniyastra, the fire-arrow – how was that possible? And what else had he remembered?

He staggered and fell to his knees amidst the pile of bones. He knew at once that these must be the remains of Senapati Madan Shastri and Queen Darya. He rummaged among the bones, smashing these disintegrating sticks into pieces – until something moved, glittering, within the pile of detritus. He reached in and grasped a smoky crystal about the size of a baby's fist and a thrill of recognition ameliorated the shattering pain for a second. It was a heart-stone, the one he himself had given to Darya back in old Mandore: a crystal that was intimately tied to her very being.

He'd been searching for it through so many lives, and never before found it. His hand was shaking as he gripped it, his mind trying to reach past the pain to the possibilities . . .

This discovery could turn *everything* in his favour; he could use it to bring down his enemies – as he always had and always would – but this time he might finally unlock the clues and find a way to right everything that had gone wrong a thousand years ago.

Clutching the gem, he crawled back to the water and let the icy flow abate the burning of his body. There had to be a way out . . .

Almost six months later, as darkness fell over Rajasthan, a black Mercedes purred to a stop in the car park beneath the Mehrangarh Fortress. The lights of Jodhpur glittered below; the civic buildings and clock-tower glowed in the night. Traffic bustled, bells tolled, horns honked and birds squalled, the racket softened by distance. Two hard-faced men emerged from the front seats and peered about warily, then one opened the back door of the limousine and a tall, dark-skinned man got out.

He was an impressive figure, with curling black hair that fell past his collar and a flowing moustache. His Armani jacket was impeccably cut to conceal the handgun in a shoulder holster. Narrowed eyes pierced the gloom; he nodded curtly to the bodyguards and strode away across the steep, uneven terrain beneath the towering walls of the fortress. The bodyguards knew better than to follow him. His name was Shiv Bakli, though the Mumbai underworld knew him better as 'The Cobra'.

Shiv Bakli now called himself a different name, an older one: Ravindra.

It took Ravindra several minutes to find the place: a tiny crevice in the slope barely large enough for a child to crawl through.

He shuddered, remembering the superhuman effort it had taken to break out, pushing through with his shoulder ablaze and only minutes to live, and his hurried efforts to conceal his treasure before that body disintegrated into ash.

From within the crevice, he felt a cold regard: a snake had found the hole and made a home. He saluted it silently and walked a few paces down the slope. A dark smear on the rocks, barely discernible in the darkness, was all that remained of his previous body. He crouched beside a rock of distinctive shape and heaved it over, as he had that night.

He reached in a hand and felt something pulsing gently. He pulled it out and held it once again: the heart-stone of Queen Darya, a gleaming smoky crystal. He couldn't resist sending a chill message of hatred and malice through it.

I am coming, little queen. There is nowhere you can hide.

Hundreds of miles away, in the kitchen in a block of apartments in Delhi, Deepika Choudhary felt a sudden debilitating tremor rip through her. The plates she was carrying crashed to the floor and she collapsed amidst the shards.

In his tiny Mumbai student dormitory, Vikram Khandavani heard his mobile ring as he stepped out of the shower. He wrapped a towel around his waist, examined the name and number on the display and answered. 'Hey, Amanjit!'

'Hey.' Amanjit's voice was taut with stress. 'Vik, Dee's in hospital.'

Vikram sank onto his bed, his legs going weak. 'What?'

Amanjit hurriedly explained how his fiancée had collapsed in the kitchen. 'Her folks have taken her to see the doctors. I'm minding the house, 'cos I've got to go to work shortly – they've called me already; she's not in danger.' He paused and then, his voice low, asked, 'You don't think it's all beginning again, do you?'

'Yeah. I think maybe it is.' Vikram rubbed at his face tiredly. 'Perhaps I shouldn't go on this telly swayamvara thing after all?'

The line fell silent for a few seconds, then Amanjit said, 'No, you should do it. If you're right and this is tied to the *Ramayana* – and we know there's a *big* swayamvara in that! – then we've got to see it through. We don't have a choice, anyway – it's all going to happen whatever we do. You've got to do it, Vik!'

The newspapers and television had been full of nothing else for months: Sunita Ashoka, Bollywood dream-queen, had decided to offer her hand in marriage to the winner of a game show based on the old-fashioned idea of the swayamvara: a contest between potential bridegrooms, like when the demi-god Rama won his bride Sita.

After what had happened in March, when they'd worked out their lives appeared to be echoing the old Vedic epic, Vikram had been especially wary of – and drawn to – such coincidences, so last week he'd joined millions of other young Indian men and sent off his application. Now he sighed. 'Yeah, I know – I do think Sunita is important. I'm thinking she might be the reincarnation of one of Ravindra's six queens – Padma, maybe. But what if it brings Ravindra down on us? We're not ready!'

'Then it's on us to *be* ready, bhai,' Amanjit said. 'And don't forget, Rama *wins* in the *Ramayana*! So all we have to do is follow the story and we'll win too – I'm sure of it!'

'I've told you before, I'm not Rama – and let's not forget that in every other life I remember, Ravindra has won. In *every* one of them!'

'Yeah, but how many have involved a swayamvara?' Something chimed in the background and Amanjit cursed. 'Damn, that's the doorbell; gotta go. Think about it, Vik: in how many other lives have you been involved in a swayamvara?' But he didn't wait for an answer. 'Bye!'

'Yeah, bye. Love to Deepika. Bye!' Vikram lay back, his wet body soaking the sheet, his mind far away, thinking about another time and another place, and how that swayamvara had turned out in the end . . .

PART ONE

A BATTLE OF HEARTS

CHAPTER ONE

The Blindfolded Archer

Vishwamitra's Gurukul, Rajputana, 1161

The bow sang, an arrow swished through the chamber, struck a wall and snapped before clattering to the floor. The young man in the centre of the shadowy chamber cursed, but the ancient man beside the door merely sighed. 'Again, my prince,' he said, in a dusty voice.

The archer bowed his head, nocked another arrow by touch – he had a cloth tied about his eyes – and half-drew the bow. The old man signalled to the only other person in the chamber, a small figure who padded from behind a pillar, hammer in hand. Dusty shafts of light pierced the gloom and refracted off the gongs hanging at the four points of the compass, each at a different height. At the signal from the old man, the small youth with the hammer reached out and chimed the northern gong, then darted behind the pillar. The arrows were round-tipped, but still dangerous at close range.

The archer's arms flexed as he turned, drew and fired in one fluid motion. The arrow slammed into the gong, denting it as it chimed. The archer whooped joyously, wrenching off the blindfold. '*A hit!*' he shouted, beaming expectantly. 'I got it!'

The ancient one bowed. 'You did indeed, my prince. A fine shot. Each day you strike the target more often.'

'That was amazing, Prithvi,' the youth with the gong-hammer exclaimed. 'You'll be the greatest known archer in the world.' He was a skinny boy with a serious face and big, luminous eyes. His clothes, the prince's hand-me-downs, were worn and ill-fitting, and his hardened hands were chapped and callused.

The young prince smiled triumphantly and his eyes strayed to the door where the light was growing fainter by the second. 'The sun is going down, Guru-ji – and I'm starving! May I go?'

'You may, my prince. You've worked hard today. But remember, you're expected by the swordmaster at dawn tomorrow. No drinking tonight! No sore heads.'

Prithvi laughed. He was a big-boned youth with an open face, the beginnings of a moustache already showing on his upper lip. 'Don't worry about the drink, Guru-ji. I can handle it! Come on, Chand!' he added to the smaller boy. 'I'll race you to our rooms!'

'I'm afraid not,' the guru said. 'Chand must remain a while longer. I oversee his learning too, and unlike you, his progress is not so swift.'

The prince frowned at being thwarted, then leaned the bow and quiver against a pillar, draping the blindfold over them. 'I'll get us some food, Chand. Don't be too long!' He turned back to the guru. 'I don't know why you drill him so hard on weapons, Guru-ji. He's only a poet.'

'That's for me to decide, my prince,' the guru replied evenly. 'Now run along.'

Once the slap of Prithvi's sandals had faded into the distance, the guru turned to the smaller boy. 'So, Chand, are you ready? Prepare!'

The slim youth draped the quiver about his shoulder, took up the bow, then allowed the old teacher to tie his blindfold. 'Need I walk you into position?' the old man asked.

Chand shook his head as he turned and strode unhesitatingly to the middle of the chamber. He nocked an arrow and went completely still. The old man paced about the room, once, twice, thrice, and then tapped the eastern gong. He didn't bother to step behind a pillar.

Chand whirled towards the east. His lips fluttered as he released and the arrow ignited as it flew. It struck the gong and burst like a ball of fire, blackening the metal. A heartbeat later his second arrow flew towards the silent southern gong, hung a foot lower than the eastern one. It struck dead centre and remained stuck there, burning. The third sheared off one of the chains holding the western target so that it swung and struck a pillar with a crash. Despite that distraction, the fourth flew true, punching a fist-sized hole through the northern gong before exploding against the stone wall behind.

'You've ruined another one,' the guru remarked, eyeing the northern gong. 'They don't come free, you know,' he added.

Chand pulled off his blindfold and glared at the western gong, hanging by the single chain. 'I missed one again,' he muttered. 'I always miss one of the four.'

'I've never heard of anyone like you, Chand. You are the finest master of *shabd bhedi baan vidya* I've ever taught. When it comes to the art of shooting blind you are kin to Rama, I swear. Perfection will come.'

'Yes, Master, it will,' Chand replied. 'But I still don't know why you won't let me show my real ability. Why should Prithvi have all the praise when I am the more skilled?'

'Because he is a prince, Chand. If you are to be his friend, then you may not exceed him in any matter, least of all one that is important to him. He tolerates you bettering him at poetry because he values it little. The arts of war are too dear to him. If you wish for his friendship, then you must not ever be seen to exceed him in such skills.'

'But it just feeds his ego, Guru-ji – surely a prince should also know humility?'

'In a perfect world, yes, but this world is imperfect. Princes become rajas, and rajas must be the acknowledged betters of their rivals, especially in battle. These are troubled times, Chand. The Rajput kings are always at war, and now the Mohammedans are flexing their muscles in the northwest. There will come a time when they will look this way and then we will need a great king, a true maharaja, to lead us against them. We will need Prithvi to be strong and unclouded by doubts.'

'But how can I help him when he doesn't know what I'm capable of?'

'By using your skills in secret, and being his loyal friend. Let him be the greatest *known* archer in the world – you will be the greatest *unknown* one. The hidden weapon is oft times more dangerous than the visible one.' The guru cupped the boy's chin and lifted his face. 'Are you his loyal friend, Chand?'

'Of course, Guru-ji. I am loyal to Prithvi for ever.'

He answered with such fervour that the ancient teacher could not help but smile. 'Then put aside your complaint. You will gain enough recognition, I'm sure. Let the whole world know that the friendship of Chand Rathod of Kannauj and Prithvi Chauhan of Ajmer is as strong a bond as that between Rama and Lakshmana and people will remember your names for ever: surely that is fame enough?'

The ashram was called Gurukul, and the princes and courtiers of the Chauhamanas, greatest of the royal dynasties of the Rajput tribes, had been coming here for generations to learn at the feet of its legendary teachers. All the vital skills of the warrior-prince were taught here: war and weapons, the equally deadly ways of politics, and the skills of art and literature. Prince Prithvi Chauhan was the third and youngest son of Someshwar Chauhan, lord of the Chauhamanas clan, King of Ajmer and Dilli. No successor had yet been named, but Prithvi was already seen as the prince with the greatest promise. His prowess could secure his succession – and in this world where kin fought tooth and claw for thrones, a lack thereof could cost him his life. Though he was only twelve, he was big for his age and could not only out-wrestle and out-fence all the other young men in the ashram, he was also acknowledged as the greatest archer of them all.

All except for – though he didn't know it – his best friend Chand.

Chand was a distant cousin, the poor son of a poor branch of the Rathod family, of the rival Gahadavalas clan. Chand was barely eligible to attend the Gurukul, and then only as a scholar – he was far too small to be a warrior. But Prithvi, perhaps because there was no rivalry between them, had befriended the skinny boy and protected him, and they were soon spending all their free time together. Prithvi was generous, and though quick-tempered and impetuous, he was swift to forgive and forget. They learned together, laughed together, minded each other's backs against jealous rivals and false friends, and forged a bond even closer than brothers, for in the courts of Rajputana, brothers were often deadly rivals. And it was never forgotten that Prithvi led and Chand followed.

They had been together at the Gurukul for six years; their time there was coming to an end.

On his last night, Chand was taken to the temple at the heart of the Gurukul. It wasn't a grand place made of white marble and glittering gold, nor did it bustle with worshippers like the temples in the town below the ashram. It was very, very old, and in truth, rather dingy, the smell of decay never quite masked by the incense.

Watching Guru-ji walk away, Chand found himself filled with trepidation. His final test, if that was what it was, was to keep vigil all night and experience what visions and dreams might come. The previous night had been Prithvi's turn – he'd claimed to have seen a vision of himself as maharaja, but afterwards he'd confessed to Chand that he'd fallen asleep and had no such dream at all. He'd been amused by the whole thing.

Nothing supernatural would dare *happen to Prithvi*, Chand thought, *but I've always had strange dreams* . . . He wasn't nervous because he was afraid of visions, though: what he feared was the morning, when he and Prithvi would go to Ajmer. The warband had arrived that week to escort the prince home to his father's court – and Chand was to learn at the feet of Jindas, the court poet. Guru-ji had warned them of courtly intrigues that would test their friendship to the limits and they'd sworn loyalty to each other, over and again, a multitude of oaths and promises. But he was still afraid.

He began his vigil sitting cross-legged in front of the shrine in the circular inner sanctum, which was barely ten yards across. There were three idols, which had been painted with ochre so often the features could barely be discerned. Shiva was on Chand's left: god of death and rebirth, lord of dance, a guide for one who searched. To Chand's right was the image of Vishnu, the law-bringer, protector and warrior, mankind's champion. 'All men find their balance between these two,' Guru-ji had told them, 'between the extremes of passion and calm. Seek your own balancing point, venerate both and live in harmony.' Prithvi always tended towards Shiva, so Guru-ji made him spend more time meditating upon Vishnu. Chand, drawn to Vishnu, was commanded to think often on Shiva.

Before him, halfway between the two male gods, was Durga, the female force: she who rides the tiger, who tends, protects and intercedes, she who bears and nurtures the child. 'She divides them, but she also draws them together,' Guru-ji had told them. 'Do not underestimate the women of the court. They have it in them to make you whole – or to rip you apart.'

Chand didn't really understand that; he hadn't seen a woman since he came here as a child. He shivered slightly at the fierce expression on Durga's face.

Prithvi liked to make jokes about girls these days. He would be married soon, no doubt, to some princess of Rajputana. Chand too would be given a bride when he went to court, which wasn't something he was looking forward to.

The early hours of his vigil were measured in the slow crawl of moonlight across the walls and floor of the shrine. The full moon was riding towards its zenith; soon it would light where he waited. That was the time when the visions would come, Guru-ji had said, if they came at all. As he waited, breathing in the faint residue of incense and the damp coldness of the night air, feeling the chill creep into his skin, an ache in his back and joints made him feel like an old man. His breath steamed and he closed his eyes. Far away in the valley, birds squabbled, disturbed in their perches by some night thing. A bell tinkled, cattle lowed and went quiet. He drifted.

Something exhaled in his face. He jerked awake, and found himself still in the temple, cross-legged in the moonlight, alone.

Not alone.

A young woman sat opposite him, her hair tangled, her eyes tawny and wild. Her clothes were ragged and she smelled – no, she *stank* – of sweat and musk. Her irises were shaped like crescent moons and her nails were long. Her frigid breath sent a chill through him.

He could see the statue of Durga through her body.

He stopped breathing as she reached out, slowly, inexorably, and touched the middle of his forehead. '*Wake up, Chand Rathod.*' Her voice was like a snake's. He jerked backwards and sprawled on his back, twitching, utterly terrified. Then she was upon him, her body pressing his down with the weight of an avalanche. He opened his mouth to scream but nothing came. Her hands gripped his temples and icy knives stabbed into his head. The ground was falling away as images flooded his mind. He spun, her eyes boring into his, filling his sight, until they were all and everything—

The visions began, but they weren't visions at all . . . they were *memories* . . .

. . . of him, reciting poems to a dreadful king, trembling, knowing one slip would mean his end . . . a tall, muscular captain clasping his shoulder . . . a young woman in a torn gown with a bow in her hands . . . a queen screaming as flames engulfed her while a lush beauty standing beside her laughed in glee as she too burned. Then darkness . . .

. . . as a peasant, Bhagwan, scrabbling for life in a dreadfully poor village, watching as a troop of mercenaries ride through, shoving captives before them. Their leader turns and glares at him with his one eye, and a whip snakes out. He howls in pain . . .

. . . which becomes a mourning cry as he is another man, chanting the death-prayers of a girl who was meant to have been his wife, though she died before he ever met her. He reaches out to her dead face curiously . . .

. . . and she opens her eyes, only it isn't her, it's a tangle-haired madwoman who follows him through the streets of a city, calling a name that isn't his, yet is. When he turns to confront her she's gone, and thugs with cudgels and knives close in. A blade flashes . . . He gasps, clutching his chest . . .

There was worse, and over and over again, and throughout it all, one face presided: one set of eyes, one being. His Enemy.

Ravindra.

The next morning Chand wondered why he had been so scared of such mundane things as court intrigues and petty politics, when there was so much more in the world to fear.

Guru-ji woke him as sunlight crept across the shrine. 'Chand – Chand, wake up!' Then more gently, 'You're safe, now. You're safe.'

Chand ignored his old master. He knew that he would never be safe again.

'They were visions of past lives,' he told Guru-ji later. He was lying on a low bed and the old man was squatting at his side, his lined face drawn with worry. Chand's vision had left him feverish and ill; he'd been lying there for two hours now, still shaking, semi-delirious. His bedclothes were damp and stinking of sweat, his own, and that of the ghostly woman from his visions – he could not purge her animal reek from his nostrils, no matter how he tried.

'How can you know that, Chand? Perhaps they were just delusions, brought on by exhaustion and cold? They probably meant nothing.' The old man didn't sound certain. Chand had never heard uncertainty in Guru-ji's voice before.

'Past lives,' he repeated. 'I know this.'

'Then who is this "Ravindra"? I don't know the name.'

'He was a king, in Mandore, maybe three hundred years ago . . . and then he was a mercenary captain who flayed me to death sixty years later. And a century later, a thug who beat and mutilated me. He is my *Enemy*. In my last life, he rode me down on a battlefield. I escaped him in Mandore, but he has destroyed me in my three subsequent lives and he is out there somewhere, waiting for me again. I know this.' He gripped his teacher's arm. '*He can't die!*'

Guru-ji's face held none of the comprehension that Chand desperately wanted to see. *He thinks I'm raving . . .*

'I'm worried for you, Chand,' the teacher said. 'Perhaps you shouldn't travel today. Go to Ajmer when you're feeling better — perhaps we can explore these visions of yours? Your friendship with Prithvi will survive a small parting, but in your present state, you may not survive the road.'

'No! I must be with him — I have to protect him!'

'You're in no fit shape to protect anyone, my friend. I'm sure all these soldiers the king has sent will be enough, if the prince needs any protection at all.'

'But you don't understand, Ravindra is also Prithvi's Enemy — he has slain him as well, in other lives! I have to be with him, to protect him!'

'You're sick, Chand. You're not yourself right now.'

'I am going with them,' Chand insisted, his voice strangely resonant and mature. 'We're bonded together, through debts that transcend the grave.' The ancient teacher could only stare as Chand rose on shaky legs. 'Our lives are at stake, Guru-ji — *all* of our lives — and I have to be with him, or it will all happen again. You've played your part, and I'm grateful. You've woken things in me that haven't been woken in any of my past lives. I will be in your debt for eternity.'

The way he said 'eternity' made the old man shiver.

There was no time to say more. The sun was rising and Prithvi and his guards were soon to leave. 'Goodbye, Guru-ji Vishwami-tra. I'll never forget you.'

'Nor I you, Chand,' the old man murmured.

'No, you will. In your next life, if not this. But me . . . now, I will remember. Farewell, until we meet again.' Chand touched Guru-ji's shoes reverently, then rose and ran unsteadily for the courtyard.

He caught up with Prithvi just as he was mounting his horse. The prince was surrounded by armoured men, their horses caparisoned for the dangers of the road: hard-faced men with no time for skinny little poets. But he strode between them, leading his mount, his eyes only upon the prince.

'Chand!' called Prithvi, surprised. 'Guru-ji said you were too sick to travel.'

'He was wrong. Here I am.'

If Prithvi thought him mad to be here when he was clearly ill, he said nothing of it, for which Chand was grateful. 'Good,' he replied. 'I'm glad to have you with me.'

Chand swung up onto the saddle and stared into the smiling face of his friend. He half-expected *something* . . . recognition, perhaps, but there was nothing, not of the sort he meant. He recognised Prithvi with complete clarity now, though: Madan Shastri reborn. He reached out a hand and the young prince took it. The soldiers drew apart, almost as if sensing something profound was happening.

'I'm indebted to you, Prithvi,' Chand told the soul inside the prince's body. 'I will always be indebted to you.' *And I'm so sorry for what I did: to you, to Darya, to Padma . . . to everyone. May the gods allow me to atone.*

Prithvi didn't understand, but he looked moved, somehow. 'You owe me nothing, cousin.' Then he grinned. 'Except a chest full of silver for all those sweets I have bought for you in the town! But I will allow you to pay me off in poetry and good service.'

'I'm your man, Lord. Always.' Chand looked about him at the waiting men, and on impulse, shouted aloud, 'Prithviraj ki jai! Hail Prithviraj Chauhan, King of Ajmer!'

The men took it up good-naturedly, but Prithvi just laughed. 'You aim too low, as usual, Chand! I will be Maharaja of all Rajputana, my friend – nothing less will do!'

He whooped, pulled his mount's head about and galloped out of the gate. The soldiers shouted, spurring their horses on and Chand too hollered for the sheer joy of being in motion, his remembered past lives fading from his attention as he pelted in the wake of Prithvi and his soldiers on the road to Ajmer – and destiny.

CHAPTER TWO

Arrows for Sita

Mumbai, October 2010

'Isn't this amazing?' demanded Jai. 'Isn't it the coolest thing you've ever done?'

Not even close, Vikram reflected – not that he could really say that aloud, because Jai wouldn't believe him anyway. 'Sure,' he muttered, thinking, *this is a really bad idea.*

Jai pulled a face. 'Aw, come on! Here we are, contestants on the greatest game show in the history of game shows and you're in a grumpy mood? Lighten up!'

Jai and Vikram had been roommates at Mumbai University since July, thrown together by chance but quickly becoming good friends. Both liked movies, books and keeping fit. Jai had a boundless optimism that was instantly endearing, and he had a large circle of friends, which had helped Vikram get settled into his new life in Mumbai, so very different to Jodhpur.

Vikram was almost unrecognisable from the bespectacled, shy youth he'd been, fresh back from Britain, only six months ago. A deluge of memories from past lives had struck him, and with it had come a maturity that had erased his boyhood. Centuries of knowledge and wisdom now lurked behind his eyes, unseen, and

yet somehow palpable. He could barely remember how teenagers were supposed to act, but he could remember what it was
to be adult, and even old. He could remember battles with
swords and bows, matchlocks and rifles; he recalled killing and
being slain. He recalled lovers from centuries past, being in lust
and love, raising children, cremating friends and wives. All of
that was concealed in his gaze, but however much he hid it, his
maturity still intimidated a lot of people. He'd changed physically, too; he'd started working out, his hair was thicker and
longer, and weirdly, he appeared to be growing out of his short-
sightedness.

But these were things he wasn't going to share, not even with
his new friend, so now he settled for rolling his eyes. Around
them, in a huge pavilion on the sports fields of Mumbai University, hundreds of cocky young men were strutting about with
their chests sticking out. The noise was deafening; they had to
shout in each other's ears to be heard. Television people swarmed
everywhere, cameras probing with all-seeing eyes. Although the
monsoon was officially over, it was pouring with rain outside and
the roof had sprung a dozen leaks.

But all this muddle was the first step in getting onto Sunita
Ashoka's televised swayamvara, and they'd all paid a thousand
rupees just to be here. It was running late, everyone was getting
more and more overheated and excitable and Vikram had
already had just about enough, secret quests to solve age-old
puzzles notwithstanding.

Finally he gave Jai an exasperated look. 'Come on, man – this
is a total waste of time. We could have done anything with that
money: dinner, movies, drinks, *anything*! Instead, we've blown it
on this rubbish!'

'Oh, come on – a thousand roops is nothing, especially for the
chance at the biggest prize in history!'

'Biggest prize in history,' Vikram scoffed. 'Huh! She's just a Bollywood has-been promoting herself in another sham wedding game.'

'Sunita isn't a has-been,' retorted Jai. 'She's the greatest—'

'She's a flake! A one-hit wonder jumping on the silliest band-wagon in Bollywood history. Hell, I don't even want to win this stupid game show – in fact, I'd rather lose! I'd rather sit at home and laugh at all the fools who've signed up.'

Jai sniggered. 'Come on, Vik: you're as excited as I am. You were on the toilet half the night!'

'That was those onion bhajis you reheated for dinner—'

'—which technically made it your own cooking!'

It wasn't the cooking that had kept Vikram awake all night. It was the fear that this might be the worst mistake of all his lives. The call from Amanjit had shaken him, and he was afraid that everything that had nearly killed them back in Jodhpur six months ago was going to happen again . . .

Swayamvara Live! was a game show, but it was also reviving a centuries-old tradition: a king would declare a swayamvara, a contest for all the neighbouring princes to compete for the hand of his daughter. The contestants would compete in tests of skill, courage and martial abilities, hoping to win the heart of the bride – or more often, catch the attention of the king himself, who was usually the real judge. The practice died out many years ago – or it had, until Bollywood had seen fit to revive it in a mix of game show and reality TV.

Sunita Ashoka was a typical Bollywood starlet, her early career little more than singing in the musical interludes in a few B-movies, and being the girl in a string of C-grade tabloid romances. But six years ago a Western film company had picked her for a leading role in *Actor's Wife*, an unpromising Hollywood/Bollywood crossover – but Sunita had seized that opportunity

with startling gusto. She'd stolen every scene, and then the
movie, which had somehow become a world-wide hit. Suddenly
Sunita Ashoka was not just a megastar but insanely rich, at least
by Bollywood standards.

It hadn't lasted: a string of flops and broken romances
followed, and a couple of drug-addled appearances at award
ceremonies fuelled rumours of mental instability. She was only
twenty-six, and this TV game show was seen by the press as final
proof that she'd completely lost it . . . but though she'd gone
from zero to hero and back in record time, the generation who
had grown up with *Actor's Wife* still dreamed of her.

The tabloids were busy speculating that she was really broke
and planning to leave the country once she'd banked all the
thousand-rupee entrance fees she'd collected, but she'd instantly
responded to that: the 'gate-fee' was only to keep out those men
who weren't going to take the competition seriously, or so she
claimed, and everyone who made it onto the show would be
refunded.

Already the newspapers had published profiles and horoscopes, trying to deduce what sort of man was expected to take
part. Some of the rules were written into the contracts: the contestants had to be five foot six or over (Vikram just scraped in;
Jai, who was pushing six foot, had no problem); he had to be over
eighteen (both were, just) and under forty (which ruled out half
the Bollywood A-list, to the newspapers' consternation). He also
had to be athletic, with all his limbs and mental faculties in place
(groups supporting the physically and mentally challenged were
outraged); and heterosexual, which annoyed the LGBT crowd –
and still didn't stop a few lesbians from turning up to make
political capital about this 'discrimination'; they had been vocal
in their protests after being turned away.

'Apparently one cannot choose the gender of one's preferred

life-partner in a TV stunt these days,' Vikram had noted with a wry smile.

The newspapers had even run hypothetical horoscopes, based on Sunita's stars, and predicted that her ideal man would be a Leo or maybe an Aquarian – Vikram was a Gemini, which seemed somehow appropriate, given how many people he was carrying around in his head these days.

The morning had been spent getting weighed and measured and doing fitness tests, which had left the contestants smelly and irritated. There were no clues at all about what she was looking for in a husband, or how the events would be judged, but the television adverts were loud on the big screens erected everywhere: Sunita was looking for THE PERFECT MAN – which assumed such a thing actually existed!

A sudden burst of hollering and cheering erupted at the entrance to the pavilion and everyone turned, almost clambering over each other in their eagerness.

'Maybe she's here,' exclaimed Jai. 'Maybe it's really her!'

Despite himself, Vikram tried to look, but everyone was taller than him, and he couldn't see all that far without his glasses anyway.

'It's Pravit! It's Pravit Khoolman!' someone shouted. 'Hey, Pravit, we love you!'

Jai was bouncing about. 'It's Pravit, it really is – he's come after all!'

Vikram snorted. 'Well, we should all leave right now – it's clearly a fix.'

Jai ignored him and shouted, 'Pravit! Pravit!' along with most of the room.

When Pravit Khoolman, the star of *Pyar Pyar* and *Yaarana 2*, had gone public a couple of days back, saying that he was going to be a contestant on *Swayamvara Live!* the papers had been full of nothing else. Terrorist attacks and global warming crises had been pushed to the middle while the scribes speculated on whether it was true: were Sunita and Pravit about to rekindle their much-publicised romance? Heaven knew, both needed the publicity!

It was another twenty minutes before order was restored and the crowd could be herded away from the star, who was cheerily signing autographs and being photographed amidst the great unwashed.

'A veritable man of the people,' Vikram observed sardonically. 'Probably eyeing a move into politics.'

'Hush, hush everyone!' shouted a functionary near the front. 'Quiet, *please*. We have a message to play for you – *quiet, please*!'

It was still another five minutes before he got his silence. The lights were extinguished and the projectors started, and as the light beamed from the metallic boxes onto a screen dangling from a wall, all voices inside the tent fell silent– except one.

'Of course I will win,' Pravit Khoolman was bellowing into a journalist's microphone, his words booming around the suddenly silent auditorium. He didn't even flinch, just smirked about him.

'Quiet, please!' the official called out from the stage. 'It is time to hear from Sunita!'

The handsome actor patted the hand of the pretty journalist, mimed a phone call gesture and winked, making her blush. Then a blare of song echoed from the PA system and the breath-taking face of Sunita Ashoka appeared onscreen. More than a thousand young men sucked in their stomachs.

'Namaskar, namaskar,' the actress trilled in the voice which had captivated the nation a few years ago. 'Thank you! Thank you all for coming here today. I greet you warmly, wherever you are. For yes, I am speaking to you live, and this broadcast is going out to contestant groups in every major city, from Kolkata to

Mumbai, to Delhi and to Bangalore, to Hyderabad, to Chennai, and even to London and Birmingham and Bradford and other Indian communities in England, Canada and Australia. Namaskar, and thank you! Thank you for coming forward to try and win my heart!'

Vikram glanced at Jai. His face was a picture of entrancement, a look mirrored on every face around him. Every young man present was caught up in a fantasy of beauty and wealth.

'We love you, Sunni!' shouted someone at the front. 'Pick me!'

The flawless face onscreen gave no sign of hearing. She smiled warmly, tilting her face *just so*. 'For my heart is truly here, truly yours to be won. This is real, let me assure you. There will be no backing out. There will be no false promises. I long to give my heart away.' She stared into the camera, leaning forward, filling the screen. 'It has come to me clearly, in my dreams and visions, that I am Sita reborn, and I am seeking you, my Rama.'

A collective intake of breath swept over the pavilion. Jaws dropped. This was somewhat insane, even by the lofty standards of Bollywood.

'Sita reborn?' Vikram muttered in Jai's ear. 'That'll set the Hindu fanatics off! Maybe she'll claim to be the Virgin Mary next, in case there are some Christians here to upset?'

Jai squirmed uncomfortably. Vikram guessed the journalists present were already scribbling words like *blasphemy* and *insane* in their notebook, while even the most ardent fans present were looking quizzical.

'I repeat,' the woman onscreen said, 'I am Sita, and this is my swayamvara. I am seeking you, my Rama, to fill the hole in my heart – and when I find you, I will give you all that I have, and all that I am. So come to me, my lover. Win my heart, and I will be yours, for ever.'

The screen went dark and the pavilion fell silent. For about three seconds, no one moved, no one spoke. And then everyone did, all at once.

'Well, that was interesting,' Vikram observed as he watched the men around him reacting in a myriad ways. 'She's clearly got a number of screws loose.'

'She's a divinity, sent to bless us,' Jai said dutifully. 'And her face . . .' He grinned. 'Well, actually, I can forgive a little madness.'

While the more fervent Hindus were storming out, threatening vociferously to riot unless they *immediately* got every single rupee back, the remaining suitors were herded into groups of twenty and taken outside to the sports fields. It had stopped raining and the ground was drying fast. They could see crowds lining the fences; most were just peering over curiously, but it looked like some had already learned of Sunita Ashoka's 'I am Sita reborn' words, because they were pushing and shoving and shouting at the policemen trying to hold them back with their batons.

Vikram couldn't help but be relieved that their group was furthest from the fences. Jai pulled his arm as they were made to stand in a line facing a row of canvas-covered shapes some sixty yards away. 'Wow, look!' he gasped. 'It's Pravit – he's coming our way!'

Pravit Khoolman was indeed walking over towards their group, surrounded by bodyguards and hangers-on. 'Hey, dat's kool,' the actor drawled – his tagline (slightly retro, and stolen from about a dozen other actors, but said in a much catchier way, obviously) – and high-fived a couple of the other contestants as he joined the group. Jai gaped at him adoringly, but Vikram was less impressed – in his past lives he'd joined Gandhi-ji on the Salt March and he'd heard Nehru speak, too. He'd seen Prithviraj Chauhan rallying his men in battle and Emperor Akbar launch his troops against the Rajputs. He'd seen the best. This guy was *nothing* compared to such men.

Khoolman wasn't without charisma, though; Vikram had to admit that at least, as the actor milked the attention with practised surety, superior yet obliging. *I've seen your sort so many times before*, he thought, watching with cool dislike as the handsome face suddenly turned his way and their eyes locked for a second in mutual disdain.

'Attention everyone, attention!' The functionary was now bellowing into a megaphone in a bid to be heard. 'Please be silent and listen to the instructions of your group leaders.'

The twenty men in Vikram's group reluctantly turned from Pravit as a pretty young woman waved for their attention. She wore a red blouse and black skirt under a windbreaker with *Swayamvara Live!* emblazoned across the back. She switched on a microphone and tapped it a couple of times to ensure it was working, while across the sports field dozens just like her were doing the same.

'Hello, everyone! My name is Aboli – please listen!' the girl started. 'This is the first elimination round, and for most of you, I'm afraid it will be your only opportunity to compete. As you have heard, Sunita is taking upon herself the mantle of Sita in this show, and she is seeking her Rama, the perfect man, to win her heart.' From her bag she produced a bow and arrow and waved them in the air. 'Lord Rama is famed throughout history as the greatest archer of all time, so it is only logical that this must be the first and most crucial test to find Sunita's husband-to-be.'

Aboli gestured, and the canvas covers were removed to reveal a row of targets. Almost everyone groaned. Jai glared at Vikram. 'That's not fair! Archery's the only sport you're any good at,' he grumbled.

Vikram ignored him, his mind racing. He couldn't work out if he was doing the right thing — or the wrong thing entirely. *Is this a mistake? Maybe I should leave?*

Aboli brandished the microphone and went on, 'Everyone will get three shots at a normal archery target, sixty yards away — all you have to do is hit the target once and you'll be through to the *Swayamvara Live!* show. Sounds simple?' She laughed and admitted, 'Well, it's not — but if you do it, not only will you get your full entrance fee back, but you'll also get free accommodation while you're competing on *Swayamvara Live!* in November — and not just accommodation; your food and drink too, all at Sunita's expense.'

A few people whistled as they mentally calculated what it was going to cost the actress to stage this show. *A fortune, that's what*, Vikram decided. *She must really want this.* But his own certainty had fled. Sunita was clearly deranged, and that could mean a number of things — none of them good. An insane woman appeared in far too many of his past lives, and her arrival always presaged disaster.

I can't draw this sort of attention to myself, he decided, *not when Ravindra is out there.*

'So,' Aboli exclaimed, 'who's going to go first? Form a line!'

Jai and Vikram let themselves get pushed towards the back and watched as the first few contestants demonstrated just how hard it was to hit a target at sixty yards. Though the rain had stopped and the air was still, most could not even get the arrow to fly sixty yards, let alone hit the target. 'She'll be lucky to get any potential husbands at all at this rate,' Jai muttered — then a massive shout erupted from another group: someone had scored a hit and was now dancing around ecstatically.

Everyone visibly relaxed: it *was* possible!

After that, hits became a little more plentiful; Vikram counted more than a dozen before Pravit Khoolman stepped up to the line. He was handling the bow with practised deftness – whatever else the actor might be, he clearly knew a bit about archery – no doubt a legacy of all those action-thriller roles. But unless he was very good, he would still need luck to hit the target from here.

Turned out, he *was* very good. After an initial ranging shot that flew narrowly wide, he scored two hits, one in the outer ring, another near the middle. His group cheered as if they themselves had struck the target, while the actor made a great show of asking Aboli for the refund on his gate-fee. 'Hey, it's a thousand rupees – I need that cash,' he laughed, before stepping aside and bowing to the crowds.

'Pravit! Pravit! Pravit!' shouted the gathered throng. Vikram mimed sticking his finger down his throat to Jai, then turned to see Pravit Khoolman staring straight at him. Vikram looked away, feeling foolish.

From then on, the actor positioned himself beside each archer and gave tips on stance and technique. 'Deep breaths, and exhale as you fire,' he told one youth, and, 'Back straight, head level and steady,' to another, an older man. Vikram was getting more and more annoyed, and when two people in their group got a hit, Pravit high-fived them with a satisfied smirk, as if it were only his coaching that had enabled them to hit the target.

Finally it was Jai's turn. 'A steady pull,' advised Khoolman from the side. 'No nerves, now.'

Jai missed, and then again.

'Last one, buddy,' Khoolman said encouragingly, one eye on the camera. 'Let it flow.'

Vikram muttered under his breath: an old phrase that Vishwamitra had taught him, a very long time ago. Jai's arrow soared . . . and struck the target.

Jai whooped and flung his arms around Pravit Khoolman as Vikram concealed a grimace.

'Hey man, good shot,' he muttered to Jai as he shook his friend's hand.

'I'm in! I'm *in*!' Jai was dancing a jig on the spot. 'I'm going to marry Sunita!'

'Yeah, you're in,' Vikram agreed, taking the bow. *And in a few seconds I'm out and I can forget all about this sideshow . . .*

As he cleaned his glasses, from the corner of his eye he noticed Pravit Khoolman staring at him fixedly. He wondered if he knew the man from another time and place. He couldn't really tell without getting close.

But who cares? It's better I remain in the shadows. He took up his stance, deliberately aiming to the left and low, and drew back.

'Hey, is that kid even five foot six?' interrupted Khoolman.

Vikram stopped and half-turned, fighting a sudden surge of temper.

'All the contestants have been measured by us and our measurements independently verified,' Aboli said quickly, in a helpful voice.

'He doesn't even look eighteen,' Khoolman continued in a low voice.

Vikram turned back to the target, took up his stance and drew the bow again.

The actor's voice dropped, but he was still clearly audible. 'I don't know why a little four-eyed dweeb like that even bothered to enter. I know what Sunita likes, and it isn't bat-faced nerds like that.' Then he shouted to Vikram, 'Come on, *little boy*, see if you can get the arrow to fly that far.'

Vikram stopped aiming and turned to the actor. 'You know,' he grated, 'when I saw you on *Yaarana 2* I thought, "That man is a plank: an inert lump of wood with all the personality of a louse." But I was wrong, because even lice have a personality, whereas you' – *thwang!* – 'are an arrogant prick' – *thwang!* – 'with about as much appeal as a smear of dog turd!' *Thwang!*

He put his glasses back on as a hundred mouths gasped and a hundred pairs of eyes swivelled from the muscular actor to the small bespectacled youth and back again. Everyone took a step back as Pravit clenched a fist.

Then Jai stepped between them, his eyes on the distant target. '*Shiva . . . Rama . . . Krishna . . .*'

At Jai's words everyone looked at the target – except Vikram, who didn't give a toss what had happened. *Do I run or do I punch him? Are the cameras on us? Damn!*

'Vik,' breathed Jai, 'you've *got* to look.'

Khoolman reluctantly dragged his eyes from Vikram – and physically staggered.

Vikram finally glanced at the target, and groaned.

The first arrow had struck the bulls-eye. So had the second. And the third. They pierced the boss in a neat equilateral triangle that would have thrilled his geometry teachers back in England.

Now what the hell did I go and do that for?

CHAPTER THREE

Hotel Hobbies

Delhi, October 2010

A steel-grey Lexus was waved through security and purred up to the doors of the Ramada Hotel on Ashok Road. The sun was a disc of glowing orange. A white-haired European in a fine linen suit helped his sari-clad middle-aged wife from the car. They shuffled inside and shook hands with some waiting dignitaries as the Lexus silently flowed away and was replaced by another luxury sedan. The bustle of the streets was just a distant murmur, occasionally punctuating the classical music flowing from the ballroom into the lobby. Everyone moved with stately dignity, as befitted yet another corporate-sponsored charity ball for the glitterati of East and West: Asians and Europeans speaking a mishmash of languages, displaying their wealth and status by their mode of dress and the gold and gems adorning men and women alike.

In the corner, Amanjit Singh was at match-point against Roger Federer—

—*whose serve fizzed down, top-spun and blindingly quick, precise and straight to the corner. If Amanjit hadn't moved a fraction of a second early, it would have been ace and game over — but he* had *moved early and*

*now he swung through his backhand, hitting a daring return low
and hard, risking everything on all-out attack.*

*The Swiss master reacted like lightning, slashing across the ball and
sending it powering across the court, but Amanjit lunged, almost diving
across the line of the ball, and with a vicious swipe, sent it bounding into
the opposite corner, just beyond his opponent's reach. Deuce! He punched
the air as the crowd roared, and his racquet gave a crackle—*

—sending another mosquito twitching to the marble floor.

'Amanjit! What are you doing?' hissed Mr Kumar, the floor
manager.

Amanjit blinked and stared down at the mosquito, then looked
up to find half the guests in the lobby peering at him, tittering
behind their hands. 'Got him!' he replied, flushing scarlet. 'Quick
little bugger, that one. Not fast enough to get away from me,
though!'

Mr Kumar put his hands on his hips and his schoolteacher face
crinkled in disapproval. 'Some decorum, please, Amanjit! This is
the *Ramada Hotel*, not some nursery playground!'

Deepika's father had got Amanjit the job, so here he was, his
muscular frame straining at the seams of a size-too-small uniform, his throat constricted by a too-tight Nehru collar. His role:
to wield that plastic electric racquet, killing mosquitoes before
they could spread malaria and dengue fever to the great and
worthy guests.

The bug-killer really did look a lot like a tennis racquet . . .

'Um, sorry, sir.'

'I should damn well think so. Mind what you're doing, young
man – I'm watching you.' Mr Kumar waggled a finger, then
stalked away. The entertainment over, the guests filed past, while
Amanjit found a pillar to hide behind.

After he'd finished school in July, it had been party after party
celebrating his engagement to Deepika Choudhary. His heart sang

every time he thought about it. But before they could marry, Deepika was going to university in Delhi and he had to get a regular job. Her family had been very generous to their son-in-law-to-be, bringing him with them when they'd returned to Delhi from Jodhpur and helping him to apply for jobs. He really wanted to go to the National Defence Academy, then join the Air Force, but he'd not yet heard if his application had been accepted, so in the meantime he'd been doing part-time jobs like this one.

It wasn't that he didn't want to work, but this job was so *boring*! After fighting for his life – with a real sword! – beneath the Mehrangarh Fortress in Jodhpur, waving a yellow electrified bug-killer around was demeaning! *If I didn't need the money, I'd jam the handle down Kumar's throat . . .*

His mobile hummed in his pocket and after checking to make sure Kumar couldn't see him, he answered it.

'Hey,' Deepika purred, and fireworks went off in his head at the sound of her voice.

'Dee! Where are you?'

'I'm at this bar in Defence Colony with Jayshree and her friends.' He could hear a distant burr of music and voices in the background. 'It's really rocking.'

'Is it full of guys?' he enquired, putting a little frost into his voice.

She giggled. 'Yeah, really handsome guys with big cars and loads of bling.'

'I'll be right there!'

'You've got a job to do – and anyway, none of these jerks are a patch on you. What time will you get home?'

'About two in the morning. Stupid job, lousy money,' he grumbled.

'Hush! We need that stupid money – every rupee is for our future.'

'Yeah, yeah, I know.' He waved the racquet at a hovering mosquito, which flitted aside. Mr Kumar was toadying around a Japanese businessman and his tiny wife. 'You have a fun night . . . but not too much fun, you hear!'

'Sure: no fun, got it. A couple of drinks, only dancing with the girls – I know the drill.' The bar noise suddenly trebled and she gushed with laughter. 'Ha! Gotta go – love you, love you! Bye—!'

'Yeah, see you later,' he started, but she'd already rung off. He looked at his watch: nearly seven. The hours stretched ahead like an eternity. He drifted into a corner where Kumar couldn't see him . . .

. . . *and it was deuce. Where would Federer put his next serve—?*

The bar was throbbing. Deepika bounced along with her girlfriends next to a towering cluster of Irish and Australian expats. They might have had flushed faces and loud voices, but they were polite and weren't hitting on anyone, so she was fine with them.

Getting engaged this young had never been part of her game plan – in fact, going to university here in Delhi hadn't been in the plan either; she'd long ago set her heart on America. *But like they say in songs, you can't plan for love*, she thought. It happened when it did, not at your convenience. That was her and Amanjit: the Delhi miss and the Rajasthani Sikh – she would have recoiled in horror at the mere thought of such a thing a year ago, but it was really happening. He'd even come to Delhi to be with her!

It was a beautiful agony, living together under her parents' roof, so close – and yet so closely chaperoned! But she'd promised her mum she'd be a virtuous bride, at least as long as she didn't have to wait too long. But it was all so complicated, even without the other stuff they'd gone through together.

What had happened in Jodhpur in March had changed *everything*. Vikram might be the only one of them who could actually remember any past lives, but neither she nor Amanjit had any doubts about what he'd told them, not after all the ghosts and thugs, and that dreadful Ravindra-raj . . . or was he Ravana, King of Demons? Deepika shuddered. No one could go through such experiences and emerge unchanged.

What their adventure had done was to bind them all together. No day went by without one or both of them phoning Vikram in Mumbai, and almost always the conversation went back to their terrifying flight through the caves beneath the Mehrangarh Fort, and the dreadful figure who'd been after them – was he dead now? Had they actually succeeded in killing him? Or was he still hunting them?

She shuddered, no longer in the mood to be out partying. The girls were fun, BFFs since their school days together, and it was really good to be back with them – she'd really missed them the year she spent in Jodhpur – but tonight she just wanted to be curled up on the couch, wrapped in Amanjit's arms, resting her head on his chest and listening to his powerful heartbeat.

Why is the bar so cold? Or is it just me? The bright lights suddenly looked like the eyes of a snake, looking into her soul . . . She could feel the blood in her veins turning to ice-water; her muscles had no strength. There was a roaring in her ears and her skin felt slick. Her friends were turning towards her, but they faded away until all she could see was one face, hovering over everyone: a cruel, fleshy visage framed by a thick moustache and long black hair that coiled like serpents. Eyes that looked like tarnished gold. A mouth that whispered half-heard taunts: *Darya, you belong to me!*

She tried to speak but the floor was moving, rising like a wall to slap her in the face.

*

Amanjit was 5-3 up in the tie-breaker when his phone rang. He pulled it out and looked at the display, not recognising the number. 'Hello?'

'Amanjit?' The voice was female, speaking fast. 'This is Jayshree! You have to come! Deepika has had an accident—'

He was already heading for the doors, not noticing Mr Kumar racing to intercept him. 'You! Amanjit Singh! Where do you think you're going? I'll see you fired—'

'My fiancée has had an accident! I have to go!'

Mr Kumar's eyes bulged. 'Don't think we'll give you a single rupee for this night, you lazy piece of—'

Amanjit turned and jammed the handle of the fly-killing racquet against the floor manager's lips. For an instant, he wasn't a big Sikh boy in a tight Nehru collar and ill-fitting coat, he was Madan Shastri, warrior, leader of men – and he was other men too, all part of his past. 'One more word and I'll smash your mouth. I don't want your damned money. *My fiancée is sick* – so get out of the way!'

Mr Kumar's eyes suddenly filled with fear, as if he could see those others. 'I'm . . . I'm sorry,' he started, but Amanjit was no longer paying attention.

'Good for you.' Amanjit tossed the racquet to the petrified floor manager. 'Kill your own bugs, Mr Kumar!' Then he ran outside, waving at the concierge to hail a taxi.

Deepika was sleeping. Amanjit left the ward, which was crowded with families of patients huddled together, talking in low tones or trying to sleep, so he could ring Vikram in peace. Dee hadn't been able to tell him much, just that she'd felt cold and fainted, and her friends swore blind it was nothing to do with alcohol – she'd barely touched her first drink.

But while she'd been in hospital, she'd been talking in her sleep, and her words had chilled him to the bone.

A bleary voice answered his call. 'Amanjit? What's up, bhai?'

He'd not realised it was three in the morning. 'Dee's collapsed again, Vik, at a bar.'

'No——! Is she okay?'

'She's sleeping. She's okay, the doctors think. But she's talking in her sleep.' He could hear how shrill his voice was becoming and tried to quell it. 'She's talking to *him*.'

'Talking to who?'

'Ravindra. She's talking to Ravindra. It's all beginning again, Vik, just like you said it would. *What do we do?*'

CHAPTER FOUR

The Fortune Teller

Jodhpur, Rajasthan, October 2010

Rasita lay on a hospital bed in the grip of a skinny metallic octopus. At least, that's how she saw all the heart-monitoring wires and drips she was hooked up to: some kind of many-tentacled creature that was slowly sucking her life away.

I shouldn't be so negative about it, she thought. *They're trying to save my life — in fact, they've already saved it several times over.* She was well aware that without the miracles of modern medicine, she wouldn't have survived so long.

She'd just heard that her brother Amanjit's fiancée Deepika was in hospital too. Amanjit had called that morning, just before she and her mother had left for her weekly tests. *Bad news for Deepika*, Ras thought, although for her, hospitals were pretty much a daily fact of life, thanks to her defective heart. She'd be lucky to get through her last year of high school — she'd barely survived three separate cardiac incidents already, but the last one, back in March, had been different . . .

No, I won't think about that—

But how could she not, when the ghost of a long-dead queen had tried to kill her in her own bedroom? *Padma*. A nice, commonplace name – not the name for such a horrible thing. The ghost hadn't guessed that while Rasita might be weak as a kitten, she was still a fighter. Ras had managed to drive a silver letter-opener into whatever passed for flesh among the undead, and she'd watched in mingled terror and relief as the ghost disintegrated right in front of her.

Seven months later, she still couldn't close her eyes without seeing that awful face. The others didn't know about what had happened to her when they'd all gone off to the Mehrangarh Fort. Though she was clearly somehow involved in the mystery they'd uncovered, they'd left her behind, deciding she was too sick to be involved. Realistically, she was – but they hadn't realised that she was in danger too. She knew it was sheer luck she'd survived dead Queen Padma's attack.

She shook her head to dispel the image and turned her face towards the window where her mother sat, wringing her hands. She croaked, 'Any more news from Amanjit?'

Kiran Kaur Bajaj looked up at her daughter. 'No, not yet. I'm sure it's just a bad turn. That girl better not be pregnant,' she added fiercely. She still wasn't sure about her son falling for that Delhi miss, all flashing eyes and tight jeans . . .

'Oh, Mum——! Of course she won't be. She's a good girl! And anyway, Amanjit treats her like a princess.'

'All Sikh men treat women as princesses,' her mother replied, 'until they get their way with them. Trust me, I know this! But not my new husband, of course.'

Amanjit and Ras' father was long dead, and Kiran had married Dinesh Khandavani, Vikram's father, two months ago. She had good reason to resent men, Ras thought, what with Uncle Charanpreet, who'd been bullying her for years, until they finally freed themselves from his influence. That was in March as well. Now Kiran was living with Dinesh in Jodhpur, and Ras had never seen her mother happier. Dinesh might not be a heroic figure from the sagas – he was a plump little man, a fabric salesman – but he had a good heart, and he clearly adored her mother. Now Amanjit was in Delhi, the household was just the four of them: Kiran and Dinesh and Ras, and her eldest brother Bishin, who ran the family's taxi business.

'I'm going for some food, darling,' Kiran said, giving her a peck on the forehead. 'Do you want anything?' When Ras shook her head, she left for the canteen.

Rasita looked around, sighing to herself. Being in a room alone in hospital was a rarity, 'reserved for our best customers,' the nurses liked to joke. Her eyes skipped over the mirror on the wall – she didn't like to look into it, not when all it showed was a girl as skinny as a famine victim, festooned in tubes and wires. Even though she had lost a frightening amount of weight these last few months, she found it hard to eat. Everyone was putting a brave face on it, trying to be upbeat, but this didn't feel like a bad patch, something she would come out of. This felt *different*.

And the ghost – *Padma*, she mouthed – was back, she was sure of it. She'd only glimpsed her, thin, pale tendrils of fog, barely present at all – the silver letter-opener had hurt her badly – but she knew it was the dead queen. Padma was hovering around her like a moth near a lamp – *or a vulture circling a dying cow,* Ras added to herself with a snort. Some nights she was too scared to sleep.

The door opened and a young man in a white coat came in, a parrot sitting jauntily on his shoulder. Chi, the fortune-teller, was small and skinny, like her, with dapper hair and smooth skin, and probably not much older. The parrot had left stains on the shoulder of his hospital-issue coat. He was holding a pile of battered cards in his hands.

'Fortune, didi?' he offered with a smile.

'Hello, Chi.' She raised a hand in greeting, careful not to disturb the tubes and wires.

Chi sat at the end of the bed and held out his arm. His beautiful fluorescent green parrot hopped down onto his wrist. 'How are you this morning, little Ras?'

'I can still make the machine go "beep",' she said, pointing at the heart monitor.

The young man beamed. 'Very good, that. Very good.'

'Getting much business today?'

'Today is slow. Everyone is asleep or being worked on.' Chi was allowed to read fortunes for the patients, provided he gave them only good news. Many of the patients believed in his mystic patter and anything that made the patients more optimistic was approved of, even Chi's odd little repertoire of sleight-of-hand and pseudo-magic. 'I don't have enough to buy lunch today,' he said in a pleading voice. 'And Muki is bored,' he added, stroking the parrot.

'Oh, you poor thing,' giggled Ras. 'All right, you can tell my fortune. There's a tenner in my jacket pocket.' She pointed to where it hung behind the door.

Chi set Muki onto Ras' wrist and she squealed softly as the parrot's sharp-taloned grip both tickled and dug into her flesh. He found the money, touched it to his forehead in thanks and tucked it away. 'Okay, Muki, time to earn your seedcake.' He showed the bird the cards before stacking them beside Ras' hand.

He muttered a little prayer, just nonsense, as far as Ras could make out, and Muki started picking up and discarding cards until he finally decided upon one, which he gave to Chi. Ras had never worked out Chi's system, but she knew there had to be one: perhaps it was done with hand gestures?

Each dog-eared, creased card had a picture of a god or goddess and some lines of verse. Chi turned over the one Muki had selected to pronounce upon her future. Ras had had this done so many times she knew that it wouldn't matter what the card was; the message was always the same: *this illness is a short-lived thing. Happiness will fill your days, so long as you are strong during this adversity*. The 'fortune' Chi dispensed was always the same. That's what they paid him for.

So she wasn't ready for the look of consternation that ran across his face. He looked accusingly at the parrot. 'Bad Muki! Where did this come from?'

Ras snatched the card from his hand as Muki squawked and took to the air. She stared, and felt her heartbeat falter slightly.

The card was utterly blank.

Chi kept protesting that the card was a mistake. He was still scolding Muki as he left, nearly running into Kiran, laden with chai and pakora. She took in Ras' drawn face and asked, 'Are you okay, darling? Did you get your fortune told?'

It took her a few seconds to muster a reply. 'Yes. It was just the usual.'

She could tell her mother knew she was lying, but she didn't say anything else – how could she tell her that she had no future at all?

CHAPTER FIVE

Guarding the Rear

Gujarat, 1165

The Chauhamanas camp stank of vomit, and the stench from the latrine trenches was even more appalling. Chand Rathod had wrapped a thin scarf about his face in a vain attempt to keep the worst from his nostrils. The dried dung that fuelled the fire beneath the metal pot he was tending wasn't helping either. The cries of the wounded filled the air, punctuated with shouted orders from the few remaining officers. Above, the sun was descending in a scarlet haze.

The day's battle hadn't gone well. King Bhimdev Solanki's Gujaratis had assailed the Chauhamanas' position in force. The Chauhamanas had set up around the only adequate waterhole in miles, but it was a poor position to defend and they had barely held against the massed Solanki assault. They did manage to hold it in the end – but shortly afterwards, hordes of their fighting men had gone down with stomach cramps and diarrhoea, and too many had died, clutching their bellies as their insides bled out. The waterhole had been poisoned, a ploy typical of Vanraj, the cunning Solanki prince.

It was four years since Chand had gone to Ajmer with Prithvi.

He might be only a little taller, but he was a man now, with serious eyes and a worldly manner. He looked far more mature than his years, which isolated him at court, as did his studies – and his secrets. He wore his hair long and affected a small beard. He sported neither a nobleman's finery, nor a warrior's steel, just functional travelling clothes. At court he was a trainee poet; here, he functioned as a scribe and historian and, intermittently, as a doctor. And he was a friend of the prince, which won him both friends *and* enemies.

Chand heard the gritty crunch of footsteps in the sand. 'Put more dung on the fire,' he ordered, without looking up.

'Er, it's me,' replied Prithvi Chauhan, Prince of Ajmer.

'I know. I recognised your tread. Feed the fire before it goes out and ruins this potion.'

He heard Prithvi snort with amusement, and then the prince was bending over the fire and tossing on a couple more bricks of dried horse dung. 'Presumptuous damned poet,' he muttered good-naturedly, then, putting a hand on Chand's shoulder, 'How goes it?'

Prithvi had grown until he was the match in stature of any man at court – and then he kept on growing. He was big-boned, but lithe as a cat, and he was already spoken about as 'the hope of the Chauhans' and 'the Chauhamanas Lion'. His father Someshwar leaned upon him more and more; Prithvi was now the acknowledged heir to Ajmer, and maybe more. His grandfather Anangpal Tomar, King of the Pandavas, had two daughters but no living son and he had not yet named an heir, but his health was in decline and he'd recently announced that he would relinquish his fortress of Dilli. That was probably to forestall attack; in truth, he couldn't hold it much longer. Prithvi's mother was Anangpal's daughter; his other daughter was married to Vijaypal Rathod of Kannauj. The king had yet to announce which line would inherit Dilli when he died – that was the whole point of this mission to

Gujarat, to win honour and fame for the Chauhans, enough to confirm Someshwar's supremacy over the Rathod line. Except it wasn't going so well right now, and if they didn't extricate themselves from this mess they wouldn't just lose Dilli, the Chauhans could very well find themselves without their royal heir.

Chand wrinkled his nose. 'I couldn't get half the ingredients I wanted, but it should settle their guts. No more than a thumbnail-sized drop per man, mind!'

Prithvi looked down at the pot, estimating, and sighed. 'It won't go far, will it. Though after today, we've got no more than three hundred capable of holding a weapon.' He reeled off the names of the noblemen slain or crippled. 'We held,' he concluded, 'but tomorrow . . .'

'Before tomorrow, there is tonight to think of,' Chand pointed out. 'They'll attack under cover of darkness.'

Prithvi was offended at the notion. 'No true warrior sneaks about like a thief at night!'

'A Solanki would – just as they would poison a waterhole. Bhimdev may lead them, but it's his son Vanraj who's their true leader.'

They'd encountered Vanraj in the past and they agreed he was a backstabbing liar – not that that distinguished him from most of the courtiers Chand knew. But what did make Vanraj stand out was his willingness to bend tradition to get what he wanted. He'd been a rising Chauhamanas general until shifting alliances took him back to his Gujarati family – with all his knowledge of the Chauhans and how they fought.

Prithvi patted the ornate hilt of his curved talwar. 'Bastard,' he growled. 'Tonight, you think?'

'Count on it.' Chand used a silver spoon and took a small sip of the potion, wincing at the taste, then offered the same to Prithvi. 'This'll settle your guts.'

The Prince downed the measure and winced. '*Ugh!* If you judge the efficacy of medicine by how badly it tastes, I doubt I'll ever be ill again.'

Chand beckoned a servant, and quickly instructed him to set about dosing the men. Prithvi waved over two of his personal guards to escort the man around the camp. 'Treat *everyone*, mind,' Chand called. 'Even those who claim to be well.' The men hurried away purposefully and Chand turned and surveyed the darkening west. 'They'll come from over there,' he said. 'Once the moon is up fully and they think we're asleep.'

'It's what I'd do,' Prithvi admitted, 'were I so dishonourable as to attack at night in the first place. It's a straight line in between that copse of trees northwest of us and that wadi just south of west. They'll use them for cover, obscure their approach.' He turned east. 'But wouldn't it be just like Vanraj to swing around and strike with his primary might from behind?'

'We've got the advantage from that side,' Chand replied. 'Except for the path we took to get up here in the first place, it's a tough climb, not one for horses, and not at night.' He looked at Prithvi meaningfully. 'A few good men with a lot of arrows could tie up any rear attack.'

'I thought you might say that. I need to be visible, to rally the soldiers. It'll be up to you to keep them off if they do as you think, Chand.'

'They will. Vanraj is Vanraj – he can't help trying to be clever.'

'Nor can you,' laughed Prithvi. 'Is that potion going to get the men back on their feet in time? Everything depends on this, you know that? If we fail here, even if I survive, the Rathods will get Dilli. They say Anangpal is dying, so this is our only chance: we must win, and win gloriously.'

'Then we shall,' Chand promised. '*Gloriously.*'

*

Silver light streamed from the face of the moon. Chand pulled his blanket tightly around himself as he huddled between two boulders some sixty feet above the narrow path that wound its way towards the waterhole. The sickness that had swept the camp was abating as rapidly as it began. It was being blamed on bad cooking, though the men only went back to drinking from the waterhole after Chand had given the priests some holy water to purify it. The gods must have been appeased, for the water now tasted fresh and sweet. Only Prithvi and he knew why.

The men had been ordered to sleep in their armour and keep weapons close to hand – though they scarcely needed to be told the latter, for Rajputs were warriors, born with sword in hand. In the Rajput court, all honour and praise and status went to the warrior. The men fought all the time: over status, position, insults, women – or just for the sheer fun of it – and they only respected other fighting men. For Chand, a minor noble with no visible military prowess, the last four years at court had been a constant struggle to stay out of the way of the innumerable vicious, cruel youths who all appeared to have a desperate need to *prove themselves*, which, far too often, took the form of putting the boot into a defenceless poet. His friendship with Prithvi only made things worse – what better way to get at the prince than by beating up his hapless cousin?

But Prithvi had quickly made it known that Chand was his, and he retaliated whenever he found his friend had been assailed. It was only when the two rode out together that Chand could drop the mask and properly practise his archery and swordplay – but even then, he had another, *harder*, mask to wear: that of the slightly inferior warrior. Only Prithvi knew that Chand was skilled in the arts of war, but even he didn't know how deep those skills ran. Chand wore all his masks well.

The tides had turned a year ago, when Prithvi's elder brothers died on the battlefield, leaving Prithvi as heir apparent. Now his former tormentors sought Chand out: sneering rivals asked for love poems with which to woo that week's chosen lady. Even the Raja invited him to sing before the court. Life was definitely getting better . . . but it would all end if they couldn't triumph this night.

The crunch of a footfall below him snapped him from his reverie. He didn't move, but his eyes swiftly found the source: one of Vanraj's scouts was checking the trail. Chand let the man go unmolested, but he marked his route. When he returned ten minutes later, the scout looked relaxed, utterly unaware he'd been seen. He retraced his steps, vanishing into the night.

Chand kept his eyes from the face of the moon, lest he lose some of his night-sight. He quietly strung his weapon, a recurved bow of bone and wood. It was larger and more powerful than those he'd trained with at the Gurukul: a true warrior's weapon, though few even knew he owned it. Beside him were six quivers, each with two dozen arrows. *More than enough for what needs to be done*, he hoped.

Five minutes passed . . . ten . . . then shouting came from the west, together with a sound no one ever forgot: the distant whirr of arrows in flight, like the hiss of a thousand snakes. The attack had begun . . . but not the *real* attack. That would be here, where he waited alone.

Ten more minutes . . .

He heard the Chauhamanas shouting urgently, but there was no panic in their voices: they were holding. Their attention was fully westwards, though. If Vanraj knew his business, it was time . . .

With a soft whickering, the first Solanki rider rode from the darkness, hooves muffled, no torches lit. Their armour was glinting softly in the moonlight – Chand would have insisted all metal was covered, but Vanraj was cocky, sure in his strategy, for which Chand was grateful. They'd be easier to hit this way.

He waited until the narrow file breasted his position. Beneath him the slope was broken and rocky, too steep to ride up. He thought of what he was about to do; it still sickened him a little, even though he'd already killed men on this, his first proper campaign. Guru-ji always said that life was sacred, not taken lightly, though he acknowledged that war was unavoidable in the Rajput world. It still troubled Chand enough to whisper a small prayer before he took aim. But when he let fly, it was with words of power streaming from his lips.

The first arrow skewered the heart of the lead horse, which gave a shriek as it crashed sideways, its rider yelping in shock. The second arrow took the next horse, bringing it down to block the narrow path, preventing advance. A third shot brought the next horse to the ground – and then Chand turned on the men.

Suddenly six arrows were flying for every pull of the bow-string, and igniting in midair. Whatever they struck instantly burst into searing flames. A shockwave ran through the Solankis and they recoiled, then someone bellowed an order and those in the middle and at the back tried to advance, even while those at the front were attempting to flee. In the ensuing chaos men and horses alike came crashing down, screaming as flesh was pierced and bones were broken. The fallen were trampled in the mêlée as Chand kept pouring his deadly arrows into the press, never missing. Occasionally an arrow from below would zip around him, but none came near; those few warriors who did manage to stand and fire as the dead and wounded piled up around them were shooting blind. He saw one man slip into the shadow of a rock; although he could see little more than an amorphous shape, he shot him through the eye. Another attempt by the survivors below to push a path through the carnage faltered as he turned his attention back to the hapless beasts, and mount after mount went down until the enemy finally began to fall back. He could hear the wounded men crying out as they tried to crawl away; their voices allowed him to pinpoint their positions and now he concentrated on methodically killing them. Finally he put the injured horses out of their misery.

The Solankis tried again, a few minutes later. Skirmishers came slinking in on foot, cloaks drawn over their heads, their faces painted with ash, heading for the position marked by the trajectory of the fire-arrows. But Chand had already shifted to a better vantage point higher up, and as they stealthily closed in on his supposed position, he shot them from behind, one by one: instant kills in silent darkness.

He left just one alive, after putting an arrow in his leg. He straddled the man and held his dagger to his throat. 'What is the signal that all is clear?' he whispered in the man's ear.

'Go to hell, Chauhan scum,' the man hissed through his pain.

Chand gripped the arrow and twisted it and the man screamed, but he wouldn't answer. So Chand did it again, and again, until finally he got what he needed.

He waited a while for the echo of the skirmisher's cries to die away, then he stood and waved a blazing torch in a circle, three times.

A second torch below flared and circled in the night as he shifted to the third position he had marked out, closer to the camp. The advance guard would have to clamber over their fallen friends to get to him, and then again in retreat.

He waited patiently.

Prithvi Chauhan strode from his tent, groomed and resplendent. He paused beside a spear, driven into the sand outside his pavilion, and stared up at the lifeless head of Bhimdev Solanki. The warrior's long grey hair was tangled in gore and flies were thick about the blood drying on the shaft. The old man should never have led the final push himself. By then his men were demoralised and wavering, quite unable to withstand Prithvi's counter-attack. The Chauhamanas had given the old king a wide berth, letting their prince have the honour of taking down the chief of their foes, but Bhimdev was in his fifties, pot-bellied and well past his prime; it had been more murder than fight.

His men cheered Prithvi as he passed with his entourage of young nobles, a mix of hardened killers and fresh-faced tyros. They said if you survived your first campaign, you'd likely live until youth faded and you got slow, like Bhimdev had. This was Prithvi's third campaign.

His nobles formed the Rajput cavalry, the core of his war party. The rest of his warriors were sons of artisans and farmers, many conscripted against their will to be spearmen. They weren't worth much in the field; most just hoped to survive and win some plunder. Often they didn't know who they fought, let alone why, but they knew their own homes and property would be for-feit if they failed, and that was enough, at least until the real terror of combat began. When the enemy cavalry actually charged them, only the veterans could keep the front ranks from rout – but after that, their hearts were won. The spearmen never talked to the men leading them, not unless they were spoken to, but they idolised them, and every man there dreamed of performing some great feat that would raise him to the nobility. They fought for the right to suffer alongside their leaders; to be part of the dream of glory and plunder.

Prithvi raised an arm towards them as they cheered him. He had kept them alive: for now, at least, they were his.

He patted shoulders as he went through the press of his noblemen, some his closest friends: Sanjham Rai, dashing and callous; Govinda, older, muscular and hard; and Raichand, himself a minor king, though of lesser lineage, shifty and quicksilver. He spoke to each, commending them on incidents he'd seen himself or been briefed upon. There was no sign of Chand, and he pretended not to notice.

The Rajput nobles ate and drank, and oversaw the plunder: piles of weapons and armour, captured horses, clothing, whole or marred. The naked bodies of their enemies were piled and burned, except for the Solanki highborn, who were prepared for collection by their enemies. Unofficial truce reigned: Vanraj had withdrawn with his remaining men to a high point not far away. By midday the stench of smoke and burning flesh filled the camp. Nearby farms were raided for food, livestock and women, all herded together and tethered, ready for the return to Ajmer.

It was mid-afternoon before Prithvi was told that Chand had returned. His intimates were more than a little drunk; Raichand was telling a bizarre story of Muslim harems he had seen in Kabul while Govinda downed yet another goblet and Sanjham had a naked slave-girl washing his feet with her long hair.

'I tell you, this old merchant fellow had seventy wives, and they were all magnificent!' Raichand insisted. 'And he was as old as all four of us put together – they were grateful for a real man in their midst, believe me!'

'So how many children did he have?' Sanjham asked, puffing from a hookah and eyeing the slave attending him.

'Only seven! From seventy women! What a waste.' Raichand smirked. 'Of course, there were probably another twenty born nine months after I left.'

They all roared with laughter as the tent flap opened. 'Ah, finally, some more drink!' growled Govinda, then blinked. 'Oh, it's only you, Chand.'

'It's only Chand,' Sanjham snickered. 'And we thought it would be someone useful.'

'Where were *you* last night?' growled Govinda. 'I don't remember seeing you anywhere, not even when the battle was won.'

'Chand was running an errand for me,' Prithvi put in quickly. He was nowhere near as drunk as the others, though he affected intoxication. 'Which I take it was delivered satisfactorily?' He looked at the young poet and Chand bowed. His hair was matted and he was covered in soot and dust. 'Then go and wash, Chand, for heaven's sake!'

He bowed once more, still ignoring the others, and slipped out again.

'Why is Chand never seen during the battles, eh?' Sanjham wondered. 'You protect him like he's your sister, Prithvi. A real man must stand on his own feet!'

'Except if he's drunk as much as you have this morning,' Prithvi replied.

'Sanjham's right,' Raichand put in. 'You mother him. People talk—'

Prithvi's eyes narrowed. 'Do they?'

Raichand suddenly looked uncertain. 'Well, not us, of course. We know you . . . But still, you shouldn't favour him as you do. He's only a scribe.'

'I'll favour whomsoever I chose,' Prithvi said, letting a little steel enter his voice. 'The court of Prithviraj Chauhan will be a place of music, poetry and culture. Any man who enhances the magnificence of my court will be valued. It will be the wonder of Rajputana.'

Govinda rolled his eyes. 'Here we go again! "Prithviraj's court, blah-blah-blah!"' He raised his voice. 'Where's the damned drink? We need more!' He looked at the laughing Sanjham. 'What's funny, you preening peacock?'

'You are! Grim Govinda: he drinks, he fights, he sleeps – he has no other function! What would you want poetry for, hmm?'

'Poetry is for women,' Govinda agreed, his eyes flicking to Prithvi. 'When you've fought as many campaigns as I have, you'll know. First and foremost of all pastimes is battle. All else is just gilt and decoration.' He half-drew his plain, straight-bladed sword. 'This has killed more princelings and strutting mummy's boys than any blade in the realm – and does it need gemstones? No, it does not. The security of the realm comes first. All else is frivolity. Remember that, my prince.'

It was no use reasoning with Govinda. Prithvi needed him, and Sanjham, and Raichand was amusing and well-connected. But he needed Chand too, and one day they'd all see why.

The whole camp was in a stupor after the celebratory evening meal; the men were either carousing or whoring. Prithvi found Chand in the surgeons' tent; his arms were covered in dried blood, his eyes were red-rimmed, his face grimy. His hands were clean though, and so were the bandages he wrapped about the bruised stump of yet another amputee.

Prithvi waited until the other surgeons had left them alone before he asked, 'How did it go?'

The exhausted poet looked at him and grimaced. 'Vanraj wasn't there – or if he was, he was wise enough to stay at the rear. Either way, once I struck, they didn't react very well. There was no planning, no cohesion – they tried to send in their skirmishers and when that failed, they stormed the slope again.' He winced. 'It was nothing more than slaughter, Prithvi – a child in his first year at Gurukul could have done it. You were better off where you were.'

'Did you clean up?'

'As best as I could. I burned them.'

Prithvi frowned. 'On your own? How many?'

'A dozen, maybe more. They had no chance. It was like shooting pigs in a pen.' Chand kept the true count – closer to sixty – and the method he'd used of burning them, the agniyastra, to himself. The former would steal his friend's glory and the latter was still a secret, even from Prithvi.

The prince whistled softly nevertheless. The poets might sing of men killing swathes of enemies, but any real soldier knew that battle wasn't actually like that. If you killed one or two men, scared away a few more and got out without being maimed, you were a hero. A dozen kills, even from a distance? That truly was the stuff of legend. 'That was a mighty feat, my friend,' he offered, his voice wistful. 'All I did was kill an old man.'

Chand grinned. 'Don't worry, that'll be a victory worthy of Rama by the time I've composed it.'

'Chand Rathod, professional liar.' Prithvi chuckled, then pulled a face. 'The others think you're a coward, that you'd prefer to wear a ghagra choli rather than a breastplate. They say you aren't a real man.'

'It doesn't bother me—'

'Yes, it does,' Prithvi interrupted. 'I'm not blind, my friend. I know you! You're burning to show them what you can do. But you know we have to keep things a secret. You're a scribe and a poet – you're not supposed to know how to fight at all!' He tapped his fingers, his mind moving on. 'You know, my friend, you should marry.'

'*Marry?*' Chand screwed up his face. 'Why would I want to do that? Women are illiterate, avaricious, twittering baby-producers, and the ones at court are even worse – they're either noble harlots or preening magpies, and they all backstab like professional assassins. When they open their mouths it's all gossip or complaints about their men or bitching about everyone else's clothes and jewellery. You can't talk to them, you can't spend enough on them and they never shut up. Why on earth would I want a wife?'

Prithvi laughed. 'If I'd known you were so keen, I'd have arranged it sooner! But seriously, I have someone in mind. She's a relative, so it would tie you to the Chauhans by marriage – and at least people would shut up about you being a Rathod. She's well-bred, she's sensible, and quiet and—'

'Kamla! You mean *Kamla*, don't you?'

Prithvi coloured a little. 'Well, er . . . yes . . . Listen, Chand, she's—'

'She's fat and ugly and a widow.' Chand threw up his hands. 'Her moustache is bushier than Govinda's!'

'No it isn't! This is my cousin you're talking about, right? Okay, she's no beauty, but she *is* a Chauhan. And she's not stupid – far from it. She may be a widow but she's still young and she wants children. She's perfect for you.'

'Because only an ugly woman is good enough for a cowardly scribe,' Chand said sulkily.

Prithvi rolled his eyes. 'Come on, Chand. What did you think? That Father would offer you my sister Pratha? You're too small to fight among the cavalry or in a mêlée, and you're too valuable to risk. It's not fair, I know that, and when I am raja, I promise I will elevate you. But for now, you need legitimacy at court, and that means a good marriage. Kamla is the best there is for you.'

Chand bowed his head. 'All right, my prince. I'm sorry, it's just . . . you know . . .'

Prithvi put a hand on his shoulder. 'Soon, my friend. Anangpal Tomar will cede Dilli to the Chauhamanas now, you just wait and see. You've won us a great victory here, my friend, and I *will* repay you.'

'Okay, okay, I'll marry Kamla. I'll give her sons to take care of. And I'll be patient. As ever.' Chand looked up. 'Now, if you don't mind, honoured prince, I've got more wounds to dress and some victory poetry to compose.'

'And I've got some heavy drinking to do.'

They grinned at each other. 'Each to what we're best at!'

A month later, Anangpal Tomar bequeathed Dilli to the Chauhamanas, to assume control on his death (although that turned out to be a long way off). Congratulations flooded in from all over Rajputana, even from the newly crowned King Vanraj of Gujarat.

But Jaichand Rathod, King of Kannauj, remained silent.

CHAPTER SIX

Swayamvara Live!

Mumbai, 1–5 November 2010

A month after the archery elimination round, those who had, by skill or luck, hit the target arrived in the ballroom of the Taj Hotel in Mumbai. The murderous terrorist attack just two years before cropped up in dozens of conversations amongst the two hundred or so competitors, who had come not just from all over India but from England, Europe, and as far as Australia and North America. Even in the excitement of the moment, it was difficult to forget what had happened here.

Not that any of them were staying at the Taj: Sunita Ashoka might have made good on her promise of accommodation, but it wasn't exactly five-star luxury: the contestants were all crammed into dormitories at a school that had recently gone bankrupt. Those from overseas were particularly virulent in their complaints. Joseph, a red-eyed young Indian from North London, told Jai and Vikram they were sleeping ten to a room on flea-ridden beds outside a major road. 'Not even beds,' he groused, 'more like pallets! I left Walthamstow for this? Trust me, I'm going to let them know all about it!'

Vikram heaved a sigh of relief that he and Jai had been allowed to stay in their own digs at uni – it might not be the Taj, but at least he knew it was clean and free of bugs.

He scanned the ballroom, looking for familiar faces, but the only one he could see was Jai. Not even Pravit Khoolman was there. *Perhaps he's getting a private briefing from Sunita*, he thought sourly. It was difficult not to think that this whole thing was a waste of time, just a massive publicity stunt, that Pravit had it all stitched up. After all, everyone knew he'd been dating Sunita before their very public – and *very* messy – break-up. Sometimes things in the current life could overweigh even the strongest past-life issues; other people's lives could get tangled up by past events. Pravit could be a bigger threat than Ravindra in this setting.

Perhaps he'll pull out, like the papers were saying yesterday? But then he spotted the actor amidst a huddle of bodyguards on the other side of the stage. *Oh well, so much for that.*

'Hello! Hello!' An impeccably groomed middle-aged man had climbed the podium. Feedback squalled as he shouted into the microphone and he winced while someone at the back started fiddling with some controls. At last it was sorted and he started again, 'Ah . . . Good morning, everyone, and thank you all for coming. I am Vishi Ashoka, Sunita's eldest brother, and I am here to oversee this swayamvara.' Lukewarm applause quickly petered out. 'Firstly, a special hello to all those who have come from overseas.' The murmur that greeted this was laden with disgruntled overtones. 'Yes, yes, your complaints about the accommodation have been heard and they will be dealt with, so let us move on, yes?'

Ironic slow-clapping came from the back corner. 'Namby-pamby Brits,' Jai whispered.

Vikram's mind was on other things; he was wondering yet again if he was right about Sunita. His gut instinct that he'd met her at some point in his past lives was based purely on his reaction to seeing her in close-up during a TV interview, the night she'd announced *Swayamvara Live!* to the press. But had they actually met before? Could she be the mad girl? Was she Gauran? *And if she is, what does that* mean? His head was spinning . . .

Jai nudged him, and he tuned back in as Vishi Ashoka announced, 'Gentlemen, you are about to embark on a *phenomenal* journey, full of thrills and spills! A journey which will see one of you here' – he leaned forward and gestured extravagantly around the ballroom – 'yes, one of *you*! Right *here* in this room! Will become the husband of the most *beautiful* and *famous* woman in all of India: *my sister Sunita*!' A screen flashed to life and a highly appreciative murmur filled the room as a bikini-clad Sunita posed provocatively on a sun-drenched beach somewhere exotic.

He waved a hand, trying to shut them up, and went on, '*But* . . . to win this *lifetime opportunity* – yes, to actually *win Sunni's hand in marriage*, you must prove yourself *worthy*! So, my fine young men, how will you do this?' He lowered his voice and said confidentially, 'This is what I will share with you now! Over this coming week, we will really be mixing it up! Yes, you will be subjected to tests, to trials and games, and interviews too: for the viewers around the world – and for *Sunita herself*! For your Queen of Hearts will be watching *every single second*!'

Vikram scoffed at that and said, 'He's talking like a bloody tabloid!' but Jai nudged him to shut up as Vishi went on, 'Highlights will be screened at 7 p.m. nightly, and Sunita herself will be commenting on them – and *yes*!' – his voice rose dramatically again – 'she is watching you *even now*! Her eyes will be upon you *every single day*, and by the end of this week, all but thirty-two of you will be eliminated!'

The young men in the ballroom looked around, counting heads, calculating odds, silently measuring themselves. So only fifteen per cent would go through. It felt as if a switch had been flicked: suddenly, everyone else in the room was a rival.

But Vishi hadn't finished. 'The following week, things *really* hot up, for now the trials begin in earnest! Yes, you lucky thirty-two will be locked in even more *intense head-to-head* competition – and now Sunita will be *here*, *in person*! You will each meet her, you will be given chances – *lots* of chances! – to impress her. And of course, the competition will *intensify*, for there will now be *daily* eliminations!' He started counting down the days on the fingers of one hand as he explained, 'On *Monday* next week, eight fine young men will be out. On *Tuesday* we will say goodbye to another eight. And on *Wednesday* eight more will go, until just eight are left.' Vishi Ashoka leaned forward. 'You think this is harsh? My sister's hand is worth far more effort! After Thursday, there will be *six* left. After Friday, just *four* suitors. And then, on Saturday November 14, my sister will announce which of the four finalists is to be *her* choice of bridegroom!'

He let that thought hang in the air, then resumed, and now his voice was intense, personal. 'Sunita will see you at your *best* and at your *worst* – but do not make the mistake of thinking that this is a beauty contest or an athletic contest, for *it is not*. This is *not* about wealth; it is not about *intellect*; it is not about *family connections*. No, this is far, far more important: this is about a *magical impulse*' – his voice throbbed with passion – 'which my sister believes will be revealed through this *ancient* ceremony. Even she doesn't know precisely what she is looking for, but she believes *most ardently* that she will know it when she sees it!'

Beneath all the *bonhomie* and excitement, Vikram could hear the scepticism in Vishi Ashoka's voice. He wondered how many family arguments there'd been before this strange event had been announced to an unbelieving world. Did Vishi hope it *would* work, or that it *wouldn't*? Would he welcome – or even acknowledge – the winner?

Vishi raised a hand to quell the rising swell of voices. 'A final thought before I hand you to the producers. We all know there have been one or two other TV shows of this nature – *and* how they turned out—'

Vikram looked at Jai, who tapped his nose knowingly; he'd already filled Vikram in on the two previous attempts at a swayamvara-style show like this, when both actresses had apparently decided not even ratings were worth such a marriage and reneged on the deal.

'You have a right to be cynical,' Vishi admitted, 'but my sister *fervently* wants this, and she has argued most passionately for it. She believes most deeply that she will find her destiny – that she will find *true love*. I exhort you to be *worthy* of this most *special*, *most precious* of women, and if there is anyone here who does not believe that he could love my sister with *all* his heart, that he could not be *worthy* of her love, he should leave *right now.*'

Was it his imagination, or did Vishi's eyes trail over Pravit thoughtfully? The tempestuous romance and stormy break-up was public knowledge; Vishi was known to dislike Pravit. But Khoolman didn't flinch.

If they were honest, Vikram thought, *half the room would leave right now. All* they *see is beauty and money. And me . . .? I don't even really understand why I'm here . . . If Sunita Ashoka really is the reincarnation of Gauran, should I be running away, screaming? Or should I be trying to help her? And is it wise or foolish to seek her out so publicly?*

Despite his inner turmoil, he stayed in his seat, desperately thinking through all the possible permutations.

'Okay, honey-buns, you're next.' A tall woman with a deep, melodic voice and wearing an outrageous sari sashayed into the studio waiting-room – and half the men there instantly turned away or pretended to be deep in conversation, rather than acknowledge the girl . . . who was clearly a guy. She patted Vikram's shoulder. 'Skip along, sweetie, we're way behind.'

As soon as Vishi Ashoka had finished his pep talk they'd leaped straight into the trials, starting with a 10,000-metre run, followed by an exercise designed to prove who could – and couldn't – dance and hold a tune. Thirty contestants had already walked out, including most of the badly accommodated foreigners, all Non-Resident Indians, who were loudly threatening to sue over what the jaunt had cost them.

'What's this session about?' Vikram asked as he followed the tall figure into what looked like it might be a make-up room.

'Screen-test, cupcake.' The ladyman looked him over thoughtfully.

'What – we can get eliminated because we don't look good on television?' Vikram snorted. 'I bet the ancients didn't have to go through that.'

The ladyman giggled, which made her Adam's apple quiver. 'Probably not, sweetums, but this is Bollywood. Now, you need to take off your clothes.' She pointed to a row of hooks on the wall. 'Just hang 'em up there and come on through.' Her eyes twinkled at Vikram's appalled look. 'Stop panicking, honey-buns! You can leave your boxers on, ah . . .' She consulted the clipboard, 'Vikram.'

He swallowed in relief. 'Thanks! And you are——?'

'Me?' She sounded surprised. 'Uma.' She fluttered a hand. 'Thanks for asking. First today.' She sashayed out, humming to herself.

Vikram looked about uncomfortably, then mentally resigned himself. He'd been running most of his life and had started taking the gym seriously a couple of years ago: he might not be a hunk, but he wasn't a stick insect either. *In for a penny, in for a pound; that's what they'd say back home in England. Not that it's home any more*, he supposed. He undressed, pulled his shoulders back and went through.

The next room was a forest of bright lights, screens and cords that coiled everywhere like snakes. Uma fluttered her eyes. 'Over here, honey. Oh my, nice abs. That's an unexpected bonus, isn't it, girls?' A flurry of giggles drew Vikram's attention to a row of young women leaning against the far wall. From their clothes he guessed they were film crew, but they looked suspiciously like they were scoring the participants.

'Don't mind them, honey,' Uma snickered. 'They're our panel of experts – they're providing *all sorts* of guidance.' She peered intently at Vikram's face. 'Nice regular features, but you're a little on the short side. I see they re-checked your height already . . . Now, let's see your teeth . . .' She giggled to herself, then asked, 'So, how're you feeling?'

'Like a new stallion at the stud farm.'

The ladyman shrieked, 'Oh, honey! My sorta guy! What're you doing tonight?'

'Dreaming of Sunita Ashoka, I imagine,' he replied wryly.

Uma feigned regret, sighing and tossing back her hair. 'My life is full of these moments. Living in the shadow of India's foremost beauty is so hard!' She gave Vikram a genuinely warm smile.

'Being number two is always challenging,' Vikram answered, making the ladyman snigger again, and recognition suddenly struck him. *She's Uday, the eunuch at the court of Mandore – meeting her could be more important than I thought* . . . 'How long have you worked for Miss Ashoka?' he asked, to cover his sudden distraction.

'Eight years. I've been with her from the beginning. I did her make-up, back in the early days. She took me everywhere with her. Now I'm more like a companion.' Her voice held a faint longing.

'What do you think of this circus?'

Uma met his gaze thoughtfully. 'Oh, I think it's *madness*, darling. All these testosterone-fuelled idiots trying to beat each other up to win her heart? But the poor girl is *convinced* she's Sita. I've never heard such a stupid thing . . . But she thinks this will give her a new start. I really hope it does.' Her voice trailed off, as if she had suddenly realised she was speaking too freely. 'But let's just keep that between us, shall we?' She studied him. 'I like you, Vikram. I hope you do well.' She clapped her hands. 'You can go home now. Be back here at nine sharp tomorrow.'

All week long they were watched by cameras and film-company girls, though none of them had any real idea of what was being judged as they played cricket and football, cycled and sang, completed forms and puzzles and personality tests. The approach of a girl in a *Swayamvara Live!* jacket came to be dreaded, as it usually presaged elimination; one by one they were thinned down, with no reason or explanation given. Some went angrily, others were as sullen as beaten dogs. They might not have seen Sunita, but they could sense her presence behind everything. Uma the lady-man *was* visible, and her word was law. Several of the eliminated men had threatened her, only to be swiftly evicted by the hefty security staff. Another was rumoured to have been chucked out after trying to kiss her – although no one could claim to have actually seen this.

The most instructive clues were gained from watching television each night. They would turn on *Swayamvara Live!* at 7 p.m. and avidly watch the day's highlights – along with increasing numbers of regular viewers – to learn why their fellows had been eliminated from the lips of Sunita herself, who was doing the voice-over for the show. They taped the episodes and pored over them, looking for hints of what Sunita liked and didn't like.

Some had clearly been eliminated because they were bad sports; others caught out by a lie. Once they realised how many men had been booted out for snide comments about other competitors, or uncouth remarks about Uma, the remaining would-be suitors started to school their tongues, to display a positive and cheery demeanour and encourage each other, never mind that they were wishing each other to fall under any convenient car, motorbike or rickshaw!

Of course the cameras concentrated on Pravit Khoolman, who clearly knew how to play the game. The actor was in every second shot, shouting support to his fellow contestants, offering a helping hand on climbing walls, massaging pulled muscles. The newspapers were all over the show and his face was *everywhere*, his popularity stats higher than ever.

Every so often, Vikram saw his own face on camera, mostly laughing with Jai, and then finally helping his friend, gashed to the bone and covered in blood, to the medical tent after he fell off his bike in the velodrome.

'Sorry, man, guess you're on your own now,' Jai whispered through gritted teeth as Vikram tried to get him upright. The pain of failure was far more acute than his injuries. 'Don't let that jerk Khoolman win,' he added.

'I thought he was your idol?' Vikram replied, wondering why no one else was rushing to help them.

'Nah. I'm on to him now. He's been tipped off; that's why he's being Mister Sunshine. But he showed his true colours at the archery event last month. He's not good enough for Sunni.'

Vikram snorted. 'Sure.'

'I mean it, man.'

'I'm sure you do. Now shut up and let's get you to the first-aid tent.'

He had to fight a path through the cameramen while an

interviewer fired questions at them; he answered reflexively, concentrating more on trying to get Jai to the first-aiders. But he didn't punch anyone, although he was sorely tempted.

Despite his expectations, no one in a film-company wind-breaker tapped him on the shoulder all week, and when he walked into the Taj ballroom on Friday afternoon he was a little shocked to be handed a number: Competitor Twenty-Six of the thirty-two finalists. Vishi Ashoka assured them there was no significance to the numbers, but everyone duly noted that Pravit was Competitor One. The finalists all appeared to come from middle-class families, or even above, right up to a raja's son, and all of them looked to be capable and confident. Vikram put aside any notion that this would be easy because of his past lives.

'I want to see you all here, *bright-eyed and bushy-tailed*, at 9 a.m. sharp on Monday morning, and with your game-faces *on*,' Vishi told them all. 'That's when the *real* competition begins! That's when this show will go *LIVE!!!*'

They still hadn't seen Sunita Ashoka in the flesh.

A burly muscleman who clearly fancied himself noticed when Uma winked at Vikram as he filed out with the others. 'I see the tranny fancies you,' he whispered in Vikram's ear. The man was one of Pravit's friends; Vikram groped for his name . . . *Kajal?* He was a professional stuntman.

'So, did you give the ladyman something special?' the big man added, grinning widely. 'Something to get yourself through? You look the sort, you little creep.'

Vikram could see Pravit watching them with narrowed eyes. 'If you're after something of that sort, you're barking up the wrong tree,' Vikram replied. 'Why don't you go and pucker up to your film-star buddy? I'm sure he'd oblige.' Then he hurried away before he got flattened.

CHAPTER SEVEN

Made for Each Other

Jodhpur, Rajasthan, 5 November 2010

Kiran, Dinesh and Bishin joined Ras, who was propped up on the sofa on a stack of cushions watching the latest instalment of *Swayamvara Live!* The show had brought their little household to a stop at 7 p.m. every night that week as they all craned for a glimpse of Vikram on the telly.

'I don't even know why he'd want to marry her anyway,' Ras told Bishin. 'She's *ugly.*'

Bishin pulled a face; her eldest brother seldom spoke, except when he was working. He always said he used up all his words during the daytime, before he gave up even telling them that.

'Ugly?' Dinesh repeated. 'She may be a lot of things, Ras, but never that!'

Ras glared at her stepfather. 'Well, *I* think she is. Her eyes are beady, and her nose looks like a beak. *And* she's had a boob job.' She shifted uncomfortably, sick of sitting down all day, but since she'd got back from hospital it was all she felt up to. She'd missed a whole month at school – her room was full of get-well cards from her classmates, but she was lonely and bored.

'Has she really?' Kiran asked. 'Not according to *People* magazine – they devoted a whole article to her breasts last week!'

Bishin perked up and fished under the coffee-table for the magazines. He grinned when he found it and brandished it aloft, just out of Ras' reach. She scowled at him and snarled, 'Chauvinist!'

Bishin ignored her, ogled the magazine with exaggerated goggle-eyes, then winked slyly.

'A shame you missed the age of silent comedy by eighty years,' she told him.

The *Swayamvara Live!* theme music began and the screen filled with Sunita's face. They sipped tea and pointed out their favourites – they wanted Vikram to win, of course, but in their hearts, none of them believed he stood any chance, especially not now a 'Pravit for Sunni' campaign was sweeping the media. Vikram had shared his views on Pravit with his dad, but Ras still thought the actor was a hunk.

The show largely followed the reality formats they'd seen on other similar shows, a mix of reality TV, documentary and game show all in one – although Vikram had told them it would be going live next week, and then things would be more normal, like *Bigg Boss* or *Who Wants to Be a Millionaire?* They couldn't see her, but they could hear Sunita's voice as she mused aloud over what was going on with the contestants onscreen – whenever she eliminated someone, she would quietly explain why – not that her reasons always made sense; sometimes there was just a little comment like, 'No, not him.' They wondered what the ex-contestants felt about having their faults highlighted on national TV; the newspapers and celeb bloggers especially were keen to give the evicted contestants plenty of space to vent.

Tonight it was a cycling race, to test stamina and character. Kiran spotted Vikram first. 'Look! Look, there he is, there, on the red bicycle— Oh my goodness!' She pointed mutely as two of the cyclists beside Vikram went down in a sickening skid and sprawled across the track, blood spreading beneath them.

Before anyone else could move, Vikram was getting off his own bicycle – *in the middle of the race!* – and was helping one of the fallen competitors off the track; the camera panned, following them as they headed towards what Kiran said was the first-aid tent. Suddenly a lens was thrust into Vikram's face and a microphone all but jammed down his throat as a cold female voice demanded, 'Are you aware that pulling out of the race could cost you your place in the show?'

'Honestly,' they heard Vikram reply, 'I don't give a toss. This is my friend and he needs help.'

'Is this a stunt? Do you think a show of chivalry will get you through?'

Vikram's mouth twisted in a very adult, very ironic way. 'So eliminate me. Now, get out of the way, please – can't you see Jai's injured and in pain?'

'No, I'm not!' said the patient, wiping blood from his face. 'I can carry on, I can!'

'That's his roommate,' Dinesh commented. 'Nice lad.'

'He is nice,' Ras agreed, trying to take her mind off how hunky Vikram looked, and how grown up – even though he'd barely noticed her, even after what had happened to her – to them all – in March. He was always too busy having intense conversations with Amanjit and Deepika; sometimes she almost felt like he was actively avoiding her.

'He's covered in blood – how can you tell?' Bishin wondered, lifting his eyes from the magazine.

'Go back to your vow of silence, dork,' Ras responded.

'Children!' Kiran warned. 'She'll eliminate Vikram and Jai for this . . .'

'You know,' came Sunita Ashoka's voice, 'sometimes it can be hard to tell genuine concern from posturing. By now, I think all the competitors have realised that I'm not interested in men with no compassion. Are this pair now milking this – or is this genuine? Because I can't stand being lied to.'

'My son doesn't lie!' yelled Dinesh at the television.

'So should I red-card these two?' Sunita asked dramatically.

'He's a good boy, you silly bint!' Kiran shrieked. 'You leave him alone!'

Then Sunita's voice grew warmer. 'But I happen to know that these two are roommates and best friends. Of course, the poor man who fell off the cycle won't recover in time to finish the competition. But I am sure that his friend's concern is real. True brotherhood: I like that in a man. The hand of destiny is intervening.'

'Woo hoo!' shouted Kiran. 'You wonderful girl!'

'Sunni, we love you!' Dinesh and Bishin cheered.

Ras pursed her lips. *That's my Vikram you're talking about, lady. He has nothing to do with you.* 'I still think she's ugly,' she muttered to no one in particular. Bishin winked at her, then pulled an amazed face at the magazine pictures – the article on Sunita's boobs, no doubt – as the telly cut away to a commercial.

Later that night Ras lit a candle and took out her holy book. She opened it to the traditional thanksgiving prayer, the Ardas, and puffed her way through it, her words a semi-audible murmur. She had felt short of breath all night, ever since seeing Vikram onscreen and hearing Sunita Ashoka talking about him.

Holy God, bless me. Lend me courage and strength. Please, I want to live.

Her mind was far away, hovering about a face too serious for its age, a face that increasingly filled her thoughts. *Vikram.* The truth was, she'd barely spoken to him, and never alone. He'd always been distracted, never really looking at her, and that made her doubt him, and herself. But seeing him on TV and realising that this reality TV show was just that – *real* – had crystallised something in her mind. *I want to see him again before I . . .*

Her phone rang and a name flashed on the screen: *Amanjit*. 'Hi, bhaiya,' she answered.

'Hey, Ras! How are you tonight?'

'I'm good,' she lied. In fact the doctors were increasingly at a loss to combat her deterioration, and every briefing was less hopeful. They didn't have to tell her explicitly that her heart was getting worse; she knew it. She was going to die, and soon. 'Today was a good day.'

Her brother knew she was lying, but he also knew better than to dwell on the negative. She loved him for that. 'Did you see Vik on the telly?' Amanjit chortled. 'Being the he-man? That was so funny! And that dopey Sunita-chick bought it—'

'It wasn't a put-on. He *meant* it.'

'Of course he did – and he'll win now.'

'Vikram? No . . . !' She tried to sound amused at the thought instead of panic-stricken.

'Yeah, he'll win, you'll see – I mean, she thinks she's Sita and he thinks he's Rama . . . they're made for each other!'

'No way! I mean, yeah, she's mad – and ugly. But Vikram doesn't think he's Rama . . . are you teasing me, Amanjit?'

'Never! But you watch: he'll win.'

'No he won't, Pravit will. It's all a fix, everyone knows that!'

'If you say so, didi. Now, how's Mum?'

She was exhausted after their ten-minute chat, but the conversation had filled her with new resolve. She pulled out a photo of Amanjit, Deepika, Vikram and her, taken earlier in the year at one of the many parties celebrating her mother's engagement to Dinesh. They were posing in the lounge. She stared at Vikram's face, wishing she could somehow wish herself to his side.

*Please, Lady, hear me . . . I think I'm dying . . . I want to do this one
last thing . . .*

She made her decision, thumbed the keypad and winced at the
sudden burst of crackly Rajasthani music, then a slow male voice
drawled into her ear, 'Hey, little Cousin Ras, what's happening?
It's late!'

'Idli! Hi! How are you?' Cousin Idli – nicknamed for his addic-
tion to the south Indian snack – drove his truck all over India.

'I'm floating high, little cousin. Been smoking the good stuff!
What do you want, some presents from the big city? I can get you
anything, sweetie!'

'No, no, I don't want . . . um—' She swallowed, and whispered, 'Idli, when are you next driving down to Mumbai?'

CHAPTER EIGHT

The Raja of Kannauj

Taragarh Fort, Ajmer, Rajasthan, 1169

'They say a man who sires only women does so because he is so dominant in his house that his wife's body responds by producing only girls, to try and balance his power,' Sanjham Rai said slyly. 'Which makes one really wonder about our friend Chand when he only produces sons!'

Oh, subtle, Sanjham: are you really suggesting I'm not master of my own house? But Chand was used to such sallies by now, and this wasn't the night to make a scene. He was the host, after all, and half the court were jammed into the gardens of Taragarh Fort for this feast to celebrate the fact that he was a father again: a third son. Chand was in his finest clothes, his matching red and white turban flecked with gold thread and set with precious gemstones. Kamla was also draped in her finest; she sat amidst a crowd of matrons. She reminded Chand of a toad on a lily-pad – all wide eyes and drooping jowls, fleshy and quivering – while about her moved slender visions of perfect womanhood, the wives of the warriors, tittering and gossiping. Nautch-girls danced, musicians played. The tables bent under their load of flesh, fruits and sweetmeats. All this was set out in the garden beneath his rooms inside the Taragarh, the Chauhans' stronghold above Ajmer.

His two younger sons were with their ayahs, whilst the newborn slept. Around the edges of the garden, the warriors lounged or strutted past, displaying their gaudy clothes to best advantage, decorative swords glittering at their sides. Most were a little drunk, but not overly – it was always better to keep one's wits about one, even at a social occasion for a minor courtier – although favoured, or they wouldn't be here at all – like Chand.

'It makes one wonder about old wives' tales, certainly,' Chand replied evenly. He was used to Sanjham by now. The man habitually baited others, but whilst he might disdain Chand, he was smart enough to realise that Prithvi favoured the poet, and therefore wasn't someone to provoke overly. It didn't silence his needling tongue, though; Sanjham just couldn't help himself.

Govinda, standing next to them, was tearing at a haunch of meat like a feeding tiger, his eyes fixed on the dancing Nautch-girls. He swallowed, and asked, 'Where's Raichand?'

'With a woman, where else?' Sanjham replied. 'His wife is away on some pilgrimage, so he is purging his lust with some whore he brought back from Dilli.' He looked at Chand. 'What did you think of Dilli, poet?'

Chand had – yet again – been negotiating Prithvi's caretaking of the realm until Anangpal Tomar's own children came of age; Anangpal was stubbornly refusing to die, which was trying everyone's patience.

'I liked it,' Chand admitted. 'Ajmer is a village by comparison. Dilli is where Prithvi should be. The Lal Kot Fortress is three times bigger than this . . . even you would be impressed, Sanjham.'

'It must gall Jaichand,' smirked Sanjham. 'The Rathod rat

must be furious. Ten years older than Prithvi, and passed over.'
He eyed Chand. 'You're a Rathod. Have you seen Jaichand lately?'

'I am a loyal Chauhan, by desire as well as by marriage. And
no, I've not seen Jaichand,' Chand replied civilly. 'But I hear that
he's as bitter as a jilted bride.'

Sanjham patted Chand condescendingly on the shoulder. 'No
one questions your loyalty, Chand,' he said, the tone of his voice
suggesting that everyone did. 'And congratulations on your latest
progeny. No mean feat, given your bride's . . . um . . . lack of
grace.' His eyes were mild, yet challenging. Sanjham had killed
four men recently, duels provoked quite deliberately with just
such doses of measured insolence.

*Just once, Sanjham Rai, I would like to smash my fist into your clever
mouth and break your pointy little teeth.* 'Enjoy your evening,' Chand
replied. 'I must attend other guests.' He walked away, seething.

'Chand, welcome,' Prithvi Chauhan said, as Chand slipped into
his friend's private chambers. The city below was dimly lit, yet
still teeming with life, despite the monsoon which had been
flushing the streets. The king was staring out of the window. They
were both twenty now: Prithvi was tall and imposing, muscular
and lithe, the very model of the Rajput warrior-class. Chand had
remained small; he was thin and harried-looking, except when
alone with his prince.

'How was your feast?' Prithvi asked. 'Is it over already?'

'It's well after midnight, Prithvi. All three of my sons are
screaming their lungs out, Kamla snores like a camel and half the
guests are unconscious in my gardens. I had to escape!'

'Three sons! I told you it was a good match. Kamla may not be
a beauty, but I think you are fond of her now. I have seen you
smile at each other.'

'I value her,' Chand admitted. 'She is uncomplaining, and she is observant of the court around her.' In fact, his wife was wonderfully insightful when it came to the machinations of the court. She was always well abreast of court gossip, and on good terms with the other women – with her lack of 'grace' they saw her as no threat, and often confided in her. He might not have chosen Kamla, but he certainly appreciated her.

'And in the dark, one woman is like another,' laughed Prithvi unkindly – then he thought better of his words and apologised. 'I'm sorry, my friend. I shouldn't say such things.'

Chand was used to forgiving his prince. 'She and I have an understanding.' He took a handful of areca nuts and ate one. 'How is your father?'

Prithvi became serious. 'He's really not well. I'm travelling to Pushkar tomorrow. They tell me he is praying, seeking moksha, so I'll go to his deathbed and pay my final respects. I must do that in strength, so I'll have Govinda on one side and Sanjham on the other.'

'Your strongman and your conspirator. You'll leave me here to keep an eye on Raichand?'

'Not this time,' Prithvi replied. 'Oh, I know Raichand has ambitions, but he's not a threat yet. If I leave him here for a short time, he won't let me down. Anyway, I need you to go and see your beloved kinsman Jaichand Rathod.'

Chand was a little shocked. '*Me?* I'm not exactly welcome in Kannauj, Prithvi – I'm the Rathod who married a Chauhan! Jaichand will ignore me if I'm lucky – and gut me if I'm not.'

'He wouldn't dare. You think your name isn't spoken in courts all over Rajputana? People *know* you speak for me. I promise you, Jaichand will listen to you.'

'So what am I to say?'

'That Prithvi Chauhan will soon be Prithviraj III, King of Ajmer and Dilli; that it is time for the disputes between us to be put aside. We should unite our houses: I have no wife and he has an unwed daughter.'

'His daughter is only twelve,' Chand reminded him.

'By the time I wed her, she will be of age,' Prithvi replied. 'A skinny little thirteen-year-old virgin, ripe for the plucking.' Like all of his caste, he saw women as little use for anything except pleasure and breeding. The high-bred were ornaments, prizes; they had their own separate wing of the palace and led almost entirely separate lives, except when it came time to assure the succession. 'Then I can set about catching up on your three sons!' He lifted a cup in an amiable toast. 'So, will you go?'

Chand sighed. 'Of course.'

Kannauj, 1169

The court of Jaichand Rathod was a palace of whispers: everyone speaking at once, but every conversation was hushed, delivered behind hands into waiting ears, furtive eyes checking to see who was observing. Vishwamitra had once told Chand that kings set the tone of their court: if that really was the case, Jaichand Rathod was a plotter and a schemer.

The king was well-built and richly dressed, yet strangely unimpressive. He sat hunched over, his head cocked as a string of shaven-skulled servants murmured in his ear, one after the other.

Jaichand and Chand were sitting in a marble-roofed cupola, the pillars carved with scenes of battles and romances, life and death. They were alone, so that their words would not be overheard – a rare honour, Chand knew, but Prithvi had been right: Jaichand had been intrigued by him from the moment he arrived in Kannauj.

The Raja of Kannauj sat cross-legged on a cushioned throne

with Chand, on a hard mat, facing him. The king's retinue – warriors, musicians and dancers, soothsayers and priests – lurked below, watching and straining their ears.

'So,' Jaichand said eventually, waving his whisperers away. 'Chand Rathod . . . is it still Rathod? Or do you use another name, now you are so ensconced with the Chauhans in Ajmer?'

'They call me Chand Bardai, for my poetry,' Chand replied. He was proud of that honorific, even though he knew it was mostly so that the name 'Rathod' wouldn't be used in Prithvi's hearing. 'I am still a Rathod,' he added.

'Are you indeed? Yet you befriend my enemy and live at his beck and call. You even marry the ugliest woman in all India at his behest.'

A warrior would challenge you for that, and your men would expect you to fight the duel yourself. But I have not even the rank to challenge you, as you know. Petty, vindictive Jaichand.

Chand swallowed the insult. 'My wife carries her beauty within,' he replied in careful, submissive tones. 'Raja Jaichand, Prithvi Chauhan bid me say this: soon he will become Prithviraj III, Lord of the Chauhamanas. The whole of Rajputana fear war between Chauhan and Rathod. But Prithvi asks, "Why not peace?" He asks, "Why should there be war, where once there was friendship?" He asks, "Why should my queen not be a Rathod?" Indeed, perhaps the daughter of his cousin Jaichand, to ensure peace, and seal it before the gods.'

A servant climbed up and bent to Jaichand's ear. *Whisper, whisper, whisper . . .*

'I have heard that your daughter is of surpassing beauty,' Chand added. 'It would honour the Chauhamanas greatly to find alliance thus. It would honour Prithvi.'

A sideways look. More whispers.

The servant backed away, bowing. Jaichand turned back to his guest. 'I will consider this. In either case, you shall meet my daughter. I am having her brought here.' He clapped his hands and servants rushed up with platters of dried fruits, raisins and dates, and edible seeds. He helped himself, then gestured for Chand to do the same.

When the servants had withdrawn, he leaned forward. 'So, Chand Rathod, proud Rathod poet and scholar, intimate of the Chauhan king . . . Tell me: are you as deep in the counsel of the Chauhamanas raja as word suggests? Close friends since childhood; keeper of his secrets, they say. Is it so?'

'We share a close friendship,' Chand agreed. 'And he heeds my counsel.'

'And he rewards this friendship well?' Jaichand leaned closer, his eyes hungry.

'Passably well, if by reward you mean being kept around as an untitled lapdog so his warriors can mock me, and forced into a marriage I didn't want.' Chand deliberately inflected his words with hints of injury and regret. 'In chambers barely big enough, and a wife always carping at how little finery I can afford. And as you say, she is no beauty . . .'

Jaichand smiled sympathetically. 'It is a shame, is it not, that a king who claims surpassing nobility would abuse your friendship in such a way, especially when you contribute so much to his thinking, and know his mind so well.' He spread his hands in a gesture of benevolence. 'I, on the other hand, know how to value those who share their knowledge to the benefit of all.'

Chand met his eye and nodded in understanding.

'It is good to have this conversation and be reconciled, Chand Rathod,' Jaichand said loudly. 'You are welcome at my court.' He half-turned, and cried, 'Ah, here is my daughter!'

A slender veiled girl stepped forth from a crowd of newly arrived women, handmaids and wives of the king. She was dressed in deep greens and maroons, shrouded and anonymous. She stopped a few yards away, uncertain, and went to kneel.

'No, no child, we are all friends here. This is my cousin, Chand Rathod, from Dilli.' The girl turned and looked at him through her gauzy odhani. 'Take off the veil, child,' Jaichand instructed. 'Chand must give report of you to Cousin Prithvi.'

The girl bowed her head, then raised slim, shapely arms and pulled back her odhani.

Chand sucked in his breath.

The girl was surpassingly lovely: big, long eyes and the most delicate bone structure, fair and perfect of complexion, lips soft and moist, a slender neck. But that wasn't what stopped his throat.

Darya!

Jaichand chuckled, mistaking his distress for lust. 'She is magnificently beautiful, is she not, cousin? Her name is Sanyogita: the fairest creature in all this world! A prize beyond prizes is my Sanyogita.'

She spoke, and the sound of her voice almost broke Chand's heart. The same music, and the same defiance of his lost Rani Darya of Mandore. 'Who is Prithvi, Father?' Then she answered her own question as her eyes went back to Chand. '*Prithvi Chauhan?* This man is from Prithvi Chauhan?' Her eyes narrowed, her voice held a slight cadence that betrayed eagerness.

They say in Ajmer that all women dream of Prithvi. Do they also have such dreams here in Kannauj?

Chand nodded, meeting her eyes.

Jaichand was suddenly displeased. 'Go, Daughter. This man has seen enough.'

Sanyogita looked back at Chand as she left, her eyes drinking him in, almost as if she *knew* . . .

Jaichand watched her go with possessive eyes and a strange

hunger that chilled Chand to the marrow. When he turned back to Chand, his face was flat and hostile. 'She is dear to me, Cousin. Dearer than all the jewels in my kingdom. So, much as I treasure the friendship of Prithvi Chauhan, we must find another way to align ourselves. He may not have my daughter in marriage. *Never.*'

Chand bowed his head. He'd been shown the girl to taunt him, and through him, Prithvi.

I hear you, Jaichand. But I know that I must reunite them: reuniting Darya and Shastri has just become the purpose of my life.

The raja clapped his hands and stood. Servants closed in. The audience was over.

Chand was reunited with his small escort of Chauhan soldiery and they left Kannauj the next day. He travelled with a bag of gold coins given him by a shaven-headed Rathod servant, apparently to secure his newfound loyalty to Jaichand. The money would come in handy, but his loyalty had never actually been for sale. He was focused on only one thought now. *Darya, I have found you!*

It was clear to him that this was a chance to right the wrongs of his past life in Mandore — and perhaps even to bring about the death of his Enemy. *I've not forgotten you, Ravindra. Your vile ritual failed because I kidnapped Darya and inadvertently brought her and Shastri together. What happens when I allow them to live together in love, as they were destined? Will that not destroy you?*

Though watching her love another will likely destroy me too . . .

He returned home to find Ajmer in uproar: Someshwar the king was dead and Prithvi had, predictably, been crowned his successor. The reign of Prithviraj Chauhan III had begun, and the queues of supplicants outside Chand's door next morning stretched far, all seeking friendship and favours from the new Raja of Ajmer and Dilli's best friend.

CHAPTER NINE

First Day Dramas

Mumbai, 8 November 2010: Day 1 of Swayamvara Live!

The change in atmosphere was palpable. This week Vikram had to shove his way through press and onlookers just to get to the top of the street where the studio was sited; he wouldn't have got any further if he hadn't put on his competitor's jacket – and from that moment, just as he'd feared, he was mobbed by teenagers and young men and women from all walks of life, pushing him through, screaming his name and waving flags. 'Come this way, bhai!' a uniformed guard shouted, 'Security is this way! Come, come!' A tiny channel opened to where a wall of security men were blocking the studio entrance. The noise was deafening, everyone shouting and cheering, and over it all, the ceaseless racing of engines and blaring and beeping of car horns. The heat of the enveloping crowd had him dripping, even though it was November and almost winter. *So this is what it's like being a celeb . . . I think I can probably live without it!*

Every few steps he passed another well-groomed reporter trying to shout above the noise; he caught snippets as he passed—

'—s is NDTV, reporting more Mumbai madness . . .'

'—saying Sunita doesn't like facial hair any more! Of the

thirty-two finalists, only five have moustaches – and favourite
Pravit Khoolman has shaved! The trend is clear . . .'

'—going to be just another false swayamvara show? Will
Sunita Ashoka *really* marry a complete stranger? Of course,
Pravit is no stranger at all . . .'

'—don't call Sunita "Ashoka the Shocker" for nothing,
Radhika! Is this the last straw? Is this the end of India's love affair
with this unusual artist – or will it rekindle our affection for her?
The next week will tell us all! But for now, it's back to you in the
studio, Rad—'

All over town newspaper billboards had been the same.

> INSIDER: SUNITA HAS NO INTENTION
> TO MARRY WINNER
> PRAVIT THE CLEAR FAVOURITE
> SUNITA CURSED FOR BLASPHEMY:
> WILL NEVER FIND LOVE
> IS THE SHOCKER'S REAL LOVE A
> MAN IN A SARI? WE PROFILE UMA!

The *Times of India*'s showbiz team had given each of the thirty-
two contestants a rating out of ten; over breakfast Vikram had
discovered that he was rated 2 stars (the lowest of any of them,
he noted with a grimace), and described as '*a local boy, too short,
too young, too naïve. Will be gone by lunchtime*'. The bookies apparently had his odds at 800:1. He cut the piece out as a souvenir.

As he inched his way through the crowd, people, recognising
him, bombarded him with comments:

'Good luck, bhai! Do it for Mumbai! Do us proud, Vikram!'

'Hey, twenty-six,' screamed a teenage girl with braces and a
garish dupatta, 'I love you!'

My first fan . . . He grinned and waved at her as he broke through into the enclosed area. A security man was patting him down when sirens blared and a shockwave ran through the crowd, spilling people in all directions. A train of limousines was forcing itself through the press with someone standing on the roof of the lead vehicle, bellowing incoherently into a megaphone. *Pravit Khoolman, making an entrance, no doubt. What a dick!* But even that was topped by another contestant who was arriving from the opposite direction: on the back of an elephant!

The raja's son, I bet. 'This is insane!' he shouted at the security guard, but the man just grinned through broken teeth and cupped a hand to his ear.

Well, maybe this is a mistake, but at least it'll be memorable.

As soon as he was through security he checked his phone and returned the earlier call – from the only person he wanted to talk to right now. 'Hi, Amanjit. Sorry, I couldn't answer before.'

'That's okay, bhai. How're you feeling? Have you made up your mind about this?'

They'd been burning all their credit on long-distance calls, talking through whether he should really be doing this or not, especially after the attack on Deepika, who was still shaky and couldn't remember a thing about her collapse.

'Until I actually meet Sunita, I won't know for sure,' Vikram admitted, 'but Dee's second collapse? That's really raised the stakes. We can't just sit around hoping nothing's going to happen, not any more. Ravindra's out there, bhai, and he wants our blood. And if this does draw him out, we have to be ready.'

'Have you recognised anyone else?'

'Other than Uday? Not so far. Believe it or not, I like the ladyman! Uma's one of Sunita's people and I reckon she's very protective . . .'

'So you're going to actually meet the goddess today, then?' Amanjit paused, then asked, 'So, what if it is her, this insane chick you've been married to in half your previous lives? What will you do if she is Gauran – run away? Or try to win?'

'I've no bloody idea . . .'

'You know what I think, Vik? We *have* to find Ravindra and deal with him; we've got no choice, right? We missed our chance in Jodhpur, so if Sunita really is your ex, then that should lure him out – and then we can nail him.'

'We're just going to "nail" Ravana-reborn?' Vikram asked sceptically. 'You've forgotten that whole "sorcerer-king" thing?'

'We can do it. We nearly had him in Jodhpur, didn't we? And now you know who you are . . . So I think if it's her, give it your best shot.'

Amanjit was right: it might sound insane, but this really was their only lead right now. 'Okay. Listen, I'll call you tonight after the show, and tell you what I've got.'

They ended the call, and Vikram headed for the studio door. To his own surprise, he was ready to enjoy himself, whatever happened.

'Right, mate, let's do you now.' The film technician was a ginger-haired, overweight, bearded Australian who smoked like a chimney. 'I'm Jez. Me mates call me Jezzer, and you can call me "sir". And if you're anything like that actor jerk I've just been working on, you can sod off right now.'

'Did Mister Khoolman annoy you . . . *sir*?' Vikram asked, trying to keep a straight face.

'Annoy? Hah! I'm told this is a *family* show, so let's just go with "annoyed the bloody hell out of me"! How's that?' he added, as he fixed a microphone to Vikram's collar. 'Apparently I wasn't female, pretty or Indian enough for your bollocking Mister Coolbutt . . . and don't tell me you're another of his adoring bloody fans!'

'For now, every contestant is my enemy,' Vikram replied lightly.

'Good! That's the attitude. Sun-Tzu, *Art of War* or whatever. Go for their nuts, I reckon, and squeeze hard.' He reached out and jiggled the wire behind Vikram's neck, and then stepped away, drawing on his cigarette. 'Okay, say something.'

'India won the last one-day series against Australia. Sir,' Vikram replied. His voice echoed faintly about him from a number of speakers. Jez cocked his ear, then came back to him and moved the microphone a little.

'So they did. Couldn't care less, mate. I'm more of a rugby man, and you lot ain't much cop at that game.' He pointed to the right. 'Far door, then left, wait your turn in the green room. No smoking in there,' he added, puffing on his cigarette again.

'I don't smoke. It's a filthy habit. Sir.'

'Whatever.' Jez half-smiled at him. 'Sod off, and good luck, mate.'

Vikram negotiated the tangled cables and discarded coffee cups littering the corridor to join five other contestants in the green room. He guessed the red light flashing on the wall meant someone was already being filmed and that no one should use the studio door.

The raja's son was lounging on a plastic chair, magnificently dressed in an elaborate turban and a full-length kurta studded with what looked suspiciously like real gemstones. He was stroking his impressive-looking moustache worriedly. 'I wouldn't shave it off, not for any woman,' he was saying as Vikram entered. 'It is part of who I am.' He glanced up at Vikram, then turned back to the man he was talking to: Pravit Khoolman, of course.

'What's next?' Vikram asked the room.

'We meet Sunita,' said a young, sick-looking youth sitting next to the door.

'And then we kill each other,' added a burly Sikh beside him with a faint grin. 'With cars.'

'Really? How do you know?' Vikram asked, ignoring Pravit's hostile face.

'Just a rumour,' the Sikh replied, with the air of one who knows secrets.

The light crackled green. 'Next!'

'That's me,' the Sikh announced. 'Don't bother to follow, boys; her heart will be mine before you even meet her.' Looking determined, he pulled himself to his full impressive height and marched out.

The raja's son leaned forward. 'Have we met before?' he asked Vikram in a puzzled voice.

'Not in this life,' Vikram replied, extending a cautious hand, which the young prince took in his own ring-encrusted fingers. 'Vikram Khandavani.'

'Alok Pandiya, next Raja of Gondwara, when Father finally decides to die. You know, there is something familiar about you . . .'

Vikram tried to mask his own reaction, but he'd instantly recognised him: *Raichand* . . . Another face from the past was a really worrying sign. There were a few people from his past he'd always liked – Tilak, the faithful soldier who'd helped them in Mandore was one. There were a few others, but not many, and he'd come to regard too many *old faces* as a bad sign. *And here they are, all turning up again* . . .

The room emptied and filled as competitors were summoned elsewhere and others came in. Some talked, some tried to get autographs from Pravit. The-next-Raja-of-Gondwara left, and then Pravit, to Vikram's relief. The actor had studiously ignored him.

'He really doesn't like you, does he?' remarked an older man who introduced himself as Mandeep Shekar, a businessman.

'It's that obvious?'

'Indeed. So what exactly did you do to upset our Bollywood hero?'

'I think he's marked me down as his chief rival,' Vikram replied with a wink.

'Perhaps, perhaps.' Mandeep chuckled. 'I think she'll go for an older man, myself. Someone to guide her, someone with experience.'

How about sixteen lives' worth of experience, Vikram thought. *Would that do?*

The green light flashed. It was his turn.

Uma greeted him at the door wearing a white mini-dress and a gold-sequinned hat. 'Hey, Vikram,' she purred. 'Like my outfit?'

'Very classic,' Vikram offered as the ladyman did a twirl.

'I think so.' She ran a critical eye over Vikram. 'Whereas you look like you've just stepped off a twelve-hour flight from a Bangkok junk-sale. Honey, you *really* need someone to take you clothes shopping.'

Vikram ducked his head apologetically. The clothes were his best: a long-sleeved grey embroidered shirt and faded cotton pants. 'Er . . . this is my nicest stuff.'

Uma winced. 'Well, too late to change now, darling. Come and talk to me later.' She put a hand behind his shoulder and gently pushed him through a door. 'This way. Come and meet Sunni.'

The studio was a blackened pit surrounding a dazzlingly lit stage, where a small bird-like woman with flowing locks had her face buried in her hands.

'Oh my. Wait here,' Uma told him, and swept past the aides and techies and cameramen to throw herself onto the couch beside the woman. Vikram watched with growing discomfort as he saw the heaving shoulders and heard the wet sound of sobbing as Uma embraced the distraught actress and wiped her face. 'Honey, let's take a break, shall we? Are those cameras still on? Well, turn the damn things off! For heaven's sake, give her some privacy, you idiots!'

'No.' The quietly authoritative voice came from the skinny figure in her arms. Sunita Ashoka sat up, the tears on her cheeks glimmering in the stage-lights. 'No. In this process there must be no privacy. The world must see everything.'

'Oh sweetie, you don't have to do that to yourself – and it's hardly fair on this young man if your mind is still doing flip-flops over Pravit, is it?'

Sunita wiped her face and peered towards the door, where Vikram was standing. 'All is Destiny. If that's what Fate dictates for him, then he must accept. I cannot make allowances for one over another—'

It was very clear from Uma's expression what she thought of this, but she waved Vikram forward with a resigned gesture.

Vikram fished in his pocket, thankful that for once he had remembered his mother's stricture always to carry a clean hand-kerchief, and he offered it to India's most beautiful woman as he stepped onto the stage. Up close, her black hair was a night-sky of stars and comets, her flawless skin was the palest coffee. Her body might be slight, but there was no doubt she worked out. He didn't let his gaze linger over her much-debated breasts, which looked real enough as far as he could tell, straining at the bodice of her gorgeous peacock-tail blue silk dress. It was her eyes, huge and heavy with tears, that drew his gaze.

It's her. All his memories rippled within him: an array of names, all just temporary labels for the single soul who had shared so many of his lives. Ancient storms of rage and joy, fer-ocious fights and passionate reunions played out again and again – he could scarcely believe she didn't feel it too, but even through so many colliding echoes, nothing stirred within her eyes, no recognition of him.

He wondered what Pravit was to her. Had the actor been important to her in the lives she had lived when he hadn't met her? Then he discarded that thought as irrelevant and concentrated solely on the woman before him: Gauran, his lost, insane love.

In a resplendent palace built of marble and gilt, protected by spiked iron and razor-wire coiled atop the twelve-foot stone wall, lurked a cobra. The palace was in the heart of the prestigious Bandra district, where politicians and film stars and captains of industry vied for the best real estate: a jigsaw of luxurious apartments and glittering hideaways, where the rich could be who they truly wanted to be when they were away from the prying eyes of the public.

The manor was neither the largest nor the smallest, but it was among the most private; Shiv Bakli insisted on that. It had been carefully designed and landscaped to ensure that even the most sophisticated snooping eye would be thwarted. With its labyrinth of subterranean bedrooms and lounges, play room, private cinema, spa and pool, it sprawled for a full block, and yet few would ever have realised it was there, for Bakli threw few parties, and when he did invite guests, they were carefully selected. Despite ever-more-elaborate attempts to shed light on this most mysterious man, no member of the press had ever got close.

So who was Shiv Bakli? Financier, entrepreneur, gangster. 'The Cobra' was all of these things – and more, for his real identity had become much more complicated of late, ever since increasingly bad dreams had turned to screaming nightmares of choking on the blood of every victim of every crime he'd committed on his barbarous rise to power. No one had been omitted, from the backstreet stabbings that had been his initiation into his first gang to the broken girls raped in alleyways and the coked-out actresses with blood-filled lungs asphyxiating on their own toilet floors. Then, however impossible this was, the face in the bathroom mirror had *changed*: terrifying charred hands had reached out of the glass to clutch at his throat, and something had crawled into his brain and taken over. There had been no witnesses to his murder, and no body – the mind behind the face of Shiv Bakli was another man's. The soul was another soul entirely.

Ravindra needed a host and that host had to be of a like mind – and Shiv Bakli was *perfect*: the sort of man who would sell his own kin for gain, who would watch his own sister choke to death on the poison he had devised and administered, without the slightest hint of remorse. Someone who could break a terrified child in a secret torture chamber in the depths of his home, and then calmly dismember and incinerate the body. A man who could donate millions to charity and accept the plaudits without the faintest sense of irony. Shiv Bakli was a liar, a torturer, a rapist and killer – and a towering egotistical hypocrite. Ravindra slipped inside with almost no resistance, and no one noticed the difference.

Tonight he was on his own, the only change his people had noted. The real Shiv Bakli had never been one for solitary contemplation, but since Ravindra stepped in, he spent more and more time alone. Tonight his only company was a highly expensive bottle of aged Scotch whisky, a jug of pure spring water and a massive flatscreen TV, currently showing *Swayamvara Live!* He was studying it intently.

'Remember what I said in Paris?' the whole nation heard Pravit Khoolman whisper to Sunita Ashoka. 'Well, my darling, I was wrong.' He stroked her cheek, and she burst into tears. The moment was replayed again and again as the onscreen presenters guessed what he might have said and discussed all the implications for the other contestants – even though no one other than Pravit and Sunita had any idea what he'd meant.

Since the show had gone completely live, it had spawned a subsidiary – *The Swayamvara Panel Show!*; a hastily cobbled-together group of 'experts' to analyse what happened and dissect the 'highlights' of *Swayamvara Live!* It ran for an hour every night after the contestants had clocked off for the day.

Ravindra studied the show for the glimpses it gave him of his Enemy: Vikram Khandavani dancing more than competently with a popular girl from the Bollywood chorus-line in a *Strictly Come Dancing in the Punjab* segment; giving Sunita his handkerchief as she wept at Pravit's words; losing at arm-wrestling in a ridiculously unfair battle against an immense stuntman. His chivalry in consoling Sunita without trying to push himself on her had been rewarded: eight of the finalists had already been eliminated, but Vikram somehow managed to cling on. It was all entirely predictable, Ravindra thought sourly.

'What exactly did Pravit mean?' the *Panel Show!* presenter was asking her group of experts – fashion designers, newspaper gossip columnists and 'insiders' – who preened for the cameras and said nothing useful at all. 'What happened between them in Paris – and what is it that he takes back? Well, I'm sure it will all come out. Keep watching, India! This show is just going to get more and more intense!'

Intense? thought Ravindra. *Oh yes, I think it will end in blood.*

He switched off the TV and contemplated the darkness. In the shadows, wispy figures writhed like ash caught in a breeze – his dead queens, vanquished in Jodhpur in March, but gradually re-forming. They too were capable of stealing another's body, but it was far harder for them, and for now, he wanted them close. The heart-stones he wore around his neck had imprisoned them for a millennia in this half-life. He had six stones, but there should have been seven; he had five ghostly queens, but there should have been seven of them too. The missing queens troubled him more than he liked to admit, even to himself.

'Let us serve you, Lord,' Halika, the chief of his queens, the one who had always been the most like him, pleaded from the shadows. 'Let me take a body that pleases you.'

'Silence,' he scolded, and Halika recoiled as if slapped. The others – pretty, doll-like Rakhi; skinny, hungry Jyoti; foolish, frightened Meena, and needy Aruna – chittered and all but dissipated like smoke on the breeze. Over the long centuries he'd come to loathe them all, even Halika, but they were bound together in this dark dance until he overcame his Enemy.

He now knew where his sixth queen was: thanks to the heart-stone he'd retrieved from Mehrangarh Fortress, he'd found Darya-reborn, or Deepika Choudhary, as she was in this life. But the seventh – placid Padma, Madan Shastri's sister – continued to elude him, and this game could not end until she too had returned to her place at his side.

'Leave me,' he told them. 'Go to your holes. Feed on bugs and worms.'

Their moaning grated on him, but they obediently faded into the shadows and vanished. Once they were gone, he turned towards the balcony, meaning to take the night air, when suddenly he stiffened.

The statue in the corner, a stone carving of a demon with a tusked mouth and four yellow eyes, had shifted on its pedestal . . . turning to look at him. For an instant Ravindra was alarmed, then he trembled in excitement as the hulking creature first stretched, as if awaking from a long sleep, then bowed low. It presented one of its four swords, hilt-first. 'My Lord,' it hissed, bowing and spreading its other three arms in a submissive genuflection.

A memory, submerged for centuries, surfaced in Ravindra's mind: a memory of Mandore. 'Rakshasa,' he breathed.

The creature sank on one knee. 'My Lord Ravindra, I have found you once more.'

'Who are you?'

'My name is Khar, Lord. I am your brother.'

'It was you who spoke in my dreams! You who revealed the ritual and its formula in Mandore – you who told me how to enchant my queens' heart-stones!'

The rakshasa bent low. In the dim light, Ravindra could see bronze armour covering dark reddish skin, horns jutting from a wide brow above slitted reptilian eyes.

'It was my honour to serve, master. I have found you, Lord, after searching through all the centuries of the world. We rakshasa have stayed faithful, as you will learn. We will not lose you again.' He pressed his stony forehead to the floor and added, 'The throne of Lanka awaits you, Lord of Lords.'

CHAPTER TEN

Mirrors and Clocks

New Delhi, 8 November 2010

Deepika Choudhary kissed her parents good night, then stole a long, lingering kiss with Amanjit before he had to go back downstairs to the guest room, where he'd be sleeping until they married. She could still taste his mouth, and feel his hands on her flesh . . . they'd promised to keep things chaste until they married, at her mother's insistence, but that was proving harder than either of them had anticipated.

It had been weird, seeing Vikram on telly. Amanjit said he thought he could win, if he wanted to, though he wouldn't say why, but he was wrong, obviously. Pravit was going to win – not just because the Bollywood star oozed charisma; clearly Sunita still loved him, or why else would she cry about him?

But she wasn't really worried about Vikram; there was another reason she couldn't relax, or sleep peacefully . . .

Night had become an unsettling place of late. She would turn out the light, but then she'd lie awake for hours, shivering with cold, no matter how high she turned up the heater. She'd become convinced that someone was watching her through the curtains, that mere cloth couldn't deflect that unseen gaze – but when she wrenched them open, there was never anyone there. Sometimes she sensed something creeping over the sheets, like a huge spider – she could feel it, but whenever she bolted upright and turned on the lights, she saw nothing.

And when she finally did fall asleep, it was as if she had dropped into some kind of waking coma: her body was rigid and unmoving, her eyes fixed, though the room was still visible. Worst of all, her mouth was babbling, some strange one-sided conversations that she couldn't hear.

She'd tried to tell Amanjit about these new nightmares, but it was hard to explain, because when she put them into words, they sounded like nothing at all, just the anxieties of a stressed-out young woman. But she wished he were here with her, because his very presence was reassuring.

She left her light on, but that couldn't stop exhaustion closing her eyes, her eyelids stinging with fatigue. She heard the traffic outside fade away as the night sounds of the house settled, a half-registered backdrop. She shivered and clutched the blanket tighter about her shoulders as she drifted away.

Suddenly her eyes flipped open and she stared down her body in terror at the *huge* spider resting on her thigh: a giant, bigger than a tarantula. She opened her mouth to scream, but no sound came. As the thing reared back she saw that it wasn't a spider at all; it was a *hand*.

The hand was dark and smooth-skinned, banded with ruby and emerald rings and tipped with yellowed nails that looked like the talons of a hawk. There was no arm, just a stump where the wrist should have been. The disembodied hand was walking about on its fingertips, not friendly, like the Addams Family's Thing, more like some ghastly arachnid, and though there were no eyes, it was watching her. She could feel its weight on her skin as it walked up her thigh, the sharpness of the nails prickling her belly as it climbed with malevolent purpose up the T-shirt she'd nicked from Amanjit to wear at night.

Then disgust gave way to fury and she jerked upright and swatted at the thing, sending it flying. At that briefest of contacts it vanished as if it had never been there – but the after-echo of a cold chuckle filled the air, emanating weirdly from the mirror on her dressing table.

The mirror wasn't facing the bed; she couldn't see if it was reflecting anything. Slowly, carefully, she crept towards it, moving as silently as she could, then, with an angry cry, she leaped in front, as if she might surprise her own reflection. She still expected – *hoped* – to see nothing more than a frightened girl with matted bed hair, drenched with cold sweat, swamped by her borrowed T-shirt. And that's what she saw—

—and then it wasn't. The longer she stared, the more the image seemed to change, though it was slow, subtle, barely discernible in the dim light of her bedside lamp. Her skin grew more pallid, her hair took on a deeper, almost purple lustre. Her lips were thinner, her eyes no longer chocolate brown but tawny.

The image was whispering to her, its eyes hypnotic, the voice mesmerising. Deepika went to shout out for someone to come, but the glittering eyes held hers as the words became a sultry, languorous murmur.

'*Go back to sleep. There's nothing here . . . you're imagining all of this . . . You're safe, right where you are . . .* Darya.'

Next morning she woke exhausted, certain she'd dreamed, but the memories had faded before she could bring them back to mind.

Jodhpur, 8 November 2010

Hundreds of miles away, through cities, villages and farms, and deserts filled with dust and darkness, another girl sat rigid with fear. Her mother and stepfather, Kiran and Dinesh, had long since retired to their bedroom and Bishin had gone to his pallet on the rooftop. Only Rasita was far from sleep.

She was dressed, not for bed, but in jeans that hung off her wasted frame, a denim jacket over a cotton T-shirt and low-heeled leather boots. A little knapsack was propped up between her feet. She was staring at the clock, willing the hands to move.

Seeing Vikram on the telly had filled her with such silent fury she could barely speak. When he gave that *ugly* madwoman his handkerchief, she'd wanted to *slap* him. What was he thinking, to comfort that shallow bitch? Let her crawl back to Pravit Khoolman – it was clearly what she desired! And all she *deserved*.

The clock finally struck eleven, she took a deep breath and reread her note.

> *Dear Mum,*
> *There is something I have to do. I will come back if I can, but if I can't, please know that I love you all.*
> *Your loving daughter, Rasita*

She propped the note up on the table, slipped out of the front door and closed it quietly behind her.

CHAPTER ELEVEN

A Song for a Princess

Kannauj, 1175

Chand Bardai slipped into the court of Jaichand, Raja of the Gaha-davalas, through a servants' entrance. A trader the king trusted made sure to give Chand the constantly changing roster of passwords each week, and now he murmured that evening's phrase while the soldiers checked his baggage, then passed him through. He slipped each a coin – it never hurt to be generous with such men.

He'd been coming here for a long time now, trading secrets for gold. His reports blended truth and subtle falsehoods, which he'd jointly composed with a highly amused Prithviraj. 'Let Jaichand believe he has a spy in my chambers,' the king laughed. 'We can use that against him.'

Raja Jaichand awaited Chand in a shaded garden, sipping sherbet imported from Persia. He greeted Chand with undisguised eagerness; though Chand smiled in reply, it was for an entirely different reason: he'd been trading secrets for a decade now, and the easiest thing about it was that Jaichand – for ever paralysed by mistrust – had done little or nothing with them.

He over-thinks everything. A great raja must know when the time has come to act.

'Look at you, Chand Bardai!' Jaichand exclaimed. 'There is grey in your beard, my friend – you are finally *looking* as wise as you are!'

'It's all the children,' Chand chuckled. 'Nothing ages us faster than our children.'

'True enough: even one daughter has turned my hair white!'

Chand heard the sadness behind the Raja's jest: he still had only his one beloved Sanyogita, despite having taken yet another wife in the hope of better fortune.

Chand had quite the opposite problem: he'd thought to stop at three boys, but life had given him more than he had ever bar-- gained for. Kamla had pushed twins from her tree-trunk body in 1170, both boys – their fourth and fifth! Then another boy had followed three years later, and another set of twins in 1175. Her fecundity was legendary: eight sons in ten years!

'Soon all the soldiers in Prithvi Chauhan's army will be the sons of Chand Bardai,' Jaichand joked. 'I hope you remind them that they are Rathod by blood.'

'When the time comes, when they are old enough to understand discretion, they will of course know their true bloodline.' Chand waited until the raja sat before taking his own seat, and they drank, toasting each other.

'So, Chand Bardai, what is the news from Dilli?'

Everyone called him Bardai now: Chand the poet, the singer, the scribe; a member of the king's privy council, one whose word carried more weight than generals' and rival kings'. But he'd been struggling for too long to let flattery go to his head now. 'The realm is stable – well, as much as Rajputana is ever at peace,' he told Jaichand. 'Prithvi has renamed the fortress in Dilli: it is now the Qila Rai Pithora.'

'How can he rename something he holds in trust for the Tomar princes?' Jaichand asked.

Chand met Jaichand's eyes. 'You think Prithviraj Chauhan will *ever* relinquish the fortress of Dilli to his wards? Would you?'

Jaichand's mouth twisted, then he said sourly, 'It was naïve to think he would honour such a promise. But tell me, is the court of the Chauhan as magnificent as everyone claims? Even the travelling entertainers are raving about it . . .'

Chand weighed his words. Nothing made Jaichand angrier than to hear praise of Prithvi, his greatest rival, but in truth, Prithvi's palace had become everything he had sworn it would be, and more. The greatest poets, singers and musicians, dancers, writers, jugglers and acrobats – in fact, anyone who could entertain – they all flocked to the Chauhamanas court. Epics were composed and sung; the great old tales were re-enacted on the grandest scale, huge shows with massive effigies, live animals and hundred-strong choruses of singers, and at the centre of it all was Chand Bardai, selecting, directing and arbitrating. Though the warriors still warred and raided, it was of the court itself that all spoke in awe: the magnificence, the spectacle, light and colour, the excess.

Chand's role was always to ensure that Prithvi's name was spoken first, last and loudest, to see that he was the most majestically costumed, the man most lauded in song and tale. Prithvi had always been determined that his reign was to be remembered as a golden age.

But that wasn't for Jaichand's ears. 'You know what wicked liars poets and singers are,' Chand said with a wink, making Jaichand laugh in that sideways, nervous way he did.

The raja signalled for more wine, then leaned forward and asked conspiratorially, 'And what do they say of my daughter in Dilli?'

Chand took a moment to compose himself. For ten years he'd watched Sanyogita as she grew from precocious girl to legendary beauty. She truly was Darya reborn, and his longing for her would consume him, if he let it. She was well overdue for marriage, but Jaichand couldn't bear to part from her. As the king's guest, Chand was often permitted to feast his senses as she sang and danced just for the king and his small circle of intimates. He knew Jaichand did this to taunt Prithvi, for he always encouraged Chand to report Sanyogita's beauty and grace back to the Chauhan king.

'My Lord, your daughter is spoken of as the greatest living beauty in the world. Young men dream of her. Young women dream of *being* her. But all wonder: when will you permit her to wed?'

Jaichand's face became tense and furtive and he signalled to a servant. A small group of young women entered the garden, decorously veiled and clad in silks of every bright hue. Then a musician struck a chord on his sitar and another man rattled his drum, the music started and the young women began to dance, stepping in time as they moved through the intricate, courtly steps of the traditional ghoomar. All of them were lovely, but Chand watched only one, scarcely daring to breathe.

Sanyogita's voice was clear and warm, her face lit like an apsara: she was truly a creature of the heavens as she sang an old love song laced with yearning. Jaichand looked down at her with a twisted mouth. When she finished, she and her companions sat down in the garden below and the raja leaned towards Chand, his long silver locks falling over his eyes. 'I must let her go,' he whispered. One still spoke mostly in whispers in the court of Kannauj, even the raja.

'She is of age,' Chand agreed. 'Long of age.'

'I know. I have resolved to announce a swayamvara.'

Chand looked up at him with unfeigned shock. '*A swayamvara?*'

'So even the imperturbable Chand Bardai can still be

surprised!' Jaichand smiled, his expression tinged with bitter-
ness. 'I am glad I retain that capacity,' he added drily.

'You certainly do! No one's held a traditional swayamvara for
years – I can't even remember the last one!'

Chand suspected that Jaichand had been torn about the best
way to marry off his prize: a kingdom with no male heir was only
a heartbeat from being rent by war. Jaichand had been ill soon
after conceiving Sanyogita, and Chand suspected the Rathod king
was now sterile – no matter how many nubile young wives he
added to his court, there never would be a male heir. *The old tradition of the swayamvara is actually not a bad choice*, he reflected. The
man who displayed his prowess before his peers would gain huge
status, and that would stand him in good stead should he be forced
to fight for the throne on Jaichand's death. A contest for the right
to be heir, which Jaichand would obviously judge, would go a long
way to ensuring that someone with strength and wit would suc-
ceed him.

*And what better man to be victorious than Prithviraj himself? Darya
and Shastri, reunited . . .*

'When, Lord King?' he asked, his mind racing.

'In six months,' Jaichand replied. 'After the monsoon, when
the roads are useable once again.'

Six months . . . Plenty of time to prepare . . .

A servant approached, a small youth of around eight, who
attended upon the women. Jaichand turned, permitting the boy
to address him directly.

'Great Raja, your noble daughter asks whether it is permitted
that they hear the famed Chand Bardai sing?' the boy asked, staring openly at Chand.

The king looked apologetically at Chand. 'You are my guest,
Cousin. You are here to confer and relax. I will not insist –
although of course, your fame precedes you.'

'It would be my honour,' Chand replied. 'What would you have me sing?'

Jaichand made an expansive gesture. 'Let your audience decide.' He sent the boy back whilst Chand went to confer with the musicians. He established a rhythm, a simple tune to sing to, while waiting for the women's decision.

They were tittering amongst themselves, until Sanyogita herself rose. 'Sing a song of Prithviraj Chauhan,' she declared in a loud voice, eyeing her father defiantly.

Her maids put their hands to their mouths as whispers ran rife through the garden. Jaichand reddened, his eyes narrowing, but there were too many eyes watching and to refuse would be tantamount to admitting a weakness – as his daughter well knew, Chand read with a measured glance.

Wilful, stubborn, and unafraid of later punishments: she really is Darya reborn.

Jaichand gave his assent with a lordly, uncaring wave of the hand.

Chand had composed many songs in praise of his king over the years, singing of his ferocity in war and his majesty as king. There were verses praising the judge, hymns to valour and courage. But this was an audience of women. He chose a simpler piece, set to a well-known tune, in praise of Prithviraj the Man, and he sang of kindness, of a strong hand that held gently, of a stern eye that softened in the presence of beauty, a heart that yearned to give. The women caught the tune quickly and swayed in time to it. His voice, once clear and high, was still in perfect pitch, but now held a timbre of maturity that lent it gravitas.

When he was done, they sucked in their breath, and then applauded generously.

'You sing well, Cousin. I would have you at my court, composing such fancies for me,' Jaichand murmured as Chand took his bow.

'I'm sure I'm more valuable to you right where I am,' Chand replied quietly, his eyes on Sanyogita, noting the way her hands bunched against her heart, her gaze far away. *Will you dream of Prithvi tonight, Sanyogita?*

Would that she dreamed of me instead, part of him retorted. He buried that thought deeply.

Jaichand turned his taut gaze his way. 'I don't blame you, Cousin,' he murmured. 'She manipulated us both. The little wretch wants for nothing, yet she humiliates me by setting herself at the one thing she cannot have. She has no appreciation of the privilege in which she dwells. You and I, who have struggled, we know what it is like to earn one's rewards. We *appreciate* them. She who is gifted everything has no appreciation of that privilege at all.'

'Marriage will teach her to value more of life,' Chand replied smoothly. 'And she will understand her father all the more when she has children of her own.'

Prithvi's children, he thought silently. *And a union of the two greatest kingdoms of Rajputana. But how can I make it happen?*

CHAPTER TWELVE

Chessboards and Wooden Swords

Mumbai, 9 November 2010: Day 2 of Swayamvara Live!

It was getting worse outside. The crowds were now hundreds of feet deep around the studio and the studio audience tickets were changing hands for tens of thousands of rupees. Millions were being wagered at the bookmakers. The *Times of India* now rated Vikram 200:1 and said he had a 'certain innocent charm' – but he was still in the bottom eight, according to the odds, and likely to be eliminated today. Vikram pinned the clipping above his bed, next to the one from the first day. This time Jai drove him to the studio an extra hour earlier, but he still only just got inside in time.

Vishi Ashoka led the briefing for the remaining twenty-four contestants. 'Good *morning*, gentlemen! Today will be *even more intensive* than the first day, I can *promise* you! Lord Rama was a *master* of strategy, horsemanship and warfare – and so to *explore* your abilities in these fields, you will be given *three tests*. This morning, you will be playing *chess* with each other, the matches drawn randomly. The *top four* will each gain a life! And this afternoon you will demonstrate *your equestrian* talents at the Mahalaxmi Riding School, and once again, the *top four* will gain lives . . .'

Vikram knew the *Ramayana* pretty well now; once he'd

realised it appeared to be telling his life story he'd read it all the way through. As far as he recalled, Rama didn't ride at all in it. *Ah well, you're not setting the rules here, they are . . .*

'Then in the evening,' Vishi continued, 'you must fence against a randomly selected opponent, live on television. Any loser without a life will be eliminated – unless reprieved by Sunita herself!'

Vikram looked around him, noting the reactions of the other competitors, which varied from sudden confidence among those who felt they were competent in at least one of these fields, to those with no experience, whose faces now wore thinly veiled panic.

'Are there any questions?' Vishi asked.

'Will those of us who couldn't have an intelligent conversation with Sunita after she had her post-Pravit meltdown last night get another chance to actually talk to her?' asked a lean Bengali, eyeing the movie star darkly. Vikram saw Kajal bunch a fist, but Pravit only smiled.

'There will be other chances, of course,' Vishi responded, 'but only if you survive today and make the last sixteen.'

The Bengali scowled, clearly unhappy. There were other questions, but Vikram was trying to remember if he had ever played chess before. Surely in one of his lives . . .?

'Checkmate,' chuckled Alok. The next Raja of Gondwara offered a ring-encrusted hand. 'You put up a good fight, Vikram.' He stroked his own cheek, a gesture that was Raichand all over.

'Yeah, thanks,' sighed Vikram. 'Well played.'

'I was on the chess team at Harvard,' Alok said apologetically. 'Whereas you, I think, haven't played for a while?'

'That's an understatement.' *By about four hundred years.* 'I suppose you're pretty good on horseback as well?'

'Of course. And fencing too.'

'No one loves a smart-arse,' Vikram said with a grin.

'You don't think? Well, someone has to give that Bollywood manikin a run for his money.' Alok smoothed his moustache with a vain little gesture. 'It may as well be me. And what about you? Have you ever ridden?'

'A little.' *Well, quite a lot, actually. The problem is, I've always been rubbish at it.*

The studio audience thrummed with anticipation. They'd just seen the highlights of the chess and horse-riding and a series of screens flashed up with photos of the contestants, shown with their accumulated lives. Alok had two. Pravit, Kajal and the Bengali had one each, as did a few others. Vikram had none.

The MC, a moustachioed former character actor called Sunil, cracked a few jokes, and they showed some of the more spectacular falls from horseback in slow motion so that the audience could laugh some more. Vikram winced as his own ignominious tumble at the water jump was shown over and over again. Then a pair of lissom girls in sequined bikinis wheeled out a glass bowl full of numbered balls.

'Coming up next, MUMBAI!! Yes, it's the draw for the *ne-e-e-xxt challenge*!' Sunil announced grandly. 'And then it's time for LIVE SWORD-FIGHTING!'

The applause went up a notch at the thought of seeing the contestants going head-to-head with edged weapons – or maybe at the possibility of real blood. The studio audience buzzed as the show went to a commercial break.

Vikram rubbed more ibuprofen cream into his ankle, wincing at the ache in his grazed and bruised right shoulder from his landing – but at least it wasn't dislocated like the Bengali's.

This fight will have to be brief.

It wouldn't be classical Olympic-style fencing, that quickly became clear. They were given white padded suits and masks, but instead of a fencing foil, the sword was a heavy curved sabre, like the classic Indian talwar, edged and tipped with thick felt to soften the blow, although the blade was probably heavy enough to break limbs and crack ribs. The felt had been soaked in red ink to provide a visible 'wound'.

Vikram picked it up gingerly. He'd never been much of a one for the weapon – he'd been an archer, not a swordsman. Around him the remaining twenty-two (the Bengali and one other contestant were too injured to continue after their falls this afternoon) limbered up with varying degrees of competence. Vikram noticed that Pravit handled his blade with confidence, and remembered with a sigh that he'd starred in several historical epics, so of course he'd been taught to handle just such a weapon.

Dear Gods, don't make me go up against him one-on-one tonight . . .

If the gods were listening to his prayers, it wasn't very attentively: he didn't draw Pravit – he drew Kajal.

Alok Pandiya destroyed his opponent methodically, and Pravit broke the wrist of his with a brutal stroke. A tall Delhi-ite and Joseph, the Englishman from Walthamstow, whom Vikram had met on their first day here, also won their bouts skilfully. The other contestants were incompetent but willing. The studio audience picked their favourites and cheered raucously, especially when someone was hurt. There was a distinct scent of bloodlust in the air.

Out of the corner of his eye, Vikram watched Sunita's reactions. She laughed and cheered with the rest, Uma at her elbow, but her eyes were far away, looking at something beyond the contest. 'She's thinking about Paris,' he heard someone say, and wondered what that meant.

He scanned the audience closely as well, but there was no one there who reminded him of Ravindra, though exactly what he was looking for, he couldn't say. A certain demeanour, maybe, or someone staring at him too intently . . . He wondered who of his family and old school friends were watching – the contestants' mobiles had been taken away that morning, so he'd not been able to call anyone.

Finally, he was up: he and Kajal were the last bout. Jez helped tie down the last straps of his padded suit and ensured the helmet buckles were set right before patting his shoulder. 'Mate, listen up: Kajal's strong, but he's not fast. I've seen him do stunt-fighting on a couple of sword-swinger movies – he likes to square up and swipe from high-right to low-left. He doesn't move his feet much. And he's a jerk.'

'Thanks, Jezzer.'

'Don't thank me – and don't call me Jezzer. Just beat him, okay?'

Vikram and Kajal walked side by side into the middle of the over-bright arena, where the cameras looked like massive micro-scopes that could see inside their souls. Kajal was exhaling deeply, twitching his head from side to side, making his neck muscles crackle and pop. Vikram slowly rotated his right shoulder, trying to loosen it without damaging it further.

'You've got no lives,' Kajal growled. 'I'm going to break both your arms and then jam this sword up your arse.' He looked more than capable of it. Vikram felt like a child walking in his shadow.

'Ladies and gentlemen, the *final bout*!' Sunil hollered. The MC was as over-excited as the crowd. 'On my left is *Kajal*! Six foot two and weighing 140 kilograms, Kajal is a stuntman from Gujarat, currently living and working right here in *MUM-BAAAAIIII!!!*' The audience cheered parochially as Kajal glowered about him, looking mean and tough.

'Facing him, five-foot-six and weighing only 62 kilograms –
and that's after a big meal! – is *Vikram*! When he's not falling off
horses into water hazards, Vikram is a student from Rajasthan,
resident here in *MUM-BAAAAIIIII!!!*' Ironic cheers and laughter
ensued.

Vikram bowed, then fitted the mask, trying not to blink in the
glare of the studio lights, which were refracted awkwardly
through the mesh. One of the stagehands waved at him and he
moved across to take his place. The stage was all fenced in by
ropes and a forest of cameras and techies. The audience looked
like a sea of eyes, but he had time to turn and salute Sunita
Ashoka, who was watching, while listening to Uma whispering
in her ear. The ladyman waved back with Vikram's own handkerchief and he grinned, forgetting his face was hidden beneath the
mask. Then it was time to face Kajal, who was flexing and stamp-
ing his feet like a bull about to charge.

'It's a good thing it's not *a wrestling match*, ladies and gentlemen!' Sunil exclaimed, 'because there would be only one winner!
But it's not: it's a best-of-three *fencing* match. Only hits to the
head and torso count, unless they are debilitating. Gentlemen,
you may begin—'

*In how many lives have I fought with a sword? Not many: I don't usu-
ally let my enemies get that close . . .*

He practised a couple of tentative figures, but scarcely felt
ready when the bell chimed and Kajal stormed at him like a
one-man stampede.

The first blow came down right to left and almost smashed his
sword from his hands. The second one hit before he could re-grip,
tearing the blade from his hand as the big stuntman laughed
inside his mask.

'Little weakling.' He aimed a vicious blow at Vikram's neck.
Vikram ducked away, but he was too slow and the sword cracked

across his buttocks, leaving a massive red stain. The audience laughed at the sight and most punched the air as Vikram went sprawling onto his belly. He felt his face burning with humiliation.

The bell rang and Kajal raised his mask, yelling at the crowd.

Vikram eased himself up, his bum smarting, and limped back to his corner. *I'm not strong enough for this . . . Or good enough . . .*

He decided his only chance was to go for a two-handed grip – his fingers were just small enough to get inside the guard – and this time when the bell rang, he moved forward quickly to avoid getting cornered. He caught the first massive blow and immediately swept back low, making the giant dance backwards, then he darted away from another overhand swipe that smacked against the floor, leaving a slash of red ink on the canvas. Kajal roared and followed him, raining down blows, one-two-three, his breath like bellows through the mask as Vikram took the first two in double-handed blocks, then quite deliberately stepped away and fluttered his blade aside. Again the big man's blade slammed into the floor, but this time Vikram darted in and landed a little red circle above Kajal's heart.

The bell chimed while the stuntman stared down at the mark on his breast in disbelief.

Vikram pulled off the mask and wiped his sweaty face on his sleeve, then dried the grip of his sabre. Kajal was showing the crowd the tiny mark as if to say, 'Surely that's not worth a point?'

But it is, big man . . .

The bell chimed again.

Last time . . . here we go . . .

This time Kajal came in slower, obviously aware that one slip would see him lose this match. Caution wasn't his natural style and he looked bewildered when Vikram began to circle him, jabbing and poking. He began to rumble, like a train building a head of steam, torn between caution and explosion.

The problem with a patient approach was that Vikram couldn't keep it up for long either: his injured shoulder was really beginning to hurt, and his reach was too short. Each lunge was coming up further away from his target, and even grasped in two hands, the blade was beginning to feel like a block of concrete.

The end came suddenly. With a sudden roar, Kajal leaped at him, his sword a blur in his massive hands. Vikram tried to dodge, slipped and went down as a shape that looked as big as a building toppled over him. He jammed out his arm and twisted his head and torso. The blade of the stuntman smashed into the canvas beside his ear with a sound like splintering wood, while an explosion of air slammed from the stuntman's lungs like a boiler bursting.

Vikram opened his eyes and peered up through the mesh of his mask.

His blade was thrust into Kajal's groin, and the man was slowly bending over double, wheezing and whimpering, his legs twitching and his hands gripping his loins protectively.

The crowd roared like Romans in the Coliseum.

Vikram had won.

Vikram stood among the last sixteen, trying to keep the next-raja between himself and the frightening glowers of Pravit and Kajal, who had a life from the riding. One by one the remaining sixteen went forward to receive Sunita's personal congratulations. He watched her converse anxiously with Pravit, and posture like a girl when Alok kissed her hand. He smiled to himself when Kajal hobbled painfully forward and was pleased to see that Sunita barely looked at the giant stuntman.

Then it was his turn.

'I'm told this is your handkerchief,' said Sunita, as Uma winked at him over her shoulder.

She doesn't remember me giving it to her? 'Yes, madam.'

She smiled faintly, not really looking at him. 'Not "madam"—what sort of suitor calls his intended "madam"? Call me Sunita.' Her voice was softer in this life, and more . . . *sedate* . . . The word triggered something in his mind: Gauran had practically lived on sedatives, as had other incarnations of this soul. Sunita's madness was less obvious than in some of her past lives, but it was there, lurking behind the bird-sharp eyes, speaking through her nervous twitches and giggles. She was taking drugs to suppress it. That was another complication.

'Sunita, then,' he conceded, trying to meet her eye, but not quite succeeding.

She held out the handkerchief. 'Here. I return it to you with thanks.'

'Keep it, please. You may need it again. And I have others.'

'No, take it. I will not be beholden to a contestant.'

'Then you should stop wearing the ring Pravit gave you,' Vikram murmured. He bowed, and walked away.

He had naïvely thought those words had been soft enough to be below hearing, but there were plenty of lip-readers happy to decipher every whisper for the voracious viewers. Before he had even realised what was happening, his words, meant for one person alone, had been blared to the watching world and spread all over the next morning's newspapers, under headlines like, 'TWO LOW BLOWS FROM VIKRAM!'

But Vikram had bigger concerns by then. When he finally got his mobile phone back, there were dozens of texts and missed calls. Rasita had run away from home.

CHAPTER THIRTEEN

On the Road with Idli

South Rajasthan, 9 November 2010

'Hey, little cousin, wake up, it's breakfast time.'

Ras flinched, peering blearily about her. 'What——?'

Her cousin was looking at her, worried. Idli was small, skinny, scruffy, unwashed, and usually so stoned on uppers and ganja it was a miracle he could see, let alone drive. He made his living taking his garishly painted Tata truck all over northwestern India and even into Kashmir. He'd crashed or run off the road more than a dozen times, but he was the only person Ras knew who could get her to Mumbai without leaving a trail.

Idli had a grumpy wife he habitually avoided by spending weeks on end on the road. Whenever he was in Jodhpur he always slept at their house – he thought no one knew he slipped Bishin moonshine and ganja leaf on the sly, though they could always tell. He treated Ras like a little sister, bringing her exotic sweets and always happy to spend time with her. He wasn't good at saying no to anyone, least of all Ras – he wasn't happy to be abetting her runaway escapade, but he just didn't know how to refuse.

'Get down on the floor, Ras,' he told her.

'Why?'

'Because we're going into a truckstop. There's gonna be around four hundred trucks and the only women here are prostitutes. If a man sees you, he'll try and do you – and he mightn't be too quick to offer payment afterwards, either.'

'*Yuck!* Really?'

'It's law of the jungle out here – I'm not gonna let you get hurt, but you've gotta keep your head down for a while. I need a pee and some food.' He stuck a foul-smelling rollie between his yellow teeth and concentrated on manoeuvring through the bedlam of the truckstop. There were vehicles *everywhere*, and the air stank of wood fires, garbage and food cooking. She had no idea where they were; they'd crawled along gridlocked roads filled with barely road-worthy battered old trucks like Idli's, all belching noxious fumes. She was dizzy from the mix of leaking exhaust and ganja.

Because the big cities were so congested, most big vehicles weren't allowed into places like Delhi and Mumbai during daylight hours, so they drove at night. She'd turned off her own mobile and confiscated Idli's – it was only dawn, but Mum must have found her note by now. Rasita teared up a little, thinking of her mother – she'd be beside herself, ringing family and friends and police, everyone she could think of. Bishin would be going crazy too – and she didn't even want to think about what Amanjit was feeling. She shook herself. Feeling guilty wasn't going to help anyone.

A man with a flag and a whistle ushered the trucks into place, rank upon rank of vehicles laden with everything from wheat to engine parts to carpets to plastic toys. She heard men calling, old friends greeting each other, laughing and shouting about the roads and speculating on which women would be here today, and what would be on the menu at the kitchen. Then Idli threw a blanket over her as she huddled in the footwell and everything was muffled.

'Don't move!' her cousin hissed. 'These doors don't shut

properly, so you have to stay out of sight. Don't trust *anyone*! I won't be long.'

She was strung out and overtired and couldn't think straight anyway. *All I want to do is sleep . . .*

Rasita woke up seconds later, or so it felt, to someone climbing into the cab. She almost cried out in fright, but then heard Idli's voice. 'Just me, Ras. Just me. I got chapatti and rice and daal makhani for you.' Then he snickered warmly. 'And I got some sweet, sweet ganja for us both.'

She groaned. 'Just the food for me, Idli. If I smoke that stuff I'll throw up.'

'Don't you go sicking up in my cab!'

'How would you even tell over all the other smells?' Ras grumbled. She struggled to a sitting position on the floor and accepted a little plastic plate wrapped in foil. Inside it, a lukewarm slop was soaking into half-cooked chapatti. 'Ugh, is this real?'

'Yes, yes, it's good. Best place this side of Sirohi.'

'Then never, *ever*, take me to the worst place!'

She felt ill, but she was starving and her stomach was growling; almost before she realised, she was gobbling the food down like a starving dog. Then she was toppling sideways, plummeting back into the sleep she'd failed to find all night.

She woke at dusk to the sound of Idli tinkering with the underside of the vehicle. Stolen glimpses through the half-open driver's door showed her sleeping men – rough-dressed, unshaven men, their skin burned almost black – sprawled in the shade of their vehicles or sitting in groups playing cards. Not the sort of men her mother would ever let near her, for which she was profoundly thankful. Most of them were smoking, the clouds pierced by shafts of late afternoon sunshine.

Finally Idli poked his head into the cab to fiddle with one of the foot-pedals, trying to coax the van through one more night without breakdown. The trucks were run into the ground by the transport companies, and the drivers were forced to work insane hours – it was no wonder there were so many accidents. But no one ever did anything about it.

Night was falling and the men were revving their engines and beginning to roll out in informal convoys. She reached into her pocket. Idli's phone had a text from her mother. She opened it and peered.

<Idli, have you heard from Rasita?>

<No> she sent back. She didn't even turn her own phone on. Who knew what was traceable these days? 'When will we get to Mumbai?' she asked her cousin.

'Tomorrow night, just before dawn.' Idli looked at her with a worried expression. 'You won't tell Kiran I helped you, will you, Ras? She'd kill me!'

'Of course not. It's our secret!'

He pulled a face. 'Don't like secrets.'

'Don't worry. We'll be fine.'

They stopped an hour later at a roadside dhaba just south of Sirohi normally shunned by the truckers for its overpriced meals and ill-mannered service. The few other customers didn't even look at them; they were all crowded around the tiny TV set in the corner and the crackly strains of the *Swayamvara Live!* theme music were filling the tiny room.

Just a glimpse of Vikram's face set her to dreaming of the impossible.

CHAPTER FOURTEEN

The Trophy Bride

Dilli, 1175

Chand was sitting at one end of a bench, grateful for the padding of a woven cushion. His wife Kamla took up the rest of the seat. Her sari left her waist bare; it was layered with rolls of fat and scarred by stretch marks. Her hair was already going grey and her face still reminded him of a tree frog. In spite of all that, it felt good to be sitting with her on cool nights like this.

Their suite in the palace was second only in size to the raja's, but it was still barely enough for his rapidly growing family. At last most of the children were abed and at least pretending to sleep. The servants were bustling about discreetly while he shared the most peaceful waking hour of the day with his wife.

'Jaichand is to hold a swayamvara for his daughter's hand, but he has forbidden Prithvi or any of his court from taking part.'

'So, how did little Prithvi take that?' Kamla was sucking on a mango – she was always eating – but she was also listening intently.

Chand looked across and met her knowing eyes. He smiled. It was very strange, his marriage: it wasn't rooted in love or desire, not on his part, and nor on hers, he felt sure, although when she desired love-making, she could be very persuasive. She had never made any secret of the fact that carnal activity gave her intense physical pleasure, nor was she shy in telling him what she needed moment to moment to get what she craved – and she was always generous in return. As husband and wife, they knew their parts, and played them well. She wanted children and adored them, a deep maternal love that Chand found utterly mysterious. Children might be little more than noisy little tempests of snot and tears to him; to her, they were a constant source of complete joy. He gave her children; she gave him heirs.

Most importantly, they had found each other as friends. Far from being the mindless creature he had dreaded, he had found she was intelligent and patient, and her mind was as thirsty for knowledge as her body was for life. She had learned to read and write as fast as he could teach her and she had always seen things at court before he did, instinctively following the currents of opinion and favour. He had come to prize her opinions above all others.

Unexpectedly, given what he knew of his past lives, he was happy. Most importantly, there was no sign of his Enemy – in fact, Chand was beginning to hope that in this life at least, he and Prithvi would be left in peace. Surely a respite was owed. Perhaps Ravindra had finally died? Or maybe the sorcerer-king was elsewhere in the land and hadn't realised that he and Prithvi were here, in Dilli? Or perhaps, given that in this life, both he and Prithvi were formidable – master archers, mighty rulers – Ravindra knew where they were, but feared to confront them?

He dared not let such hopes cause him to ignore the danger. He constantly studied the journal of Aram Dhoop, trying to understand what had occurred so long ago, and sifted through his memories of other lives. He meditated upon Padma's heart-stone, wondering if – or *when* – she would re-enter his life. And most importantly, right now he sought to unite Shastri and Darya in their current incarnations as Prithvi and Sanyogita.

'How did Prithvi take that?' Chand echoed and laughed. 'How do you think? By throwing the tantrum to end all tantrums. He shouted for to wake the gods, and threw a marble bust across the room. He threatened all manner of revenge – in fact, he was on the verge of summoning the Kannauj ambassador to execute him before I managed to calm him down – once I got the others to shut up.'

Kamla tutted. 'Silly boy. Let me see . . .' she mused, reaching for a handful of seeds to nibble. 'Govinda wants war, because he's impatient with all this peace that's broken out. Sanjham thought it amusing, and proposed going in Prithvi's stead. Raichand volunteered to cut Jaichand's throat. How did I do?'

'Are you sure you weren't listening at the door?'

'I'm too fat to sneak around. Anyway, men are obvious, especially those ones!' She patted his knee. 'And what did the wise Chand Bardai advise his king?'

'To forget her, that she wasn't worth it, that no girl is worth plunging the kingdoms of Rajputana into war for.'

'Good advice,' Kamla commented. 'Naturally, he didn't take it.'

'Of course not.'

'And your next suggestion?'

'That we cheat.'

Kamla rumbled with laughter. 'You also are predictable, husband.' She cocked an eye at him. 'But you amuse me. Come to my chamber. I want more sons, and this garden is too public for love-making.'

'But we already have eight sons!'

'I want more,' she purred, reaching across to stroke his thigh. 'Many more.' Her eyes filled with laughter as her hand stretched up to his groin. 'Obviously you do too, for I can feel you are steeling yourself for this part of the process of making them.'

Prithvi had once remarked thoughtlessly, 'All women are the same in the dark!' It was a cruel twisting of an important truth: that if you actually cared for someone – the personality within the flesh, the soul or the essence – then their physical appearance receded towards irrelevance.

He knew what love was – he would never forget Darya, or her effect on him. What he and Kamla shared wasn't anywhere near the same, but it came close enough to give them both content-ment, and after the lives he'd lived, it was more than enough, for now.

Kannauj, 1175

Jaichand's swayamvara a true spectacle, Chand had to admit: ele-phants and tigers, rearing stallions, endless music and lithe, beautiful dancers at the feasts that were held every night; effigies of the gods, effigies of the king, even traditional Rajputana puppet-dolls sporting Sanyogita's likeness . . .

Chand was the official ambassador of the Chauhamanas, the only representative of Prithviraj Chauhan's court permitted to attend the swayamvara for Sanyogita's hand in marriage. There were many other highly ranked men from all over the north of India, representing the Paramaras and the Guhilas, the Tomaras and Chandelas – there were even Mohammedans from the Punjab. Southern princes came, their skin almost black, their cheeks and lips full and rosy. There were Eastern lords from beyond Bengal, with slanted eyes and flat faces. The swayamvara had caught the imagination of men far and wide, all seeking this opportunity for power and influence. The town itself, as well as the temporary city of tents and pavilions which had sprung up outside the walls of Kannauj, was filled with everything from exotic traders selling spice and slaves to penniless girls selling themselves. It felt like Kannauj was the centre of the world.

Throughout the days of the contest, which was scheduled to run for two weeks, the ranking nobles watched men compete in every way imaginable, from horse-riding acrobatics to martial displays with swords and exacting tests of archery. A bow representing Shiva's bow — which Rama broke when he won the hand of Sita — was made as a test of strength, though the bowyer did his job so well that none could bend it. There were competitions in song and dance and poetry that Chand himself helped judge. Chess matches. Wrestling. Running races. Men fought each other in duels both sanctioned and secret as slights boiled over into violence. Dozens died each day.

Chand found himself itching to compete — he was only twenty-six, despite being a parent eight times over, and though he cared for Kamla, Sanyogita was Darya-reborn, the love of his first life. *Am I not the best archer and poet of all the kingdoms? Surely I would win . . .*

But his sense of duty to Prithvi stayed strong, as did his conviction that bringing Prithvi and Sanyogita together would mend everything that had gone wrong in Mandore four centuries ago.

Despite the excitement of the spectacle, it was in the evening, a swirl of public feasts and secret trysts, that the real business of the swayamvara was done. Jaichand met with all the real contenders, those from families of power and wealth who had something to offer the king. His own goals were twofold: the survival and growth of Kannauj, and the overthrow of Prithviraj Chauhan. The negotiations, masked in pleasantries and fine gifts, were intense.

Chand, Prithviraj's representative, was seldom privy to these meetings, but he was openly busy himself, identifying threats to his master and issuing threats or bribes in response. And he was watched constantly, of course – but he was a master of slipping about unseen, and had long ago discovered the secret ways of Kannauj.

He also knew a hidden passage that opened into Princess San-yogita's chambers in the palace . . .

Chand knocked twice, and heard a sudden intake of breath. The bolt shot across silently and eager fingers pulled the panel open. Sanyogita had her fingers to her lips for a moment, then she whispered, 'They've gone at last.'

He crawled in and straightened gratefully. He'd been stuck inside the tiny passage for more than an hour. 'Everyone?'

'My maid is here – but don't worry, she's asleep by the door, and she's . . . well . . . moon-touched.' Sanyogita tapped the side of her skull, her expression sympathetic and dismissive all at once. 'Please come through here.'

She led him to a small chamber, a pentagonal room of cool stone, hung with tapestries to soften it and warm it at night. Rugs were piled on the floors, and huge candles burned in all the niches in the wall. She patted a large cushion, then sat opposite him and offered grapes and wine. He glimpsed a tiny girl asleep by the door: presumably the moon-touched maid.

'So, Lady, what do you think of the contenders?' he asked, his voice playful.

'They're all fools,' she replied. 'The ones who can fight can't sing, and the ones who can sing can't fight. The intelligent men are feeble of body, and the strong of body are feeble of mind. Those with status are broke, and the wealthy have no status. No wonder I'm unmarried!'

'Unfortunately, in all these wide lands, there is only one per-fect man left . . .'

She clasped her hands together, her eyes coming alive in the warmth of the candlelight at the thought of a man she'd never met. For an instant he yearned, with all his heart, for her to look at him that way – but how could anyone compete with an idealised fantasy?

I can't let my own desires distract me: that's what caused this mess in the first place! That's why I can remember past lives, and why a murdering jadugara *called Ravindra is on my trail! Look away!*

'Thank you for your courage and kindness, Chand Bardai,' she told him. 'You know, if it weren't for Prithviraj, it might have been you I wanted,' she said, with a naïve sincerity that struck his heart like an arrow. He ducked his head, flushing, but she barely noticed. 'So, Master Poet: tell me of Prithviraj! Do you have word from him?'

He reached inside his tunic and brought out the latest poem from Prithvi – although, in truth, he'd written them all himself. Prithvi wished to claim the girl solely to annoy his rival; Chand knew that, but he also knew that once they met, that would change. That thought sustained him.

'It's called "In Praise of the Sita of Kannauj",' he told her. 'Prithviraj Chauhan wrote it for you.'

CHAPTER FIFTEEN

Singing for Sunita

Lodi Gardens, New Delhi, 10 November 2010

Beneath the sun-dappled trees, as morning sunlight bathed the ancient tombs, leafy copses and well-watered grass of Lodi Gardens, it was difficult to believe that anything could be wrong in the world. Joggers ploughed along the running tracks while families walked dogs and couples meandered, catching some peace before the working day began.

Deepika and Amanjit, walking hand in hand, were far from tranquil, though lost in thought. Deepika had seen Amanjit confront the burnt-out living corpse of Ravindra beneath the Mehrangarh, but she had never seen him look as afraid as he did now. Her fiancé looked torn in two; his mother and brother were close to breakdown. Rasita, who meant the world to them all, had crept out of the family home and was who knew where now. The police were doing next to nothing, and there had been no word from any other family members. She knew Amanjit was aching to jump in a car or a train or a plane, whatever would get him back to Jodhpur the quickest, so he could be there for his mother, or to go off and track his sister down. His whole body was quivering with the need to act. The only thing that was keeping him here, Deepika knew, was worry for her.

She felt sick to the stomach herself, helpless and frightened. *Ras, Ras — where are you?*

Everything was going wrong. Deepika kept having strange, barely remembered dreams, something about a spider and mirrors, but she could never recall the details next morning; all she knew was that she couldn't be doing a lot of sleeping, because she was *utterly* exhausted. There were dark hollows under her eyes and her skin was breaking out. Her mother kept offering her sleeping tablets, but she was scared of not being able to wake up. She was so angry she could barely stop trembling — but she had no idea how to fight back, because she didn't even know *what* she was fighting.

'What are we going to do, love?' she asked eventually.

Amanjit stopped and pulled her to him. 'I don't know,' he said, and she knew how hard admitting weakness was for him. 'I don't know. Pray, maybe.'

'We're doing that already. We need to do more! We need to strike back!'

'My warrior-queen!' Amanjit said, without a trace of mockery. 'You know I feel the same way — I wish I could be in two places at once. But Ras might be coming here . . . and you're exhausted, Dee.'

'I'm holding you back,' she muttered bitterly.

'No! You're keeping me strong. My God, if there were some task we had to do, well, we'd both be doing it — it's this not knowing I hate. If it's really — you know, *Ravindra* — behind this, I wish he'd just step from the shadows where I can see him!'

'If he's done something to Ras, I'll . . .' Deepika's voice trailed off as she failed to articulate the depth of her anger. 'But listen, Ravindra never even *saw* Ras in March, did he? We don't even know that she's really involved, so I'm sure he doesn't either, even if he knows her name. It could just be coincidence.

She's been so sick – maybe she just needed time to herself for a while?'

'No one matters more to her than her family!' Amanjit sounded completely bemused. 'And I don't believe in coincidences. If Ravindra is all that Vikram suspects, he'll be just the sort to prey on the weak.'

Deepika hoped he was wrong, but the truth was she agreed with him; she was pretty sure Ravindra knew far more about them than they wanted to believe. But neither of them dared to speculate further, striving to protect each other from their own fears. He lifted her face to his; she kissed him back, hard, feeding off his strength and giving of hers.

'I love you,' he said aloud. 'And I'll never let anything happen to you. Ever.'

'Back at you, Sikh-boy. I love you too. Only you, always you, for ever.' She set her jaw. 'We're going to beat this, and if that means hunting down that bastard Ravindra, we'll do that too.'

Mumbai, 10 November 2010: Day 3 of Swayamvara Live!

Vikram hadn't slept, and it showed. Uma pulled a face when she saw him, and Jez asked if he'd been 'out on the turps', which he assumed was Aussie for on the lash. What he had been doing was trying to reassure Dad and Amanjit; and to get the Missing Persons Bureau at the Compound of the Office of Commissioner of Police in Mumbai to list Ras and to check on Shodh, the railway police's online portal, though he'd not been having much luck. If they would only issue a BOLO – but would a 'be on the look-out' be any good when there was nothing to indicate that she might be coming this way?

The rest of his time had been spent in bitter self-recrimination. *I should have included her!* Now that Ras was missing it was obvious that she was involved somehow. Hadn't the ghost of Padma seen her — and fled from her? *Surely that should have told me something?* But none of them had wanted to include her, not because they were selfish, but because her health was so fragile. And he'd never got the sense that she was someone he *knew* in any of his past lives. So they'd believed it was better to stay away from her, to exclude her . . . though he liked her a lot; her immense courage in the face of daunting ill-health filled him with admiration, and he always enjoyed her deadpan humour.

We thought we were doing the right thing . . . but what if we were utterly wrong?

But there was no time to dwell on it now, not when the newspapers were trumpeting his victory over Kajal in the fencing, and reporting on the developing rivalries between the contestants with growing relish. Pravit's odds were lengthening, and the *Hindustan Times* was now championing Alok Pandiya — Raichand-reborn — as the dark horse in this race. ALOK GETTING UNDER PRAVIT'S SKIN their headline had shouted. The *Times of India* had dropped Vikram's odds to 80:1, and spoke of 'grit, pluck and resource — still a long shot, but he's winning hearts'.

That morning the crowds had been even denser, and there were riot police lining the road to the studio. Jai came with Vikram to the studios to help him fight through the crowds, and when people spotted them, they cheered Vikram, shouting out his name and patting his head and back, blessing him, touching him, encouraging and claiming him as one of their own. Four more girls had shouted their undying love for him, and one even looked older than fourteen. Still, it felt good to be moving through a friendly crowd — apparently people had thrown rotten fruit at Kajal.

The wear and tear of the physical trials was taking its toll: his ankle was sore, his shoulder scabbed and purple, and there was a thick welt across his buttocks worse than the caning he'd got from the bullies in Year Ten. It really hurt to move – so his spirits sank when he found that today's test was going to be all about movement . . .

'Rama was a *master of dance and language*!' Vishi Ashoka told the remaining sixteen contestants. 'You will be composing a *song and dance* routine to perform tonight for Sunita! *That* is today's test – simple!'

Vikram saw Alok smile to himself, and Pravit clenched a fist triumphantly, but most of the rest of his rivals looked ashen. Jai, in the studio audience, looked worriedly at Vikram, but he gave his friend a thumbs-up.

I've been court poet to many different rulers. If I can't pull this off, I'm a disgrace to my past selves!

But then Ras' face flashed across his mind and his concentration collapsed.

Each contestant was given a techie to pull together the music, and Vikram was delighted to find Jez was going to be helping him; the Australian had already started pulling different instrumental tracks from the Internet for him to listen to and select. But his biggest challenge was keeping Vikram focused.

'Mate! Hello? Are you still with me?'

'Uh . . . 'course!'

'We're playing this little game where you could get to marry the richest fruit-loop in India, remember? Are you still keen?'

'I . . . um, yes, I suppose . . .'

'You "suppose"?' Jez threw up his hands. 'Crikey, mate, I'm trying to help you here, but you're not even paying attention. Has this one got you freaked? Can't you sing? Or dance? I thought all you Indians could do that?'

Vikram took a deep breath. 'No, no, it's nothing like that. It's just . . . my stepsister – that's my dad's wife's daughter – she's run away from home.'

Jez's face fell. 'Aw, that's terrible. How old is she?'

'Seventeen – but it's worse: she's really ill . . . she's got this heart condition—' Vikram found himself choking back the tears he'd been keeping bottled up.

'Mate, that's awful. I'm *really* sorry. Are the cops on it?'

'Maybe – well, I don't know. Hundreds of people go missing every day here, Jez, so until there's a ransom demand – or a body – they won't do much. They're not even treating her as a missing person yet.' He buried his head in his hands. 'I just feel so *helpless*.'

'I'll tell Uma,' Jez said, standing.

'No! You know what people are like – they'd just say I'm making it up to get sympathy. I have to keep it secret.'

'Mate, no one would think that except that cretin Prankwit Coldsore – hey, you don't think he's kidnapped her, do you?'

Vikram looked up, his mind churning over the possibility, then he reluctantly discarded that idea. 'No. I'm sure even he wouldn't do that.' He grabbed Jez's arm. 'Please don't tell anyone. I'll try and focus now, I promise.'

'Okay, mate, but if you don't want to do this, I'm sure I could get you some kind of dispensation.'

'No, you won't need to. I can handle it. Play that last track again, please?'

Applause flooded the studio. The audience was on its feet, stomping and clapping, singing along with Pravit as though the number were an old favourite, not something they'd only just heard.

'You're sure it's an original?' Vikram whispered to Jez, standing next to him at the side of the studio auditorium. *That asshole probably has A. R. Rahman and Simon Cowell on speed-dial*. He fiddled with his turban and straightened the vivid orange kurta Uma had looted from the wardrobe department. It was the least sequin-encrusted one there, Uma insisted – Vikram had his suspicions about that, but he didn't have much choice, so it would have to do.

'Define "original",' the big Australian drawled, tipping back his fourteenth coffee of the day while Pravit milked the applause. 'All Hindi songs sound the same to me. But why does everyone look like they know the song already? He only just wrote the damned thing!'

'Because it's only got four lines and the tune is from one of his own movies. It's easy to pick up.'

'Bugger. Wish we'd thought of that.'

'I've not been in a lot of movies,' Vikram admitted. 'Less than one, in fact.'

Jez glanced at Sunita, who was clapping along. 'What're the words? My Hindi is pretty crap.'

'They're *rubbish*, all about wanting to be "Sunni's Accessory". You're lucky you only speak English.' He turned away, too dispirited to watch any more. 'So, how come you're working in India anyway?'

'Gotta go where the work is in this industry,' Jez replied. 'I spent five years in New Zealand on the *Lord of the Rings* shoot, then back to Oz for the big *Australia* movie. Then the recession hit and work got harder to find so I came here – I keep telling myself it'll look good on my CV. Though to be honest, this place has kinda grown on me, the madness of it all. I'm in no real hurry to go back to Sydney.'

'Maybe after this show you could run your own swayamvara in reverse, have all these hot Indian babes competing to marry you?'

Jez guffawed aloud and clapped Vikram on the shoulder, though the sound was lost in the shouts of 'encore' chorusing from the studio audience. 'Mate, I've got my own portable swayam-vara show: my Australian passport.' He looked down at Vikram and frowned suddenly. 'Which is a sad thought all round, if you think about it for too long.'

Then Uma signalled from across the stage. 'Okay Vik, "Private Coleslaw" is done and you're on next. Knock 'em dead. Literally, if you have to.'

The spotlight found Vikram as the audience noise died down and suddenly he felt alone on the planet. It had been years – well, *lives* – since he'd last sung solo, and he'd forgotten what that rush of nerves felt like. Especially as his was *nothing* like the previous crowd-pleasing number.

The music that began to lilt through the speakers whilst Sunil introduced him ('Here's Little Vikram from MUM-BAAAAIII!!') had no drums, and the instrument was just a sitar. Which probably meant he'd lose the studio audience immediately. But that didn't matter; only one person's opinion counted here. He looked up at her and bowed. For the first time in the whole contest, he felt the stirrings of something and realised that this mattered to him too now.

Do you remember this one, Gauran? Technically, it *was* his own song – and he'd written it for her. But he'd written the verses more than eight hundred years ago, when his name was Chand and hers was Gauran, and adultery was in his heart.

> *Oh my eyes, dusted in sand*
> *They long for your face, as mountains long for snow*
> *And oh my lips, they long for yours*
> *As holy men long for God*
> *Oh my skin, kissed by starlight*
> *It longs for your fingers, as dust yearns for dew*
> *Oh my fingers, they long for skin*

As flowers yearn for rain
Won't you please come home
Won't you please turn around
Won't you please come home
To where my hearts awaits.

He knew that if Rasita was watching, she would know that the chorus – the only new words in the song – was for her: *Won't you please come home*. He prayed that if others with darker intentions watched, they wouldn't understand.

He opened his eyes to polite applause, but he didn't look at the audience, just at her. She was watching him with frightened eyes and a hand over her heart.

We had some good times, didn't we? Do you remember, even if it's just a strange feeling of déjà vu? Do you remember what we sometimes had? My Gauran . . . we shared something so intense, so real . . .

Shiv Bakli tossed back another Scotch as he stared up at the screen where talking heads swathed in couture were babbling and waving their hands around. The *Swayamvara Panel Show!* was meandering through conversational circles. Benny Nimi, the foppish host in the glittering silver shirt, was speaking. 'Anita Rai, is this the night the game got serious?'

'Oh yes, Benny, I am thinking so. The previous nights have been for the boys, with all those swordfights and masculine nonsense. Tonight was for the girls: tonight, we finally began to see past the macho-man masks to the real men inside. I think Sunita will see it that way, too.'

'Absolutely!' exclaimed an anonymous veiled woman in a sari so bedecked with gold that she must be built like a wrestler just to be able to stand up in it. 'Up until now, it was just about ratings and cutting down the numbers to a manageable level. From now on, we will see the things we *girls* want to see – men showing us their *real* charms. We've seen their muscles, now we want to see their moves! So who's got the moves, Benny? That's what we want to know!'

'Absolutely!' gushed Anand, a fashion designer from MUM-BAAAIII!!! (as everyone was calling the city these days). 'Well, who were the big winners tonight, Anita? Who will the papers be talking about tomorrow?'

'Oh, Alok, Alok, Alok! Absolutely Alok! I was charmed! Totally besotted! That, ladies, was how old-fashioned gallantry works. A master-class!' Anita made a great show of fanning her face.

'And Pravit of course,' put in a skinny actress who had been smiling at the cameras and blowing kisses, but hadn't yet managed to say anything intelligible. 'What a fun boy he is! I love him, I just do!'

'I was also impressed by Kajal,' said the Insider. 'He has a strong baritone, real power.'

'I was surprised he wasn't singing falsetto after what little Vikram did to him last night,' giggled Benny. 'Right in the goolies, heh heh!'

'Yes, and what about little Vikram?' said Anita, looking around. 'That was . . . *different*. He continues to survive, doesn't he? Despite, well . . . *everything*. He's such a *runt*!'

'Yes, yes, slumdog millionaire etcetera blah-blah-blah,' said the Insider. 'I think he's just been lucky. You'll note that the audience vote last night placed him last, but Sunita kept him on. The life she gave him kept him in the contest. Which brings me to this next clip—' She waved a hand meaningfully at someone offscreen, the panel disappeared and suddenly the TV screen was filled cheek-to-jowl with an angry-looking Kajal.

'Vikram is homosexual,' the stuntman stated in a flat tone.

'We all know it. We can't prove it, but every one of the competitors knows. And let me tell you this: he gets favours from Uma. No one else does. What favours does he give in return? At best, he's compromising his manhood to win. At worse, he's lying to Sunita. I can't abide that.' The big man spat. 'He's going down—'

The camera flickered back to the panel, who were all, apart from the Insider, staring with open mouths at their studio monitors.

Shiv Bakli turned off the flatscreen with a wave of his hand. He had heard enough. Let the fools chatter; he knew what was really going on.

He set down his glass and went outside to the marble balcony, surveying the city while taking in the relief of the cool night air. The ugly demon statue in the corner came to life and became Khar once more. The creature claimed to be a rakshasa – in Hindu lore that meant a demon, but Khar claimed he wasn't a demon in the sense the world understood: the rakshasas were lords of the Asura. Ravindra was appalled, but not by the things Khar told him – by the fact that he didn't remember them in the first place.

'Khar, how could I have forgotten you?'

'Lord, with every change of body you make, you lose more of your memories – more pieces of yourself – and that makes you hard to find. We lost you, and you forgot us. The last time I personally saw you was in Mandore in the eighth century. Others have had fleeting contact, but you have forgotten even those instances. And you have been secretive – rightly so – and so are we; had this swayamvara not provoked our notice – and had you not invested in the production company – we might still not have found you.'

'Then I'm grateful for your vigilance. My enemies have also surfaced – souls from long ago are arising again.' Ravindra stroked a necklace of dark crystals at his neck. 'I have found the Darya heart-stone. I now have six – only Padma's stone eludes me. This life feels of greater significance than any other I remember.'

'Yes, Lord. Many things are aligning.'

'Where are your brethren, Khar?'

'Scattered, Lord. Some still search for you; others wander, serving their own purposes. Many are waiting in Lanka for your return.' Khar narrowed his eyes. 'Some cannot be trusted. I have sent word to those I do trust and aid will arrive, but it may yet be some days. In the meantime, I will guide and protect you, until you come into your full power and recall all that you once knew.'

It occurred to Ravindra that Khar might be concealing his presence from his brethren for his own purposes, but he knew too little and he wasn't confident he could coerce the beast-like figure if he needed to, for all that Khar appeared to serve him. For the time being at least, he was in the rakshasa's hands.

'Then we shall begin the next phase,' he decided. 'It is time I reasserted my dominance over Queen Darya.'

'Yes, Lord.' The thought of abuse had Khar leering eagerly. The rakshasa leaned closer and its stale reptilian odour filled Ravindra's nostrils. 'Tonight, you must break her down and bring her to us. Are your queens in place?'

Ravindra had sent his queens forth with explicit instructions to steal the bodies they needed to get close to his prey. 'They are waiting on my word.'

Khar's teeth glittered in the darkness. 'Then let us proceed as planned, Lord of Lords.'

Ravindra settled himself cross-legged on the ground before a huge mirror reflecting his chamber, which was dominated by a massive canopied four-poster bed draped in antique silks. Golden urns sat in the corners, and the air was heavy with incense issuing from an array of braziers standing before the mirror; some contained coals, some water, some coloured powders, all to lubricate the spirit world. Khar observed him from the corner, looking more like a statue than a living being.

For hours Ravindra had been meditating, preparing his mind for the arcane purposes of the night, using powers lost somewhere down the centuries of body-jumping. If it hadn't been for Khar, reminding him of what he had once known, he would never have been able to manage this . . . When the sorcerer-king finally opened his eyes, it was after midnight. He breathed upon the mirror and the reflection changed, revealing another room entirely: a small, simple bedroom containing just a single bed, and a young woman lying upon it. She was twitching and grimacing, in the grip of a bad dream that was about to get so much worse . . .

Ah, my Darya, can you feel me coming for you?

His mind coursed over every memory of her he had, spitting and fighting and clawing as he broke her, time and again. Her body was fuller in this life, but the spirit was still the same. He licked his lips. It had been a long, long time since he'd drunk from this particular cup. With a growl of anticipation, he took a cloudy crystal pendant from his pocket, raised it over the braziers and started to speak the ancient words. Immediately the braziers came to life, some smouldering, others starting to smoke and steam. One bowl of water simmered while another froze solid.

He studied her face again, imagining how her mouth would taste, and the sounds she would make as he reclaimed her. And how her last breath would tingle on his skin . . .

He reached out, pushing his right hand through the glass of the mirror, which sucked it in like a pool of mercury. Then his hand appeared inside the image in the mirror, floating across the room towards the sleeping girl. It pulled back the blankets and hovered above her face.

With his left hand, he plunged the pendant into the bowl of water just as it began to boil. The girl on the bed silently convulsed, her skin at once drenched and scalded. Her eyes flew open in agony and terror, but his floating right hand grabbed her face, smothering her scream.

Darya, my queen. Welcome. What games shall we play tonight?

CHAPTER SIXTEEN

Detectives Mean Bigger Bribes

Highway 8, Gujarat and Maharashtra, 9–10 November 2010

Idli and Ras drove all night again, part of a two-lane convoy of trucks that never got above thirty miles an hour. The night air was dense with exhaust fumes and ground mist and as there were no windows on either door, they both wrapped scarves around their noses and mouths just to breathe. Ras dozed most of the night, half-stoned from Idli's cigarette fumes, but Idli himself was hyperactive, singing, bouncing on his seat, tooting at anything that attempted to cut across him.

The road itself was India in motion. In amongst the colourful trucks there were elephant work-gangs and bullock-carts, tiny three-wheeled auto-rickshaws and whole families teetering along on scooters. They passed a convoy of military vehicles parked on the roadside just north of Ahmedabad, the troops smoking and posturing lazily beside their tank-transporters. At one point traffic in both directions was held up for twenty minutes while a drover moved his herd of camels across the highway.

The landscape that greeted them at dawn was very different to home. Gone were the desert sands, the sparse trees and the wide-open pallid blue skies. Morning rose under sullen clouds, revealing muddy farmsteads grazed by big black buffalo with curved horns. The villages they passed through looked much the same, though: half-finished concrete structures, open-fronted, with people sleeping like corpses under thin blankets on bamboo-framed rope-beds. Dogs ran or hobbled about, sniffing at the rubbish piles, and monkeys squatted on fences, picking at themselves.

Idli finally noticed she was awake. 'Hey, Cuz, you back with us?'

'Yeah, just woke up,' she replied, not entirely truthfully. She'd been conscious for some time, but conversations with Idli tended to be like talking with an eight-year-old. 'Where are we?'

'Just out of Valsad, on the coastal road to Mumbai. MUM-BAAAIIII!!! Heh heh.'

She groaned. 'How far to go?'

'About sixty miles, I think. But this is a real busy road, so it'll be slow. And we've got to stop soon anyway, no trucks allowed inside the city until after dark.'

'Really?' *Not again* . . .

'Yeah. Too much congestion, otherwise, with all the city people and their cars. And I need sleep.'

She peered at his skinny face with the bloodshot eyes and glazed expression. *Yeah, you sure do, Idli. How do you live like this?* 'So, another truckstop?'

'Yeah, good one coming up. They do great samosas at the dhaba. Hungry?'

She pretended enthusiasm, but the truth was she felt sick to her core: the constant fumes, the motion, the noise: they were all crushing her. She could barely remember why she was doing this. Something about Vikram – telling him something important?

They used a filthy toilet behind a roadside dhaba before pulling into a truckstop that was even larger than the one the previous day. They ate in the cab again, and then she had to crawl to the floor of the cab, despite the heat of the engine making the cab almost unbearable. As she curled back under her blanket she was tempted to turn on her mobile, to see how much panic she'd caused, but she didn't have the energy. Idli slumped on the seat above her and was snoring in seconds. Despite the heat and the racket, soon she was too.

That evening they found another dhaba with a television, this one in colour, and watched Vikram win through to the next round with his stark, traditional Rajasthani song. She felt queasy. He'd made it through to the last eight. She worried that his head would be turned by the scent of success; that she'd left this too late. While around her the other travellers puzzled over what it meant when he chided Sunita for still wearing Pravit's ring, all she could think of was how sweetly he'd sung. And the song was for her, clearly: 'Come back home . . .'

I'm coming home, Vikram. Just not the home that you mean. I'm coming home to you . . .

They left immediately after the show, so they missed Kajal's outburst on *The Swayamvara Panel Show!* Idli sang and she joined in with her thin voice – she'd never been much of a singer. But Idli was in a happy mood and she felt herself lift despite everything, even as the traffic crawled ever more slowly south as the roads became more and more congested. The sky ahead was aglow with city lights reflecting in the coastal smog of the world's most populous city. Somewhere to their right, out in the darkness, was the sea. Her belly felt queasy from the last meal and her heart was fluttery. But she was nearly there!

Just then Idli cursed mildly as a man with a glowing pink light-stick in his hand stepped to the side of the flow and waved at him, directing him into a siding. 'Damned police,' Idli sniffed. 'I thought we'd get through without being pulled over, for once.'

'Are they looking for me?' Ras wondered, worried.

Idli's face contorted – clearly he hadn't thought of that. 'Doubt it, Cuz. Just routine. They pull some over, check our papers – we all carry baksheesh for the cops.' He patted his breast pocket. 'Happens most trips that someone stops me. Damned uniformed thieves.'

He wrenched the steering wheel and pulled the truck out of the queue inching south and into a siding where three police trucks and a sleek-looking black sports car were clustered. The cop with the glow-stick gesticulated impatiently at the truck behind Idli's, making it pull in too. Then he waved Idli to the far side of the lay-by where a pile of rubble abutted an unfinished wall. Judging from the weeds growing through it and over it, the builders had stopped work on it during Partition, half a century ago.

A tall, slim man with lank hair and a black leather jacket was leaning against the sports car, smoking. He gestured the police towards the second truck while he walked to theirs. Idli turned off the ignition, and swore softly as the engine rattled and shook its way to silence.

'What?' asked Ras anxiously. 'Who is he?'

'Detective.' Idli cursed. 'Detectives mean bigger bribes.' He patted his pocket ruefully, grabbed a fistful of documents from under his seat and climbed down.

Ras hid her face while the detective went through the papers, asking rapid-fire questions. Then he glanced up. 'You too,' he told Ras. 'Out of the truck.' His voice was melodious, yet shot through with steel. His lean, long-chinned face was clean-shaven but for a fine stubble. He looked young, but he spoke with authority.

'This is my cousin,' Idli answered the unspoken question as Ras clambered down to join him. 'Travelling to Mumbai. MUM-BAAAIII!!! Heh heh . . .' The laughter died on his lips as the detective looked at him with frosty eyes.

'I wish to see your cargo. Open up the back.'

'Um, well . . . It's just carpets and dhurries from Kashmir. No real need, eh?' Idli reached into his pocket and flashed some money.

The detective's mouth twitched and then he looked away. 'Just open it up.'

Idli rolled his eyes. 'Time is money, Detective-sahib.' He sauntered to the back and fumbled with some keys until he'd managed to unlock the padlocks that secured the main bolts. 'Just carpets. Just dhurries. Saw them loaded meself.'

The detective looked at Ras. 'What's your name?'

She met his eyes and swallowed. He was dreadfully handsome – there was no other way to put it: he was so attractive it filled her with dread. He moved like a cat, full of languid grace, and something in his motion and demeanour ticked boxes inside her skull. His face filled her vision, and she suddenly felt as if she was the centre of the world and only she mattered. 'Uh, Rasita,' she managed to squeak.

She waited fearfully for some look of recollection on his face, but instead he just looked at her with a gentler expression and his voice became soothing. 'I am Detective Inspector Majid Khan of the Narcotics Bureau. Are you really Mister Singh's cousin, Rasita? Or are you a working girl?' He met her gaze sympathetically. 'Say the word and I'll take you away from him – I'll take you anywhere you name.'

'I am not a prostitute!' she hissed, affronted.

'I mean no offence,' the inspector said. 'Many girls on the road are.' His eyes ran over her slight form. 'You have the looks for it,' he added roguishly. 'Lovely face, classic northern nose and cheekbones, but you need to eat more, round out a little.'

This detective inspector could have graced any of her movie posters in her bedroom. He was the embodiment of all her young fantasies – but such words made her stomach turn and heightened her mistrust. She turned away as Idli climbed down from the back doors of the truck and pulled them open. Majid Khan moved to her side, gesturing over his shoulder to a towering policeman with an imperious moustache and a chest like a refrigerator. The policeman strode over, a suddenly threatening presence.

'So, Mister Singh,' Majid Khan said, 'think about this question very, very carefully. Did you oversee the packing of this freight, and is there *any* possibility that there could be something in there that you yourself did not pack?'

Ras could see Idli's mind ticking over. 'Anything possible, Detective-sahib, yeah?' the driver said eventually. 'But I swear, I only saw carpets loaded.'

'I understand, Mister Singh. I understand perfectly. And what about you, Rasita?'

'I wasn't present, Detective Inspector. Idli – er, Mister Singh picked me up later.'

Majid Khan leaped athletically onto the back of the truck and quickly disappeared into its depths. They saw a torchlight flicker on, and heard him snort at the smell.

Ras looked across at Idli, who looked anxious. 'Is there a problem, Idli?' she whispered.

The little man looked sheepish. 'Maybe. My boss, he and his boys do the loading. I dunno what's in there either.'

'But there won't be anything bad in there, surely?'

Idli ducked his head. 'Might be. The boss, he don't tell me nothing.'

The detective inspector reappeared at the doors of the container compartment. 'Both of you, climb up, please. Constable, you remain there,' he added to the towering policeman watching over them.

Ras shot Idli a frightened look, but he wouldn't meet her eyes; he just swallowed hard, then spat.

Oh no! Her heart was racing so hard she thought it would burst. *What's in there?*

After Idli had clambered up, the detective inspector reached down and offered her his hand. She refused it pointedly – touching him seemed somehow perilous – and his eyes met hers knowingly. Then he turned away and shone his torchlight onto a small box that had been buried beneath the carpets that were stacked against the back of the cab. He'd opened it and taken out some of the contents: shrink-wrapped packages of white powder. She felt her throat empty of air and her fragile heart shudder. Beside her, Idli whimpered and sank to his knees.

Detective Inspector Majid Khan looked at them both, his face as impassive as a temple idol.

He led them away behind the ancient wall, where the only light was his torch, and indicated a low part of the wall where they could sit. The policeman walked behind them, swishing his cane and whistling softly. Ras, frightened, huddled with Idli by the wall; the net was always full of the most terrible stories about corrupt policemen.

Idli sank to his knees. 'Please, Detective-sahib, it wasn't me. I didn't know it was there, *I swear*. Please – I'm a simple man, I don't break no laws. Please ji, *please!*'

The policeman drifted in behind him, swishing the cane in a way that made Ras cringe with fear, expecting it to fall brutally across her cousin's back at any moment. She fell to her knees beside Idli and wrapped her arms around him protectively. 'Don't you touch him,' she shouted, trying to sound brave.

'Do you know what you're carrying?' Majid Khan demanded. 'About four kilograms of opium, fresh from Afghanistan, I would guess – it carries a street value of more than sixty thousand – oh, and when I say sixty thousand, I mean *dollars*. US dollars. Probably destined for Mumbai's bars and nightclubs . . .'

Ras looked at Idli, her head whirling. Her cousin would have been grovelling at the inspector's feet if Ras hadn't been hanging on to him. 'I didn't know, ji! I didn't know!' he kept repeating, bobbing his head as if bowing to the policeman.

'Drugs buy armaments, you see,' Majid Khan continued conversationally. 'The drugs trade keeps the Taliban afloat. It finances Al-Qaeda and Isis. Maybe you are linked to these organisations, yes? We don't like terrorists in Mumbai, especially since 26/11.' The detective inspector's face was impassive, his voice flat and implacable.

That made Ras angry. 'You don't think that,' she snapped. 'You're playing with us, you prick!'

She felt rather than saw the police constable behind her shift and growl, but the detective inspector raised a hand and she guessed he had just saved her a thrashing. *For now.*

'Mind your language, Rasita. My friend takes offence easily.' He looked away for a second, then down at the two of them cowering at his feet. 'Get up, both of you.'

Ras pulled Idli to his feet and turned back to the detective inspector. She didn't like the way her face flushed despite her fear when he looked into her eyes. She didn't like the way her throat choked up and her belly went hot and cold, the way her palms went sweaty. She tried to think of Vikram, but right now she couldn't even picture him.

Finally Majid Khan put his hands behind his back and said, 'Maybe you didn't know about the drugs, Mister Singh. I'm inclined to believe you, though I doubt a judge, looking at you, would feel the same. As for you, Rasita, the court might possibly believe you to be innocent of this crime . . . but there are other things we could make them believe of you, understand?' Looking at Rasita's blank face, he clarified, 'We sometimes turn a blind eye to prostitutes and ganja, but laws are laws, yes? Sometimes they must be enforced, particularly when people are uncooperative. Understand?'

Ras was a big fan of *Orange is the New Black*; she knew all about life in women's jails. She wouldn't survive even a week. 'I understand,' she said woodenly.

The detective inspector sighed, as if he had no real taste for what he was about to say. 'Sending the naïve and foolish to jail is not something I do lightly, and certainly not when there are better alternatives. What I *want* is to secure your assistance in tracking the final destination of this load. If you will work with us, and deliver as instructed, we will protect you, then let you walk away. So what do you say?'

Idli fell to his knees again and begged, '*Yes*, ji! Yes, ji! Please, ji!'

Ras eyed the detective inspector. 'What guarantee can you give us that you'll not include us in your arrests?'

'None. If we get nothing, this conversation never happened and you'll go down.'

'That's a no-win!' she exclaimed.

'It is, yes,' he agreed pleasantly.

She wished she could slap his face, wipe that insouciant confidence away. 'Then what's to stop us just walking away?' she asked.

'I wouldn't imagine a life on the run would suit either of you – and especially not when people know that their merchandise was entrusted to you both, and where your families live.'

She clenched her fists, suddenly frightened for everyone she loved. 'You bastard!'

'I'm not the one running drugs.' He looked down at Idli. 'Do we have a deal, Mister Singh?'

Idli nodded miserably, but then found the courage to say, 'But no Ras. She's not involved, detective-ji. Just let her go home!'

'No!' Ras gasped. *I have to get to Mumbai! I must!* 'I'll look after you, Idli. You'll need family close by.' *If I have to go home now, I'll never have another chance . . .* Suddenly Vikram's face filled her head again, and she felt ashamed that he had ever left her thoughts.

'I agree with Mister Singh,' Majid Khan said, looking at her with something like compassion. 'I think you should go home. This is not your world, Rasita.'

Idli clutched her leg. 'Yes, yes. Listen to the detective-ji, Ras. Go home.'

'No! I'm staying!'

'Very well,' Majid Khan said. 'Mister Singh, return to your truck and repack the merchandise. Officer, oversee him.'

Idli climbed to his feet, pulling a fierce face. 'I won't leave you alone with her. She's my cousin! She's *family*!'

'I acknowledge your concern, Mister Singh, and I give you my word she will be safe with me.'

Looking at that angelic face, Ras didn't feel safe at all. Her legs felt weak and shaky. She'd already spent what little strength she had on pointless defiance. He could do anything to her that he wanted and she wouldn't even have the breath to scream. And she knew that somehow, he knew that.

Reluctantly, Idli let the policeman lead him away. As they disappeared, the detective-inspector stepped close to her and cupped her cheek in his right hand. He smelled of musk, tobacco and danger. 'Well, Rasita. Seeing a damsel in distress brings out my latent chivalry. I get all protective. So why should I let you go with him and place yourself in danger? I can get you home, or if home isn't safe, anywhere you want.'

She swallowed with difficulty, wanting to swat his hand away, but scared to make such a move against him when he so clearly held her future in his hands. *It's the cannabis smoke and the tiredness and the fear . . . I can't think clearly.* 'I can't go back home,' she said. 'This is my only chance.'

'Your only chance? Why do you say that? Is there a boy involved?'

She said nothing. *Let him think what he likes.*

He exhaled in frustration. 'I see so many girls like you, Rasita: brave, innocent, naïve, cocky – but the city always breaks them. And the next time I see them they are cynical hags in young women's bodies, living like parasites on the arms of evil scum. Or they are battered corpses found half-buried in rotting garbage. I get so few opportunities to actually intervene, to save someone. I would like to save you.'

His words sounded so much like a script that they made her feel ill. But she couldn't turn back now. *Nothing else matters but Vikram.* 'I'm going with Idli,' she said firmly. 'Don't try to stop me.' As she fled, she was gouging her nails into her palms to try and stop herself from shaking apart.

CHAPTER SEVENTEEN

Jaichand's Surprise

Kannauj, 1175

A shaven-skulled servant whispered in Chand's ear, 'Lord, the raja wishes to speak with you tonight when he retires.' The man waited for his nod of assent, then slipped away, the very embodiment of discretion.

Chand ran his fingers through his hair, then went back to listening to the tedious war-tales of a Mehrauli prince with particularly foul breath. Tomorrow was the last day of the swayamvara, and the announcement of the victor – and it was also the time when most could go wrong, when he would be unable to react in time to unexpected changes to their plan. He found himself wishing that his wife was there to talk to. She might not be a beauty, but she could always ease his worries.

Nevertheless, he threw himself into the conversations, dispensing advice and telling his own anecdotes, being the consummate political diplomat. Finally, he left to seek the Raja of Kannauj. His route took him past the gates to the great courtyard, where a statue of Prithviraj stood, placed there as a jest by Jaichand ('his Majesty Prithviraj the Self-Regarding was too busy at table to compete, so he sent along this image in his place,' the king had explained, causing a storm of laughter). The mocking words and obscene symbols that defaced it made Chand scowl, but he said nothing as he followed the servant to the secluded little chamber where the raja awaited him.

'Ah, Chand, come in. A drink? A shisha-pipe?' Jaichand sounded in a fine mood.

'I am replete, Majesty,' Chand replied, a little warily.

'The ever sensible Chand,' Jaichand said, waving away the proffered refreshment. 'We are alike, you and I, Cousin. We are planners, thinkers. We keep our heads clear and remember what is at stake, unlike others, who are invariably caught up in the emotions of the moment. We are men of *dis*passion. We calculate, and decide with heads, not hearts. A rare breed, I think you would agree.'

It was always good to agree when a ruler flattered you. 'A Rathod trait, perhaps?' Chand suggested.

Jaichand smiled at that. 'Indeed. And so, I have a mission for you, my friend – perhaps the most important thing I have asked of you. I need you to explain my choice of victor in this swayamvara – this . . . *performance*, this *charade* – that we have so expensively entertained the world with, these last two weeks.' Jaichand met his eye. 'You must understand the choice, Chand, for you must convey it to Prithvi, and make him understand.'

Chand felt his whole being quivering in anticipation. 'What must he understand, Great Raja?'

Jaichand looked at him intently. 'Prithvi Chauhan must understand that my choice of husband for Sanyogita is not a challenge to him but a *warning*. For five years he has been chipping away at his borders, trying his neighbours' strength and gradually making all the lesser kings into his vassals. It must stop, this campaign to subjugate us all. It *must* end, and it *will*: tomorrow.'

'How will this marriage change Prithvi's policies, Majesty?'

Chand asked. There had been whispers that a younger brother of Vanraj might be chosen, to bring the Gujaratis into Jaichand's fold. Others were speaking of Ballal's grandson Nigam, from Bengal. Either option would be a threat to Prithvi.

The king's next words were not what he'd expected at all.

'The chosen candidate will be Raichand of the Tomaras.'

'Raichand! But he's not even here!'

'I can so very rarely surprise you,' Jaichand smirked. 'Yes, Raichand, your king's good friend and comrade-in-arms is here, really! He's been competing under an assumed name, in disguise. Does it not embody the finest tradition of romance? A secret identity, the true prince revealed in the dramatic finale, all for the sake of love!' He laughed at his own cleverness. 'Sanyogita is pleased – she was rather taken with the idea when I told her this morning. And most importantly, it divides the Chauhamanas court. It also legitimises Raichand as the rightful ruler of Dilli, as the late Anangpal's twin sons will have to cede their rights to their more powerful kinsman – so Prithvi will have to relinquish the fortress at last. Without Raichand and Dilli, his kingdom is confined and weakened, the balance is restored and Rajputana remains as it has always been: strong, independent kingdoms, answering to no overlord, perpetually ready to unite and fight for its freedom against the outsider.'

'What outsider, Lord?' Chand asked, to buy thinking time. *Raichand? Prithvi will go mad! He'll have the fool's head.*

'The Mohammedans, of course! Have you not seen them, Chand? They're everywhere, watching us, spying out our strength, while pretending to trade. The Punjab is already under their sway. Rajputana is next. We must be ready for when they attack.'

Chand was blindsided by this new thought. 'No, surely not? They've been ensconced in the Punjab for generations and never assailed us. Their warriors are poor; just Turkic nomads from the steppe lands far to the north. They have no belly for a real battle—'

'Not so, Chand. I have eyes and ears in the north. They have grown strong.'

'Then isn't unity under one king better?'

'No, my friend, you fail to understand the true strength of Rajputana. Our might lies in the tension between us, in our constant readiness, blades poised but not drawn. Try to conquer a Rajput and he will fight to the death! Prithvi's ambition will be our downfall; the union of Tomaras and Gahadavalas through the marriage of Raichand and Sanyogita will restore the balance of power and keep us strong.'

Chand swallowed, then feigned impressed agreement – for what else could he do? To show further dissent would be to risk the trust that he had built between them. But he did ask, 'Why tell me your choice now, before it is announced?'

'Because as soon as Raichand is announced as victor, you must be ready to ride, Chand. *You* must be the person Prithvi hears this from, and you must have all of your powers of persuasion deployed. You must utilise all that logic and reason to prevent Govinda and Sanjham and all the other Chauhan hawks from starting a bloodbath. Do you understand?'

Ah . . . I must be the one who salves the slap to Prithvi's face and prevents war.

'If you can prevent a sudden retaliation, you will save us all, Cousin,' Jaichand added. 'There is no winner in war.' The raja stood, and as Chand did the same, he stepped towards him and embraced him. 'It will be your diplomacy, the magic of your words, that will keep Prithvi on the leash. I'm relying on you, Cousin Chand.'

CHAPTER EIGHTEEN

The Man in the Mirror

Mumbai, 10 November 2010: Day 3 of Swayamvara Live!

Jai was still awake when Vikram got in around midnight. He pushed the door shut on the crowd of shouting journalists outside and slumped against the back of the door, which rattled with hammering fists. Somehow they'd found out his address and had been lying in wait for him when he got out of the film company car.

This celebrity lifestyle sucks . . .

The first journalist had seized his hand as he disembarked from the taxi and bellowed into his face, 'Vikram! Well done, my friend! Can I buy you a drink?' But before he could react, a woman in jeans and a low-cut blouse who could have been Kareena Kapoor's body-double was purring into his neck about an 'exclusive interview', and then the rest of them hit him like a tidal wave, shouting demands for his reaction to 'what Kajal said about you' – *Which is what?* he wondered. He was jostled from camera to microphone and back in a bewildering mêlée. It took him ten minutes to fight his way clear; he still had no idea what he'd said to whom, but somehow he had three business cards in his breast pocket and eight in his jeans. All this on the university campus! Where was Security?

'Hey, Vikram!' Jai waved at him from the couch. 'What do you think about that bastard Kajal, eh?'

'Not you too.' Vikram shot the deadbolt on the door, begged through it for peace and then staggered to the fridge. He grabbed the last beer, pulled the tab and chugged half of it in one. Finally he drew breath and looked at his roommate sprawled on the couch surrounded by pizza boxes and empty Kingfisher bottles. 'Did you have a party while I was out?'

'Sure. These girls wanted to watch the show, so I invited them round. If you'd got here twenty minutes ago they'd have still been here. Including Dipti Sharma, yum yum yum!'

'Dipti Sharma came *here*?' Vikram looked around the flat with embarrassment. Dipti was Jai's current lust object, but she was also a ravenous gossip. She'd probably been surreptitiously photographing the apartment to sell to the press. He sighed, and finally got to ask the question that had been plaguing him since he got out of the car. 'So, what exactly did Kajal say about me, anyway?'

'You don't know?' Jai looked apologetic and angry at the same time. 'He gave this interview where he said you were screwing Uma to stay on the show.'

The beer went sour in Vikram's mouth. 'He said that? *On live television?*'

'Yeah, he did. Now most of the nation thinks you're either a bastard or a gay or both.' Jai sounded unperturbed by the allegations. 'Hey, maybe the film company will send round some real security to escort you tomorrow morning, guys with AKs and armoured cars — that'd be cool! And anyway, I've got an early lecture so I can't drop you off tomorrow.'

Vikram groaned and stared at the door, which was still rattling. A melodious voice purred through it, 'Hey Vikram, I'd still love that exclusive. You could *prove* those rumours aren't true,' she added in a low voice, which promptly started off an angry shouting match outside until, finally, mercifully, the university's security men arrived and the threat of violence drove the press pack away.

Glorious silence fell.

Vikram finished the rest of the beer can in a second long swig. 'You're right. I probably will need extra security.'

Jai leaned forward mischievously. 'So, did you?'

'No!' Vikram responded angrily, then laughed as he realised Jai was just winding him up. 'No, it's all a pack of lies. I do have principles, you know!'

Jai pulled a dubious face. 'Hey, to get Sunita the Shocker in my bed and a billion in the bank? I'd do almost anything!'

'Yeah well, I've got something you might have heard of but clearly don't comprehend: *integrity*.'

'Integrity is a poor man's affliction, bhai. But there are cures, like giving that REALLY HOT reporter outside a hands-on demo of your hetero-ness!' Jai reclined on the couch, looking very pleased with himself. 'You know, I had Dipti tucked under this arm and her hot friend Lipika under the other and they were feeding me potato chips with their fingers. It's been a very good night!'

'I suppose you need me to keep winning to maintain this new-found popularity?'

'Obviously! So whatever you're doing, just keep doing it, bhai!'

Much later, Vikram sat on his bed, spinning an arrow on his fingertip. Beside the ancient quiver propped against the wall was a re-curved bow, an almost circular masterpiece of wood and horn. When strung, the open hoop could fire arrows with enough power to penetrate steel. He could empty an eighteen-arrow quiver inside a minute – not that he'd ever let anyone see him doing that.

But for now, all he needed was the arrow. Aram Dhoop's journal beside him was open at the section where Vikram had noted down Chand's secret education with Vishwamitra. He had wanted to remind himself of the spells, although as it turned out, he'd scarcely needed to; the words were etched into his soul. He spun the arrow on his finger as the ancient phrases tumbled from his lips. The actual *words* didn't really matter; they were just there to help him focus, to ensure the energy was channelled carefully. That was why magicians used 'spells', to help their mind separate idle thoughts from deliberately directed intentions. His mind was focused on a skinny girl he should have spent far more time with during the summer, someone he now felt certain was important, although he still didn't yet understand why.

Where are you, Ras? And who were you?

The arrow was pointing north when it stopped, just as it had every other time he'd done this, but there was no indication of distance. 'North' could mean any number of things – including her coming here, because Jodhpur was more or less due north of Mumbai.

The more he thought about it, the more sense it made, especially if Ravindra was somehow behind her disappearance. His Enemy had to be here somewhere. He swallowed and stared at his mobile for a long time before ringing Amanjit.

Deepika sat up in bed and tried to think, though her mind was so foggy she could recall nothing more than a nightmarish blur.

There had been another dream, hadn't there? A spider, crouching on her left breast and pointing at her with hairy forelegs. But the memory was hazy and indistinct, and the more she tried to grasp it, the more it slipped away. Finally she rose on unsteady legs, went to the bathroom and washed her face. Her skin felt dirty and her throat and breasts felt bruised, as if someone with filthy hands had been mauling her. The thought made her feel like vomiting, but she swallowed and tottered back into her bedroom. According to her alarm clock, it was nearly four o'clock in the morning.

She looked in the mirror – and convulsed in shock.

There was a man there, wearing black silk pantaloons, with a gold crown on his head and a chain of smoky crystals about his neck. He had a cruel, fleshy face, with heavy moustaches and big, intense eyes that leapt as her gaze met his. Some trick of the light made it look like he had too many heads, all reflecting back on both sides of his skull – and when his arms moved, there were many limbs too, like a spider. But it was when she saw his big, hairy hands that she *knew*: there had been no spider – *just his hands*, stroking her and pinching her, half-throttling her in her sleep.

She tried to back away, her mouth flying open.

Too slow!

An arm came through the glass and seized her neck, pulling her headlong against the glass. Her face smashed against the mirror, almost hard enough to crack it, and her nose exploded with a sick, wet crunch. Another arm came through the glass and wrapped around her waist, pinning her to the mirror.

A malevolent voice slithered into her ears. '*Ah, Darya, my queen. It has been so long.*'

She'd heard his voice only once before, in the cave beneath the Mehrangarh Fortress. It made her flesh shudder. '*Have you missed me?*'

She tried to pull away, but two more arms wrapped about her, then another placed its finger against the middle of her brow and dark light exploded, knocking the strength from her and mashing her against the cold glass. She could see his body, a fraction of an inch from hers, but mercifully, couldn't feel it, apart from those horrid arms that held her in such a bruising grip.

'*No!*' If she had nothing else, she still had her pride. '*Let me go!*'

Ravindra chuckled in her ear. 'Darya, my queen. I have found you again. Deepika Choudhary of Safdarjung Enclave: see? I know who you are and where you are. I know all about you and your family – shall I visit them tonight too?'

Fear for those she loved froze her blood and stole her breath. 'No,' she whispered.

He held a pulsing crystal in his hand, a grey stone shot through with darker veins; its vibrations appeared to be beating in time with her heart. 'Do you know what this is?' he purred. 'It is your heart-stone, Darya – the heart-stone *I* gifted you! With it, I can make you do anything I want. *Anything.*'

She tried to scream for help, but nothing came and Ravindra kept speaking. 'This is the same stone you wore in Mandore, the one you lost beneath the Mehrangarh Fort. It is the very thing that keeps you bound to me, life after life. It is the core of your soul, and it is in my hands. I could kill you with a thought. I could command you to dance naked for me, or to slit your own throat, and you would do it. I could make you murder your family in their beds, and you would do so.' He chuckled. 'Shall I?'

She shook her head mutely, pleading with her eyes.

'Then you must give me something in return for such clemency.' Those golden eyes glittered, filling her vision, as one of his hands stroked her cheeks, brushing at her tears.

She gagged, weeping.

He laughed again. 'Hmm. What will you give me? There is only one thing you can give me that I value, little Darya – Deepika, as you are now. Do you know what that is?'

The cruel, leering face bent as close as a lover, just millimetres away, through the pane of glass.

No, please . . . not again—

'I want *you*, little queen.'

Please . . . no . . .

'You will agree to come to me tomorrow, or this morning you will awaken to find everyone else in your house torn to pieces, and their blood will coat your own hands.' His voice was redolent with arrogance and lust. 'Will you give me what I want?'

She saw the amusement in his eyes, the curl of his thick lips, the sharpness of his teeth so close to her throat through the haze of tears.

If he can reach me so easily, what can I do?

She bowed her head in assent.

'You will tell no one of this conversation,' he warned in his skin-crawling voice. 'And believe me, I will know if you do! There is nowhere you can hide your loved ones that I cannot find! Go to Humayun's Tomb before midday and remain there until you are contacted. If you tell a soul, I will know and your parents and Amanjit Singh will die.'

She struggled to hold back tears but failed, felt them running down her bloody nose and cheeks, until his hands were suddenly gone. She fell, the back of her head struck the floor hard, a flash of white light obliterated her thoughts and she sprawled on her back, senseless.

CHAPTER NINETEEN

The Drop-Off

Mumbai, 11 November 2010

Idli's truck crawled into Mumbai on Highway 8, a huge multi-lane procession of overpasses that reared over the jhuggis and slums of the city like the path of a skipping stone before snaking its way into the centre. The traffic was gridlocked and filled with the fumes from immobile vehicles, but the air was different from Jodhpur. Here, it *moved*: a coastal breeze that tasted of salt, rotting fish and seaweed gusted over the lines of trucks and cars and pushed the diesel fumes away in shredded clouds. The city lights went on and on for ever, like every festival of the year was being held right now, burning amidst the seas of blue tarpaulin that sheltered half the citizens of India's most populous city. They squatted beneath their flimsy shelters, wrapped in every item of clothing they owned, warming callused hands over tiny cooking fires. Further in, lights glowed from buildings and streetlights, apartments and shops and hotels and on into the distance – if she hadn't been so scared, it might just have been the most beautiful sight Ras had ever seen.

She sat silently in the passenger seat, trying to erase Detective Inspector Majid Khan's face from her memory. The whole encounter had left her frightened – no, not just frightened, *terrified* — and her heart was still thudding dangerously. Even now, she could feel his eyes — she really could, because the truck was now rigged with his top-of-the-range surveillance gear, no knock-off gear for the inspector. Perhaps he was watching her right now as she bit her nails and tried to stay calm for Idli.

Her cousin was chattering non-stop, talking rubbish to mask the silence. 'Just in, deliver, out,' he kept saying. 'Easy. Easy. Just in, deliver, out. No problem.'

Ras wished he'd shut up, but she couldn't bring herself to say so.

They came off Highway 8 north of Juhu district and wound through a tangled web of roads. The traffic here swarmed like flies, vehicles darting into every available space with an aggression that bordered on the suicidal. All the while, Idli was becoming more and more hyperactive, bouncing on his seat and shouting at other drivers, in between babbling about what he wanted done with his belongings if someone shot him.

Finally, she couldn't stop herself shrieking at him to be quiet, frightening him into silence.

'Sorry Ras,' he said at last. 'I'm just scared, me . . .'

She bit her lip and tried to pretend she wasn't just as afraid. The minutes crawled, until they turned into a small cul-de-sac at the mouth of a warehouse that looked like it had survived an air raid. Beside the roller-doors was a group of men, smoking and playing cards by the light of a single lamp. A fire burned in an oil drum beside them. They all looked up as the truck rattled to a halt.

Idli was sweating like it was the middle of summer. 'You stay in the cab,' he told Ras. 'Don't talk to them. Don't get out.'

'Stay calm, Idli,' she replied. 'Don't talk too much. Just act normal.'

'I *am* acting normal.'

There were seven men waiting for them; the one who leaped onto the footplate outside Idli's door was on his mobile. He had a shaven skull and dead eyes. 'Turn off. Get out.' His eyes narrowed. 'Who's she?'

'She's my cousin. She's okay, just along for the ride.'

'She gets out too.' He ran a measuring eye over her, making her skin crawl.

'She's my cousin. She has to stay in the cab. Boss said so.'

Shavenskull raised a sceptical eyebrow, but relented. 'Let's get this done.'

Idli held out a key and passed it to Shavenskull. The man jumped down, and with an anxious look back at Ras, Idli followed him. They vanished behind the truck and a dark-skinned, bony man with a thin moustache and an unhealthy smile appeared beside Ras' window. 'Hey babe, you wanna drink?'

She realised he was very young, scarcely her own age. She gave him her most withering look. 'No.'

'Just asking.' He looked hurt. 'What's your name?'

'Ras.'

'Ras? Funny name. What's it short for?' He tried a grin that showed teeth discoloured by paan.

'None of your business.' She turned away.

'I'm Dil,' he said, staring at her with big eyes.

'Good for you.' She heard noises at the back, and the sounds of unloading. Most of the men were there, but Dil just kept looking at her, smiling inanely. She lost patience. 'What do you want?'

To her surprise, he flinched. 'Just being nice. Don't get to talk to girls much. Not real ones like you.'

'There's sixteen million people in this city. Half of them are female. Go and talk to them.'

'No time – I'm too busy, me. You sure are pretty. Skinny like a model.'

Shavenskull walked back around the front with Idli in tow. Another man stalked behind them, a hulk of a man with wild hair.

Something about the way they were moving gave Ras a chill, but Dil just babbled on, 'It's tough, being busy all the time. And I've got no real job, so no marriage prospects, but I got a little money.' His voice dropped shyly. 'You like movies, Ras?'

For goodness sake! She was about to snap at the boy, when Shavenskull looked up at her, then back at Idli. His voice carried through the open window.

'Were you stopped on the road?'

Idli laughed. 'Oh no, straight through. No problems.'

Shavenskull cocked an eyebrow, and Ras saw the right hand of the man standing behind Idli reach inside his jacket in a gesture straight out of an action movie. Her fragile heart began to pound again and she licked her lips as Dil prattled on, 'I like Pravit Khoolman – he's the best! Do you think he and Sunita Ashoka will get back together?'

No, I don't. She turned and forced a smile. 'Dil, could I have some water, please?'

He stopped and beamed at her. 'Sure! Yes, Miss Ras, yes, of course.' He scurried towards the warehouse; Shavenskull looked at him irritably as he went past and then gestured towards the cab.

Another man suddenly appeared at her window. He had a red bandana about his head and a worldly stare, when she dared meet his eyes. 'The boss wants you to climb down, girlie, so get your arse down here before I come in and move you.' He grinned as though he thought she would somehow find that to be an appealing notion.

Ras tossed her head defiantly and climbed out by herself, ignoring Bandana's offered hand, her heart thumping unrhythmically. *Have they guessed something?*

She tried to look in all directions without appearing to be concerned at all. A sleek black Porsche cruised into the turning bay and she found herself praying it was the detective inspector, even though the car was different. But three strangers got out, two in dark suits flanking a middle-aged man in an outrageous Hawaiian shirt. He walked up to Shavenskull, ignoring her.

'Well?' the newcomer said. 'Are we compromised or not?' He looked cheerful, as if this were nothing more than a pleasant outing.

Ras turned back in time to see the big man behind Idli pull out a gun and place it against the back of her cousin's skull.

Idli froze.

'Just seeking that clarification, sir.' Shavenskull turned back to Idli, and in a terse voice said, 'You see, Idli, we have men watching certain lay-bys on the highway, and one of our watchers swears he saw you stopped and searched, just outside of Mumbai. He gave us your number plate.'

Idli looked on the point of collapse and Ras felt a tightening in her chest.

If I have a seizure now, I'm dead, she thought. *Where's that damned detective?*

The big wild-haired man behind Idli glanced at Bandana standing next to Ras with his hand inside his jacket. Some signal passed between them, then Wildhair grabbed Idli's shoulder and lazily pushed him to the ground. Bandana gripped Ras' arm before she could react. 'Lie on the ground beside your cousin, girlie,' he told her in a flat voice. 'Face down and don't move.'

She swallowed, and lowered herself to her knees, trying not to think. *Just breathe, just breathe. It won't hurt. It won't hurt a bit*, she whispered to herself, mantra-like. But she couldn't help twisting her head, trying to watch, even if it meant seeing her own end coming.

Bandana looked at the newcomer, the boss man, and said aloud, 'Ready?' The word echoed about the front of the warehouse, too loud, as if he weren't talking to those with him at all, but someone else—

—and Wildhair lifted his gun and shot Shavenskull in the chest: once, twice. The man staggered backwards, his mouth falling open as the shots resounded about the confined area. As Wildhair fired, Bandana knelt over Ras, his body shielding hers, and shot the first of the newcomer's bodyguards in the head.

'Under the truck, girlie!' Bandana shouted. 'Now!' He snapped off another shot as men dashed from the warehouse and suddenly bullets were spraying everywhere.

Ras slithered like a snake, strangely calm, just as she had been in that horrible moment when the ghost had reached for her back in March. *Breathe, breathe. Don't think, act.* A bullet whined past her head and another pinged off the cab. Idli was babbling incoherently. She saw the man in the Hawaiian shirt standing paralysed in the middle of the crossfire, looking more scared than she was.

All of a sudden loudspeakers were blaring and policemen were flooding in. She lay flat, willing her heart to slow, while beside her Idli hugged the ground, whimpering.

Then Detective Inspector Majid Khan, wearing a faded brown leather jacket, was reaching under the truck. 'Rasita, are you all right?' he asked in a calm voice, his face almost expressionless. She let him draw her out and pull her to her feet, supporting her with one strong arm.

She saw Bandana pressing the boss-man into the dirt, a gun at his temple. An armed policeman was bent over young Dil, who was crying. There were three other men lying in growing pools of blood that soaked into the dirt. The air smelled of acrid powder and metallic blood, a nauseating mix that made Rasita gag. Wildhair and Bandana — they must be undercover policemen, she realised — grinned at each other cautiously.

'Where's the stuff, Tanvir?' the detective asked.

'It's still in the back,' the man in the bandana answered.

'Good. Let's get these cops out of the way. This is still our investigation; we get the prizes, not them.'

'Onto it, Majid.' Tanvir glanced at Ras, who was clinging dizzily to the detective's arm. 'We need to get this one processed down at the station.'

Majid put his arm about Ras in a way that she found both comforting and disturbing. 'All in good time. The priority is safety – let's get her to Safe House Five.'

'Sure thing, boss,' Wildhair said, leering at Ras, while Tanvir's face hardened. Ras shrank instinctively against Majid Khan, then cringed inside at the realisation of what she'd done.

Why am I like this with him? It's like I've always known him . . .

Majid turned to Tanvir. 'We'll go together. Grab the merchandise.' He looked down at where Idli was crawling out of the dust beneath the truck on his own. 'Both of you, come with us.'

Tanvir drove, and Ras sat huddled in the back of the large sedan. Idli went in another vehicle, but she soon lost track of it in the unending traffic. The new-car smell of the vehicle seemed unreal after the horrors of the gunfight. Majid Khan sat in the front passenger seat, soft music wafting from the speakers as they wound their way through the labyrinth that was Mumbai's centre. Though there were vehicles and faces everywhere, no eyes penetrated the tinted windows and no beggars importuned them at the traffic lights. It was as if they were riding in a ghost-car.

Finally the detective looked over his shoulder. 'I apologise that you were exposed to danger, Rasita. We will now look after you and ensure your safety, whilst you recover from what must have been a traumatic experience.'

Ras had no idea if this was standard procedure. 'Where are you taking me?'

'Safe House Five,' he answered. 'It is better you don't know the address. It's not in a fashionable area, but it's secure. You'll get medical attention and be able to wash, eat and change. I'll need your mobile phone, though. Mobiles are traceable, and our enemies have many contacts.'

Ras barely followed the words. Now that the danger had past, her body was belatedly reacting: she felt suddenly drained, the shock of the gunfight leeching away all her vitality. She had never had much energy anyway – her illnesses had always stopped her from doing much in the way of physical exercise. All she wanted to do now was sleep, but she managed to stay awake long enough to walk unaided when they arrived outside a bungalow with a grilled front door with a poorly kept lawn out front, shrouded by tall trees hung with anaconda-like vines.

She forced herself to walk by herself – it was a matter of pride. She didn't like the way Majid Khan had held her before—too possessive, too presumptive, from such an attractive man.

He knows the effect he has on women. Especially ones like me.

A woman in a pale green nurse's uniform opened the door and took her hand when she faltered on the steps. She didn't remember much of what came next, except for a bath full of steaming hot water, and the nurse helping her to undress. She realised she was naked and in the bath a few minutes later, but the moments between were a blank. The woman had kind eyes and an attentive manner. Her demeanour embodied safety and reassurance.

She closed her eyes. *I'm alive. I'm safe.*

She wondered where Vikram was. Had he survived another night on *Swayamvara Live!*? Would she be able to call him tomorrow? But when she tried to picture his face, the only visage that floated behind her eyes was that of Detective Inspector Majid Khan.

She woke up in a thin hospital nightie in bed, minutes or hours or maybe even days later. All she could do was roll over and go back to sleep.

CHAPTER TWENTY

Sanyogita's Choice

Kannauj, 1175

The courtyard of the palace thronged with people and noise rose in waves, assailing the senses, as warriors, princes, servants and functionaries jostled together. In the middle were the competitors, arrayed in their finest and standing in two lines leading down from the gate and the defaced statue of Prithvi. A solitary footman stood beside the statue. Princess Sanyogita would descend from the royal plinth overlooking the square and garland the man of her choice . . .

. . . who would of course be Raichand.

Now he knew where to look, Chand could see through the disguise easily. He was furious at himself at having missed it. He feigned not to recognise him still, despite Raichand winking at him furiously as he walked past. *Raichand, you fool! You* imbecile! *Do you think you can climb so high and not fall?*

He walked to the gates, where a couple of the raja's secretive slaves were hovering. He motioned one man closer. 'All is prepared?'

The man bowed, eager to appear efficient. 'All is ready. Just outside the gates here, Lord, are six horses, so you need never tire a mount fully. We've blocked off the road through to the gates, to allow you a quick departure, and given your description to the men who guard the Dilli road. Your passage will be unobstructed.'

He thanked the man sincerely and slipped him a gold coin. 'Such efficiency should not go unrewarded,' he whispered. The obsequious man beamed, pleased to be singled out, and hurried away.

Chand went outside to see for himself that the horses were there and being held by his own retainer, then returned to his post by the door. There was a big footman standing there, shifting uncomfortably, his head bowed. The man's impatience was replicated everywhere. Contestants eyed each other. Boasts were exchanged. Wagers were made. People whispered and bounced and twitched.

Only Chand Bardai remained perfectly still.

Finally, trumpets blared, drums rolled and a huge elephant trumpeted balefully as it led the royal procession into the courtyard. The elephant was caparisoned in red and gold, the colours of weddings, and carried a magnificent howdah on its back. In the howdah, under a screen, rode Jaichand's first cousin, chief of his generals, Arumpaal, leading the household cavalry, Jaichand's sworn men. The raja came next, on a huge open palanquin borne by eight slaves, followed by Jaichand's wives. Finally, he saw Sanyogita, in the horse-drawn carriage in which she would depart the ceremony with her selected husband. She was scarcely visible beneath the traditional veils and garlands of marigolds of a bride, but her demeanour was demure, her head downcast, as befitted a virtuous bride.

The crowd hushed as Jaichand ascended the royal platform and presided over the seating of his wives and daughter on his left side. Then he welcomed the chief guests, the kings escorting their sons competing for Sanyogita. When the platform was full, the profusion of men and women glittering like a mosaic of every colour on earth all sparkling in the sunlight, the trumpeters and drummers once more pounded a fanfare and the king stepped forth.

Jaichand was bristling with excitement, clearly enjoying this moment of destiny. When he spoke, his trained voice was pitched high to reach all corners. 'My fellow rulers, I welcome you all. You honour my house. Brave competitors, I thank you, for the courage, the skill and charm you have displayed in these past weeks. Truly, people will speak of this great swayamvara for a thousand years. You are all magnificent, the very embodiment of the Rajput warrior, princes of the world!'

They all cheered him, for they were cheering themselves too. There was much more self-congratulatory praise, for his kingdom, for his beautiful wives, and for the daughter his favourite wife had presented him, and for himself. Then still more speeches were made as those whose rank afforded them the right to reply did so, while contestants and the watching crowd sweated and fretted, their emotions like tinder before a flame. Outside in the streets, the common people were thronging closer, like an encroaching sea, desperate to be part of the occasion.

Chand grew anxious, worried the streets from the gate might be blocked after all, but his gold-bought court official was already getting the soldiers to push people back, keeping his escape route clear.

Finally, Jaichand reclaimed the stage. 'I thank you all, with all my heart! And now, the moment has come!' He turned and offered an arm to his daughter, who walked forth clad in the heaviest red-and-gold brocaded cloth Chand had ever seen. 'Princes of Rajputana, of Bengal, of the South and the North! I give you my daughter, the flower of the realm, the most precious of jewels, the heart of this kingdom: Sanyogita Rathod, Princess of Kannauj. By her choice, this kingdom will gain an heir and I will gain a son. May this herald a new age of peace and prosperity across all the realms of this great land.'

They cheered louder still, drowning Jaichand out. Chand saw the competitors gaze at Sanyogita in awe and understood that regardless of the reasons they had entered the competition, greed or ambition or simple competitive spirit, they were all infatuated with her right now, in this legendary moment. To be able just to say, 'I was there! I competed!' would be enough to carry to the grave. To be the victor, that would be beyond price. It was to become a living legend. He felt his hands go sweaty, and his heart begin to pound.

Come on, get on with it . . .

Sanyogita pulled the huge garland of marigolds from her neck and walked to the edge of the platform. At the last second she turned and gestured behind her, saying something that didn't carry. A tiny girl, clad as a doll-like smaller version of Sanyogita herself, leaped to her feet and ran to take the princess' hand. The crowd tittered and sighed.

What on earth? That's her maid, isn't it? The moonstruck girl she favours? Chand quivered, fretting at this unexpected moment. *What's she doing?*

Sanyogita surveyed the two columns of men carefully and then descended the steps and walked to her right. Chand felt his belly clench as she came to the first of the competitors. Each hopeful face was etched onto his memory.

The princess walked the line of men, looking carefully into each face, the tiny girl trailing behind her. Some men smiled, and some almost fainted in the heat of the moment. Some went stony, as if facing an enemy charge. Some blushed and ducked their faces. And as she passed them by, some looked relieved, others crushed.

She neared the end of the line, where Raichand waited expectantly, the last man in this column. His false moustache was slipping ridiculously as his perspiration loosened the glue. He was visibly shaking with anticipation and excitement – and fear, too, as Sanyogita neared him, the little girl beside her.

Why is the girl with her?

Sanyogita stopped in front of Raichand and the whole courtyard quivered. Something passed between Raichand and the princess, then, with a faint bob of the head she stepped past him. He looked dazed, but not put out. Chand felt as if the tension was crushing his lungs.

Then Sanyogita was before him and passing him without a glance. The little girl looked up at Chand and pulled a face. Chand poked out his tongue, making her grin. Sanyogita paused, right beside the doorway, and the crowd fell utterly silent. Then she stepped to one side, beneath the shadow of the gates, as if she were about to go back to Raichand . . .

. . . but instead, she garlanded the statue of Prithviraj Chauhan.

The whole gathering recoiled in shock.

Suddenly, amidst the stillness, came an explosion of movement. The big footman nearest the statue burst from the shadows and flung something that whirled at Chand's face and instinctively, he snatched it out of the air. It was his bow, fully strung. A quiver of arrows followed. He nocked an arrow instantly. The footman, bellowing merrily, tore the helmet from his head and roared with laughter. The crowd gasped as he seized Sanyogita about the waist.

'Thank you for your daughter, King Jaichand!' roared Prithviraj Chauhan.

The entire assembly gaped, stunned with shock and wonder. Chand scanned the closest men, seeking those likeliest to attack.

Raichand gulped and backed off in the stretched moments of paralysis as Chand's retainer clattered in with his string of horses. Then everyone's head turned back to the raja, standing on the royal platform with his mouth hanging open, gasping like a fish on land. Everywhere were soldiers tensing for action, but frozen by their leader's immobility.

Prithvi swept Sanyogita onto one of Chand's horses and seized another for himself. The princess threw her legs from side-saddle to fully astride with confidence and turned back to the little girl. 'Come! Come to me!'

Chand lifted his aim and focused straight upon Jaichand, just as the raja raised his hand to signal the attack. Jaichand stopped, and across the courtyard their eyes locked.

The first arrow is yours, Jaichand . . .

The Raja of Kannauj didn't move. Across the square, Chand could sense the man wondering whether a poet could hit him at one hundred paces.

You know me, Jai, better than most. You've always suspected that I'm more than I seem, haven't you? You know I won't miss. So don't move; just let us go. Rely on your men to capture us when you're safely out of harm's way.

Jaichand didn't move, except to slowly lower his hand.

Chand took a step back, then another. That was enough to provoke mayhem. The nearest competitor howled a battle-cry, drew his sword and charged. Chand pivoted and fired, and the man stumbled backwards, clutching the shaft that had slammed into his chest. But the spell had been broken, and everyone moved at once.

Chand shouldered his bow and snatched up the little handmaid, clutching her in one arm as he swept from the steps to the saddle in a single leap. He almost lost her — and his seat — as the horse danced erratically. *Damned creatures — I hate horses!*

Everything lurched sickeningly, but somehow he held on as behind him, the thwarted competitors roared and hundreds of swords were pulled from scabbards in a metallic rush.

Another bow whirred, but this was Prithvi's weapon, sending a shaft into the breast of the nearest competitor. Chand glimpsed Raichand hesitating as the others surged forward, then his attention was snapped away as his retainer shouted and Prithvi slapped Sanyogita's horse. It leaped, sending the princess lurching, but she kept her seat and they were all thundering down the specially cleared path. Chand caught a glimpse of the servant he'd paid staring open-mouthed. He grinned and waved, then all became a blur as they careered away towards the city gate.

Outside Kannauj, Chand and Prithvi met the crowd of Chauhamanas warriors awaiting them and the pursuit, poorly organised, drew off. At last they were able to slow to a trot, and the men began to smile. They eyed Sanyogita curiously – she had kept her veil over her head during the ride, retaining her air of mystery. The girl on Chand's lap had wriggled around until she was facing forward; she was singing to herself and wouldn't respond to any of Chand's questions.

Finally they reached a village where Govinda waited with more of Prithvi's warriors. The big man was clearly having a fine time, having driven off a small contingent of Rathod cavalry. Prithvi swung from his saddle, clasped Govinda's hand, then hauled Chand from the saddle and bear-hugged him. His whole frame was trembling with excitement.

'Did you see his face, Chand? Did you see Jaichand's face! And they even let us station horses and cleared our way for us! After all the hours we spent trying to work out how we could get horses close enough, Jaichand gave them to us himself! Incredible!' Prithvi pummelled Chand's back, convulsing with laughter.

Everyone was beaming, whooping and dancing excited little jigs. Chand wondered if he'd ever seen a happier day.

Prithvi cuffed Chand's cheek gently. 'Magical, my friend! *Magical!* That is how you win a swayamvara.' Then he turned and went to Sanyogita, who was standing aloof with the girl clutching her legs. He dropped to one knee. 'My Lady of Kannauj, my apologies, that I was unable to compete fairly for your hand. I wish only that your father had allowed me to attempt to win you openly.'

The girl stood silent for a moment and then said, her voice clear, melodious, 'My Lord, I would also that you had been able to win my hand fairly, before the eyes of the world. But my father would not allow it. And now, here I am: my reputation ruined, my family's honour stained for ever.'

Prithvi's face became grave. 'My Lady, your reputation is as precious to me as my own. Gentle words have we exchanged in verse and letter. Gentle words I speak now. I will return you to Jaichand, untouched and pure, rather than have you take a further step unwilling. I would even place my head upon the block, rather than have your name tainted. All that I have done, I have done for you. And though I have not seen your face yet, still I hold myself bound to every promise I have written.'

The soldiers had gone quiet and their raja's words hung in the air. Even the villagers had crawled from hiding to witness the scene being enacted in their humble square. Sanyogita stood before the kneeling king, her posture erect. The girl at her side peered at the king, and then up at her princess. No one spoke.

Slowly, carefully, Sanyogita lifted her hands from the girl's shoulders and pulled back her own veil. Every man there licked his lips, drinking in the smooth skin, the full lips and the bewitching eyes. Her face was hung with jewellery, chains from ear to nose, earrings of pearl, necklace of diamonds. But even unadorned, she would have taken their breath away.

Prithvi stared up at her, and Chand saw the moment ripple through his friend's heart and mind and knew that nothing would ever be the same. For an instant, he was back at that bridge beneath the Mehrangarh, watching Shastri and Darya fall to their deaths: different faces, but the same beings. He was certain neither remembered, and yet he could see inside them the echo of love lost and now regained. Their hands rose and then fell, not quite touching, as each tried to understand what it was that had drawn them to the other. Words half-formed fell away unspoken, but their eyes spoke, more eloquently than he, court poet, ever could.

Finally Prithvi found his voice. 'Now that I do see you, I understand. You are the most beautiful of women, the purest, the most wondrous, who has ever lived. I am not worthy. Say the word and I will return you to your father. Or stay with me, and I will love and honour you for ever.'

'I am just a woman, my Lord. And I will stay, and return your love, measure for measure and beyond, in this and every life.'

Somewhere, far away, something rumbled in the air: a distant thundercloud, perhaps. Everyone heard it, looking about them, except for the two lovers, whose every sense was consumed with each other.

The little handmaid looked about her, then detached herself from Sanyogita and threw her arms around Chand's waist. He absently stroked her head as he watched his friend, trying to read the moment, to comprehend whether this gamble, in which he had purposed to free himself and Shastri and Darya from the burdens of his choices, had achieved that aim. It was impossible to say, but he saw many reasons for hope.

'They love each other,' the girl whispered to him.

'What do you know of love, little bird?'

'That it makes people crazy,' the girl replied. She looked up at him. 'You love her too, but you're giving her up.' She sounded disturbingly old and wise, suddenly. 'You are like a cat, with many lives. Ghosts haunt you, and all your arms and legs are wrapped in spiderwebs.'

He looked down and sucked in his breath. *She must be someone from another time. But who?*

'What's your name, child?'

'I'm Gauran,' she replied, looking up at him curiously. 'Jai-chand is my father, but my mother was just a serving girl. He refuses to acknowledge me – but Sani is my friend.' She looked up at him and her eyes narrowed. 'Don't look at me like that,' she hissed, and buried her head in her odhani.

But Gauran stayed with him for the remainder of the journey, and would speak only to him. When they got to Dilli, Kamla threw her arms about Gauran and vowed to care for her – a daughter at last! Chand agreed reluctantly, because the girl made him uneasy, but the choice was no longer his. Like the cobwebs the girl claimed she saw, his movements felt wrapped up in destiny, for he had finally recognised her, seeing who truly lurked behind her eyes, unknown even to her. She was Padma reborn. Padma; the Queen of Mandore whom he should have saved so long ago, when he was Aram Dhoop.

But he also saw, quite clearly, that Gauran was moon-touched, and irrevocably mad.

PART TWO

THE HEART OF BATTLE

CHAPTER TWENTY-ONE

The Ravages of Time

Dilli, 1192

'Husband, what are you thinking?'

Chand looked up from his writing desk on the shaded balcony, the sunset glowering distantly, his expression melancholic. He had been penning a stanza, part of a new play, commemorating that swayamvara seventeen years ago. 'I was thinking that all things end sadly, even if they begin with happiness and high hopes.'

Kamla grunted, unimpressed. 'Then I am thinking that it is poets who are sad, and that poets who spend their days brooding on the past are the saddest of all.'

Chand couldn't deny the charge. He surveyed his desk, piled high with erasable slates that were etched with crossed-out words and half-written verse. 'It's my *Prithvi-raj Raso*: this history of Prithvi's life is taking all my time, and it's forcing me to re-examine all that has gone before. It makes me wonder whether I did right, all those years ago.'

Kamla rolled her eyes. 'Not this again! You mope too much, Chand. You scribble and cross out and sigh. You stare into space. You don't come to bed at night. You forget to eat and drink. You neglect your wife.' She looked at him reproachfully. 'Both of them.'

The hurt in her voice made him cringe. He ran his fingers through hair that had gone grey and begun to thin. *When did this happen? Where did my youth go? Where did our happiness go?*

He was only forty-three, but the accumulated sorrows of the years since the glorious swayamvara had worn him down. His shoulders were thinner now – he hadn't fired an arrow in anger for years, and didn't even practise any more. Kamla was right, too. He did neglect her. He neglected himself. Even his sons, all ten of them, were strangers to him. The eldest four were brawling barbarians, warriors obsessed with swords and horses, typical Rajput fighting men without a poetic soul between them. The younger ones were on their way to the same destiny, except perhaps his fifth, Jalhan, who was scholarly – but even he treated Chand like a stranger and a rival. He barely knew his boys.

Where did the time go?

He knew the answer, though. Sanyogita's abduction had pitched the Chauhamanas into four years of war with Kannauj, as Jaichand launched campaign after campaign, attempting to regain his daughter. The marriage of Prithviraj and Sanyogita had become the greatest love story since Rama and Sita, but it was also the bloodiest. The flower of Rajputana manhood hacked each other into lumps of dead meat for the jackals to feast upon in the name of that love, until finally attrition won and they could fight no more. They did not so much declare a truce as reel away from each other like brawling drunks so dazed and battered that they were barely able to stand. It was a peace of exhaustion.

They all licked their wounds, but by 1182, Prithviraj was ready to fight again – his depleted treasury made it a necessity; their own lands had been ravaged during the fighting and they desperately needed plunder. There was a new generation too, warriors desperate to emulate their fathers and older brothers, to win 'glory'. So Prithvi declared a grand digvijaya, a military campaign to conquer all of Rajputana. He started gobbling up minor kingdoms in Haryana and the borderlands of the Punjab, then pushed east into Bengal and south over the Narmada River — small battles, steady conquests, sacking and pillaging as he went. His legend grew, not as a lover, this time, but as a conqueror. He lost friends and gained subjects. His enemies proliferated on all sides.

To Chand fell the task of documenting it all and making it glorious, writing the history of Prithviraj Chauhan, safeguarding his friend's name for all time. He composed endless stanzas on his victories, like the one over King Parmar of Mahoba, though it had been a near-defeat. He documented the death of friends, like that of Sanjham Rai, loyal to the last despite his sarcasm, though his had been a squalid end, dying horribly of snake-bite while skulking in a quarry, protecting his wounded king after an ambush.

And then there was Raichand . . . at the end of the Kannauj War they had finally settled matters with the wayward king, bringing him back into the fold, with much back-slapping and pledges of loyalty. But Raichand had turned on them again, this time trying to trap Prithvi and murder him. Prithvi took Raichand's head himself, but it felt like a defeat.

But last year, 1191, had brought the battle that redeemed them all and restored some of Prithviraj's tarnished glory. *The Battle of Tarain!* The Mohammedans had finally invaded, an army of Turkic warriors led by Muhamed Ghori. Prithvi had placed Govinda in command of the advance guard, following himself with the main body. He hadn't been needed; Govinda defeated the invader himself, but Chand was careful that the glory accrued to Prithvi first. The legend of Prithviraj was restored: Protector, King and Lover.

'Chand,' said Kamla, 'you're doing it again.'

'Huh? What?'

'Staring into space like that idiot girl does.'

He winced. He didn't want to think about Gauran. *I should never have taken her in. I shouldn't have married her when she came of age. It destroyed our happiness.*

Kamla waddled over to him. Like himself, she was greying, a woman in her forties, unlovely, lined and worn. She put an arm about his head and pulled his face into her bosom. 'Come to my bed tonight, husband. You think too much. You need to forget.'

If only I could. He pushed her away gently. 'I have to write, Kamla. I *must*! The king expects progress every day.' *We're running out of time*, he thought. *Can't you feel it?*

She looked down at him and stroked his hair. 'When will Prithviraj give me back my husband?' She sighed. 'I miss him.'

He worked late again that night. Paper – that brilliant innovation for capturing phrases that had first crept into Rajputana in the time when he was Aram Dhoop of Mandore – was still expensive. A poet had to choose his words carefully, for each sheet was too precious to waste on errors and misjudged words. His history of Prithviraj and his reign, begun as a labour of love, had become a tedious burden.

Like our friendship. We go through the motions, we pretend, but we're no longer content in each other's company any more. Not when she is present, and all I can think is that each night he has her, whilst I have Kamla . . . poor Kamla.

The swayamvara had not just destroyed Rajputana, miring it in ruinous wars of retribution, but Chand's own self-regard, his love for Prithvi and the fragile happiness of his marriage to Kamla.

I thought it was what destiny required of me: that after bringing

Darya and Shastri together in this life, that I could achieve the same with Gauran. So I raised her, poured all my love into her, never intending more than to heal her troubled soul.

Instead she'd pulled him into her circle of madness. She'd become obsessed with him – as he had with her. The worst thing was, he could feel the ghost of what should have been: the real love that Aram Dhoop – he himself – should have shared with Padma. At their best, she was almost whole.

But at her worst, she was manipulative, conniving and vicious, poisoning his marriage, seducing him with her eyes and her pretence of innocence, then waiting until he'd stayed up one night too late, when she'd waylaid him . . . and he'd been too drunk . . .

After that, they'd had to marry – a minor scandal, but she wasn't his *actual* daughter, and he was far from the only man in the world to take a younger ward as wife when she came of age. At court, he was powerful enough to be above criticism.

But he'd broken Kamla's proud heart, and she hadn't deserved that.

Nor had it cured Gauran's troubled mind. It was as if there was a void inside her, where her soul should have been. It was as if she was half a person.

With a sigh, he put down his quill and pushed aside the latest sheet.

It was the middle of the night, with all of the servants and junior scribes long asleep, before he crept along the corridors of the second floor, below the chambers where he and Kamla slept. Faint discordant singing trilled from behind a curtained room, dimly lit from within. He placed an eye to the gap in the curtains.

A skinny young woman in a shift with tangled, matted hair sat tying a doll made of twisted flax. A lock of grey hair was wrapped about it. Her bony shoulders were bare, her shift many sizes too big. Beneath it, she was skin and bone. She sat cross-legged, looking exactly like the being he had dreamed of, that night in Gurukul when he had regained his memories of past lives.

No, she was *that girl.*

He could smell her across the room — for she seldom remembered to wash — all sweat and dirt and musk, strong, unpleasant, yet still enticing. It reminded him that humans were animals too. Her teeth were yellow, her body and face scarred from her lapses when she'd torn her own flesh. Her eyes were a thousand years old.

Everyone thought her a witch and no one except him would come near her any more. His loyalty to her made sense to no one except himself, and sometimes, to her. She needed him and he needed her, though he couldn't say why, and he doubted she could either.

Maybe it was compassion or mistaken destiny back then. Who knows what it is now?

'I know you're there,' she giggled. 'Won't you come in?' His mouth went dry, his skin hot and prickly, but he still stepped through the curtains. She lifted the doll. 'Do you know whose hair this is?'

He shook his head, reaching out to take it, but she snatched it out of reach. 'Kamla's hair. I'm trying to kill her. With magic spells. But the fat toad won't die.'

The room had been pristine when he had settled her here. He had given her all the finery he could afford, but she treated it all as garbage. The room stank of stale sweat and mould and her. Mostly of her, of her blood and bodily fluids. She beckoned him, pointing to the ground before her, and he knelt before her, hoping tonight she might be a little sane. On a silver chain around her throat dangled her heart-stone. He had given it to her years ago, thinking it might solve something — he thought she was a little calmer when she wore it, but she didn't often do so. She said it gave her bad dreams.

A small girl with huge eyes peered from the door to the inner room: his one daughter, Gauran's child. 'Rajabai,' he called, like coaxing a wildcat. She hissed, then looked at her mother, who beckoned her until she shot from the shadows and flopped into Gauran's lap.

'See, it's only your father,' Gauran reassured her. 'He won't hurt you.'

The grave eyes of the little girl shone in the candlelight as she studied him. Tentatively she crawled out of her mother's arms and approached him, perpetually on the brink of flight, until with the greatest reluctance, she leaned in and pecked his cheek – then she scampered away into the shadows, leaving him clutching at empty air.

'She has your eyes,' Gauran murmured.

'Her eyes are nothing like mine,' Chand disagreed. 'They're not even the same colour.'

'Not in this life,' Gauran replied. 'The same as when you were Aram of Mandore.'

He swallowed, his heart shuddering in his breast. It was the little moments like this that gave him hope that she might some-how be truly healed.

But a few seconds later she was back chanting her dark little ill-wishes at her doll, as if that moment of true recognition had never happened.

Next morning, Chand paused outside the audience hall of the king, feeling something of his old vigour and confidence. *I am still a counsellor*, he reminded himself. *I still have the ear of the mightiest man in Rajputana*. He squared his thin shoulders and strode inside.

Prithviraj Chauhan rose to greet him with a small grunt of

exertion. Time had been kind to neither man. 'My friend, my friend. Come, sit.'

Prithvi had always been big with muscle; it was beginning to run to fat. His belly protruded beyond his chest, and he no longer leaped up and down stairs with the same light feet. His face was fleshier, its once-fine chiselled features dissipated – too much rich food, far too much drink. But he still had his hair, though now it was darkened with dyes. And he remained a man to fear, an awesome presence. They were both middle-aged, but Chand still felt like a child in his friend's embrace.

They embraced, for old time's sake, and exchanged measuring looks. Prithvi's eyes still shone, but they were crow-footed, wrinkles appearing during the years of war and struggle. Of late, Chand had noticed they held an air of doubt. 'It's always easier to take a throne than sit upon one,' Vishwamitra had once told them. Chand thought that Prithvi was finally beginning to understand the old guru's words.

As they settled onto cushions opposite each other, Chand noticed for the first time a third person in the room. He bowed warily to Kola Chauhan, Prithvi's son and heir. With such parents the young man could scarce be anything but eye-catching, but there was a languorous cynicism about him that sat ill with Chand. Kola reminded him more of Sanjham Rai than of Prithvi, and he recalled the words of Jaichand: that those who have never known struggle don't value what they have.

'Prince Kola,' Chand greeted his ruler's fifteen-year-old son.

'Counsellor,' the prince replied. Kola and Chand seldom agreed, and frequently clashed.

'What is it, my Lord?' Chand asked, turning back to Prithvi.

The Maharaja went straight to the heart of the matter. 'Ghori has returned.'

Chand felt himself go cold.

'Then Ghori is a fool,' Kola sneered from the shadows. 'We will defeat him again. It will be just like last year at Tarain.'

Chand ignored the prince, focused on Prithvi. He knew what his king was thinking: that all mistakes come back to haunt those who err.

Last year, Prithvi had arrived on the field just as Govinda's men forced Ghori into retreat. A younger Prithviraj Chauhan would have led the charge, ploughing his cavalry into the broken enemy, and come back with Ghori's head on a spike. But the older Prithvi, overweight and exhausted from a day's riding, had stopped. Govinda was injured, his men battered. Prithvi's force had marched all day; they were thirsty and tired. So he'd not followed up with a vigorous pursuit: the Mohammedans had already been taught a lesson and were in retreat.

Now Ghori was back.

'A messenger came in just after sunset from Ajmer,' Prithviraj said. 'Ghori sent a parley there. His emissaries are coming here to Dilli, desiring negotiation. The scouts say his forces are very strong. He has already stormed my fortress at Sirhind and is marching southeast, right for Dilli.'

'The scouts always overestimate,' Kola commented. '"A man running away counts his enemies thrice",' he quoted. 'Receive the emissaries, and send back their heads. That will be an eloquent reply.'

Prithvi waved his son to silence and looked at Chand. 'My friend, what do you counsel?'

Kola scowled at not being immediately heeded.

'I recommend that we keep the emissaries at arm's length, my King. We need to muster and provision. We don't want his emissaries to come here and see that we aren't prepared for instant battle. Last time he underestimated us. He won't do so again. We'll need more men this time. Many more.'

'We have no more, my friend.' He knew Prithvi was digesting the implied criticism – that he had been complacent, that he was unprepared, that he had spent too much time in banquet and not enough on the business of war. Govinda had been ill since he'd been wounded at Tarain last year, and without the general's single-minded drive, the Chauhamanas had become slack. 'We don't have more men to send.'

'Jaichand does.'

Kola snorted from the corner. 'Jaichand is a gutless woman!'

'Jaichand has repaired his kingdom carefully since the truce began, Prithvi. He has many men. With him at our side—'

'At our side?' Kola interrupted. 'Jaichand would rather sever his own cock than help us!'

'He would fight for Rajputana,' Chand replied.

'You're an old fool if you think that,' Kola snapped back. 'Jaichand will never forgive, and he'll never risk his neck. We should have destroyed him when we had the chance.'

'No, we should have *reconciled* whilst we had the chance.'

To Kola's visible and vocal resentment, it was Chand's arguments that swayed the king. Prithvi sent him to meet Ghori's emissaries while he despatched conciliatory messages to Jaichand. Those messages were still unanswered when Chand rode with a small escort into a tiny village north of Jaipur, and met a Turkic outrider.

He was small, the Turkic rider, with a thin moustache and the leathery skin of the nomad. But he rode his horse as if it were an extension of his own body. There were furs adorning his cloak that spoke of colder places. His eyes were so narrow as to be slits, and his skin a dark amber hue. He spoke in rudimentary Punjabi, telling Chand that Mehtan Ali, Ghori's emissary – who was a Mohammedan holy man, an imam – awaited him. The Turkic rider led Chand's party to a pavilion pitched atop a small rocky hill and bade Chand enter alone and unarmed. His host was waiting for him outside the tent, similarly unarmed.

Mehtan Ali was a big man with a flowing grey-black beard dressed simply in white. Apart from his beard, his hair and moustache were shaven, and he wore a close-fitting round skullcap, embroidered with Islamic prayers. As Chand approached, he saw that the man's face was horribly scarred as if from old burns. Then he met the man's eyes—

He staggered. It was Ravindra.

'Come, sit, Aram Dhoop.' Ravindra's voice rolled, deep and strong. 'We must preserve the forms, after all.' Hatred rolled off him in waves, yet his gestures were courteous and calm. 'Time enough to destroy you later.'

'We will remain out here, where my men can see me,' Chand panted, his throat suddenly as dry as the desert about them. The thought of being out of sight of his escort was suddenly terrifying.

Ravindra gestured carelessly. 'As you wish.' He sat on the ground, imperturbable. Chand reluctantly did the same, facing him. 'I know who you all are, of course,' Ravindra said. 'You and Shastri and Darya – and I knew we would all meet eventually.'

'How can you, a Hindu, become a Mohammedan cleric?' Chand demanded, trying to gain some foothold in the conversation.

'I find one god much like another, and it was the best way to get Ghori to do as I wanted. The man is something of a fanatic. The means do not matter, in the end, only the result. So, how are our little lovebirds? Only one son, I notice? Is their union not as happy as you hoped, "Chand"?'

'They are as deeply in love as they have always been. The number of children is not a measure of the degree of love – not that I would expect you to know anything of the subject.'

'If it were, then Chand Bardai would be spoken of as Krishna himself,' Ravindra rumbled. 'Ten sons!' He pulled a bland face. 'Ten more ways to hurt you before you die.'

'State your business, Emissary,' Chand retorted.

Ravindra smiled mockingly and pitched his voice in a formal fashion. 'These are the terms of Muhamed Ghori, offered to Prithviraj Chauhan: surrender your kingdoms, disband your armies and convert to Islam. Acknowledge the overlordship of Muhamed Ghori and pay tribute to him. Fight at his command. Anything less, and he will raze your temples, enslave your people and occupy your lands for the rest of time.' Ravindra spoke with relish, taking pleasure in the words of conquest and destruction.

Chand raised his head defiantly. 'Those are not terms.'

'They are all the terms you'll get, Aram Dhoop.'

'Then this is not a negotiation.'

Ravindra smirked. 'It never was, Aram. I just wanted you to know who you faced.'

'Then you can take back the reply of Prithviraj Chauhan: there will be no surrender. Withdraw, and return no more to Rajputana, or face destruction. This time, there will be no mercy.'

He almost hoped this might enrage Ravindra and provoke violence, though his Enemy could probably break him like a twig. *Surely my escort would ride him down, and if I could get to my bow . . .*

But Ravindra only smiled. 'Excellent. We will await you at Tarain. Ghori is desirous to exorcise the ghost of defeat, so the same field of battle would be ideal.'

Chand rose, regaining his defiance. 'I'm going to kill you personally, Ravindra. You've made Ravana your patron, but I know the secrets of Rama, Ravana's nemesis. I swear I will kill you myself.'

Ravindra met his gaze blandly, then suddenly he stepped forward in a fluid motion, seized Chand and embraced him. He didn't resist, first in shock, and then caught by the brutal strength of his foe. 'I could break your neck right now, Aram Dhoop,' the sorcerer-king of Mandore whispered in his ear, 'but killing you might frighten your king into terms, and frankly I don't want terms. I want battle. I want *blood*. And then afterwards, I will take my women back.' His eyes twinkled. 'Do you think I don't know about Padma? Poor, insane Padma . . . What's she called in this life? Gauran, yes? She will give *excellent* sport.'

Chand stared. *How can he know?*

'See you at Tarain, Aram Dhoop. Pray that you're not taken alive.'

CHAPTER TWENTY-TWO

Papering Over

New Delhi, 11 November 2010

Deepika awoke on the floor before anyone found her, showered, then threw on some jeans and a T-shirt. Her mother was in the kitchen and her father still washing, so she slipped downstairs and knocked on the guest-room door.

'Amanjit!' she whispered, letting herself in.

Amanjit was half-dressed, one leg in his trousers; he looked up in surprise, staggering a bit, and began a cheeky remark, then he saw the expression on her face. 'What is it, Dee?'

She closed the door behind him and flew to him as he rose, melted against his muscular chest as she clung to him. 'It's Ravindra! My nightmares, they're all Ravindra!'

His big arms enfolded her protectively. 'What do you mean?'

She described her terrifying through-the-mirror encounter with Ravindra. 'I think he must have been doing something to my memory, and I'm certain he's been doing this for some time,' she admitted, quivering with rage. There were bruises on her breasts, but she was afraid to show the to Amanjit, knowing the anger it would provoke. She needed to be cool, needed him to be the same. 'He'll kill you and Mother and Father if I don't meekly surrender! But like hell am I going to do want he wants!'

She slipped from his grasp, the better to talk. 'I don't know if he can make good on his threats,' she told her fiancé, 'but I'm worried that he can, so somehow, we've got to make sure my parents are safe.'

He frowned. 'Can we call the police?'

'I'm not sure: *"Officer, I'd like to report a thousand-year-old sorcerer with god-delusions, who's been sending me nightmares through the mirror. What form do I fill out?"* – they wouldn't take us seriously, not for a moment!'

'Fair enough. But we could make it sound a lot more credible than that.'

'And have a bunch of strangers come into our house – how would we know some weren't working for him? He had ordinary men working for him in Jodhpur in March, didn't he?'

Amanjit bit his lip. 'What if we all left the country?'

'To where? For how long?' She put her hands on her hips. 'I'm not going to run away from that bastard for the rest of my life!'

'Nor me!' Amanjit assured her. 'But you're right, we need to make sure it's between him and us. At least we've got some idea what we're getting ourselves into. I've fought him before, and I've still got Shastri's scimitar.' He walked to his wardrobe and pulled the weapon out, still in its old scabbard.

Seeing him with the weapon brought back the memories of March, in the caverns below the Mehrangarh. Deepika took heart from the sight. 'Then we fight back.'

That resolved, the next step was to make sure her parents left the house with no suspicions. That proved easy enough – her professor father had a busy day ahead, and her mother was going shopping with her sisters, Deepika's aunts, in Gurgaon.

She and Amanjit waved them both off, smiling, and then they turned to each other.

'Ravindra's been stalking me for days. Somehow he's prevented me from remembering, but he's been attacking me at will.' Deepika felt nauseated at the thought – and enraged. 'I was once a queen!' she gritted. 'How dare he think he can do this to me!'

Amanjit buckled on the scimitar, beside his kirpan. 'I'm right with you, Dee. But what's the plan?'

She remembered the crystal pendant he'd taunted her with. *My heart-stone.* Vikram had talked about them – he hadn't known where hers was, despite searching in many lives; she knew he'd hoped it wasn't important: but it clearly was, especially now Ravindra had it.

'Let's call Vikram. It's only eight a.m. – he shouldn't have gone into the studio yet.'

But Vikram didn't reply and she couldn't imagine what he was doing right now. 'Stupid bloody television programme!' she fumed. 'We need someone who understands these things!'

Amanjit forced a smile. 'You'd think in a country with a million swamis and gurus and mystics, we'd know dozens of people who could help.'

Deepika settled for leaving a text message: <Rav in Mumbai. Attack thru mirror. Call me!>

Check your phone, Vikram! Now!

Abruptly she turned back to Amanjit. 'Well, my love, if he can reach us through the mirrors, then they have to go! The maid won't arrive for another hour – I'll phone Jinta and tell her not to come, then we'll blank out the mirrors, and work out what to do next.'

He stared. 'Are you sure?'

'No, but it's worth a try – he was watching me through my

dressing-table mirror, and reaching through it! Let's at least pre-vent that.'

Jinta, her parent's maid from Bihar whom Deepika had known all her life, never picked up, but that wasn't too surprising; she was probably already en route, sitting in a noisy bus bringing her from the poorer neighbourhoods at the edge of Delhi. Deepika left a text telling her to turn around and go home again, while mentally composing excuses in case Jinta made it all the way here before checking her phone.

Then they set about blinding Ravindra to their movements. They armed themselves with masking tape and newspapers and started in her room. Once they'd covered her mirrors, they moved on to the bathroom and the hall before heading for the other rooms. It would almost have been fun if it hadn't been for such a frightening reason. They worked together – they'd watched too many horror movies to do that 'splitting up to cover twice the ground' thing that got teenagers slaughtered in Holly-wood. At each new mirror, Deepika felt like she was looking at a crazier version of herself in the reflection.

Around 9 o'clock, Amanjit's mobile rang and he put it on speaker so they could both talk to Vikram.

He sounded tired. 'Hey, I got your text – what's happened?'

She briefly updated him, then explained what they were doing. 'There's no way I'm going to let him bully us into submission. I think if we can cover the mirrors, he'll be blind to us, at least for a while. We don't know how to strike back, but I'm thinking if we create a blind spot where he can't watch us, we'll have at least enough time to organise something – worst case, we'll take a train and come and join you, or go to Jodhpur and help find Ras.'

Vikram went silent, then just when she and Amanjit were wondering if the connection had been lost, he said, 'I can't think of a better plan right now, except, I'd start thinking about

Mumbai – I'm here, Sunita's here, and I've seen a few other old faces. Whatever's happening will be here, so I'm betting Ravindra's not far away.'

'What about my parents?' Deepika asked.

'Perhaps persuade them they need a break at a nice hotel down south?' Vikram suggested, adding, 'I hate this feeling of being hunted.' Then he changed the subject. 'Have you seen the *Times* this morning?'

Amanjit chuckled. 'Yeah, I was reading it online before I got up. Heh, heh.'

'It's not funny.'

'Yes it is, bhai! It's a scream! I'm picturing you in a sari and nearly wetting myself.' Amanjit winked at Deepika, who rolled her eyes and went back to blacking out the hall mirror while still listening to the conversation.

'Yeah, thanks,' Vikram said tersely. 'I knew I could rely on your sympathy and support.'

'You have my full support, and I'll completely thrash that Kajal character if I ever meet him.' Abruptly the banter left Amanjit's voice. 'Any news of Rasita?'

'No, but I think she might be coming here. You know that thing I told you about, where I can track direction? Well, looks like she's on her way to Mumbai. It's not foolproof, though.'

'Yeah, I thought that might be the case – and Cousin Idli isn't communicating, and he's supposed to be on the road from Jodhpur to Mumbai this week. He's expected in tonight, according to his boss.'

'Okay, I'll check again then . . .' Vikram paused, then added, 'Hey, I've arrived – another day of madness awaits! Good luck – and keep me posted, okay? My phone will be confiscated, but I'll see if I can send you one of the techies' number in case of emergency.'

'We'll be fine,' Amanjit insisted. 'Don't worry about us, please – look after yourself! Archery is all very fine, but military technology has moved on a little since then. Don't underestimate Ravindra's ability to hurt you, Vik.'

'I'd never do that.'

'Good luck, Vik,' Deepika called.

'Thanks. I'm not sure what "good luck" actually means in this case. I'm pretty sure now I don't want to win, and this whole "drawing Ravindra out" plan isn't working too well. But it feels like I have no choice now, not when the whole country is watching me.'

They hung up, and Amanjit looked at Deepika heavily. 'This is spiralling out of control. Let's finish blacking these mirrors, then we need to make arrangements for getting to Mumbai. Can you call your father and tell him we're needed there, do you think?'

'Sure. They'll think we're just helping find Ras.'

They'd just begun to debate how they'd overcome that, when they both heard a sound from her bedroom: paper being torn . . .

Mumbai, 11 November 2010: Day 4 of Swayamvara Live!

Vikram rubbed the grit from his tired eyes, yawned and stepped from the studio car into a storm of flashlights. He'd been up most of the night, casting seeker-spells to try and find Ras, and the phone call with Deepika and Amanjit had consumed the rest of his faculties. Big security men shepherded him through the press pack; they really did seem like a pack – of jackals.

There had been a copy of the *Times of India* on the back of the car, as usual: the front-page story was all about what Kajal had said, with reactions from various celebrities (who were caught between being politically correct about homosexuality, and condemning Vikram for lying to Sunita: which he hadn't done, but everyone appeared to believe Kajal had spoken the truth). There were no comments from anyone who actually knew him, though there were angry denials from Sunita's camp, on behalf of Uma.

He made it to a dressing room, slumped in a chair and closed his eyes. One last moment of peace. *But the show must go on.*

And as it turned out, that morning's challenge on *Swayamvara Live!* was a piece of cake. And a cup of tea, with Sunita.

The remaining contestants were all herded into more limousines – Vikram shared with the businessman, Mandeep Shekar, the oldest remaining contestant, a quietly capable man in his late thirties who looked far too sober and sensible for all this madness. After a few minutes of silence, Vikram asked, 'Why are you putting yourself through all this, sir?'

He smiled reflectively. 'My son told me to enter.'

'Oh, you've been married before?'

'I have – my wife died four years ago, after a long illness. We had one son – he's thirteen now, and he told me to enter the show.' He grinned, which took years off his face. 'It's been rather fun – you see, I was a decathlete when I was younger, and in the training squads for the Olympics, though I wasn't selected. So all of this is well within my capabilities. And we all want to be our son's hero, don't we?'

Vikram thought about the sons he'd had in his past lives: not many, in truth; Ravindra had usually come for him before he'd had time for family – apart from his life as Chand Bardai, in the twelfth century, when he'd had *eleven* children – the ten sons with his wife Kamla, and a daughter with poor Gauran.

Was I their hero? I think not – except maybe Jalhan's. He finished the Prithvi-raj Raso *for me. Perhaps he remembered me fondly . . .*

'Do you think this show is rigged?' Mandeep asked him.

Interesting that you should ask me that, Vikram thought. He sensed that Mandeep saw maturity in him and respected him as a competitor. 'I don't think so,' he said, 'but it's not a level playing field either. Pravit is either favoured or doomed by his and Sunita's history, don't you think?'

'I think you are right about that — and if all along she's been playing us false and just using this as a means to get back together with him, then my lawyers stand ready — while it's been fun, I don't take kindly to people wasting my time.'

All that sounded ominous, but Vikram knew the real game was quite different to the one Mandeep thought he was playing, so he didn't comment. In a few minutes, they arrived at the Taj Hotel, where he and Mandeep found the other contestants in a private lounge, awaiting their turn for a one-on-one filmed cup of tea with Sunita. It was what passed for an 'intimate encounter' — just the contestant, Sunita, a dozen or so film crew people, lighting technicians, sound technicians and assorted flunkies. And the eyes of millions, later that night.

Looking around the room at the seven others, Vikram felt a new kind of tension in the air. Alliances were either fraying or becoming stronger: Kajal and Pravit sat alone together in one corner with a pile of newspapers between them. Alok, the next-raja, was nursing a coffee — the bookies had just slashed the odds on him winning to 5:1, the closest anyone had come to Pravit. Joseph, the NRI from Walthamstow, was nearest him, but he too sat in silence. The Punjabi and the Bengali were having a cheerful conversation. Mandeep nodded amiably to Vikram, offering him a bottle of water.

Vikram nodded thanks, but walked straight up to Kajal and Pravit. There was no point in beating about the bush on this, he'd decided. 'You're a dirty liar and I demand that you make a public retraction,' he said in the most coldly formal voice he could,

while the handlers scuttled off, looking for someone senior. Out
of the corner of his eye he could see the security men converging
on them.

Kajal flexed an arm. His fists looked huge and he was wearing
rings that could easily double as knuckle-dusters. *Bruises all over
my face will look great on television* . . .

'Or else what?' the stuntman growled.

Good question. Fortunately Vikram didn't need to answer it.
Vishi Ashoka bundled in, looking cross. He had a copy of the
contestants' terms and conditions under one arm and an
anxious-looking lawyer with him. 'Kajal Dilkishan, I need to see
you, right now, in my office.'

Kajal looked up at him, then at Vikram and Pravit. He made
no effort to move.

'Now!' snapped Vishi.

For a moment Vikram thought the big stuntman would continue to ignore him, but he rose slowly, scowling at Vikram, then
followed Vishi and the legal team as they marched swiftly away,
their heels clicking on the marble floors.

Hopefully he won't come back, Vikram thought. He slumped into
an empty armchair, feeling edgy, ready to shout at the first person who spoke to him.

No one did.

'So, is there anything you need to tell us?' Sunita asked him, her
voice amused. She fiddled with her teacup, which she had not yet
drunk from – but then, this was the fifth 'morning tea' she had
sat through; she probably wasn't all that thirsty. She hadn't
touched her cake either.

'I'm not homosexual,' Vikram replied in as dispassionate a
voice as he could manage, keenly aware of the cameras pointing
at them both from all sides. 'I'm all in favour of homosexual

rights, but I'm not gay. I've never been accused of being gay before, and when I heard it I was as much amused as angry.'

'I take it you and Kajal don't get on,' she said, her bird-eyes glinting.

'Not since the swordfight, perhaps not ever.' Vikram forced a smile at the woman across the table from him and sipped his tea. She had a faraway look on her face, though only the tiny coffee table divided them. *An intimate cup of tea*, he thought sarcastically. *This is about as 'intimate' as a cricket test. How do you get intimate with all these people around — and this damned table between us?*

Sunita leaned forward suddenly. 'Why are you competing, Vikram?'

He blinked, a little bit surprised at the directness of the question. 'To marry you, of course.' He thought about that a little. 'If it turns out that I like you.'

'Does that matter?'

'More than anything else. I really don't care about money, and fame seems to be a burden, not a blessing.'

'That's easy to say when you've never had them,' she observed. Her eyelids were fluttering, her pupils oddly dilated, which made him wonder what medication she was on. In the lives he'd known her, she'd always needed some kind of drug to function.

He had in fact experienced both fame and fortune in several past lives, and they'd not turned out well. He'd settle for love and not being gutted by Ravindra in this one. Not that he thought for a moment that mad, needy Gauran could ever give him real love. She never had before.

'Then I won't miss them,' he replied. He decided to take the initiative in this conversation. 'I can see how running this show could give you an insight into who we are, and no doubt you'll pick a favourite. What I don't understand is how we get to know you.'

'Through moments like this. And afterwards.'

'Afterwards may be too late, if you choose wrongly.'

She laughed, a little self-consciously. 'But I am *Sunita*. Every-one knows me. I belong to everyone, and that is my curse. Some of the contestants know me socially, anyway.'

Vikram could work out who: Pravit, of course. Kajal, possibly. Maybe Alok, or even Mandeep, if he did business in Bollywood? 'That's hardly of use to me. I only know you from movies.'

'In which I bare my soul!' Sunita replied passionately. Then she tittered and sat back, as if she'd not intended to become so involved in the discussion. 'This is my swayamvara, not yours.' She looked down at a piece of paper, a list of questions, as if determined to talk of something else.

So they talked about trivia, what he liked and disliked, places he'd visited – nothing useful. At moments he thought there might be some little rapport established, and when they kissed each other's cheeks as he left, he thought there might be something that flickered behind her eyes at his smell and the touch of his lips to her cheek. He hoped so, because she'd certainly made an impression on him.

As he stepped away, still facing her, his buried memories relayed many other such greetings and partings with the same woman in a dozen different bodies and hundreds of settings. Her scent and her touch washed over him, and suddenly – daringly – he turned his head to one side and brushed her lips with his.

She looked up at him, and something subliminal and deeply buried truly *saw* him.

Hello, Gauran. Hello, Jane, and all you others. It's me.

CHAPTER TWENTY-THREE

Waltzing on Broken Glass

New Delhi, 11 November 2010

Deepika and Amanjit whirled to face her bedroom door as the sound of ripping newspaper carried into the hall.

Idiot, she thought, *it's only paper! Why did you think it could stop that monster!*

She lunged for the toolbox, snatched up a hammer and started for the door, but Amanjit beat her to it. He stormed into her room and over his shoulder she caught a glimpse of a dark-skinned, muscular arm protruding from a mirror half-covered in newspaper, tearing the rest of the veil aside.

Then Amanjit slashed at the arm and someone bellowed in shock as the blade hacked through, severing the hand, which dissolved and vanished before it even hit the ground, as did the blood that sprayed from the wound. Then she came alongside, saw a furious face in the cracked glass and smashed the hammer at it; the glass shattered and fell from the plywood backing and crashed to the floor.

The largest shard reflected her: a crazy woman with a hammer.

'It's not enough!' Amanjit shouted. 'We have to break them all!'

This time they did split up, because there were too many mirrors and not enough time. She flew into her bathroom, glimpsed wide white eyes and a dark moustachioed face and hands ripping through, then her hammer-head crunched into the glass.

Smash! Glass sprayed everywhere, tinkling as it fell to the ground. Broken shards fell against her jeans, but barely pricked. She bent and pounded at them, grunting at the exertion. She saw blood amidst the fractured glass and didn't know if it was hers or someone else's — she had a glass fragment stuck in her right cheek, and drops were slipping down to her chin.

Now try and reach us, you bastard!

From the hall came the sound of Amanjit, shouting as he smashed the hall mirror. She ran out to join him, bypassed him and entered her parents' room, brought their dressing mirror crashing down, then shattered the glass panel in their en suite bathroom into a sea of fractured glass. Her shoes crunched through the mess satisfyingly. Then back to the stairs, where there was a large decorative mirror, a present from her father to her mother. She paused before it, and lifted her hammer.

'Miss Deepika?' shrieked a woman from the foyer below. Jinta's narrow East Indian eyes were wide in shock, her angular face dismayed. She clutched her bag of cleaning equipment to her chest. 'What is wrong?'

Deepika half-turned, her mouth opening to try and dissuade the maid from panicking, when a sudden movement caught her eye. The mirror! She spun and saw Ravindra glaring through the glass at her. Then his face blurred into many and his hands and arms began to multiply horribly. She saw her heart-pendant; she saw grasping hands and a curved blade, and fires burst to life around him. She shrieked in defiance and hammered at the mirror.

Jinta screamed as glass cascaded down the slate-tiled stairs in a strangely musical torrent of destruction. Deepika didn't even notice. There was only Ravindra and his reaching hands. She saw blood erupt as one hand tried to wriggle through a large fragment that flew apart as she struck it, and she heard him shout in fury and pain.

'Dee?' Amanjit shouted from upstairs.

'Get out of the house,' she called to Jinta. 'Get out! *Run!*'

She whirled about. What other mirrors were there? She stormed down the stairs and the maid backed away, squealing for help. 'Just get out!' she implored Jinta. 'Everything is fine! Don't call the police!' But the maid just fled into a storeroom and slammed the door behind her.

Damn her anyway! She couldn't stop now: there were other mirrors downstairs! She ran into the lounge, saw a huge black eye peering from a hand-mirror on a bookstand. She swung and the steel hammer-head sent it flying, trailing a comet's tail of broken glass.

She heard Jinta, shouting incoherently. *That's right, there's a landline in the maid's room.* She glanced up the stairs, saw Amanjit coming to join her, but she was worried Jinta was calling the police, so she motioned for him to stay where he was. 'Hello? Jinta! It's all right! But we have to break all the mirrors, to keep Ravana from the house! Let me in!'

Despite her *perfectly rational* reassurances, the door remained locked.

'You have to let me in. Open up!' Deepika raised her hammer to pound at the lock, then decided that would just panic the maid more. *It's Jinta! I've know her for years! What must she think?* 'It's all right, Jinta!' she called again. She waved Amanjit away, pointing to the kitchen, and he backed off and went looking for more glass.

This is insane, she thought, but she tried to fill her voice with reassurance. 'Jinta, listen, you're perfectly safe, I promise, I just had to break all the mirrors, to keep the Demon King out. I'm not crazy, I swear! Please, hang up the phone.'

There was a long silence, then she heard the click of the receiver being replaced. Then the lock clicked and the door opened a crack. She saw a narrow eye peering through. 'You are not making sense, Miss Deepika.'

'I know,' Deepika admitted, 'but I swear, I'm protecting the house – from the Demon King. He's trying to enter this house through the mirrors, so we have to smash them all, to save us from harm.'

'You swear you won't hurt me?'

'Yes, I swear. I think I've got them all now anyway. See, I'm putting the hammer down.' She placed the tool on the bench beside her, signalling to Amanjit, who'd reappeared at the kitchen door, to stay still. 'Who were you talking to?'

Jinta opened the door, her flat face confused, but steady – surprisingly so, maybe, but Deepika was just relieved she wasn't screaming. 'No one, Miss Deepika. I was just frightened.'

Deepika saw something on the wall behind the maid, inside her room: another mirror. She was reaching for the hammer when Jinta's eyes rolled back in her skull and her voice became throaty and cold. '*You missed the one in here.*'

Her features changed dramatically, from East Indian to Rajasthani, from plain maid to a dusky and deadly beauty: Halika, dead queen of Mandore. Her arm shot out and she grasped Deepika by the throat. Deepika had time to scream once before the woman struck her across the face with brutal strength, snapping her head sideways and scrambling her senses. She slumped against the wall and Halika-Jinta bore her to the floor and leaped on top, pinning her with horrific strength.

'*Hello Darya,*' purred a voice that resonated from out of time.

Deepika stared up at the face that haunted her nightmares, then sensed movement behind her: Amanjit reacting, raising his sword.

Halika-Jinta's hand dipped to a pocket and came up with a squat metallic shape that spat fire and lead. Deepika flinched at the crack of the gun as Amanjit bellowed and staggered sideways. Her ears were still ringing from that shot as another flew through the kitchen door. She tried to hurl Halika-Jinta off her, but her arms were pinned beneath the maid's shins and she couldn't get any purchase.

'*Back off, Shastri! Or the next bullet goes in Darya's mouth!*'

Something more than the dead queen's weight was pinning Deepika down, because she couldn't move her body at all. She twisted her neck and caught a glimpse of her fiancé pressed into cover behind the doorframe. 'Amanjit!' she called, 'are you okay?'

'I'm okay,' he called back, but his voice was strained with suppressed pain. 'You?'

Deepika went to reply when a dark hand clamped over her mouth. She saw the maid's skin rippling, a tiny outward sign of the struggle of two beings in one body, then Halika's features settled firmly onto the top of the maid's, and she drooled over Deepika's face. 'Shastri,' she called to Amanjit, 'come out or I'll shoot.'

'I'm not stupid!' he shouted back. 'If I come out you'll shoot me anyway.'

Halika-Jinta's canines became long and thin as snake fangs as she growled at him from deep in her throat, then her voice became sly. 'Then stay, for all I care. I have what I want.' With Deepika powerless to move, she buried her face in her neck and bit savagely. The initial shock became a numb, floating sensation as venom pumped into Deepika's veins, deadening her senses.

She dimly saw the demonic visage as it rose with her blood on the dead queen's lips, then grey shapes whooshed over them both, from inside the maid's room, towards the kitchen. 'Amanjit—!' she tried to scream in warning, but all that came out was a mumble. Then the door slammed shut, and three thin voices yowled.

Halika chuckled. 'Well, here we are again, dear Darya. It feels good to have a body again, even one as pathetic as this.'

As if from far down a winding tunnel, Deepika heard Amanjit cry out, but she was floating away. Halika stood, but she still couldn't move. *Am I dying?* she wondered, as the world faded away.

Three spectral shapes like windblown exhaust fumes in the shape of dead girls streamed from the mirror in the opposite room and through the air towards Amanjit, as the maid with Halika's face buried her face in Dee's neck.

It only took one bullet to kill, and he'd probably used up his luck with the one that had grazed his left shoulder, but he erupted from the door, his mind full of one goal: to rescue his beloved. He charged full-on into the cloud of darkness flowing from the maid's room, blade raised, but that darkness picked him up like the outflow of a jet engine and hurled him backwards into the kitchen.

His back smashed into a chair and it broke apart, leaving him sprawled on top of the debris, winded and dazed. The wood stabbing into his back had ripped cloth and punctured flesh, but then the fighting instincts and reflexes of the long-dead Madan Shastri kicked in and he rolled free as the smoky remains of the dead queens flowed towards him. He swished his scimitar blade through them, heard them shriek from the touch of the silvered blade, buying him a moment to find a more effective weapon against these foes: he'd seen the way these beings hated fire in the caves below the Mehrangarh, so he slammed his free hand down on the nearest dial of the hob.

The gas ignited first time with a whoosh, a tiny tongue of flame, but enough to make the gauzy, web-like witches clinging to him draw away. He grabbed a tea towel and dropped one corner onto the element, where it began to smoulder. They hissed and drew back, emaciated faces semi-visible in the swirl of ash, like ruined negatives of a photograph imprinted on the air. Only then did he realise that everywhere they'd gripped him — bony handprints on his arms, numbing nail-rakes on his cheeks — was numb with cold, and he was feeling dizzy.

Then the tea towel caught fire and he brandished it. The wraithlike figures yowled and blew, turning the air about him to ice and all but extinguishing the flame, but he threw another tea towel on it, then another. *The building's stone*, he decided; *it won't burn easily.* 'Dee!' he shouted. '*Dee!*'

They came at him in a rush, trying to overwhelm him and pummel him to the ground, as they almost had when they threw him into the room, but the first caught fire and yowled, and their attack fell apart. They backed away again, watching one of their number burn into nothing, and suddenly the remaining pair didn't look so eager to get close.

'Stay away!' he shouted, edging forward. He could hear footfalls outside now, female voices, cold and hard. '*Dee!*'

A bullet ripped through the kitchen door, narrowly missed him, and buried itself in the tiled wall, cracking it apart. He flinched away as two more shots followed. The two wraiths poured like gas out through the bullet holes and were gone, but as he reached for the door handle, another bullet splintered the timbers and he pulled back, pressing himself to the stone wall beside the door, desperately shouting, '*DEE!*'

There were at least two women out there — not ghosts but real people – and he realised he knew the new voice – though it was being used in different ways, the normal melodic tones now guttural and harsh . . . it was Deepika's best friend, Jayshree.

Two of the dead queens have stolen the bodies of her friends . . . Ravindra's known we were here for days . . .

But the galling thing was, he couldn't do *anything*. If he could get close enough, he was sure he could take them, but they'd have a bullet in him the moment they glimpsed him.

He hauled out his phone, tried to call Vikram, then realised the emergency number Vik had given him was written down upstairs. He swore under his breath.

He heard movement, then silence, but the moment he reached for the door handle, another bullet punched through the wood, just inches from his wrist. He cursed again.

Take a bullet, or let them take her? He ground his teeth furiously. *If I could get close enough* – then he thought that one through – *I'd have a chance – if I'm not shot first – of killing a maid whose body is being used as a puppet by a ghost, and maybe Jayshree too.*

With a disgusted growl, he dialled Emergency and asked for the police.

Mumbai, 11 November 2010:
Day 4 of Swayamvara Live! *(Afternoon)*

The contestants spent the afternoon tackling an assault course on a police training base. Vikram came second to last after slipping and getting tangled in a rope net – which was extra frustrating, as he'd been coming third until he fell. The sleek Punjabi came last, but to many people's surprise – though not Vikram's, now he knew a little more about the man, Mandeep came second behind Kajal, with Pravit third. The giant stuntman had been allowed to compete only after taping an apology and full retraction of his homosexuality allegations against Vikram.

Vikram and the Punjabi spent a tense evening. If they'd made no impression at the 'intimate' morning tea, they would be eliminated if they messed up that evening. They were left largely alone, apart from being costumed and made-up for that night's TV session, then settled in to watch the *Swayamvara Live!* show begin with a run-through of the day's activities.

The first half hour featured 'highlights' of the morning tea. Vikram saw the studio audience titter knowingly at his denials — most still appeared to believe he was gay. But the camera caught his light kiss on Sunni's lips, and lingered on her face when he pulled away; he saw something troubled in her gaze. They all saw Pravit kiss her like an old lover, and they all laughed at the way Alok had immediately shifted his chair around the table, removing the barrier to intimacy that Vikram had so struggled with in an instant: simple, but a masterstroke.

The contestants were led away without hearing how they ranked. The second segment, that wretched assault course, played out while they were changing into tuxedos. They would each dance a waltz with Sunita, they had found out that afternoon. *Strictly Come Dancing at the Swayamvara!* A waltz! Vikram had never waltzed. In this life.

But as he stepped onto the waxed wooden floor, and the orchestra struck up Mozart's *Eine kleine Nachtmusik*', it all came flooding back . . .

. . . Calcutta, latter days of the Raj. Red uniforms and punkah-wallahs. His medical knowledge had got him co-opted onto the Governor's staff. He called himself Chand in that life too, though it wasn't the name he was born with; he'd adopted it after his memories came back to him when he was fifteen. The soldiers simply called him 'Doc', and it stuck. He was

married to a Bengali girl and having an affair with another, who was
Kamla-reborn. He had never thought to meet Gauran-reborn there, and
certainly not as a white woman: Lady Jane Grace-Cowan, born in Calcutta to a young English military couple sixteen years earlier. The other
women called her 'Crazy Jane' for her night-wanderings, strange utter-
ances and off-key singing. She couldn't read or write, couldn't even speak
properly: an embarrassment to her family.

Her father, the Colonel, came to Doc, pleading for him to look into her
case. He'd diagnosed dyslexia immediately, combined with hearing problems, which accounted for many of her communication difficulties. She
was possibly also schizophrenic. Her medication was wrong, and he set it
right. He taught her to read. She taught him to dance: waltzes, polkas,
tangos.

He fell in love with her.

The evidence that convicted him came from a one-eyed spy in the service of a local raja: his Enemy, of course, and One-Eyed Jeet reborn.

It wasn't Doc who raped Crazy Jane, but it was Doc they hanged
for it.

. . . and Vikram found he could waltz after all. He and Sunita
moved perfectly, their eyes locked because there was no need to
look away and they just knew which way the other was about to
move.

'Where did you learn to dance?' she whispered.

'I haven't. It's easy, though. We move well together.'

She coloured, disturbed, almost agitated. 'You're so young.'

'So are you.' *She's what, twenty-six? What's that to someone who
can remember all his past lives?*

'I don't know you at all,' she said, looking away. He could feel
that she was trembling faintly.

'Isn't that the whole point of this? To find something new?
Something different, to change your life? What would be the

point of just going through the same old motions – doing the things that failed before?'

That hadn't stopped me doing just that in life after life, he acknowledged with bitter irony.

The music came to a finish and he bowed and kissed her hand while the studio audience thundered. 'I hope we will dance again,' he murmured as they parted. He glanced up at the screens as he left the stage. Her face was thunderstruck, and she looked like she wanted to flee the stage rather than dance once more. Uma hurried past, flashing him a perturbed look as if seeing him differently, and the screen went to a commercial break.

'Well, aren't you full of surprises?' commented Alok as Vikram returned to the waiting lounge. The next-raja didn't look even faintly put out, but for once there was genuine respect on his face. For an instant, Vikram felt a trace of guilt, as if he had cheated. At least Alok had packed all his accomplishments into one life. Pravit looked away, a haunted expression on his face.

When all of them had danced they were summoned onto the stage. The atmosphere had changed completely. The studio audience cheered him loudly, and he scored in the top two in both dancing and the morning tea, more than enough to prevent his elimination, despite the assault course failure.

The assault course scores saved Kajal, who finished bottom in both the morning tea and the dancing. The Bengali and the Punjabi were eliminated, and only six remained: Pravit the Bollywood star, Kajal the stuntman, Alok the raja-to-be, Joseph the Englishman, Mandeep the businessman, and Vikram. There was real electricity in the air as the closing credits played and the studio audience, now half-filled with Bollywood luminaries, clapped wildly. What had started as the Pravit Khoolman Show was developing uncertainties and twists: the drama television audiences (and executives) so loved.

Vishi briefed them afterwards. There were only two nights left and lives would no longer be issued. Tomorrow they would each spend time with Sunita in a secret location, and then face a mystery test that night. *Sleep well*, they were advised. *Dress well. Tomorrow you must give your best.*

As he got into the film company car that night, Vikram was finally able to switch on his phone. He was besieged by messages, which he read with growing horror.

Deepika — no! Now Dee is missing as well?

Mumbai, 12 November 2010

Ras woke from a dreamless sleep into silence and just lay there for a few minutes, scarcely daring to think. Bloody images of the men and their guns haunted her, and chilling memories of the havoc a tiny bullet could inflict on a body.

Eventually she found the nerve to open her eyes and look around. The room was plain, with white walls and old knocked-about wooden furniture. The sheets were soft but the mattress was hard, now she was conscious enough to notice it. She used the bathroom and vaguely recalled a nurse, and being helped to bathe. It was cold, but she was clad just in a nightdress. Her clothes were gone.

There was a small window on one wall, hidden behind musty curtains and covered with a blackened grille. All it revealed was a tangle of power-lines and a tiny alley below. An old homeless man wrapped in a dirty blanket and a colourless turban was all she could see, huddled unmoving in a doorway. There was a trail of thin smoke wafting from his cupped hands. She went to the door, afraid it might be locked, but it wasn't. She found herself on a small landing above a staircase. There were no decorations, nothing to personalise the house at all.

This is Safe House Five, she recalled dazedly. It was utterly faceless, and it didn't feel safe at all.

'Hello?' she called tentatively.

Almost immediately a woman's shoes clipped across the crushed marble tiles. A skinny South Indian nurse with a bobbed haircut peered up at her. 'Yes?' she replied, sounding bored.

'I'm . . . Ras. I'm a . . . um . . . a guest. Do you know where my cousin is? And my clothes? And am I allowed to leave yet?'

'No.'

Ras frowned. '"No" to which question?'

'All of them. Your cousin is in a different safe house. Would you like some chai?'

Idli isn't here? 'What time is it? And can I use my phone? I need to call someone.'

'No, no calls allowed. It's only for a day or two. I can bring a magazine?'

'No! I want my things! I want my phone! Where's Majid? I want to see him!'

'He'll be here soon. There's a TV room below. It's nearly six on Friday, so you must be hungry.'

Six! I've slept all day! 'I'm cold,' she complained, determined to make this cow of a nurse do something for her. 'I need my clothes.'

'There's a dressing gown in your room. We're laundering your clothes; they'll be back tomorrow. Probably.' She made an uninterested gesture. 'I'll get someone to send food to the TV room.'

Ras glowered, but the woman walked nonchalantly away, leaving her with no choice but to peevishly stalk back to her room, find the thin towelling dressing gown, wrap herself in the ill-fitting garment and slip downstairs.

She found the television room off a short corridor. It was small, with nothing but the telly and a pair of worn sofas. She perched in one and wished that damned nurse would bring her food quickly. Finally the woman came with a tin plate of channa daal and a vegetable curry that tasted utterly bland. She gave her a plastic spoon to eat it with, as if she were some kind of self-harm risk. It made her ache for home; her mother cooked the most wonderful Punjabi feasts. She missed her mother suddenly, and wondered what she was going through, worrying after her wayward daughter. She nibbled guiltily at the chapatti, until the heat and substance of the meal suddenly hit her stomach and she wolfed everything down.

She had barely finished when the door opened and Detective Inspector Majid Khan entered. Tanvir stayed by the door, pulling off his sweaty bandana to reveal a shaven skull. As she stood up, horribly conscious of the huge towelling robe swathing her, Majid Khan swaggered towards her. He was dressed in his leathers and looked wolfish and mesmerising.

'Rasita, you are okay?' He clutched both her forearms in his long, smooth hands and bending over her, asked, 'Are you recovered? We were concerned for you: there are medic-alert cards in your wallet.'

She wanted to remonstrate with him for going through her possessions but was silenced by the perilous beauty of his face. 'I'm okay. I just woke up. Can I go soon? Where's my mobile?'

'I'm sorry, but until you're fully debriefed you need to stay here, with no outside communication.'

'Then let's get on with this "debriefing" thing then.'

He grinned apologetically. She noticed that he hadn't let her arms go yet. She felt like a child in his grip, but his hands were warm, and a comfort when she felt so isolated. 'Not so easy, I'm afraid. These things take time. But it'll only be a day or two, I promise.'

'A day or two! But—'

'I'm sorry. It's just routine, don't worry,' he said, as though 'routine' absolved everything. He glanced sideways at Tanvir, who frowned, but left. She felt a sudden mix of alarm, to be alone with this arrestingly handsome man. There was no mistaking it: the detective inspector had a presence that overpowered thought. But he also had a warmth and sincerity that went some way to overriding her nerves.

Yes, I'm a little close, and a little flirtatious, his eyes said, *but tell me you don't like it . . .*

Majid sat on Ras' sofa, his manner suddenly languid. 'So, Rasita. Tell me how you are doing.' He patted the cushion beside him.

Ras eyed the sofa a little nervously, but sat dutifully. She found herself looking up into his bewitching eyes, while confused impulses spilled through her mind and body. Why did this stranger affect her so? Because on one level it disgusted her, that he could be so forward towards a vulnerable girl – but there was also something about him that she wanted to believe in. Even Vikram's face faded when Majid was so near.

'I think . . . I'm okay. I guess,' she said hesitantly.

He put a hand on her knee and her spine locked with fright, even as his heat warmed her skin through the fabric of the dressing gown. 'Where are you from, Rasita? How did you come to be here?' His breath was spice on her cheeks.

She tried to look away. 'Jodhpur. Idli's my cousin. I . . . I ran away from home.'

'Was there a problem at home?' he asked. With his free hand, he brushed a strand of hair from her face. 'Something I can help with?' The hand on her knee was now pressed to bare skin. Somehow her nightgown had become bunched up around her thighs.

She found the strength to speak. 'I . . . I have health problems. And I wanted to see a friend of mine, before . . .'

'Before what?' He put an arm around her. She felt as if she had no volition any more, that he had sucked the power to move from her limbs. He had the face of a Krishna. 'Before what?'

'Before I die,' she whispered, as tiny acid tears sprang from the corner of her eyes. 'I wanted to see him before I die.'

'Him?' The hand on her thigh – *how did it get there?* – stopped its stealthy climb. 'Who is "he"?'

She blinked up at him and the part of her that wanted to kiss him and let him do whatever he wanted warred with her pride and loyalty. Her belly was in turmoil, and below her belly, something stirred that made her feel aching and hollow. *What's wrong with me?*

A voice caught her ear and a face swam onto the television screen. She clung to it, a buoy in trackless seas. It gave her just enough strength to twist away and jab a finger at the screen.

'Him. I came to see him.'

The detective stopped and stared at the screen. While he was distracted she disentangled herself and almost fell to the floor, before she caught herself and stood. He suddenly looked merely human again, just a man after all.

She found the strength to be angry. *I wonder how many 'witnesses' you've brought here to play with, Majid Khan. I wonder how many girls have given up themselves to you in your 'safe' house.*

'His name is Vikram Khandavani, and I *love* him,' she stated, to her own surprise, and then realised it was true. She *did* love him – not a mature, thought-through love, more like a girl's crush, but real, very real right now, when she badly needed something to anchor her.

She walked to the television and turned up the volume, then deliberately settled on the other sofa to watch the show. She didn't look at the detective as he left the room.

New Delhi, 12 November 2010

Pain drew Deepika awake: her throat was aching dully, centred around two swollen scabs an inch apart. She found herself lying on her back in a narrow, body-sized box, the wood faintly warm beneath her. She opened her eyes cautiously and looked around, but it was difficult to make out anything. There was a weight on her chest, and an unpleasant smell. Instinctively she remained still, letting her eyes flicker about.

The air was dark, though a little light filtered through a carved stone lattice high on one wall that lit the chamber dimly. In the distance she could hear cars and shouting children, and in the dark corners there was a squeaking. She wrinkled her nose as the rank odour of rodents reached her: rats, or maybe bats. She bunched her muscles to sit up, and the weight on her chest moved.

It's alive.

She went still as recollection of how she'd got here paralysed her. The weight on her chest shifted, pressing down harder. Someone moved close by, on her right.

'Ah, the sleeper awakes.' Halika's cruel voice slid from Jinta's throat. A light flared: a cigarette lighter, it was applied to a candle, and then another, and now she could see Halika in Jinta's body, with those ghastly blackened eyes almost glowing. 'Don't move, girl. You might anger my little friend.' She shone the candle over Deepika's prone form, cackling softly, and Deepika raised her head and found herself staring into the gleaming eyes of the cobra lying coiled on her chest. She stifled a scream.

'We are in the catacombs beneath Humayun's Tomb. See? Your stupid defiance accomplished nothing. You are here anyway, right where the master wants you.'

Abruptly, she realised that the box she was lying in was a coffin. Halika lifted its lid. 'Scream,' she purred, 'or even move, and my little friend will bite you.'

'What are you going to do?' Deepika panted. The cobra shifted and lifted its hooded head.

'Can't you guess?' The dead queen chuckled. 'I'm packaging you up for a journey. We're taking you to Mumbai to see Lord Ravindra.'

She lowered the lid, leaving Deepika alone in the lightless coffin with the cobra.

CHAPTER TWENTY-FOUR

Parley

Tarain, Haryana, 1192

'Has it come to this? Must our court poet fight?' Govinda shifted uncomfortably in his saddle, eyeing Chand's slender form. The bulky warrior, veteran of hundreds of battles, looked at once amused and disturbed. He grimaced painfully – he'd lost half his teeth at the first battle here at Tarain. Today, there was a nervousness about him that Chand had never seen before. Govinda had finally realised his own mortality.

Chand had to remind himself that Govinda, though a lifelong colleague, had never seen him even train. 'All must contribute, General. I will do what I can.'

'You old woman – can you even shoot?' the general chided. Then their attention was drawn back to the centre of the plains, where Prithviraj was parleying with Ghori. The king had gone forth with Khande Rao, his junior general, as Govinda was more apt to start a fight than diplomacy in the parley tent. Chand had asked not to accompany them – he really didn't want to confront Ravindra again – though Prithvi wanted him to go. But he had insisted that Prithvi tell Ghori the presence of Mehtan Ali wasn't acceptable, and Ghori had agreed. With his friend safeguarded from Ravindra's presence, Chand felt it safe to stay behind.

'Chin up,' Govinda growled. 'They might not even fight. We have them outnumbered four to one.'

It was true, they did outnumber Ghori – and this was Tarain, blessed Tarain, where they had already defeated the man once. They both knew it wasn't that simple, though. Only a fifth of their force mattered: the Rajput cavalry, and the phalanx of fifty war elephants. The rest were ill-equipped footmen, recently conscripted and untrained. By contrast, Ghori's men were veterans. The Rajputs had spent an unnerving afternoon watching the Mohammedan army at worship, wave upon wave of men on their knees, bowing and chanting. That they did so facing the west and away from the Rajputs made the act both worship and a fine display of disdain for their enemies. Their priests' wailing chants had carried eerily across the battlefield; both sight and sound were profoundly unsettling.

Real men do not do thus, the Rajputs told themselves. *Our gods do not demand such abasement. It is unmanly . . . these Mohammedans live on their knees*. But everyone was uneasy.

The village of Tarain lay away to the east. The Rajputs held the high ground, overlooking the devastated farmland, already trampled into ruin by men and horses. The scrub interspersed with occasional trees concealed much of the armies from each other, making estimation of numbers difficult. Govinda held the centre with the nobles and their horses, the elephants arrayed to his right. The footmen on both flanks lolled about, bored and frightened, a dangerous combination.

At sunset, trumpets blared, banners lifted and the parley was over. Chand saw Prithvi riding hard, and wondered if anything had been agreed upon. He followed as Govinda rode out to meet the king, still awkward on his mount: he'd never quite managed the art of riding and horses still made him nervous, even after all these years.

Prithvi had a look of exultation on his face. 'Govinda! Chand!' He stormed up before reining in his horse, making it rear dramatically. 'Ghori has backed down! They're retreating!'

Chand stared. '*Retreating?*'

Prithvi pulled out a heavily inked scroll and brandished it. 'We have terms. They're pulling back. They saw the size of our armies and won't risk battle. They've ceded the Punjab to me! He will retreat west and consolidate his realm there.'

Listening soldiers cheered, and Chand saw the words of the king ripple through the lines. Men waved their weapons and started raising their hands to the heavens and chanting thanks to the gods. Part of him wanted to do the same, but this was too easy. *What part is Ravindra playing in this?*

He edged his horse awkwardly closer to Prithvi. 'What of Mehtan Ali, my Lord? Was he there?'

Prithvi turned to face him. 'The imam is out of favour. Ghori said he's been banished to Lahore for insulting you and delivering the wrong words. He offered to send me his head.'

'I hope you accepted!'

Govinda laughed. 'Our poet is suddenly bloodthirsty, now that the battle has been called off – whereas me, I'm just thirsty!'

'Then we shall *drink*, my friend!' Prithvi roared. 'This deserves many cups!' He turned to Khande Rao, who was grinning boyishly. 'Send for our best, Khande! Only the best!'

Prithvi and the generals dismounted and Govinda clapped Prithvi on the shoulder. Chand watched them wager each other something as they swaggered off towards the tents. Something in the sight made him anxious. The old Govinda would have been haranguing the king to attack anyway, not just let the enemy walk away. The old Prithvi would have listened. Neither of them would be celebrating a parley.

He went to follow, but as the smiling throng of young nobles closed about the king, he knew he would just be wasting his time. These young tyros, raised on pleasure, knew war only through the easy victory here at Tarain last year and Prithviraj's digvijaya, which was in truth just a procession of victories against vastly outnumbered local foes. They believed themselves invincible.

Had Ghori really dispensed with Ravindra and lost his nerve? Or was he buying time for a larger campaign next year, having realised just how great the army was confronting him?

Possible . . . but even that doesn't feel *right.*

CHAPTER TWENTY-FIVE

Long Odds

Safdarjung Enclave, New Delhi, 12 November 2010

Amanjit met Professor Choudhary as he ran from his car to the front door. Behind him, the house was swarming with policemen. Professor Choudhary grabbed his arms, his face full of dread. 'Tell me you know where she is,' he begged Amanjit. 'Tell me this is a game. Tell me you're eloping! I won't care – just tell me she's safe!'

But Amanjit couldn't give him that assurance. He couldn't even speak, just looked away as the policemen surrounding him stared. They'd been treating him as the number one suspect from the moment they arrived.

'Professor, you can vouch for this man?' one eventually asked.

'My *son-in-law*,' the professor said firmly, and placed his arm around Amanjit's shoulders. 'Yes, I do vouch for him, without question: Amanjit loves my daughter – and she is a good girl. A fighter. Someone has done this to her and it was not Amanjit. He loves her as much as we do – more, even.'

'We have more questions for him,' the policeman said, motioning for his men to escort Amanjit away, ignoring the professor's protests.

*

The police questioning went on for *hours*, round and round in circles. Amanjit had to restrain himself from punching his inquisitors — especially when they tried to take his kirpan away. Angrily, he quoted Article 25 of the Indian Constitution: '— which recognises the carrying of a kirpan as part of the Sikh religion, which you very well know!' He was allowed to keep it, a minor triumph, and finally they let him go, leaving the detectives looking at each other with guarded, puzzled expressions.

Great. His mobile battery had run down while he'd been repeating his story, again and again, to the cops. He put it on charge and sat in a chair, simmering. Finally, the professor was given clearance by the police and the forensics team to clean up, and as soon as the police left, they started. It was something to do. They vacuumed and mopped and scrubbed for a long time.

When the detective leading the investigation phoned again, it was to report that Jinta's family had neither seen nor heard from her since she'd left home that morning, but Jayshree had been found in her car, dazed, and with no memory.

Finally Deepika's parents hugged Amanjit, hard, and invited him to pray together at the family shrine. The icons of Ganesh and Saraswati listened impassively, and though Amanjit was a Sikh, he had never felt so close to his God than at that moment.

Dee, we'll find you! We'll find you . . .

Then the professor took his wife to their bedroom and shut the door. Amanjit could hear her crying. He waited as long as he could, then steeled himself and knocked on the door. When he walked in, they were still holding each other. They stared at him — and the scimitar, which had been hidden in the ceiling cavity in his room.

'I know this is going to sound crazy,' he told them, 'but I think I know where Deepika has been taken. It's all about Vikram, and the *Swayamvara Live!* show . . .'

He didn't tell them the truth, of course – they'd have had him locked up for lunacy, for a start – but he'd come up with a plausible scenario before he called the police. 'Vikram thinks some Mumbai gangsters have been looking for leverage over him, before he costs them a fortune,' he started. 'Apparently there's a huge business in illegal gambling on the results of the show. Vik was warned they might target those he cares about – but we didn't for a moment think anyone would ever come here!' He felt wretched, lying to these good people, but they would never have believed the truth. He wasn't sure *he* would have believed the truth.

'So what do you plan to do?' the professor asked him.

'Fly to Mumbai – I need to get there as soon as I can.'

The earliest flight was the next morning, so he spent the remainder of the day cleaning and packing, then phoning his mother and brother in Jodhpur. Rasita was still missing, of course, and there had been no news.

It wasn't until ten that night that Vikram had his phone restored to him. Amanjit grabbed his mobile the moment he recognised Vik's number. 'Bhai?'

'Amanjit! What the hell's happening? Bishin's texted: now Deepika's missing too? I tried calling her, but her number's offline?' Vikram sounded worried to the point of exhaustion.

Amanjit brought Vikram up to date, describing the fight that morning in between cursing himself for not been able to do more.

'Should I withdraw from the show?' Vikram asked seriously.

'No, bhai – we're going to fight. You're in Mumbai, Ravindra's in Mumbai, and I'm betting the girls are too. I've already got my ticket – I'll be there mid-morning.'

Mumbai, 12 November 2010: Day 5 of Swayamvara Live!

Vikram's car came for him at dawn, though he'd been ready for hours. There were no press to be seen, he noted gleefully as he ran for the vehicle. Amanjit had called as he was waiting for his flight; he'd be in Mumbai by ten. That thought strengthened him. Shastri and Aram; Chand and Prithvi: they'd be together again. It gave him a feeling of potency: they weren't helpless – they could get through this.

He could feel the game changing. This time, he dressed in loose-fitting army fatigues and stashed his bow and quiver of arrows in his sports bag. The contest with Ravindra could become a war very quickly and he dare not be unprepared.

'Well, good morning, cutie,' a voice purred as he opened the car door to find Uma in the back seat.

'This will look good in the papers,' he said lightly as he joined her. The ladyman's perfume assailed his nostrils. 'What're you doing here? Oh, and good morning to you too!'

'Well, aren't you the born celebrity – first thing you think of is your public image! Just four days into your show-business career, and you're too important for your old friends.' Uma looked away, feigning deep offence. Then she reached forward and tapped on the glass dividing panel. The driver accelerated away from the curb.

Vikram forced a tired smile. 'Sure. Um, did Jez tell you about——?'

Uma turned back quickly, the humour falling from her face. 'About your stepsister? Of course. I get to hear everything, darling. Any news?'

Vikram swallowed the lump in his throat and tried to sound brave. 'No . . . and now my stepbrother's fiancée – one of my best friends – has gone missing as well, from Delhi.'

Uma jerked as if she'd been struck. She reached out and touched Vikram's arm. 'Oh my, that's awful! You poor thing!' She put her other hand to her mouth. 'You should withdraw, Vikram. This is too much. The show doesn't matter, not compared to what you're going through.'

'No, I have to go on.'

'You're a fool, Vikram. You should be with your family and friends. If the press knew, they'd brand you heartless. I'll bet some of those bastards would even start "hinting" that you've been staging their disappearances as a way to hold Sunita to emotional ransom!'

'But you won't tell anyone, will you?'

'No, sweetie, of course not — but it just takes one cop to put two and two together and it'll hit the press and the telly like a bombshell. It'll be out of control.' Uma fell silent as they wound their way through the increasingly heavy traffic. They clearly weren't heading for the studio.

After a while, Vikram asked, 'So, apart from that, how am I doing?'

'You're in the last six, honey. Your parting gift, even if you're eliminated tonight, will be the equivalent of most people's annual wage.'

'Really?' He hadn't known that the eliminated finalists were given gifts.

'The combined value of the parting gifts at this stage are about ten lakh. You lived in England, didn't you? So that's around ten thousand English pounds. Not bad for a student, don't you think? It'll pay for the rest of your education.' Uma ruminated for a while, and then said, 'As long as I don't tell you about the upcoming tests, there isn't a problem.'

An off-the-record chat . . . with Uday the eunuch, Vikram thought. 'Okay.'

'Sunita's a little scared of you, Vikram,' Uma said. 'The others don't worry her at all, even Pravit – he's a known quantity, of course. Alok is comforting: he's traditional but modern, multi-talented – and the people like him. He'd be a good choice. Of all you contestants, he is certainly the most accomplished. But she thinks he's all surface. As for the others: she had a very ill-advised fling with Kajal Dilkishan a while ago.' Uma wrinkled her nose. 'It was during a particularly low period. She doesn't like to talk about it, and we've managed to keep it out of the papers. It'll come out if he doesn't win, of course, but she's prepared for that. She'll eliminate him at the first opportunity – he's been lucky to have won enough lives up until now to keep him in the game.'

Vikram digested this in silence. *Gauran, you were always wayward. There were always other men.* He'd expected there would be. *But Kajal? Ugh!*

'As for the other two, Mandeep is nice, a safe choice, and talented too. But Sunita Ashoka doesn't do *safe*. Joseph is a nice fellow too, but he's an *Englishman*. He's really just there to keep the overseas channels on board. Sunita is indifferent to him.'

Vikram listened to this cold and clinical appraisal with growing apprehension. If this is what they thought of the multi-talented men he was competing with, what on earth did they make of him?

'And then, honey, there is you: the underdog, the left-field character.' Uma looked at him intently. 'Everyone saw how Pravit *immediately* identified you as a threat, right at the start, and sought to get you eliminated. And everyone knows Kajal is Pravit's man, they know where the "gay attack" really came from. But you survived that, and now they've seen that you can affect Sunita with just a look and a few words. They don't know how you do it – and neither do I! Sunita's an experienced woman. Teenagers don't leave her flustered: she's eaten men twice your age! She's

Ashoka the Shocker!' Uma glared at Vikram as if demanding an explanation.

He squirmed, knowing the truth would be impossible to explain.

'Sunita was adamant her Rama would rise through the field through prowess and destiny,' Uma went on after a moment. 'She said we might not recognise him at first, but eventually we would.' She looked at Vikram. 'She was aware there might be an age difference and she is prepared for that emotionally, although she thought it would go the other way – a far older man. She is also ready to have her choice scrutinised and second-guessed by one and a half billion people. But she's still afraid of you.'

Vikram took that in silently, then dared a question as they pulled into the forecourt of an impressively large hotel surrounded by security and film company vehicles. 'Does she take as much medication as the papers say?'

'The papers talk rubbish! I tell you, she doesn't do drugs any more!'

Vikram decided the ladyman might be telling the truth, as far as she knew it, but he'd once been Doc Chand, and he knew what he'd seen. *She's doing it behind your back, Uma. Sorry.*

She seized Vikram's hands in her own, big mannish hands. 'I shouldn't say this, but she is *desperately* unhappy, Vikram. If this swayamvara doesn't give her what she wants, then I am *very* afraid for her. I need to know: are you *genuine*, Vikram? Are you here for *her*?'

Oh Gauran, I've always been the only one who could heal you. Looks like I'll have to do so again.

'Yes,' he said firmly. 'Yes. I am.'

The daytime test, a 45-minute tête-à-tête with Sunita, was held at one of the trendiest bars in *MUM-BAIII!!!* The garishly

decorated Go-go Ra-ra Bar overlooked the harbour from thirty
storeys up. This time the contestants had to invent a new cocktail
for Sunita. The cameras would be rolling the whole time while
she was chatting with the contestants about their cocktail, and
the editors would turn the footage into an entertaining montage
for the night's programme.

They were told nothing about the evening's test, which would
go out live.

Vikram drew second slot after Mandeep. Personally, he
thought ten o'clock was a bit early in the day for drinking, but
none of the Bollywood types seemed to think so. Alok got the
lunchtime session and Kajal pulled the mid-afternoon session,
which would be beside the hotel's rooftop pool – *another opportunity for him to look good in trunks*, someone muttered darkly.
Joseph had the next slot, and Pravit was last up, by which time
Vikram hoped Sunita would have passed out.

At least they didn't have to wait together. The competitors
were separated after the draw, given tea or coffee, magazines and
the timetable for the day. What they didn't get was internet access,
in case they used it to research little-known cocktail recipes.

Vikram didn't give the whole cocktail thing a moment's
thought. The instant he was alone, he took out an arrow and his
map, pinpointed the hotel and then spun the arrow, murmuring
the words he had learned all those lives ago. He focused on Ras
and the arrow spun on his finger and pointed north–northeast.
Using the shaft of the arrow as a ruler, he carefully drew a line
across the map, then a circle around the area where the line met
the one he'd drawn before he left that morning. He kept the circle large – this method wasn't totally accurate. And of course, if
she'd moved since he'd last used the spell at dawn, it would be
totally useless anyway.

The triangulated reading indicated that she was now in either the Bandra or Juhu district, where the wealthy lived. Then he did the same for Deepika, but got nothing at all – although that wasn't altogether surprising; he was certain Ravindra knew all the counter-spells to prevent such divination. He put the arrow aside and for a moment just sat there, his head in his hands, and tried to deal with his fears for her.

Someone knocked, and he quickly dropped the map and arrow to the floor beside his chair as he called, 'Come in!'

'Gidday mate, whatcha doing?' Jez brandished a wireless microphone unit.

'Just waiting.'

'Sometimes that's the hardest part. Stay relaxed, mate. We're all countin' on you.'

'Really?'

'Absolutely. I've got a lazy hunner on you at 250 to 1.'

'A hunner? Do you mean a hundred rupees?'

'Nah, mate. One hundred Australian.'

Vikram did the maths. 'So you stand to get 25,000 Australian dollars if I win? Far out! That's a *million rupees*!'

Jez grinned. 'Sure is, give or take. So just stay cool, man. We're cheering for you, big time.'

'We?'

'Uma and I. We saw your triple bulls-eye that first trial, made a note of your name and got some money on you as soon as the bookies started taking odds.'

'I saw 800-to-1 in the papers.'

'Yeah, but that was just paper-talk. The real odds were never higher than 250-to-1. All the big money went on Alok and Pravit early, and at low odds. The bookies will take a real bath if you or Joseph win, but I think they're covered on the rest. I doubt anyone bet on you except Uma and me, at least until Thursday, and by then the odds were way down.'

Vikram cocked his head. 'Isn't your betting on this something like insider trading?'

Jez tapped the side of his nose. 'It's a corrupt world, mate. But there's always a way.' He waved the wireless mike. 'Now, let's get this fitted.'

What am I missing? Jez had left him alone and now Vikram was thinking about Mandore and about what was *really* going on.

Was Ravindra *just* attacking them all because of what had happened at Mandore? Was every past life just a continuation of his feud against them? Surely there must be more to it than that? The failed ritual at Mandore had left Aram, Darya, Shastri and Padma trapped in a cycle of death, but it had also left Ravindra and his other queens stalking the world as eternal ghosts, stealing bodies to hunt down him and his friends in life after life. So Ravindra must be seeking some kind of release from his own existence, mustn't he?

So, what does he need? What are the victory conditions for Ravindra — and for us?

Also, intriguingly, there was the link to the *Ramayana* to consider, for surely there must be one? Rama won Sita at a swayamvara, and Prithvi won Sanyogita in one. Now here he was, competing for the hand of Gauran in her current guise of Sunita Ashoka, and Gauran was Padma reborn, the woman he should have courted and rescued back in Mandore.

But who is Ras? I swear that I've never met her before, in any life. Never. Was her disappearance just a coincidence, opportunism, just another way for Ravindra to hurt him? Or was there something more going on?

He picked up a writing pad from beside the hotel bed, took up a pen and jotted down the salient facts. He'd always thought better with pen and paper.

RAVINDRA (= Ravana?)
Me = ARAM. Chand. Bhagwan. Doc. 11 others.
Amanjit = SHASTRI. Prithvi. 7 known others.
Deepika = DARYA. Sanyogita + 5 known others.
Sunita = PADMA. Gauran. Jane + 8 others (4 past wives)
Uma = UDAY + 4 others.
Alok = Raichand + 2 others.
Ras = ????
??? = Kamla . . .?

He tapped the pen in frustration, staring at the names until they blurred, but no insights came.

Who were you, Ras? Where have you been all my past lives?

Finally he put the pad aside. *I need to think about Gauran.*

The original Queen Padma of Mandore had been infatuated with him, even though he was just a lowly court poet, but he'd been besotted with Queen Darya and had barely noticed her. Every other incarnation of Padma he'd met, like Gauran, like Jane, had had severe mental problems, despite which he'd usually formed a romantic attachment with them.

Is it something to do with the heart-stones? he wondered suddenly. Padma was the only one of the seven Queens of Mandore who had died separated from the strange pulsating crystal talisman Ravindra had given each of them. She'd given hers to her brother Shastri to give to him: the unworthy object of her affections who'd never even noticed her love.

What did that do to Padma? Did it damage her psyche, even her soul?

That made him sit up: in this life – and several others, now he thought about it –he'd met the ghost of Padma as well as an insane incarnation of Padma! So perhaps when Padma died, her soul had not just been damaged, it had somehow *fractured*, split into two parts, or maybe even more than two?

Ras? He picked up the pen and drew a dotted line from her name to Padma's. *Maybe?* It felt right. His heart beat a little faster, as if he were finally on the right path.

Then he started to think about what he'd have to do in the next few days if they were to avert disaster. *We must find Deepika.* In March, Ravindra's aim had been solely to capture his errant Queen Darya, so she had to be in the most immediate danger – unless Ravindra also suspected Ras was important. But if it was just Padma's *ghost* haunting Ras, then perhaps he didn't know yet?

I need four of me if I'm to do everything: protect Sunita, find Deepika, find Ras, fight Ravindra. But I can't be everywhere! Get here quickly, Amanjit. I need you with me—

There was a knock at the door. It was time to mix cocktails for Sunita.

Cocktails, Vikram decided after a few minutes, were quite fun, especially when you had Sunita Ashoka propping up your bar.

He'd not spent a lot of time thinking about the challenge, but he'd decided his game plan pretty quickly: he was going to go with an iced tea drink, but with some Indian spice to liven it up. This life had scarcely included drink at all, but some of his past ones certainly had, especially those where he'd been married to the Gauran-soul. His unhinged ex had always been a drinker . . .

'So, I'm thinking a little masala, kind of "Long Island Iced Tea" meets "Mumbai chai-walla",' he said, speaking to Sunita but keeping his words clear and his face turned to the camera.

'Daring,' Sunita remarked. She looked half-cut already from Mandeep's efforts, and she still had a full day to weather. 'But spice and spirit don't always mix well. I should know.'

'Jamaican spiced rum works,' Vikram countered, trying to sound knowledgeable but not too expert. He threw in a measure of this and a bit of that and gave it a shake, then garnished it with mint, leaned across the bar and proffered the drink.

Sunita took the glass daintily. 'Let's see, shall we?'

She sipped it carefully . . .

. . . then sprayed it over the bar. 'Dear Gods, that's hideous!' she exclaimed.

Ooops . . .

He offered her a napkin, trying not to laugh. 'Shall I have another go?'

'Heavens no! Step away from the bottles.' She giggled as she wiped herself and the bar-top down. All round them, the film crew and associated flunkies snickered behind their hands or looked appalled, but Vikram saw that Sunita wasn't upset or even put out. He poured her a soda-water, and one for himself.

Probably best if she paces herself anyway . . .

'So, I guess we've established that I won't be mixing the drinks on honeymoon.'

She laughed, and sipped the soda with a look of relief. 'I have people for that sort of thing,' she said, offering a silent toast. 'If you really knew what you were doing with cocktails at your age I'd have been worried.' She studied him silently for a moment. 'May I ask you a strange question, Vikram?'

'Of course.'

'Thank you.' She eyed him up and down, then asked, 'Do you believe in reincarnation?'

As she asked, Sunita tilted her head sideways, the way Gauran always had. They even looked alike: thin, but curvaceous, with a narrow beak-like nose and bird-face; the same, glinting bead-eyes, the ringlets, and the same love for turquoise. Her jewellery glittered like a field of stars as she shifted her head from side to side unconsciously.

'Yes, I do,' Vikram answered. He was very conscious of the

cameras peering at them and the microphones attached to both their collars. He was dressed in the tidy but casual cotton jacket and outfit Uma had sent to his room.

'Because I am Sita, reborn, you know.' Her voice was totally certain, yet as casual as if she were discussing the daily news. 'I have lived many times, seeking my destined husband. All my lives have been focused towards that goal. So whenever I meet a man, I ask myself: is he my Rama?'

Vikram pictured the way this blasphemy would be received in the press and in the homes of millions of Hindus. He hoped that the programme editors would excise it, but suspected she was going to repeat this statement to every contestant, to gauge their reactions.

'I don't know,' was the only sane answer.

'But then, Rama himself did not know that he was the avatar of Lord Vishnu until the end of his time on Earth,' Sunita commented. Gauran had always been like this: full of grand delusions and blind faith in the impossible. She was pricklish, and as elusive as she was lovely. He found himself sinking into her eyes anyway.

'I guess I wouldn't know either then,' he said.

'You're very young to aspire to win my affection.'

'But with great potential,' Vikram responded brightly, relieved the conversation had left the arcane.

'What do you want to be when you leave university?'

'A poet and an artist and an adventurer. I will see the world, and take care of it.'

'That sounds very romantic. And impractical.'

'It doesn't cost much to live. And I don't really care about possessions.' *I've had wealth*, he almost added, *but it didn't buy me anything I needed*.

'What if you win this contest?'

'I'll still want to travel. You can come too,' he added with a smile.

She responded involuntarily, girlishly ducking her head. 'I don't travel light. I'm a city girl.'

'It's not so hard.' He thought back to the times when it had been just him, travelling all over India – and other countries too – often trying to escape or hide from Ravindra, or some other lesser enemy while hunting for clues that might unravel the mystery of these linked lives. Sometimes the Gauran-soul had been at his side for a while: rare, happy days together. 'You'd like it, I'm sure.'

'What sort of poetry do you write?'

'Whatever comes into my head. Whatever is important at that moment.'

'What do you think when you see me?'

If only I could tell you. 'I see a lovely person who yearns to be whole.'

Her eyes caught his. 'Can you do that? Make me whole?' she asked, only half-teasing.

'I think so.' It was a promise he'd made before to her, though he'd never yet succeeded in keeping it.

When it was time to leave, she stepped close and her lips brushed against his cheek, her breasts against his chest, her arms entangled with his. She inhaled, sniffing at him cautiously. 'They say that if someone smells good to us, they would make a good mate,' she whispered. 'You smell good, like leather and salt. Like something from my childhood. Something I can't quite remember.' Then she kissed his lips, quickly, not quite impersonally, and backed away.

She smelled of expensive perfume, and tasted of hope and fear.

*

That evening all of India watched the highlights of the day's cocktail meetings. They heard Sunita speak intimately with each contestant. They heard little phrases, caught looks and smiles and frowns; evaluated nervous ticks and stammered responses. They assessed each man's demeanour, and measured the partings. They rolled their eyes when Sunita looked like she needed to be carried out of the studio after the last cocktail test. They laughed raucously over her reaction to Vikram's abysmal drink, and jotted down the recipes for Alok and Mandeep's efforts.

They saw Alok kneel and kiss her hands in a grand gesture of worship and adoration and sighed at tradition upheld. They saw Kajal dismissed with a polite wave, and Joseph bend over her hand with a look of resignation. They saw Mandeep kiss her cheeks confidently, murmuring something that made her giggle. They saw little Vikram, barely taller than her, standing rigid as if in fright as she gently kissed him. Some snorted, but others sensed something *happening*. Most of all, they saw Pravit Khoolman, the last contestant and therefore the one who had her basically drunk and pliant already, seize her and kiss her passionately, bending her backwards, his arms holding her up, her body arched into his. Most murmured about ardour.

Jai watched from their sofa with two girls tucked under his arms and a dozen friends on the floor cheering their fellow student. They punched the air and exulted as Kajal and Joseph were sent home.

Vikram was one of the four finalists!

Dinesh Khandavani watched his son get through with mixed reactions. He, Kiran and Bishin ignored the media horde hammering on the door, hungry for background and exclusive information about Vikram. But they couldn't celebrate, not with Rasita still missing. Everything felt hollow, surreal, a strange dream.

*

Professor Choudhary sat beside the bed, watching Vikram's success on a small television while his wife slept the deep, dreamless sleep of the tranquillised. He prayed Amanjit could bring their daughter home.

Amanjit watched *Swayamvara Live!* on the dusty old telly in his tiny hotel room. As usual, Delhi's Indira Ghandi Airport had been in disarray, with dozens of delayed flights, and it had been a long, boring day of hanging around in crowded departure terminals, but he finally got to Mumbai. He had 15,000 rupees in his wallet and his sword in his checked-in luggage. Airport security had been somewhat perturbed by it, but it wasn't technically illegal to own or travel with it, provided it didn't go into hand luggage. Right now he was waiting for Vikram to get off air so he could call him, but his mind was on the girls. *Deepika, where are you? And you, Ras? Are you here too?*

Rasita watched the episode intently, sitting alone in Safe House Five, her body still quivering from fright at how close Majid Khan had come to overwhelming her. She wondered how long she could resist him; she was relieved he hadn't come back. She cried when Vikram and Sunita looked at each other, knowing she was losing him. It was breaking her heart more surely than any medical condition.

A growing certainty was filling her thoughts, that she would die the moment Vikram was announced the winner of the swayamvara. And if he did win, she would welcome that death.

CHAPTER TWENTY-SIX

Identifying the Body

Mumbai, 12 November 2010

Vikram was in the final, Amanjit as predicted, along with Pravit Khoolman, Alok Pandiya and Mandeep Shekar. Kajal had apparently stormed straight to the *Swayamvara Panel Show!* studio after being eliminated. The stuntman was in a towering fury and was busy dishing dirt on everyone, much to the delight of the interviewers and the studio audience, who were lapping it up. The tickertape of quotes crawled across the bottom of the screen:

KAJAL: I WAS SUNITA'S LOVER
KAJAL: PRAVIT IS 'VIRTUALLY IMPOTENT'
KAJAL: I FILLED IN FOR PRAVIT ONSCREEN,
    AND IN SUNITA'S BED
KAJAL: *SWAYAMVARA LIVE!* FIXED!
KAJAL: SUNITA PROMISED ME VICTORY!

Bollywood would be in uproar for months to come. Well, days, anyway. The TV people were having a field day. It was a promoter's dream: the press were going mad. Tomorrow's final show would break all records. Already there was speculation on which B-list actresses might offer themselves for sequels. *Sway-amvara Live!* was the new *Bigg Boss!*

Amanjit was watching Kajal's interview when his mobile rang, less than half an hour after *Swayamvara Live!* went off-air. 'Hey bhai, congratulations! One more night, eh?'

'Sure.' Vikram sounded flat, and very anxious. 'Listen, I've got an idea about where Ras could be, but I can't get a fix on Deepika. The arrow just keeps spinning.'

'What does that mean?'

'It means she's either a long way away or that my spell is being blocked. Neither is good.'

Amanjit's hand sought the grip of his sword. He desperately wanted to lash out at something. 'Vik, let's hire a car and try and find Ras tonight. Bring your bow.'

Vikram clearly needed to act as well. 'I'll be there inside half an hour.' As he hung up, Amanjit saw a text from Bishin: <Call me>.

After that call, he hung his head and prayed for revenge.

Vikram spotted Amanjit leaning against the wall of his hotel, his bag over his shoulder. He knew what would be inside it. He asked the taxi driver to wait and got out to wave to Amanjit, who strode through the jammed evening traffic. They embraced, thumping each other's backs. He'd never been so relieved to see his best friend, now his stepbrother – in this life, at least.

'Good to see you,' he started. 'First, we'll go to—'

'No,' Amanjit interrupted, 'first we have to go to the morgue.'

Vikram stared in shock, his heart lurching. 'What do you mean?' he whispered.

Amanjit's expression changed to one of horror. 'No, *no!* Sorry, I didn't mean to scare you! It's not the girls! But it's not good either. The Mumbai police found my cousin Idli face-down in a sewer. There was no ID on him, but some bright spark in Missing

Persons matched his description to the report you filed. They want me to identify him.'

Vikram hugged Amanjit again. Idli was a jovial man, not smart, but happy and fun-loving. And he'd adored Ras . . .

'I'm so sorry. I didn't know him that well, but—'

'Idli was a bit of an idiot.' Amanjit agreed with Vikram's unspoken thought. 'Easily led, but good at heart.' He didn't speak the other thought that they both were wrestling with: if Ras had come south to Mumbai with Idli, where the hell was she now?

They arrived at the St George Hospital morgue as the clock chimed midnight. The cold corridors were empty, with only a skeleton night staff on duty, but ambulances came and went regularly, depositing more and more bodies. Yama, the Lord of Death, took a high toll every night in Mumbai. The desk clerk showed them through to a small room, where they waited until finally the door opened and a tall, thin policeman with a pencil-line moustache entered.

'Mister Singh?' he looked enquiringly at them both. 'And Mister Khandavani?' He looked at Vikram curiously, as if matching the figure whose face was all over the news with the small youth before him. 'I am Sub-Inspector Ravi Bachram. We wouldn't normally allow the public in after hours, but I understand there is some urgency in this case.'

Sub-Inspector Bachram was the man who had efficiently and intuitively matched Idli's name to a body dumped in a sewage outlet, and Vikram felt a surge of gratitude. The man's attentiveness may have given them a chance to save Ras. He shook his hand warmly, then followed him to the morgue. The room was filled with medical trolleys on which sat human-shaped mounds draped with white cloth. A doctor waved them in and led them to the third trolley.

The policeman pulled back the cloth with a business-like manner.

Amanjit swallowed. 'It's Idli.'

His cousin's skull was caved in at the back. His face and chest were mottled nearly black with patchy discoloration. 'He was left face-down, hence the blood settling to the front,' Bachram told them. 'That will fade by the time he is ready for cremation.'

'How did you know it was him?' Vikram asked.

'There were no papers on him and he was naked. Even his tattoos had been partly obliterated, probably deliberately – but there was enough ink left for us to match to the photos from his previous arrests.'

'Previous arrests?' Amanjit's eyebrows went up.

'He has three counts of driving under the influence of cannabis. In each instance he was photographed. I used to work in narcotics before my transfer here; I was looking through the photographs on another matter and his rang a bell.' Bachram's tone was bitter, and Vikram wondered at his 'transfer'. It didn't sound like a promotion.

A door opened behind them and a tall, lean man stalked in. His thick wavy hair was worn long, his stubble the fashionable kind, and he sported a full-length leather greatcoat. Behind him was a muscular man wearing a red bandana. 'Bachram, what's going on here?' he snapped.

Ravi Bachram stiffened. 'Detective Inspector Khan, these are relatives of the deceased. They've formally confirmed the body as that of Idli Singh—'

'I was told that body wasn't identifiable,' the detective inspector snapped. 'Why was I only just informed?'

Vikram and Amanjit faced the newcomer warily, and when he looked back at them, they all felt something ripple unseen between them: he too had shared a previous life with them. This time Vikram had a name to go with the sensation: Jaichand of Kannauj.

Jaichand . . . slippery, charming, a womaniser . . . kinsman and enemy . . .

But it went deeper than that: Jaichand was someone who could have been an ally, if not a friend, in different circumstances. He was always someone it was important to cultivate.

Then his eyes went to the man in the red bandana and that brought another surprise. He too was someone reborn: Tilak of Mandore, Shastri's friend. It was strange to see him with Jaichand-reborn, but he sensed a wariness between them.

Two men from the past — is everyone I've ever known here in this life?

Vikram concealed his nervous tension and introduced himself. 'Detective Inspector, I'm Vikram Khandavani and this is my stepbrother, Amanjit Singh Bajaj. Amanjit is the deceased's cousin.'

The detective inspector had visibly quailed as he too felt that moment of connection, but he had recovered quickly and was pulling out an ID card to mask his momentary confusion. 'I am Detective Inspector Majid Khan, Narcotics.' He indicated 'Tilak'. 'This is my partner, Tanvir Allam. We've just been informed that the deceased may be linked to past cases.' He looked at Ravi Bachram. 'The body and its related evidence must be re-assigned from Missing Persons to Narcotics. You are not required henceforth on this matter, Sub-Inspector.' He didn't offer a single word of thanks or praise to the more junior officer, Vikram noticed; did they too have a history?

Vikram pointedly thanked Ravi Bachram before the Sub-Inspector left the room. When he was gone, Vikram turned back to confront Majid Khan. *So, Jaichand! You're here too. Is everyone coming together? Is this the life where all the skeins are finally untangled?*

They stared at each other, waiting to see who would speak first. Vikram could feel Amanjit struggling to control himself: he didn't remember his other lives, but he could probably feel sub-consciously that this man was a very personal and real enemy. He could see that the detective inspector was going through something similar. This situation could turn to violence so easily, and only he would know why.

But on the other hand, Tanvir – Tilak of Mandore – had been a friend in every life. He might have no idea of these hidden connections, but he was looking at Amanjit and Vikram with interest and sympathy.

So Vikram spoke quickly, in a placatory voice. 'Detective, are you able to tell us more about this case? Idli may have been travelling with a seventeen-year-old girl – Amanjit's sister, my stepsister. She has been missing since Tuesday.'

The detective studied his fingernails, then responded in clipped tones, 'We find dead girls all the time. None have been identified as your sister. We'll take your details and get in touch if we require further assistance.' He half-turned, almost as if fleeing the room, but Amanjit laid a hand on the man's shoulder to stop him.

'Wait! That's it?'

The detective brushed Amanjit's hand off. 'For now. I'm a busy man.'

'I want to find my sister!'

'As do we all,' Majid Khan said, sounding completely uninterested. 'So if you will let me get on with it—'

Vikram grabbed Amanjit's other arm before he did something rash. 'Thank you, Detective Inspector. Please keep us informed.' He offered a hand, which Majid Khan reluctantly took. He fixed the man's face in his mind as he left, in case he needed to track him later. Even Tanvir looked surprised, giving Vikram and Amanjit an almost apologetic look as he followed his superior out the door.

'That prick doesn't give a damn about Idli or Ras,' Amanjit growled. 'All he cared about was Bachram showing him up. Bastard!'

'I know. Let's find Bachram again. We need to talk to him.'

'What about?'

'About Majid Khan.'

Sub-Inspector Ravi Bachram was more than happy to talk. His career in Narcotics had been heading upwards until two years ago, when Majid Khan had pulled strings to get him removed to Missing Persons. 'It was nothing I could prove, but there was word on the streets.' Bachram dropped his voice. 'They said Majid was in deep with the Bakli clan.'

The name meant nothing to Vikram. 'Who's he?'

'Shiv Bakli and his brothers run drugs through Mumbai and smuggle arms back to terrorists in Kashmir and beyond. They also have a nice little side-line running girls, child labour and illegal immigration rackets, not to mention all the casinos and fixed betting rings, and any other criminal activity you care to mention. But they do it all through intermediaries, so nothing can be proved, and just to ensure that doesn't change, he has his people deep in the Maharashtra bureaucracy. The Bakli boys have always been careful to pretend legitimacy.'

'And Majid Khan?'

'A womaniser, a playboy cop, but he's sharp and smart. He likes his girls young, innocent and vulnerable. He's been *very* successful, got plenty of arrests to his name – mostly Bakli's rivals, funnily enough.' He sniffed. 'Lots of big drug hauls, too, but you know, they're always smaller than our sources led us to expect, if you know what I mean?'

So Majid Khan is skimming the captured drugs for his true master – or for himself . . . 'And Tanvir Allam?' Vikram asked.

'He's a decent man, as far as I can see, though he does little to curb Majid – but Majid's got rank on him, of course, and we all need our careers.'

That all fitted with Vikram's own past-life experiences: Majid-Jaichand the crooked one, and Tanvir-Tilak, a follower, but with a core of decency. 'What happens to the girls he takes?' Vikram asked.

'Most end up in one of the brothels run by Bakli's people.'

Amanjit growled, and Vikram placed a calming hand on his arm. 'We'll find her, bhai. It won't come to that.'

'If he's laid a finger on her, I'll kill him.'

They thanked Bachram again, then went out to their waiting taxi. Vikram spun an arrow, now focusing on Majid, and they followed the detective inspector as he wound slowly south across the city to Byculla district, where he pulled into the drive of a perfectly ordinary bungalow in a quiet street. Vikram had the taxi driver pass them without stopping: he counted three cars outside, and a dozen or more armed police guarding the front door – and they were just the visible obstacles.

He spun the arrow again, concentrating on Ras this time, and the arrow pointed straight at the house.

Amanjit bridled, his big form quivering. She was *here* – but to get her out would start a bloodbath. 'What shall we do?' he asked. 'Shall we go in?'

Vikram glanced at his watch. It was two in the morning and he was almost out on his feet. The taxi driver was nervous and curious, constantly looking at them over his shoulder and trying to listen to their conversation. 'This isn't like the Mehrangarh,' Vikram said after a moment. 'That was an ancient place, with ancient forces in play: remember how modern torches and guns failed there? They won't here. We've got a sword and a dozen arrows. And these men may be innocent, with no idea what Majid Khan is doing. We can't kill them for that – even if we could.' He looked at

Amanjit helplessly. 'I'm sorry bhai, but I don't think we can do anything.' He put a consoling hand on Amanjit's shoulder. '*Not yet.*'

Shiv Bakli answered his mobile in his solarium. Few people had his number, but Jaichand of Kannauj had been a useful contact in so many lives. 'Inspector Khan,' he said smoothly, 'what can I do for you?'

'Sir, the two youths you warned me about showed up at the mortuary. They're making connections . . .' He paused, then added a little nervously, 'There's something about them . . .'

The uncharacteristic hesitancy in Majid Khan's voice was interesting. 'Where are they now?'

'I don't know – the man I had tailing them lost them in heavy traffic an hour ago.' He paused, then went on cautiously, 'Sir, meeting them made me realise something else.'

'What is that?' Bakli enquired in a dangerous voice.

'There's a girl in my possession, Master. Rasita Kaur Bajaj. I think she will be of interest to you. She is sister to one of the two youths.'

'How long have you known her connection to this case?'

'I've only just found out, Master!' The detective's voice was pleading for forgiveness. 'I didn't realise – how could I? Those Sikhs all have the same names – they're all Singh and Kaur – how could I have known—?'

He let the man stew in silence for a while, then hissed, 'Have you *despoiled* her?'

He heard the guilty pause, then, 'No, Master. No.'

'She managed to resist your charms, did she?' Bakli laughed. 'You're losing it, Majid.' Then all mirth left his voice. 'Guard her well. And bring her to me, untouched, tomorrow morning.'

He hung up and stroked his chin. Everything was coming together – and this girl, whoever she was, would be useful leverage to paralyse Shastri's sword and Aram's bow. Another ace to play in an already strong hand. Queen Darya was en route; his private jet had landed already. All the other queens except Padma were aboard, and if he was right about Sunita Ashoka, then even that lost queen would be in his hands soon. Then nothing would stop him killing them all and completing the ritual begun so long ago in Mandore.

But he'd been in this position before in other centuries. In every life he had watched Aram die – and in most, he'd killed the runt himself. He'd often slain Shastri too, and in several he'd even tasted Darya's blood – although never with her heart-stone present. And as for Padma, he'd found her and killed her too, a number of times, but without her heart-stone, that had been a futile exercise. And there was something else missing: she was Padma, but incomplete, somehow.

As he reflected, the exultation drained from him, leaving him tense and brooding. 'What else?' he asked the night. 'What am I missing?' To be so close to fulfilment was eating away at him. Even Khar was still and silent, his stone face shrouded in darkness.

This other girl, perhaps: Rasita . . . Sita . . .? He thought long and hard, and finally he smiled as he made the connection he had failed to understand down through the centuries.

Of course, everything is simple when you know the answer.

This time, he really would be totally victorious. This time he would find release. Tomorrow night, when Sunita was revealed as Padma, he would bring them all together and complete the ritual.

He would finally, truly, *fully*, become Ravana, the Demon-King.

CHAPTER TWENTY-SEVEN

The Second Battle of Tarain

Tarain, Haryana, 1192

Chand Bardai knew he was dreaming of Mandore, though somehow it felt *real*. It was night, and he was in the middle of the court, and all the frightened courtiers were peering at Ravindra, who was sitting upon his throne. The queens were all present, half-hidden behind the carved screens of their viewing balconies, but he could see Halika leering at him hungrily. Padma waved to him . . . but she was Gauran too, beckoning him with mad eyes . . . Even Darya was there, sullen and angry, her face bruised. They were all looking at him as they argued over what entertainment they wished for.

Then Ravindra decided for all of them. 'Sing for us! Sing, Aram Dhoop! Sing for me the *Prithvi-raj Raso*.'

The queens exclaimed, and the courtiers shouted and clapped their hands. 'Yes! Yes! Your masterpiece, the *Prithvi-raj Raso*! Sing it for us! Sing! Sing!'

Ravindra smiled like a tiger and called, 'Wake up, poet! Wake up! It's time to play!'

Chand woke to a servant shaking him and the sound of shouting outside, too much to comprehend, and the intermittent beating of steel on steel — and the slithering, air-ripping sound of arrows in flight, and the screams of horses in agony.

He understood in an instant. *We're under attack.*

He slung a quiver, strung his bow and was looking for his sword-belt when his tent caught fire. He cursed as he frantically belted the blade to his waist. He cast about, but he saw nothing of true value; everything that mattered to him was in Dilli. The journal of Aram Dhoop and Padma's heart-stone were safely hidden. Little else mattered in the end . . . and he was suddenly sure that this was the end of this life.

Cursing his defeatism, he drew his sword and slashed his way out of the tent as it was engulfed in flames. He staggered out of the smoke into a Turkic spearman in filthy rags, gutting him before the nomad could react. The camp was awash with enemy warriors; he'd never get to his horse. Waves of attackers were crashing against a hastily formed squad of footmen who were stabbing back furiously. Then a group of mounted archers thundered out of the dust and morning mist to deliver a volley of arrows into the Chauhamanas line which instantly brought down eight or nine men.

The line of defenders disintegrated and the men went running helter-skelter towards the rear.

Chand planted his sword point-first in the ground, drew his bow and shot a Turkic rider who'd spotted him and was taking aim, impaling him straight through the belly. The rider doubled over and his horse bore him away, but Chand was already in motion, thrusting his sword back into his scabbard and running for the king's pavilion.

'Prithvi! Prithvi!' He burst through a cloud of dust left by a troop of Rajput riders trying to mount a counter-charge as the pavilion went up in flames. *'Prithvi!'*

He saw Govinda trying to organise a defensive line, but the

Rajput warriors were on foot and skittish as riderless horses in a storm. 'Crouch! Shields up!' the burly warrior was roaring as the enemy horse-archers wheeled and fired. Shafts flew wide and dozens went down, struck in the legs or shoulders, the parts left unguarded by the wood and wicker shields. 'I said *crouch*, you turds! Now fire! *Fire!*' Some shot back, others just gazed about, swaying, drunk and disoriented. The enemy riders dashed in again, shooting in volleys and swerving away from contact, each sally leaving more and more dead.

We'll never hold!

Chand ran behind the line, seeking Prithvi, and found the king being patiently armed by his retainers: helm, chainmail, breast-plate, greaves. He saw Chand and growled, 'Where's your armour? Get some steel on you, for my sake!'

'Fire-arrows burned my tent, my Raja. I had to leave every-thing behind. What's happening?'

'You tell me! Damn you, Muhamed Ghori, for a treacherous dog!' He grabbed Chand's arm. 'Get to Khande Rao on the right, tell him to re-order the line and push forward, wheeling inwards. Govinda has the centre. Samatasimha has the left; he too must hold, then drive inwards. He'll know what to do! We have more men than Ghori, we can envelop him!' He glared about him. 'Damn this fog! I can't see more than fifty yards!'

'My horse is gone!'

'Take one from the corral – any horse! Go! Go-go-*go!*'

Chand started to run, then he stopped and cast a look back. This could be their final parting. But Prithvi was looking the other way, so he went on, sprinting back through the gradually forming lines. The corral was almost empty; very few horses remained unclaimed – as many were fleeing as fighting. Pockets of Turkic and Afghan tribesmen were breaking through, running amok in the sick-tents and burning the supply wagons. He took down a man with a fire-arrow to dissuade the group before making for one of the few tethered horses left. Fortunately for him, this was a pliant beast and he was soon galloping north.

The visibility was dreadful, and he rode right into a contingent of war elephants. He sent them southwest, crying, 'Hit the flanks of the enemy advance! Rally to the king!' On he galloped, barely managing to keep his seat, but for once not thinking about how much he hated riding. All along the line the Rajasthani footmen were staggering back under the ceaseless volleys of arrows; they mostly ignored his imprecations to turn and fight. One even threw a spear at him as he spurred on.

He found Khande Rao floundering, a mile to the north. His footmen were breaking all along the line as swirling groups of Turkic riders circled and fired in front of them. When he saw Chand he wailed, 'They're cutting us to pieces, and I can't touch them! I need cavalry! The king must send cavalry – send me Rajput warriors!'

'Our horsemen are pinned down in the same way,' Chand shouted back. 'Our mounted archers were all gathered in the king's pavilion last night, drinking until dawn – they're drunk as sots! You must hold, then swing south!'

'I can't! We can't hurt them! I have no archers. They won't come close. They just fire and flee, fire and flee!' Khande was almost weeping in frustration. 'I need *cavalry*! I need *bowmen*!'

Chand seized the man's hand. 'Khande, you must attack! If you stand, you will fall. You must make your men charge, and force the enemy into close quarters!'

'I can barely make my men stand!' Khande looked back at the line and shrieked a warning – '*Watch out!*' – as another volley struck the line. The footmen, armed only with spears and knives, without even shields or armour, were mown down in front of them, and this time many broke and ran.

Khande pounded back to them, crying, 'HOLD, *HOLD!*', but the enemy had already disappeared into the mist, shouting in their jabbering tongue.

Chand trotted after him, soothing his mount, trying to personify calm. 'Who is to the north of you?'

'I don't know! It's supposed to be the Tomaras. Chand, this is a disaster! I must have cavalry!'

Chand gripped the general's shoulder. 'You must advance, Khande! You must! This mist won't last – soon you'll see the terrain. Push forward and left. Drive them, Khande!'

The general's despairing face told its own story.

He can't do it! He's too green. Chand gritted his teeth and hauled on his reins, galloping on to seek men who would fight.

All through the morning he rode along the right flank, trying to convince the unit commanders to push forward – some would, some wouldn't. Other riders came with other orders. Attacks were planned but never launched; others went unsupported, and left isolated, were chopped down. By midday, a cloud of brown dust covered the battlefield. The Rajasthani line was barely intact. Wherever the footmen gave way, the Turkic riders sheathed their bows, drew sabres and charged, slashing at the unguarded backs of the fleeing men, cutting them down in their hundreds. But mostly the enemy fought from a distance, destroying the Chauhamanas with their inexhaustible volleys of arrows.

Chand tried to keep the officers calm; only when alone did he use his Gurukul-taught powers. Around midday, near the centre, he found the elephants plodding forward, pushing back the Turkic riders and crushing the few footmen Ghori had deployed in their path. Then he burst in on a small mêlée and found Prithvi himself, unwounded, a grim light in his eyes. He appeared to have regained some of himself in the heat of the fray. When he saw Chand, he waved him forward. 'Chand! What news of the right, my friend?'

'They hold, barely.'

'Hold? They must *attack*!' Prithvi clenched a fist. '*They must attack!*' He pointed forward to where the enemy was drawing off. 'We're winning, Chand! We're driving them. The right must attack!'

'What about Samatasimha in the south?' Chand asked.

Prithvi's face fell. 'He's dead. The left broke, damn them all to hell. But we're winning here! *Here!* This is where victory lies! We've got to push on!' He waved his arm, eliciting a tired cheer from the Rajput nobles who were fighting on foot in shielded skirmish lines. 'Tell Khande Rao he must attack, Chand. Tell him the moment is now!' The king turned away and strode on. Chand fixed the sight in his mind: this was the Prithvi of old, his invincible friend, advancing to victory.

He turned and rode north again, mapping out the battlefield in his mind. The Rajputs advancing from the east were pushing forward in the middle against little resistance, but their flanks were folding. It felt like a noose being drawn about their heads. He could almost hear Ravindra's laughter.

We must break the trap before it closes about us! He spurred on his exhausted horse once again.

All afternoon he flitted from skirmish to skirmish. Here, a unit held under withering fire; there, another had stalled, leaderless and lost. He sent them all south, towards the centre. At the place where he had last seen Khande Rao, a group of rider-less Rajputs huddled together as Turkic horse cavalry circled them, picking them off one by one. The trapped men were too frightened to move. A Turkic officer saw Chand, and that cost him his horse and half an hour to a deadly game of cat and mouse in a copse of trees as a dozen men combed it for him. He left half of them dead in there, their bodies smouldering from the agniyas-tra, then crawled away down a farm drainage channel, caked in mud, his quiver empty.

He finally overtook Khande Rao, who was being carried off the field on a horse-drawn cart. An arrow protruded from his belly. The general barely knew him. Chand blessed him, hugged him and said farewell. A belly shot was slow death; they both knew it. Infection was inevitable. It would have been more merciful to have cut his throat.

He rode back to find Prithvi's advance had ground to a halt, pinned down below a defensible ridge where Muhamed Ghori's banners flew. The massed archers were pressing Prithvi on both flanks. The whole of the Rajput position was in range of enemy bows, and Prithvi looked close to erupting as Chand tossed aside his reins and pushed through the crowd.

'We must break them here! Send in the elephants again!' The king thumped his fist against the mailed chest of his captain of war elephants. 'Attack!'

'I cannot, my King! They've spiked the hillside – I've lost too many already!' The man was openly weeping. 'When they die, their cries are like children!' The captain turned away, overcome.

Prithvi seized Chand and asked desperately, 'What news of the right? Where is Khande Rao?'

Sleeping with the gods already, or close to. 'The general is wounded, sir. He is retiring.'

'Retiring? *Retiring?* I ordered an advance!' Prithvi's voice cracked.

Chand bowed his head. 'Sir, the general is near death.'

Prithvi's eyes went blank for an instant in mourning. 'Who commands the right now?'

'There is no right, my Lord. It has fallen into chaos.'

He saw Govinda groan softly, and the other generals flinched.

Prithvi punched his fist into his palm. 'Damn him! *Damn* this treachery!' He strode away a few paces and stood staring out through the dust. All about them came the clash of steel and the shrieks of the fallen. 'All the enemy do is feint. All they do is fall back and shoot, fall back and shoot! How can we be losing to these *cowards*?' He looked back at Chand. 'How long do we have before we are cut off?'

'Half an hour. Less, maybe. You must either break through here, or retreat and form a new line.'

Prithvi hung his head, wringing his hands. He looked at Govinda. 'What strength do we have to attack, my friend?'

'Too few horses. Exhausted men. Enemy disposition unknown. An hour of daylight left, and the camp in ruins. My Lord, we must retreat. There will be other days.'

Chand blinked back sudden tears. *No, there won't*, he thought, and it felt like prophecy. But he couldn't say it aloud.

Prithvi bowed his head. 'Then we must pull back and create a new defensive line.' He drew himself to his full height, trying to impart confidence and courage. 'We still outnumber them and they're in hostile territory. The people will rise against them – the Rathod and all the Pratihara will come, the Gujaratis will come, and all the east and the south! There will be a new alliance, my friends: a grand alliance! Rajputana has seen the threat and now we will rise against it. There will be another day!'

They cheered, but those cheers were suddenly drowned by cries and trumpets and drums. A messenger galloped back and arrows once more fell about them like avenging bolts of the gods. 'They come! They're attacking!'

'It's a feint!' Prithvi shouted. 'All the bastards do is feint and run. Hold your ground!' He turned to throw an order at Govinda when he suddenly choked, and stiffened. The generals gasped as they saw the shaft jutting from the king's thigh. The ground trembled, then a torrent of Turkic horsemen thundered out of the mists, their sabres glowing in the rays of the falling sun.

Chand saw Govinda go down, smashed to the earth by a riderless horse, then lanced in the belly as he tried to rise. His own eldest sons, Sur and Sunder and Sujan, were cut down side by side. The captain of war elephants was crushed by one of his own panicking beasts. Then Chand was running, trying to reach his friend. *'Prithvi!'*

A huge stallion burst from the cloud of attackers, its rider a colossus armoured in silver and robed in white. *'PRITHVIRAJ!'* shouted Ravindra.

'No!' Chand screamed, and his hands blurred. A spell burst from his lips as he fired, but Ravindra swept aside the fire-arrow with his sword, then slashed brutally and Prithvi went down, clutching his face. Ravindra reared his horse, casting about him, and his sabre snaked out towards Chand.

'That one!' he roared. *'It's Chand Bardai! Take him alive!'*

The Turkic warriors turned and spurred their horses towards Chand.

CHAPTER TWENTY-EIGHT

Let the Show Begin

Mumbai, 13 November 2010:
Day 6 of Swayamvara Live! *(Final Night)*

Vikram didn't go home that night. There were too many people watching his dormitory – the newspapers, the TV people and all the other celebrity-stalkers, all hungering for a glimpse or a word, anything remotely newsworthy. Instead he stayed with Amanjit in his cheap hotel, a shabby, smelly room with a blocked toilet and two musty single beds.

The few hours of sleep he managed weren't anywhere near enough and he woke tense and frightened, although not for himself, but for all those he loved. Amanjit lay on his back on the other bed, twitching in a semblance of sleep.

Today was the final night of *Swayamvara Live!*, the day that would decide it all – but nothing was going right. He was failing again, just as he always failed. The faces of everyone who had depended upon him in past lives floated before him. Many had the same souls: men he'd led to defeat in battle, women he'd let down, whose hearts he had torn apart, people he had promised redemption, then led to destruction.

How can we win?

His phone rang: an unknown number. He answered tentatively, 'Hello?'

'Vikram Khandavani.' The voice was resonant, confident and calm. It made his skin crawl. 'Do you know who this is?'

He felt a sickening lurch in his stomach. 'Ravindra.' Amanjit started upright and looked at him. Vikram thumbed the speaker and Ravindra's voice filled the room.

'The very same. What a civilised age this is, when enemies can converse via electronic toys instead of only beneath flags of truce.' The Raja of Mandore chuckled. 'There is so much we could talk about – so many shared memories . . .'

'What do you want?' Vikram demanded. His voice came out much shakier than he wanted it to.

'The usual: your destruction, and that of everyone you love and hold dear. Nothing has changed there, Aram Dhoop – but then, perhaps something *is* different this time? Do you feel it? We're all here, Aram. *Everyone*. Me. You. Shastri – who is no doubt at your side at this very moment. The lovely Darya, all my queens. Even Padma . . . How fares your wooing, Aram? Have you won Sunita's heart yet?'

'Say what you have to say,' Vikram told him. 'I don't want to listen to your gloating.'

'Very well,' Ravindra purred. 'You are probably wondering if you should just run, or whether you should somehow fight. I know you, and I know how you think. You are certainly considering not going to the final of the swayamvara and instead hunting for your womenfolk.'

It was very much what he was considering, Vikram admitted silently.

'But you will not shirk the swayamvara,' Ravindra said, as if giving orders to a wayward subordinate. 'You will fulfil this part of our destinies. You will awaken Padma within Sunita Ashoka and complete the circle. If you fail, then I will destroy Deepika and Rasita. I will ravish them and then I will butcher them. Do you understand me?'

'You'll do that anyway,' Vikram pointed out, while Amanjit clenched his fists.

'No, I will not,' Ravindra replied. 'For I have puzzled it all out, Aram. I understand now what went wrong in Mandore and how to fix it. Give me Sunita, fully awakened as Padma, and I will let these others go free.'

'What guarantee—?'

'I give no guarantees, crawler! You will do as I say, or your beloved women will suffer!'

Vikram looked miserably at Amanjit, whose face was awash with fear and fury. 'Yes, yes, all right. I'll compete.'

'Good,' Ravindra replied. 'And keep that oaf Shastri away from things, Aram, or I'll make these girls pay in ways that will haunt them for ever.' He raised his voice. 'Do you hear me, Shastri?'

Amanjit gritted his teeth. 'I hear,' he said in a murderous voice.

'Excellent. I will call again after your televised victory, Aram Dhoop. Break a leg!'

He hung up.

Vikram rolled onto his side and stared through stinging eyes at the grimy hotel wall. 'He's got us, brother. He's got us.'

For once, Amanjit could find nothing positive to say.

They called the film company and arranged Vikram's pick-up from the hotel, then went looking for breakfast. No one recognised Vikram, though one or two people stared at his face as if trying to recollect who he reminded them of. But no one looked for celebrities at little paan-stalls and dhabas. They bought some chapatti, daal and rice and ate with their fingers on the side of a dirty street as the early morning office traffic crawled past, puffing out fumes.

'I can't think properly,' Vikram moaned. 'I'm so tired.'

'Then let's have some coffee, bhai!' Amanjit replied as the food began to restore his spirits. 'This is the day, Vik – we've got to be on top of our game!' He looked at the piece of paper Vikram had given him, filled with names and places and lives and Rama- yana incidents, with lines snaking here and there. 'Why have you got a line from Ras to Padma?'

Vikram looked up, his eyes red-rimmed with exhaustion. 'I don't know. Just a feeling.' He straightened and looked at Aman- jit thoughtfully. 'You see, I've realised that in several of my past lives there's been a woman I've been betrothed to unseen, the engagements arranged at birth, but in every instance, the girl died. In the 1600s this happened, and twice in the 1800s, girls from neighbouring villages who died before I even met them. Oh, and I was briefly betrothed to Jaichand's cousin, who fell sick and perished before I met her. If not for that, I'd never have married Kamla.'

His head reeled at the new line of possibilities.

'Who's Jaichand?' Amanjit asked.

'It doesn't matter,' Vikram said. 'It's the girl who matters – *the girl who always dies*.' He looked at Amanjit with shining eyes. 'Tell me about Rasita's health.'

'Ras? Um, she's had at least three near-fatal heart failures and if it wasn't for the doctors she'd be dead.' Amanjit's eyes went wide. 'You think she's—?'

Vikram slapped the wall beside him. 'The girl who always dies! Only this time, she hasn't: modern medicine has kept her alive long enough for me to meet her. No wonder I didn't realise she was significant – I've never met her before!'

'But who is she?' Amanjit asked confusedly.

Vikram's face was alight. 'Don't you see? She's *Padma*!'

Amanjit looked at him uncomprehendingly. 'But we've only

been going along with this whole swayamvara thing because *Sunita* is Padma—'

'I think they *both* are! I think when she died without the heart-stone in Mandore, Padma's soul must have somehow broken apart.'

'That's crazy!'

'Yes, but I think it might also be true. Somehow, her soul fractured into a girl who's insane, another who's sickly . . . and a ghost who haunts them both, seeking to be whole.' His voice trailed off as he thought aloud: 'All these lives we're sharing? They're like that movie, *Groundhog Day*. Remember? The one where Bill Murray is trapped doing the same day, over and over, until he gets it right. *That's* what's been happening to us! We wrecked Ravindra's ritual in Mandore and left him stranded, a living-dead man, and each time we've been reborn he's recognised us and tried to correct things by killing us again – it's all he knows. But he's never been able to move on, because he's never had the real Padma, or rather, the *whole* Padma. So he just ends up hitting "reset" and starting the cycle again.'

'But this time he has Ras, and Deepika too,' Amanjit said, comprehension growing on his face. 'Do you think he knows this?'

'Perhaps – he sounded very sure of himself, and he was gloating at having us all gathered together. I think he senses it too, that this could be the life when everything is resolved, for ever.' Vikram drummed his fist against his thigh. 'This time, he can win. *But so can we!*'

'Yeah, well, so far he's doing a lot better than we are.'

'So he is, brother. We've got to fix that.' Vikram looked at his watch. 'Come on, the car will be waiting. We've got to go.'

It occurred to him that the ancient notebook was still under his bed in the dormitory. *If I die today, I've done nothing to ensure that I'll find it in my next life – if there is one.* But there was no time to rectify that now.

'So we're just going to play along? Do what he wants?' Amanjit asked. 'Is there nothing we can do?'

'We have to play along for now, bhai. But we'll have our chance, I'm sure of it.'

Vikram used his status as a competitor to get Amanjit into the studio, and without their bags being checked: just as well, as they were full of swords, arrows and his re-curved bow. Vikram introduced Amanjit to Uma and Jez, and he was allowed to stay with Vikram. Alok, Pravit and Mandeep were in the neighbouring rooms, but he didn't see them. It was down to the four of them now, and the organisers obviously wanted to keep them apart.

A stack of newspapers was strewn over the coffee table. The headlines blared out at them in huge letters:

SUNITA CONFESSES: 'I SLEPT WITH KAJAL'
DOCTOR: PRAVIT HAS A 'MANHOOD' PROBLEM
PRAVIT DENIES IMPOTENCE, TELLS FEMALE
JOURNALIST HE'LL 'PROVE IT'
MYSTIC PICKS ALOK FOR LOVE-MATCH
RECORD TV AUDIENCE PREDICTED
SHILPA SHETTY BACKS MANDEEP FOR VICTORY
WHERE DID VIKRAM SPEND THE NIGHT?
UMA DENIES ALL!

There was a little new information among the gossip and rumour, most importantly, the admission by Sunita that she'd had a brief affaire with Kajal. She denied that it had caused her break-up with Pravit in Paris, which was then revealed to be over children: she wanted them, he most definitely 'did not want kids cramping his style'. It was irrelevant now. The real things going on within *Swayamvara Live!* had nothing to do with any of that.

It's all about Aram and Padma, Chand and Gauran, Doc and Jane. It's about me and Sunita. And maybe, it's also about Rasita Kaur Bajaj.

The day dragged by, through hairdressing sessions and fittings and re-fittings for several outfits of increasing garishness. Tonight was entertainment and showbiz, pure and simple. The tests would be perfunctory – more archery, table-tennis, a song-and-dance routine – but the results would be largely irrelevant, with no points or lives at stake. It now came down to one thing: who would Sunita choose?

Vikram found, despite the dread of what might be happening to Ras and Deepika, that he could relax now. He joked with Jez and Uma and the make-up artists. He practised his steps with Oviya, the pretty dancer from Bangalore who'd been assigned to him for the dance routines. At every opportunity, he spun the arrows, thinking of Deepika, of Ras, and of Majid Khan. As the day progressed and they neared the beginning of the finale, the arrows converged along one single line that ran through Bandra district. Amanjit made a call to Sub-Inspector Ravi Bachram, asking about a certain person's address, and circled the spot on the map. It aligned with Vikram's arrow-lines. They gave a grim smile. Shiv Bakli's house. They had a target, finally. Now they had to find the opportunity to attack.

TV schedules permitting, of course . . .

'So why do we have to go through with this bloody sideshow?' Amanjit snarled, once he'd talked to Bachram. 'What's our priority here?'

'Ravindra wants us to complete the show, which implies it's the one thing we *shouldn't* do. He'll have spies here, though, to tell him if I leave. But you're right, we can't tamely play into his hands!' Vikram went to the door and called down the corridor, 'Uma! I need your help!'

'For you, darling, anything!' The ladyman sashayed in, then paused as her mobile rang. She looked at the screen, mouthed an apology and answered. 'It's about time you rang me back! Listen, you leech! I've got Alok acting like he's already won and Mandeep wanting to sue us over fixing allegations. Pravit is hiding in his room waving his will at people and threatening to kill himself unless Sunita takes him back, and—' She stopped and glared at the phone. 'That *matachod* hung up on me!' Then she shrugged and was abruptly as calm as a pond on a still day. 'Hey, Vikram, nice suit. You look good, honey.'

'Thanks. But I need to see Sunita.'

Uma waggled an admonishing finger. 'That's not allowed, Vikram. She's got—'

'Uma,' Vikram interrupted, weaving a persuasion spell into his words, because he knew that Uma was scrupulous about fair play, 'I *have* to see her. It's a matter of life and death.'

Uma succumbed to the spell without a word and scuttled off while Vikram ducked back into the room to wait with Amanjit. Uma returned with Sunita, who was fretting like a nesting sparrow. 'Vikram, I can't see the contestants before—'

Vikram met her halfway and seized her shoulders. 'Sunita, there's no time for that. We have to do something, or people I love are going to die. Maybe worse than die.'

She looked up at him, her face going from surprise to shock to anger. She was a Bollywood star – people didn't just grab her! She opened her mouth to shriek something at him.

There's no time for that crap. I have to force the issue. He kissed her.

He didn't just *kiss* her, though. That was just the physical act. He gripped her shoulders, pulled her to him and pressed his open mouth to hers. She quivered and struggled for an instant, shocked and outraged, but there was no time for that either. He reached inside and filled his mind with thoughts and memories of her: her as Padma, as Gauran, as Jane, as all the others. Then he pushed those memories into her head, memories of love, of hate, of children, of laughter, of pain. Lives together, lives apart, failures, large and small; short, tragic lives laced with tiny triumphs.

Remember who you are, my love. Remember who I am . . . Remember it all . . .

She fell against him, her face against his chest as her legs gave way. He heard Amanjit and Uma gasp, but he waved them away with one hand while supporting her with his other, propping her up. He held her and fed her strength, wishing her back to thought and consciousness, all the while horribly aware of the ticking clock, the evaporating minutes until the show went on air. Outside in the auditorium, the studio audience would be present, the cameras playing, the musicians warming up, the sound-checks finishing. They had less than an hour to go.

'Sunita,' he whispered as she stirred against him. 'Sunita, I'm here. It's okay.'

He met Uma's eyes. The ladyman was clearly frightened for her charge, and utterly confounded by what was happening. 'Who *are* you?' she whispered.

'I am Sunita's destined lover and I need to take her away from here – she's in real danger here. And we need your help, to save others.'

'Honey, we're due on stage in forty-three minutes,' Uma said, retreating to the known.

'I know.' Vikram had a plan bubbling up from the back of his mind. 'Listen, Uma, get Jez, and the producer. We'll need their help.' He made his voice crack with authority. 'Uma, GO!'

She stared at him as if he'd gone mad, but then something

instinctive took over. 'You'll take care of her, won't you?' she implored. 'She's so precious.'

'As best I can,' he replied, and Uma ran for the door, shouting for the producer.

Amanjit turned and looked at Vikram with wide eyes. 'What're you doing, bhai?'

'We're taking the fight to the enemy, to save the girls.'

'But Ravindra has them – how can we do anything against all his bad voodoo?'

'We're in *Bollywood*, Amanjit. They do magic here, too.' He cupped Sunita's chin and pulled her out of her dream.

'Rama, you've come for me,' she slurred. Then her eyes focused. 'What's happening, Vikram? What's going on?'

'We're in a hurry, my love. There's a man who means to kill you. We have to go.'

'Then I'm coming with you!' she demanded, her face suddenly frightened at the notion of him going.

'It will be dangerous!'

'I don't care! I belong with you, Aram . . . *Aram!* Your name is Aram!'

Gauran . . . You're awake – what have we done?

'Yes . . . yes it is. I'll explain in the car.'

She cocked her head in a familiar gesture that stirred so many memories and gave a tinkling laugh. 'I'm a star, darling. I don't *drive*. I *fly*.'

Ras lay in bed, too scared to even think, until mid-afternoon, when two nurses came for her. They gave her a pure white evening dress to wear, a designer name she'd sighed over in magazines. They stood over her, making sure she cleaned herself up properly, then did her hair and put jewellery on her that weighed like real gold. She had no choice – if she hadn't been so ill she could barely stand, she might have fought back, but she realised that all she could do was show dignity in the face of the beast. It still made her feel sick, turning herself into some kind of trophy.

Then they frog-marched her downstairs and into a limousine where Majid Khan waited, looking dangerously handsome, but smoking nervously. Two cars preceded them and two followed; their convoy of black-glassed cars wound through the streets, leaving Byculla and travelling westwards to Bandra. She refused to speak and the detective inspector didn't press the matter. He looked scared to touch her now, almost ill at ease to be so close. She was glad of that, because his beauty now disgusted her.

He's tricked me out as a virgin whore, she thought. *One use only . . .*

The small convoy slid through wrought-iron gates and along a driveway, then parked on the carriageway of a marble palace. Gold lion statues guarded the massive carved wooden double doors. Uniformed guardsmen awaited and shepherded them inside. Ras couldn't help noticing all the men were armed.

Within was a massive lobby with a huge staircase and gleaming balustrades spiralling down from above. It was crowded with statues: carved gods and warriors and women in bronze and gold and marble and black basalt. They all looked poised on the verge of movement.

'Just the girl,' a woman said, descending the stairs. Ras didn't recognise her. Weirdly, her face kept rippling between an East Indian visage and a sultry desert beauty. She was clad even more richly, in a heavily embroidered traditional sari of red and emerald green. She spoke like a queen.

'Who are you?' Majid Khan asked her.

'Someone beyond you, my pretty peacock. Create and maintain a perimeter. No one enters except those guests we expect.'

Majid looked troubled, but he hurried away without a backwards glance at Ras.

The lordly woman seized Ras' forearm with freezing, pincer-like fingers. 'Pretty little Padma,' she said in a silky voice. 'What a wonder, to see you again.'

Ras found a name for the woman, lurking in her mind – *Halika* – but that was impossible, so she refused to acknowledge or speak it.

'Come with me, sister,' the woman ordered. Her strength was frightening as she half-carried Ras up, flight after flight, to the top storey. The décor became ever more opulent, but Ras took little in. Fear of Halika made her want to retch. She had to fight hard to keep her heartbeat steady.

Then she was pushed into a shadowy room dominated by an enormous platform shrouded in silk drapes of silk and piled high with carpets and cushions. Behind her, Halika stepped backwards, and then suddenly went stiff and lifeless, as though she were a marionette and someone had just cut the strings. Her face became vacant, and something pallid stepped from her, as the body – now an East Indian woman once again, collapsed. The pale thing that had left her body leered at Ras as she was joined by four other spectres. Ras was shocked to realise she *remembered* them: the dead queens of Mandore, Rakhi, Meena, Jyoti and Aruna . . . and she recalled that Halika had been the worst of them all.

A deep voice ripe with sensual power sighed, and she whirled in fright, her eyes trying to penetrate the gloom. Flames flickered, running around the limits of the room, as rows of candles and stands ignited. As they illuminated the space she saw that the walls were thirty feet high or more, and composed entirely of copies of the relief-statues at the temples of Khajuraho: erotic carvings of antiquity. Here, out of their religious context, they looked lewd and disturbing – and they seemed to be moving at the corner of her sight, only falling still when she looked directly at them.

Then one of the statues did move: a demonic thing with tusks and horns, eight feet tall, carved from some reddish stone. It was wearing four swords at its waist: one blade for each of its four arms. Its four slitted yellowy eyes were the only non-stone part of it she could see, and they were watching her thoughtfully. The impossibility of this was dulled by the atmosphere of unreality that pervaded the air here.

I've stepped into a nightmare.

The dead queens herded her forward with icy hands, towards the canopied darkness. She stumbled over cushions and rugs towards the centre of the platform, where she could dimly make out another statue, one sitting cross-legged, sculpted from darkness. She felt the strength drain from her legs and she fell to her knees. Then this statue moved too.

At a gesture, more candle-stands lit, illuminating Ravindra-raj in all his chilling power. It could only be he, the man Vikram, Amanjit and Deepika had been whispering about when they thought she wasn't listening. He wore a crown, pantaloons of cloth-of-gold and a necklace hung with six smoky crystals, nothing else. The candlelight lit his oiled skin, giving it a dark, coppery hue. His musculature was awe-inspiring. His face was smooth, his moustache thick and sweeping. Long hair tumbled from his brow in black waves. His eyes glistened like black pearls. His voice was a resonant rumble, the voice of a dragon.

'Rasita. Come, sit.' He gestured to a cushion at his right. Somehow his words went straight to her limbs and they moved of their own volition until she found herself crouched at his feet, trembling, terrified to move, appalled at what that massive body and cruel mind might do to her. And all the time, memories flooded her mind . . . other lives, other times: Mandore – seven queens, and a poet she loved hopelessly, and a brother whom she worshipped, but who gave her in marriage to the monster at whose feet she crouched. She felt herself sway at the chillingly familiar beginnings of a seizure, the hammering heart, the fiery swelling, the pumping rivers of blood inside.

She welcomed it. *Yes, let me die!*

'Calm yourself, my queen. Be still,' purred Ravindra, and horribly, her body betrayed her again, now listening only to him. She felt her heartbeat calm immediately and become regular. That was somehow more frightening than everything else around her.

Ravindra said to the ghostly queens, 'Behold, your lost sister is restored to you.' They turned and she saw their dreadful, hungry eyes on her, heard their cold laughter and sighs. 'And who else joins us?' He gestured to the door and it swung open. The ghostly queens turned and hissed as another woman walked slowly through the doors, as alive and mortal as Ras. She was clad in gold harem pants and a gold-sequinned bikini top. Draped over her shoulders was a cobra that writhed languidly, caressing her neck with its head.

Ras swallowed a sob at the sight of her soon-to-be sister-in-law Deepika.

Deepika walked as if on puppet-strings until she passed between the ghostly queens and the four-armed demon and knelt beside Rasita, at Ravindra's feet. Then she looked at Ras, her eyes flew wide and she gasped. '*Padma*'

'Darya,' Ras replied unthinkingly, and then clutched her mouth. *Darya? No,* Deepika! *What's happening to me?*

'You are awakening,' Ravindra answered her unspoken question. 'Both of you are remembering who you once were, long ago. You are remembering Mandore, when you both belonged to me.'

With a sudden ripple of cloth, a flat white curtain fell, covering the doorway and facing wall, and from somewhere above, a projector hummed to life and a huge rectangle of colour appeared on the white curtain. Almost deafening sound swelled from hidden speakers: the opening music of *Swayamvara Live!* filled the room and Sunita Ashoka's delicate, lovely face appeared.

A huge hand fell on each of their shoulders and Ravindra lowered his face until it hovered above and between them. He leered at each in turn. 'Now, take your seats, my queens. Let the show begin!'

CHAPTER TWENTY-NINE

A Bolt from Above

Mumbai, 13 November 2010:
Day 6 of Swayamvara Live! *(Final Night)*

'I don't know why I'm trusting you. I barely know you. This is insane!' Sunita looked like an excited schoolgirl despite her gloriously groomed face and very adult figure. 'I feel incredible . . . I can remember a past life as a queen! I always knew I was a real queen, you know!' Then her voice faltered. 'And there was an awful man . . . the raja . . .' She looked at Vikram, a panicked expression flaring on her face. 'Who is he? What's going on?'

Vikram tried to compose his thoughts. They were huddled together in the lee of a wall while Amanjit hovered anxiously nearby. The studio had a helicopter pad – ('Because you're no one if you don't arrive by chopper, darling,' Uma had told him) – and the chopper was being frantically readied. Inside, the show was about to begin, without its star and one of the competitors.

'You need to remember, Sunni. I'm going to speak some names and I need you to hear them and *remember*. Are you ready?'

Sunita looked at him with a face lit by wonder and trust. 'What names?'

He reeled them off: Gauran, Jane, Virani, and all the others he recalled, and he saw the names hit her like punches. 'Do you remember?' he asked anxiously. 'Do you understand?'

She looked up at him, her eyes wet. 'There's always something wrong with me. There's always something wrong . . .'

She's beginning to regain actual past-life memories. He caught her face in his hands and tried to send calm. 'What we're going to do is fix that. We're going to make you whole. But there are risks. Do you understand? Terrible risks. This could kill you. This could put you in the power of Ravindra for ever. But if you're not present, I don't think we can save the others.'

'I don't understand. But I trust you, Doc. You're my physician.' Then she heard herself, and her face became even more bewildered.

Doc and Jane . . . Holy Gods, this is getting messy . . .

Uma came up from below just as the rotors began to turn. 'I have to go – the show is about to start! Please tell me this isn't happening!'

'I'm so sorry,' Vikram told her. 'Will you manage??'

'I'll try! It's chaos down there,' Uma drawled. 'Alok is drunk on celebratory champagne, Pravit is blubbing and Mandeep is locked away with three lawyers. But the producer and Jez are on to it. We can go ahead.'

'The show must go on.' Vikram grinned.

'Why no police?'

'Because one of our baddies is a cop – a very senior cop. There's just no time to find a safe channel, so we have to do this ourselves.'

Uma kissed Sunita's cheek, and then his. 'Bring her back safe, Vikram!' she growled, in an almost masculine voice.

Amanjit grabbed Vikram's shoulder. 'Come on! We've got to go!'

They bowed their heads and ran for the helicopter.

On the rooftop of Shiv Bakli's mansion, Majid Khan stood in a corner and looked out over the gardens. Bakli had some two dozen armed men below, lounging against the walls – he'd said he couldn't rule out an attack. Behind him, a helicopter sat on the rooftop helipad. Satellite dishes festooned the northeast corner, facing the hinterland. To the west, the Arabian Sea gleamed like rippling metal under darkening skies. All around him lay Mumbai, Mother Bombay, begrimed jewel of India. Gentle winds carried sounds and scents and the taste of salt and smoke.

But Majid's mind kept travelling inside. Beneath his feet, in a massive auditorium he'd seen once before, Shiv Bakli would be having his way with that girl, Rasita. He could taste her name on his tongue. What was it about her that set him off? He'd had hundreds of girls, the younger the better, and the very, very youngest, the very best – indeed, he'd made a sport of conquering them. They were the weakness he couldn't put aside.

But he'd fumbled his handling of Rasita Bajaj – and the odd thing was, when confronted with the moment when he could have taken her, something had held him back, the ghost of a moral code he'd long left behind . . . but now she was lost to Shiv Bakli.

He gritted his teeth. It wasn't the only thing he'd lost to Bakli. He'd given up his pride, his honour, his integrity, in return for wealth and – maybe – his life. There were no illusions, though: one slip would be all it took. He would never grow old. He sighed, pushed his fingers through his hair . . .

. . . and thought of her, just a few yards below him, her frail virginal body being used and broken.

He licked his lips nervously and wished he had the courage to do what his heart told him. He cursed himself, taunted himself with all manner of names, but made no move.

I'm a coward. I always have been.

Below Majid Khan's feet, on the top floor of the mansion, Shiv Bakli's hands stroked the bare backs of the two girls at his feet as he stared avidly at the screen. *Soon, it will be soon . . .*

He'd thought he was merely bringing in a girl with whom Vikram Khandavani had formed an attachment in this life, a bargaining chip only, but as soon as he saw her, he *knew*, and the suspicions he had formed over the centuries – that Padma's soul had fragmented in the débâcle at Mandore – were confirmed in that instant. Even the rakshasa Khar had not realised the truth.

All he needed now was for Sunita to publicly acknowledge Vikram, and the transformation would begin. The sundered souls of Padma would reunite, and one of the two women would die. His powers would sustain Rasita, and therefore it would be Sunita who died, live on television – a promoter's dream, no doubt. And then he would have every one of his queens present and whole for the first time since Mandore. Only the absence of Padma's heart-stone would prevent his ascension, and he had a plan for that, a way of circumventing the need for that jewel. There was a way.

This time, he would claim the powers of Ravana himself and ascend, a god.

Around his neck was a gold chain from which hung the six heart-stones he'd recovered – one for every queen, except Padma. They each burned like ice. His ghostly queens could barely take their eyes off them, knowing what they were. Deepika and Rasita also stared, as if they could sense the power in those jewels.

He watched the show with mounting frustration. Some fools in garish suits sang and the studio audience were invited to get up and dance. Vishi Ashoka spoke endlessly. Another song. He growled with impatience. *Must they milk it for so long?* What need was there of a two-hour extravaganza when the only moment that mattered was when Vikram claimed Sunita and her mind flew open?

He glanced at four-eyed Khar glowering beside the pavilion, only his eyes betraying animation. Again, he wondered if the rakshasa truly had contacted his brethren for aid, or if he was keeping Ravindra's existence secret for his own purposes. What little he recalled of rakshasas suggested such behaviour. Once he gained his full powers, he would rectify that.

It was Rasita who troubled him most. It appeared that she could sense the moment of her death coming – she was so weak, and he was having to pour more and more magical energy into her just to keep her alive, keeping her heart regular, keeping her breathing. It made him uneasy; it was almost as if the transformation from two souls to one had already begun. He couldn't let the girl die, for then Vikram would hold the one true Padma and the balance of the game would be altered dangerously in the young man's favour.

Where is our star? Show her to me!

But then Sunita Ashoka herself was onscreen, waving, smiling, accepting flowers, bedecked in an incredibly ornate bridal gown, her features barely discernible through the veils. Her body language was vibrant though, and filled with excitement. He felt a tinge of relief. All was well.

Get on with it, you preening bint! Finish your damned show and die!

The pilot took the helicopter in high, so that the sound wouldn't alert anyone prematurely. Vikram jabbed a finger down: the Bakli house. Amanjit felt a curious calm overtake him in the onset of battle. Sometimes daily life left him impatient for the ability to act directly, to face danger. He loosened the scimitar in its scabbard as he studied the terrain.

'There's a chopper on the roof already,' Amanjit noted. 'The garden's full of trees – there's nowhere to safely land.' He could see a man on the roof in a long black coat – he could guess who it was. *The dirty detective – Majid Khan, right? Good! I was hoping you'd be here.*

Sunita looked at Vikram anxiously as he reached inside his bag and pulled out a heavily curved piece of lacquered wood and bone. 'What's that, darling?'

'It's a bow,' he replied calmly.

Amanjit stared, thinking, *Come on, Vik, you can't be serious.* 'Bhai, the down-draft from the rotors will screw up your shot!' he shouted. 'Even you can't—'

Vikram strung the bow. 'Of course I can.' He leaned towards the pilot. 'Can you get us directly above that helicopter? Stay high, though – I don't want them aware of us yet.'

The pilot nodded uneasily, and the chopper swung about and swooped.

Majid Khan looked up as a helicopter, one of the little city-hoppers the rich used, came into view high above. It was hovering at about three hundred feet, just a silhouette. He frowned. It was a little close for comfort – was it lost? That wouldn't be unheard of in the Mumbai night sky. He squinted, peering at it, as something tiny flared, briefly illuminating the cabin.

Is that a man up there on the landing struts? What's the idiot doing?

Then something flew straight down – his first instinct was 'rocket-launcher', and he shouted in alarm, hurling himself to

the stones and burying his head. Something went *thwunk!* into
the fuselage of the helicopter on the roof-top pad beside him . . .

. . . and nothing happened.

Majid looked up nervously from the ground. What he saw was
surreal: an arrow was sticking from the cabin of Bakli's chopper.
An arrow? But it was glowing like a coal. *What on Earth?* He got up
slowly and carefully took a couple of steps towards it.

As if in slow motion, the helicopter bulged, expanding like an
inflating beach ball, as the fuselage split apart in all directions,
billowing fire blossoming from every fissure. The concussion hit
him and before he knew what was happening, he was flying backwards. His heels caught the rim of the roof and he cartwheeled,
over and over, into the darkness below.

The pilot stared, aghast. He was now clutching a silver crucifix –
he was clearly a Christian – and saying '*Jesus!!*' over and over.

Vikram grinned. 'Okay, there's room now! Take her down,
fast as you can!'

The man stared from Vikram to Sunita, who gave her approval.
'But . . . he just . . . you just . . . *Jesus Christ!* You just blew up that
chopper!'

'We're rescuing two queens! We're saving the world!' Sunita
shouted. 'Take it down!' She looked at Vikram, her face alight. 'I
love a big entrance.'

The pilot swallowed and his eyes glazed over, as if reminding
himself that this was Bollywood – so it was just special effects,
right? None of it could be real.

They plummeted earthwards.

The whole room shook and plaster cascaded in a choking cloud
from the ceiling. For an instant, Ravindra felt an appalling fear.
The five ghostly queens turned to him, hands to mouths, even his

dauntless Halika, and Deepika and Rasita instantly started fighting his mental control. He reasserted it quickly, gripped their heads and turned them back to the screen where *Swayamvara Live!* was continuing its tortuous finale. Much of the footage was composed of flashbacks to earlier episodes as the audience of millions relived the highs and lows of the contestants' journey to this point.

Rasita looked close to death. Her frail body was wracked by a coughing fit; her skin was almost as pale as the ghosts hovering about her. Deepika had crawled over and was cradling her, oblivious even to the cobra about her neck, which was licking anxiously at her cheeks like a witch's familiar.

To Ravindra's surprise, for all the power he was feeding into Rasita, he felt stronger all the time – he realised with a sudden smile that having all seven queens here had opened new doors for him already: new knowledge, new powers and strange memories, older even than Mandore, were flooding into him. He trembled with excitement, but also with fear: he felt incredibly potent, yet he sensed heightened danger too.

Seizing his mobile, he rang Majid Khan to demand an explanation for the explosion, but there was no reply. The cacophony from the television screen drowned everything as yet another singer came onstage: Shah Rukh Khan – yes, SRK himself! – brought in to spice up the big finale.

Ravindra snarled furiously and stood. A rattling sound penetrated his triple-glazed windows: small-arms fire outside. Onscreen, Sunita Ashoka was clapping her hands joyously as SRK began one of his hits. Ravindra stared at her . . .

. . . and finally realised the game being played: though Sunita's face was still buried beneath that heavy veil, her hands were visible, and they were wrong: too big, too *masculine* . . .

He swore virulently, left his queens and strode out from under the canopy, ripping the gauzy curtains aside and heading for the doors to the stairwell. The puppet-body of the Bihari maidservant Halika had possessed lay there, motionless. He snarled and gestured, and suddenly Halika looked out from the woman's eyes once again. She climbed to her feet, her eyes betraying alarm.

'What's happening out there?' he demanded, the sound of gunfire still reverberating through the building, now interspersed with cries of fear from the gardens below. 'Find out!' he ordered.

Even as Halika hurried from him, a door opened above him at the top of the stairs to the rooftop helipad. A slender shape stepped through: Vikram Khandavani, bow and arrow in his hand. There were other people behind him. Ravindra roared in disbelief as an arrow shot towards him. He was too far from the chamber, so instead, he threw himself forward into the stairwell, and felt the arrow sweep harmlessly past his shoulder, then he was plummeting down. His arms opened like wings, long-forgotten spells pouring from his mouth as he fell.

Above and behind him, Halika snarled like a wild cat, and Vikram shouted, his words indiscernible. As Ravindra dropped, distance shredded his control of the minds of the girls. Around him the house exploded with life as men flooded in below. But behind Vikram's bow and Amanjit Singh's sword, he'd glimpsed a face he knew, and his heart soared.

Sunita Ashoka is here! The fools have brought her to me!

CHAPTER THIRTY

Bearer of Bad Tidings

Dilli, 1192

Chand woke and flinched in dread as a hand touched his. A circle of faces surrounded him, weathered, frightened faces. An old man with black skin and white hair bent over him, apparently trying to see if he lived. They drew back with a sudden exhalation, as if they all used the same lungs to breathe.

'Ji? Ji? Pani?' The old man thrust a waterskin nozzle against his lips and Chand gulped gratefully. Then he remembered the past hours of terrifying flight.

Somehow he'd got to his horse and galloped from the fray even as Ravindra's men were closing in. Enough Chauhamanas warriors managed to hold their ground, on foot and fighting for their lives, to delay his pursuers, allowing him to escape before Ghori's men overwhelmed them. He could still hear Ravindra's furious cries, fading into the distance.

After that, everything was a blur. He'd fled along roads choked with broken, exhausted footmen wary of men looking like officers. Some recognised him and looked to him for guidance, but his mission was more urgent than saving small groups of refugees and deserters. He had to get to Dilli before news of the defeat. It helped that few had managed to keep their horses, and fewer still were fleeing to Dilli, the apparent destination of their foes. The army had disintegrated, and there was no one to pull it together; each man was intent on returning to his own home town. The few Rajput warriors he found were as frightened as the peasant soldiers, seeking only to get to their own ancestral fortresses, where they could feel safe again.

The hardest job was keeping his horse alive. Without the knowledge he had learned at the Gurukul, hard-won under Vishwamitra's stern eye, they would both have faltered, but he kept them going, leaving the refugees and deserters far behind. All through the day they rode slowly, conserving strength, while he sang mantras to enhance the energy and sustenance of their meagre rations. They slept through the hottest part of the day and woke at dusk to find this peasant family gathered about him.

'What tidings, ji?' the old man asked him.

He sought a way to soften the news, while still making sure they understood the full import of his words. 'The Mohammedans were victorious,' he told them.

They cowered, and the old man asked, 'What must we do?'

'Get out of the path of their army. They'll come down this road, and if they find you, they'll take all you have. Go north or south, find shelter with the Tomaras or the Gahadavalas. Stay away from Chauhamanas lands.'

'What of the raja?' the old man asked, in a quavering voice.

'Prithviraj Chauhan is dead.'

They took this in silently, and then the old man's wife began to wail.

Chand slipped into Dilli anonymously, an hour before dawn, two days after the battle. He had traversed a hundred and fifty miles, mostly under blazing sun, on a single horse he'd never ridden before the battle. It was a great feat, but it would be meaningless if he hadn't arrived ahead of the news of defeat.

The Qila Rai Pithora was eminently defensible if fully manned – but the flower of the Chauhamanas nobility were dead at Tarain, along with all their allies. Prince Kola held the fortress with only a token force, just enough to dissuade opportunist raids by other tribes. It was simple enough for Chand to climb the walls and slip past the sentries. It would be simpler still for Ghori to storm it.

He went first to his own apartments, stealing through the servants' entrance like a thief, past dozing guards, mentally scolding them but thankful they slept all the same.

He slipped into his second wife's room. The young woman was tossing in her sleep, moaning in the fit of some vision. 'Gauran. Hush. It's me.'

Gauran woke instantly, and clutched his hand. Her room reeked from the hot, sweaty musk of her body. 'I saw the bad man! The bad man has come!' Her whisper was raw, filled with dread. She clutched the dark crystal at her throat. 'Ravindra has come!'

He had never spoken the name of his Enemy to her; hearing it on her lips now frightened him more than anything. 'Listen, Gauran, you must run! You must run, and *never* be found. If the bad man catches you, it would be better to have never lived.'

'Go?' She looked panicky, and then abruptly she was sly. 'Will you come with me? Will you finally leave that ghastly slug Kamla and come with me?'

A kind of future opened up to him: they could flee south, she and him, and find refuge, safe from Ravindra, safe from Ghori. Bengal maybe? Or the far south, far from the Rajput lands. She and him . . .

Kamla would miss me, and I her . . . but she would go on. And I would

never see Sanyogita again, but she has never been mine . . . . Perhaps that's
the best we can salvage from this life.

'Yes,' he whispered, 'yes. But first I must warn Prince Kola.
He must know what has befallen us.'

'No! Come now!' Gauran implored him. 'I don't trust that
snake-eyed turd.'

Neither do I, but he is a Chauhan, and his mother is now in deadly
peril.

'At the very least, I must tell Queen Sanyogita.'

Gauran's eyes blazed. 'You're still in *love* with that condes-
cending pleasure-saturated mirror-watching Rathod? She *still*
owns your heart!' She shoved him. 'You bed me and your fat ugly
Kamla and yet you're still in love with that whore!'

'No! No, I'm not, Gauran – I've let her go!'

Liar, his conscience jeered.

'No, you haven't!' Gauran screamed, then she pulled herself
into a bundle, turning her head away. 'Go! I don't need you. I
don't want you. You're pathetic, Chand Bardai! You're nothing to
me! Run to your *fucking* Sanyogita, now her husband is out of the
way!' She tore the crystal from around her neck and flung it at
him. 'Take your ghastly trinket away and don't ever come near
me again!'

She slapped away the hand he reached out to her, then scram-
bled to her feet and fled into the maze of the zenana. She was too
fast for him to follow, so he let her go.

Instead he went and woke Kamla, and told her the news of the
battle in the calmest tones he could muster. He retrieved the
journal of Aram Dhoop and scrawled page after page of notes
while she cried, then wrapped it in greased leathers, bound the
Padma heart-stone within, its mysteries still unplumbed, and
gave it to Kamla.

'Dearest Kamla, you must go to your kin in Pushkar. Hide this in your home, beneath the house-shrine. I will find it at need. Go now, before news of the battle reaches the city and panic blocks the roads.'

'I don't understand. My place is with you.' Kamla swept him into a tight embrace. 'Husband, where are our elder sons? Sur, and Sunder, and Sujan? Tell me where they are!'

He swallowed, tried to find words, but she read the tale in his face. 'No,' she whispered. '*No . . .*'

'I must go,' he said, feeling every grain of sand that passed in the hour-glass. 'I must tell the queen, and Prince Kola. I must help prepare the defence of the city.'

'No!' Kamla replied. 'Come away with me, Chand. I am your *wife*: I *need* you. Your remaining children need you. Come with us! Live, for all of us!'

He turned away.

'I'll kill myself,' Kamla whispered. 'I can't live without you.'

'Of course you can,' he replied, not believing that, at least. 'Don't be foolish, Kamla. Pack up the house, only the essentials, and go, now! I'll see you in Pushkar, I promise!'

She seized on that vow. 'You *promise* – truly?'

'Of course,' he lied.

Chand went to the royal enclosure as the sun rose, riding so that anyone observing would not realise he'd been here for hours already. The walls of the Qila Rai Pithora were burnished by the first rays of light of the new day. The streets were still quiet, a ground mist covering the hollows and turning the distance into haze. The city slept, unaware that its days of glory were already gone.

He tried to think how long it might be before other messengers came, but his brain was foggy from being awake too long. Gauran's face haunted him, but she had vanished and no one had seen her leave. He had the skills; he would find her later, and in his mind, his plan still held: they would run and hide, live out their days together in peace. He would find a solution to her madness. Kamla was packing in secret; she would take their remaining sons — and Gauran's daughter Rajabai — to safety. They would soon be gone. From then, it would be only a few hours before the news that the court poet's family was fleeing Dilli would be everywhere.

The sleepy guards looked startled as the renowned Chand Bardai swung from the horse, no entourage in sight. A few asked questions, but he waved them off, pulling aside a servant and asking to see Queen Sanyogita.

He was shown to a small, latticed turret overlooking a garden, where the queen sat with two ladies-in-waiting. She waved them away as he approached, and his heart almost broke to see her. He'd been avoiding her for years, no easy feat in a palace in which both had important roles, but women led largely separate lives from the men, so it was possible to establish and maintain distance. But her face still made his head swim and his heart pound. She had aged gracefully; in her mid-thirties she was still considered the beauty of the realm, Prithvi's greatest jewel. Childbirth had not harmed her figure and few lines marked her face; those that did lent dignity, enhancing and not marring her loveliness.

'Dear Chand,' she called as he knelt. She bade him rise, and seized his hand. 'What news?'

He swallowed, unable to speak as he was suddenly forced to confront the truth. When a king died, so too must his wives. *Sati! It is Mandore, all over again!*

Better she die than fall into Ravindra's hands, said the logical part of his brain. *But what if she ran too?* it added cruelly. *What if she ran with me?* Wasn't that his wildest dream? But he knew she would never consent. She knew her role: all this splendour and glory had a price.

'My queen,' he began, as tears stung his eyes. 'My queen, my queen . . .' Abruptly, all the strength left his legs and he found himself on the ground, the wet grass soaking his knees as he clutched at her waist, burying his face in her dress. 'My queen, they're dead. They're all dead.'

She held him to her, rocking like an unsteady statue. When he dared to look up, she was a goddess of sorrow, tears streaming from a face carved in marble. Distractedly, she looked down at him and pushed him away gently. 'I must go,' she said vaguely. 'There is so much to be done.'

She walked away, leaving him kneeling on the wet grass, trembling uncontrollably.

On shaky legs, he clambered upright. He staggered back into the main palace, seized the arm of the first guard he encountered and demanded to see Prince Kola.

He was shown to a chamber and left alone. Clearly the guard didn't believe he was who he said, and long minutes crawled by until booted feet stamped into the room. 'Get up, you!' Kola snapped, swallowing from a goblet. His hair was awry and face groggy. He was still in his bed-shirt and looking around the room blankly. 'Where is Chand Bardai? I'm told he—'

He suddenly stared at the travel-stained figure before him. 'Chand? Is that you?'

Chand wiped his hands over his face, leaving it streaked and dirty. He could almost hear the young man's heart hammering as his complacent cynicism fell away. 'My prince, I have bad news. The worst news of all.'

Kola slumped onto a bench, his face going slack. 'Father?'

'They're all dead, Kola. Your father, Govinda, Khande, Samata-simha: all of them are dead. The Mohammedans were victorious.'

He shifted until he knelt in formal obeisance. 'You are raja now. King Kola, long may you reign.'

I'd estimate you have around one week.

Kola convened a meeting of those counsellors who had not gone to fight, and they argued the morning away on a fruitless discussion on whether to defend the city or flee. Servants came and went. Chand chafed, dying to go, to find Gauran and get her to safety, but he couldn't in honour leave just now, not openly. The prince would have been within his rights to arrest him if he'd even suggested it. So instead he had to join these debates that just ran in circles. Then a eunuch bowed his way in and whispered in Kola's ear. The young prince stiffened, then buried his head.

'My Lord?' asked the eldest of the counsellors.

Kola looked up, his face pallid and slack. 'My mother the queen is dead. She has committed jauhar, together with her handmaidens.'

Even though this was the news they were all waiting to hear, Chand felt his own face crumple. Yet again he had let everything he held dear slip from his hands. Sanyogita – Darya – was lost once more on the circle of samsara.

He tried to pray, and found he couldn't, not when the gods had so betrayed them.

Some immeasurable time later a messenger came. He was a young Rajput of the Tomaras, a prisoner released by Ghori to deliver his messages to Prince Kola. Kola saw him alone, and when the prince emerged, it was with a dozen soldiers of the royal household at his flanks. He strode into the council chamber where Chand was conferring with three greybeards, fretting over whether Kamla had got away and wondering where Gauran might be. They all turned as Kola entered.

'What are the demands, my Lord?' Chand asked for all of them.

Kola sucked in his bottom lip as his escort fanned about the room. At last he sat down, as if aware that he was standing like a recalcitrant boy caught stealing sweets. 'The invader is generous,' he said finally. 'More generous than I had expected.'

The other three counsellors exhaled with some relief. Chand waited, because he knew it would not be so easy as this.

'We keep our own kingship,' Kola went on, 'so long as we acknowledge the overlordship of the Mohammedans. They will occupy this fortress. Conversion to Islam will be required among the ruling class. But we keep our possessions. We retain our rank.' He sounded lost, disbelieving. 'There are some other, minor prices . . . but fair . . . Ghori is fair.'

Chand looked at him, struggling to keep the strain from his voice. 'What minor prices, my Lord?'

Kola wouldn't meet his eye. 'Nothing I cannot afford, Chand Bardai.' He made a small gesture to someone behind Chand and a mailed hand fell on his shoulders. 'You and a few others, delivered alive.'

It took a moment for him to respond. 'I'm to be sent to Ghori?'

'No. To the imam, Mehtan Ali.'

They chained Chand inside a foetid cart that a farmer had used to carry his poultry to market. He struggled to breathe without pain – a soldier's boot had broken two of his ribs when he'd tried to flee. Without his arrows and without the strength of youth, he was no match for the fighting men. Kola had put it about that Chand had betrayed Prithvi's battle plans and that was why he was being handed over. It made a better story than the truth when Kola needed to look strong and prevent panic among the people. Better to blame someone else for the failures of the Chauhamanas line.

The cart joined a train of similar caged vehicles going north on roads choked with refugees, but after a time Chand stopped looking at those he passed. It was better to hide his face in the thin cotton blanket and concentrate on just breathing. Time ceased to matter. They gave him food but wouldn't unlock his chains, forcing him to eat with his face pushed into the bowl like an animal. There were two toilet stops a day, which weren't enough. Even that wasn't the worst of it.

The worst, the very worst, was that Gauran was in the next cage.

She sat cross-legged, singing through bloodied lips, her fragile mind completely gone. She was so filthy now that even the soldiers wouldn't touch her. He tried to call to her at night, but she never responded. Nothing he said could reach her.

The journey took three days, until they rolled into a country lane lined with soldiers and mamluks – the soldier-slaves of Ghori's army. The wagon-train had clearly arrived at a time of worship: did these Mohammedans do anything else but pray? He had the bizarre experience of being driven past rank upon rank of Turks kneeling and bowing towards him and he marvelled again that these men, poorly equipped and hardly armoured at all, had been able to withstand the might of the Rajputs.

The logical part of him supplied answers: discipline, cohesion, unity. Total belief in their ultimate victory, better tactics – and utter ruthlessness. Their commander was not constrained by the ritualistic niceties that ruled the Rajput warriors.

War is just a game for us: a sport with casualties. These people are different. We fight to score points. They fight to win.

They left behind the ranks of praying warriors, the weird calls of the priests fading as they rolled into the courtyard of a beautiful mansion festooned with Turkic and Afghan banners. The caged wagons rattled to a halt. He looked all about until he finally spotted Gauran's wagon, but her head was buried in her blanket, as usual.

'Chand Bardai.' He looked up through the bars at Ravindra's leering face.

'I told you not to be taken alive,' the false imam told him. 'Now you're going to find out why.' He turned to the nearest officer. 'This one – and that girl! They belong to me!'

CHAPTER THIRTY-ONE

Into the Fray

Mumbai, 13 November 2010:
Day 6 of Swayamvara Live! (Final Night)

Uma looked at the crowd from beneath her heavy veil. The studio audience was fizzing with impatience, now they had finally realised they were being toyed with. At every advertisement break they shouted for the contestants. Some were even demanding a refund. The stars they'd brought in to entertain the crowd and give the event more status were looking about them anxiously.

Everybody was shouting now. *Where are the contestants? What are the tests? When is Sunita going to choose?* The clamour grew louder by the minute. The media pack was frenzied, demanding action. The producer was having a nervous breakdown. Pravit was weeping in his room like a child. Alok had passed out drunk. She'd had security evict Mandeep's lawyers and locked him in his suite. And Jez kept looping footage, laughing hysterically to himself about 'twenty-five grand down the drain'.

This was chaos even by Mumbai standards. This was career-wrecking.

*

Almost before the chopper had landed on Shiv Bakli's roof shots began to zip around. Vikram kicked the door open as they landed and was out and moving, shooting impossible arrows that flew around corners and vanished. A man screamed below, and then another. Amanjit grabbed Sunita, his sword in his other hand. 'Stay behind me!' he shouted, then looked at the pilot, who was clearly torn between loyalty to Sunita and self-preservation. 'Stay here as long as you can! We might need to leave this way as well!'

The man nodded, his eyes bulging with fear. Amanjit leaped out, then reached back for Sunita, who looked at him with enthralled eyes. *She's insane*, he thought. *Vik and I are storming a gangster's fortress with a bow and a sword and a demented actress . . . sorry, who am I calling insane?*

He gripped the sword tighter and pulled her along behind him as they followed Vikram towards the door that had to lead down into the mansion.

Let's just go with it then, he thought, asking himself if a sane person doing the insane could still claim sanity. And then he wondered what the difference between mad and sane really was.

Deepika caught Ras as she slumped sideways and her eyes rolled back in her skull, while her chest quivered: it looked to her horribly like the onset of a heart attack. '*Ras!*' she cried desperately, trying to bring her to consciousness, '*Ras!*'

The gods seemed deaf to her pleading, as Ras' limbs twitched, her chest heaving. Her skin was cold and slick, foam was bubbling from her lips. The cobra Dee had momentarily forgotten was coiled about her neck peered in, disquieted by her movements. For a moment Deepika froze, but that helped no one, and as Ras arched her back and began to convulse she grabbed her, calling her name, with no idea what to do but determined to save her.

The snake about her shoulders tightened its coils and reared back, hood flaring and fangs bared.

Vikram sent a volley of astras into the gardens below. The homing-arrows hunted out the men hidden from sight, giving him time to kick open the door and dash down the stairs. Amanjit and Sunita were right behind him. When a massive figure strode through the doors below he fired on instinct, without an astra prepared – it was Ravindra, who dodged, flinging himself forward and outwards and vanishing down the stairwell. Vikram cursed. There might not be another chance.

Where are the girls?

A narrow-eyed East Indian woman in an ornate sari stood on the landing below. *One of the gangster's women?* He ran down the stairs, shouting, 'Get out of here, you! *Get out!*'

Too late he realised his mistake: the woman's dark face split open around fangs that would have scared a sabre-toothed tiger and multiple arms tipped with barbed claws erupted from her sides. Her legs bent and she sprang at him, shrieking like a fiend as she came flying across the central void in a single bound.

Ravindra landed at the foot of the stairwell amidst a crowd of his hired thugs, who gasped as he came crashing onto the marble-floored lobby like a dropped piano, smashing the tiles beneath him. He felt them bend over him and one called, 'It's the boss! He's dead! Shiv Bakli's dead!'

The hell he is. He pulled his body back together and rose, re-knitting flesh and bone as he did so. All about him men quailed and started backing away, their faces overcome with terror. 'Get up there and kill them all!' he roared, snarling and spitting blood. He invoked all he was, all the power and terror of a deathless wizard-king.

They panicked, those at the back the first to flee screaming.

He seized the closest and ripped his head from his torso, punishment for his disobedience. One or two raised guns, but he spoke a word that froze the mechanisms. They all stood stock-still for an endless moment – and then they ran, these bullies who terrorised Mumbai, gibbering in terror.

A movement caught his eye: a man in a red bandana, one of Khan's men, vanished out the front door. Then he heard a ghastly female shrieking, and cries of pain from a male throat – some fool had fallen into Halika's grasp. He snarled and rose through the stairwell air, floating upwards on spells and hatred. As he rose he conjured an extra pair of arms that sprouted from his shoulders, then a bow and quiver, and a sword for each new arm.

He roared in defiance as he ascended the air, '*I am Ravana! And I am coming for you, Aram Dhoop!*'

The snarling, spitting woman-thing struck Vikram like a tiger and they flew together through the air and smashed against the curved stairwell wall. The arrow snapped in his hand; his bow was lost in the impact. Black stars exploded in the back of his head and he fell, dazed, as this ripping-hating-creature pinned his body down and started tearing at him.

'Got you!' it shrieked in Halika's voice.

Then Amanjit's boot connected and sent her flying, crashing onto the landing below. Amanjit leaped over him, shouting a battle cry from ancient Ajmer, and landed, perfectly balanced, his weight forward, on two stairs. He swung his sword, and Halika leaped aside, moving at a bewildering speed, more like a bug than a person. Amanjit's blade carved air as she sprang to the railing. Her limbs bunched, and then she leaped for Sunita, standing alone at the top of the stairs.

Vikram tried to make his stunned body respond, but the back of his skull felt like paste and he could hardly see. Sunita's mouth flew open and she barely had time to scream. In slow motion the creature unfurled its taloned arms as it flew through the air with deadly grace.

Amanjit's warrior reactions saved them: a flash of silver whirled past as his sacred kirpan knife spun through the air and sank into Halika's side with a wet punching sound. She shrieked and contorted as she flew and instead of enveloping Sunita, she smashed into the railing, clawing for purchase, spitting blood as she bounced on the stairs and slipped down towards Vikram.

From beyond the open double doors they heard Deepika, shouting in anguish, and with a cry Amanjit turned and ran down the stairs, brandishing his sword and calling her name. Then a voice echoed from the stairwell like the roar of a train rushing through a tunnel.

'*I am Ravana! I am coming for you, Aram Dhoop!*'

With a curse Vikram snatched up his bow, reaching for an arrow with his other hand, then dashed to interpose himself between Halika and Sunita, who had the 'damsel in distress' look nailed effortlessly.

'Sunita! Stay down!' he shouted, as he launched himself towards her.

CHAPTER THIRTY-TWO

Her Fractured Soul

Mumbai, 13 November 2010:
Day 6 of Swayamvara Live! *(Final Night)*

Majid Khan came to, half-buried in the recently turned soil of a flower bed on Shiv Bakli's ornamental roof-garden two storeys up, two floors below the main roof. His back and skull felt like they had been pummelled with a massive mallet. His face was seared red-raw and his ash-covered leather coat was still smouldering. He stared at the sky, astonished to be alive, then he sat up, still dazed.

Who the hell uses arrows in the twenty-first century? And why did that chopper blow up anyway?

With a roar a helicopter took off from the roof and lifted erratically into the night sky. Majid staggered to the outdoor stairs and peered down. On the lawn below were three of Bakli's men with arrows jutting from their breasts. He didn't know them, and didn't care. He fumbled for his gun, and its weight reassured him, although his first instinct was still to run. Instead, he hurried down the stairs and found himself at the corner of the house.

I can turn the tide. I'll earn Bakli's gratitude – or put a bullet in his back.

With a crash, the main doors of the house flew open, disgorging a clump of Bakli's thugs running for their lives, and his momentary resolve wavered again. *What the——?*

A red bandana appeared at the doors in the wake of Bakli's fleeing men: Tanvir! Uncharacteristically, his unflappable lieutenant looked dazed, which added to Majid's alarm. He called to him and Tanvir's head whirled before he ran towards Majid, shouting, 'This is insane, sir. We've got to get out!' Behind him, the house rocked with voices that sounded barely human.

'What's going on?' Majid demanded.

Tanvir looked bewildered. 'Bakli . . . *it's not real.* We've got to get out of here!'

'No!' If Bakli found out they ran, it would be their death warrant. 'What about Shiv? Is he dead?'

Tanvir's expression shifted to horror. 'No. But he's . . . I've never seen anything like it.'

Majid Khan bit his lip. *If he's not dead, I have to go in. I have to be seen to be helping!* 'Tanvir, call in back-up! Call in every man we've got!' He brandished his Glock. 'I'm going in.' When Tanvir looked at him like he was insane, he said, 'Do it!' and turned to the house.

I'll be the man who saved Shiv Bakli – I'll be a gangland hero! Then try calling me coward!

Deepika watched Ras striving for each gasping breath and urged her on with more prayers and invocations. 'Sister! *Sister! Ras! Live! Please!*' She pumped at her chest, puffed air into her mouth. The cobra peered down at her, looking from one to the other as if puzzled, almost human in its confusion, but it didn't bite. Shiva wore a cobra about his neck, she suddenly recalled: the symbol of his power over life and death. *Lord Shiva, hear my prayer! Save her!*

The four-eyed stone demon stood over them, also watching her, indecision on its monstrous face. Slowly its limbs flexed and it opened its mouth, revealing a purplish tongue that licked its stone lips. But it didn't attack, or even speak.

The four remaining ghost-queens hissed and snarled, pawing at Deepika with wispy fingers but never quite touching her. They looked lost without Ravindra or Halika. 'Sister? Sister?' they whispered. 'What are you doing?'

From the open door, confusing sounds billowed and throbbed, half-drowned by sound of the live climax of *Swayamvara Live!* — but it was beginning to look more like a riot. The television studio appeared to be in uproar: the crowd was storming the stage. She saw Bollywood stars, her idols, her heroes and heroines, shouting and pointing and shoving at angry fans. Was that Vishi Ashoka, trying to punch someone? But it meant nothing; all that mattered was that poor Rasita, who had barely lived, was dying, and she couldn't save her.

Then Amanjit leaped through the doorway, a sword in his fist and his face aflame with courage, and she almost died of love and terror. As one, the four queens flexed their half-seen claws, calling, 'Lord Ravindra, it's Shastri!'

A dark voice echoed from the stairwell, 'Rip his heart out.'

The four queens spread out, teeth bared like jackals, and the stone-demon swirled its arms and drew its four swords in a terrifying whirl of steel.

'Sunita!' Vikram called, tearing up the stairs while readying another arrow, 'Get behind me!'

But Sunita was paralysed, lost in the terror of seeing Halika unleashed. The dead queen howled her possessed body up over the railing, then went at the actress again.

Vikram threw himself upwards in a desperate lunge to get in

front of Sunita, and was just in time to have Halika slam into him again, bearing him downwards onto the marble stairs. Four taloned arms plunged into him, ripping his shirt and the skin beneath, while a rib cracked and his hip was gouged by the hard edge of the marble step. In the numbing impact he lost the arrow, but flailing, his right hand caught her chin just as she was trying to plunge her fangs into his shoulder.

Halika screeched, spittle and blood spraying over his face, and thrashed about, seeking to free herself, still trying to bite and tear at him.

His left hand dropped the bow and he pulled Amanjit's kirpan knife from the woman's side, then slammed it in again. She screamed in his face at the blow, her face exultant.

Then a bejewelled arm jabbed past his face from behind him and plunged his lost arrow into the left eye-socket of Halika's crowing face. The dead queen shrieked like a banshee, her human arms clutching impotently at the arrow, the others pulling away from him and trying in vain to wrench out the shaft. She staggered backwards, struck the low railing, toppled down the stairwell – and was gone.

Vikram twisted back and saw his rescuer: Sunita looked aghast, disbelieving. He almost swooned in gratitude and pain, and his hand flew to his belly, whispering spells of healing, trying to keep body and soul united. Sunita stared down at his torn shirt and the blood welling through and swayed dizzily.

'It's worse than it looks,' he panted. 'Stay with me, Sunita.' He looked down the stairs. With a silent, agonised struggle, he lurched to his feet, picked up his bow from where it had fallen a few stairs below and staggered back towards Sunita.

Why did I bring her here? Then he remembered the hope he'd had of healing a centuries-old separation.

Ras! Where are you?

But as he opened his mouth to shout, Ravindra rose inside the stairwell, brandishing a bow in one set of arms and two swords in a lower set. He hung in the air, majestic and deadly. Rotating to face Vikram, he wasted no breath on taunts: his arrow burst into flames as it flew at point-blank range straight at Vikram's heart.

Deepika was nowhere to be seen in the smoke-filled, silk-hung pleasure-dome Amanjit found within the double doors, but he heard her shout as four pale things with slavering eyes swam through the air towards him. The spectral queens were almost enough to paralyse him with fear, but there was something more: something big and strangely shaped, lurking behind them.

Fire! That's what worked last time . . .

He brandished his scimitar while sweeping up a candelabra and jabbing the candle flames at the silk canopy. The queens lunged at him, but he hacked off a handful of the burning silk and waved it in front of him in a desperate attempt to defend himself. Talons raked at him, and one slashed his back to the bone, making him arch involuntarily. He swivelled reflexively and jammed the burning silks at the ghostly spectre that had struck him – she ignited as well, and backed away, shrieking.

'Amanjit!' Deepika's cry reached him from somewhere inside the canopy which he'd just set ablaze.

Dear God, I'll burn us all to death! But there were no other options he could think of. He swung his wad of burning silk at another of the dead queens and drove her backwards until she was spinning like some kind of pyromaniac gymnast, then forced the other two spectral women away and darted between them. He still couldn't see what it was, but he was instinctively giving the dark shape behind them a wide berth.

Flames closed behind him and earned him a momentary respite as the dead queens drew back, mewling in frustration. Then a face flashed in the sullen firelight and pierced his heart. 'Deepika!'

She was kneeling over a prone form and shouting for him, and his heart lurched. '*Ras!*' He was running to join her when Deepika screamed a warning and he spun to see the immense dark shape he'd glimpsed, now twelve foot tall and apparently carved of stone, lumbering towards him with four flailing blades.

'*Lakshmana*,' the thing rumbled, 'I am Khar: your nemesis.' The swords whirred in a synchronised blur, cleaving the air to shreds as the monster closed in on Amanjit.

Amanjit tried to distract it with a flick of burning silk and almost lost his arm as he barely managed to evade the slashing blades. He stumbled backwards, parrying with his one blade against two and then three blades at once. He darted away, more mobile than his giant assailant, madly flailing his burning cloth about him to force the remaining queens away from his back as they tried to close in on him again.

Then the massive statue-thing stepped from beneath the burning canopy, its four eyes blazing and its swords poised to strike.

Vikram moved like he'd never moved before, his right hand sweeping Amanjit's kirpan across his chest.

If the arrow had not been ensorcelled to go straight for the heart, he would have been impaled by it, but instead, the point struck the kirpan blade like a thunderbolt, exploding against his chest and searing his shirt. The blade chimed and vibrated, but it didn't break – just as well, because Ravindra leaped onto the balustrade, pulled back his right lower arm and swung the sword it held with all his strength. Sunita shrieked and backed away up the stairs as Vikram parried with the knife, ducking as he deflected the blow over his head so Ravindra's sword shattered against the stonework, sending fragments flying.

'Sunita! Stay behind me!' Vikram shouted. *If he gets to her, we're sunk . . .*

The blade in the sorcerer-king's lower left hand swept around to slash at Vikram's neck. Again, he ducked low, letting the blade sing over his head. He could see Ravindra angling towards Sunita, his leg muscles tightening, ready to launch himself at her. But even as Ravindra took off, Vikram was lunging with the kirpan outstretched. Ravindra tried to block him with his broken right-hand blade, but Vikram lunged past it and buried the kirpan in the sorcerer's thigh. Ravindra bellowed as Vikram thudded into him, his whole body weight hitting his Enemy smack on the knee. He hadn't the bulk, nor momentum enough to knock him over the edge, but he did manage to make Ravindra fall short of the actress as his knee-joint buckled and some kind of tendon or ligament snapped.

Ravindra bellowed in pain and stumbled sideways as Sunita backed away up the stairs, her eyes huge. Vikram scrabbled to get to Ravindra before the huge man turned on him and blocked another massive sword-thrust, but this time Amanjit's kirpan flew from his hand, dislodged by the force of the blow. He heard the knife skittering down the marble steps, now out of reach. Vikram, scrambling for purchase, grabbed blindly and ended up hooking his fingers in a necklace around Ravindra's neck, but it snapped and he fell, tumbling to the next landing and sprawling, the string of crystals still in his hand.

Ravindra spun away from Sunita, lifted his bow and sent an arrow flashing into position. He was ten yards away – and Vikram's hand blurred as he lifted the necklace he was holding. He glimpsed the dark crystals in his fist, at first acting purely on instinct as he raised it, and then realising that he was holding the necklace of heart-stones. The arrow struck his palm – and the heart-stone he was gripping.

Purple light dazzled him, knocking him backwards as it radiated outwards, towards Ravindra: a soundless wave of force as the stone shattered. From the large room below came a deathly screech from one of the ghost-queens: a sound that reverberated through the entire mansion.

Ravindra staggered as the shockwave of the heart-stone's destruction struck him. Beyond him, Vikram saw Sunita had reached the door that led to the helipad, but the concussive force punched her into the wall and she slid down it, dazed. His left fist was numbed and seared, but he ignored that and took a moment to touch each stone until he gained a flash of a familiar face. He tore it off the chain and pocketed it.

He seized a third and lifted it like a shield, just as Ravindra fired again.

This time he actively called Ravindra's arrow to it and the two warriors were thrown apart once more by another violent concussion . . . and another ghost-queen died for ever in the room behind him, howling for the last time as her long, ghastly existence finally ended.

He raised the necklace again as he backed down the steps and retrieved Amanjit's kirpan, then an old spell popped into his brain from past lives, and he uttered the words that transformed the knife into a curved sword. 'Want to try again?' he panted. 'Three stones left. Three dead queens.'

Ravindra brandished the bow and his remaining sword. 'You think they matter any more, boy? They're *nothing*! I've done what was needed with them! The only two things that matter here are Darya and Padma – and only *one* Padma will matter in the end. The swayamvara was about finding out which one.' He grinned fiendishly. 'Let's narrow the odds, shall we?' He turned and fired.

Sunita and Vikram cried out in unison as an arrow struck the actress in the right breast and spun her around. She looked down at the shaft jutting from her, her eyes suddenly huge, then slid down the doorframe like a discarded doll.

'One down,' snarled Ravindra. He looked beyond Vikram to the double doors leading back to his private lair. Smoke was billowing out, but he ignored that, flexing his huge legs, ready to jump. 'Let's collect the other!'

As he leaped Vikram was momentarily torn between the stricken actress and those inside. Then he sprang to try and cut Ravindra off, his heart swelling with rage and despair.

Majid Khan ran on shaky legs, angling towards the front door. Behind him, Tanvir was shouting into a phone to the men they had stationed outside awaiting their summons. 'Roll! Roll! It's on! Bakli's house, *now!*'

Majid paused at the double doors and shouted back to his colleague, 'Go around the back!'

Tanvir threw him a look of disbelief. 'Wait for back-up, sir! It's madness in there!' His red bandana was dark with sweat.

'We can't,' Majid told him. 'I'm going in!' *If I say it often enough, perhaps I'll find it in me to do it.*

Tanvir stared – no doubt reflecting that Majid had *never* stuck his neck out for anyone before – then nodded. 'There's a servants' entrance out the back. I'll take that – we'll meet at the top.' He checked his handgun, then sprinted around the nearest corner, heading for the rear.

Inside the front doors, Majid immediately smelled smoke and heard shouts and screaming, all coming from above. He peered into the gloomy stairwell and looked up, catching furtive movement. The lobby here went all the way up to a glassed dome on the roof, five flights up. There was a great din coming from the very top: fighting, women screaming, and increasingly dark clouds of smoke.

As he watched, a small shape fell from above and plummeted to a sickening impact at his feet, bones shattering in a wet, meaty sound that brought bile to his throat. It was a skinny little woman, a Bihari, perhaps, incongruously dressed in a sumptuous sari. He took a step towards her, then stared: there were *four extra arms* protruding from her spine and out on either side, as if she were some kind of mutated insect-creature. One of her eyes was open, fixed on him. The other had an arrow jutting from it. She spat blood and reached towards him with one mangled arm – and then she visibly withered and died. Her mouth fell open and a stream of dark smoke blew from it, then dissipated.

He turned aside and vomited. Beside him the awful creature's mutated arms melted away until she was just a normal woman caught in the wrong place. Somehow that made it worse. With a choked cry he turned and ran. He thought he had intended to flee, to pretend this had never happened, but instead he found himself climbing the stairs, shouting in a deranged frenzy.

It didn't feel like courage at all.

The massive stone thing calling itself 'Khar' came at Amanjit like an out-of-control windmill, its blades carving at him from all sides in a synchronised dance of steel. There was no chance of parrying all four, only evasion as he backed away, then abruptly ramming the burning cloth in his left hand into the face of another of the ghost-queens, trying to sneak up on him. She ignited with a hideous shriek and flew backwards to strike the stone wall of the room. Like the other he'd managed to set alight, she was discomforted but not overly damaged. Still they circled, waiting for their chance. Amanjit ducked another sweeping series of blows from Khar, but managed to snatch a massive wrought-iron candle-stand up in his left hand: it was as long as a spear, and he brandished it, whirling it about him. Two blades chimed off the iron and though it vibrated and bent in his grasp, it held.

'Not enough blades, Lakshmana?' Khar rumbled towards Amanjit, whirling his swords bewilderingly as he came on like a piece of terrifying machinery. 'I have trained for millennia for this re-match!'

Re-match? Lakshmana? What's he raving about? In fact, what is he?

But this wasn't the time to work that out; Khar was coming on to him like a rearing elephant, his steel blades flashing dull orange in the firelight, the marble-tiled floor cracking under his weight. Amanjit rammed the candle-stand into the middle of the flailing blades. With a sound like a machine breaking down, the swords smashed and clanged together as they bent and battered the iron-work out of shape, twisting it beyond recognition.

But Khar's blades were stuck there, trapped in the tangled metal. The rakshasa gaped as he tried to pull his weapons free.

Too slow.

Amanjit gripped his own sword two-handed and thrust the blade into Khar's open mouth, up and into his brain until the tip punched out through the back of the monster's skull. 'Shame about all the training.'

Four eyes abruptly focused on one silver length of steel that ran from the Sikh's hand into its mouth, then winked out as the giant collapsed, sliding backwards and off the blade as it crashed to the marble floor, already crumbling into pieces.

Amanjit whirled to confront the ghostly shapes that were flitting behind him. The remaining queens shrank from him and without another look he dashed into the flame-licked canopy before him, shouting, 'Deepika! *Dee!*'

She turned, struggling with something like a rope at her neck. At her feet, Rasita was clutching her own chest, her face

contorted as it had when she'd had her last heart attack. He felt a
burst of terror as he reached for them both.

Too late, he saw that the thing around Deepika's throat was no
rope but a snake. Its hood flared, its mouth gaped, the twin nee-
dles inside jutting in a fatal curve as it reared and then struck at
him while he stood there, caught in helpless surprise, with no
time to react.

But Deepika was already moving; with both hands she grabbed
the reptile, pulling the serpent away from Amanjit. As she lurched
backwards, the snake turned in her hands and struck, and she
cried out in shock and pain as the fangs buried in her left shoulder. She tried to throw it off as she fell, but it bit her again.

Amanjit grasped the cobra around the base of its skull. It coiled
around his arm, its tail thrashing as it sought for purchase, but he
squeezed, then hammered its head into the nearest pillar until the
snake's skull shattered against the stone. It continued to convulse
as he flung it away, but he ignored it, instead running back to
Deepika, who was sitting down, staring at the bites. 'Dee!'

Beside her, Ras saw him. 'Amanjit?' she whispered, then she
went into shock, her mouth falling open as she kicked twice, her
back arching.

Behind him, one of the dead queens shrieked, a terrifying
sound torn from her throat like a last breath, and a stream of light
flew from the queen into Ras' chest. She convulsed again as she
was momentarily engulfed in a light which seemed to re-start
her, like jumper-leads on a flat car battery. A few seconds
later, another scream from outside the burning curtains tore
the air and another bolt of light flew from the other side of the
chamber – this one struck Deepika full in the chest; she sucked
in some air and rolled into a foetal ball.

Holy Father! Amanjit saw that another of the dead queens
had vanished. So just two left, and they were whimpering and

clinging together, obviously mortally terrified. Beyond them, from the stairwell, Ravindra's voice rolled and thundered.

Amanjit turned back to his fiancée and his sister. Ras had rolled against Deepika and they were holding blindly on to each other, their eyes glazed. But they were both breathing.

The remaining dead queens faded into the shadows. Khar was nothing now but a shattered pile of rubble. But smoke was filling the chamber, and from the door came the renewed clash of blades, while the two most precious women in his universe lay stricken at his feet. Amanjit sucked in a smoke-laced breath and was moving to their aid when a door in the back wall flew open and a man with a gun stepped through.

Vikram reached the double doors just before Ravindra and blocked a weighty overhead blow that made him stagger; the transformed kirpan was nearly dashed from his hands as he parried two more blows which made his knees buckle. He was going under. In desperation he dropped the remaining heart-stones behind him and gripped the hilt with both hands to avoid losing it. Ravindra's sword struck his weapon with such power that the steel belled and throbbed. The sheer weight of the sorcerer-king's blows staggered Vikram backwards into smoke that tore at his lungs. Vikram felt a familiar sinking feeling: of losing, of failure, just as he had in every past life. He tried to launch his own attack, but Ravindra's fist lashed out and he was smashed backwards to land on the threshold of the doorway amidst the swirling smoke, winded and fighting to breathe. He writhed away from a thrust that would have skewered him where he lay, then convulsed as a boot smashed into his side. Suddenly he couldn't move. He stared up at the towering figure above.

Every previous death he'd experienced swarmed through his mind: as Chand, as Doc, as Bhagwan, and all the others too; a litany of failure. Ravindra had *always* been better than him, he was always a step ahead, with mind *and* body. The hopeless unfairness of it all was crushing.

Ravindra smiled as if he too was experiencing the same rush of memories. He bent down and picked up the necklace of remaining heart-stones from the ground. His sword-point hovered above Vikram's chest, then as he prepared to thrust, he snarled, 'You lose for the last time, Aram Dhoop.'

Three realities warred before Detective Majid Khan's eyes.

In one, he paused at the second-to-top landing of the main staircase in time to see Shiv Bakli, the man who owned his soul, preparing to skewer Vikram Khandavani, the *Swayamvara Live!* contestant.

In another reality, he was Jaichand of Kannauj, watching his treacherous cousin, Chand Bardai, face death.

In yet another, a multi-armed beast with a heart of darkness prepared to destroy one who dared oppose him.

Then someone groaned painfully and he glanced up and saw the Bollywood star Sunita Ashoka, skewered through the chest by an arrow, soaked in blood and pale. She saw him and whispered, '*Jaichand* . . .?'

He staggered in the rush of memories of lives he'd never before remembered – and now he knew her, as she knew him. And he knew himself too, to the bottom of his soul.

I've been a faithless friend. I've let men and women suffer to salve my pride. I've destroyed every woman I've ever had in my power, in life after life, because the one I've lusted for in all those lives was always unattainable . . .

. . . because she was my daughter.

And now he remembered the woman on the stairs as a child – *Gauran, my daughter* – although he had never acknowledged her, in his selfish cruelty and pride, refusing to admit he'd misused a serving girl. It had taken his beloved daughter Sanyogita and the treacherous Chand Bardai to give her any kind of life at all . . .

And now Shiv Bakli's going to kill them all . . .

Detective Inspector Majid Khan did the first selfless thing in his life. 'Freeze!' he bellowed, his gun pointing at Shiv Bakli's back and thumbing it to automatic. 'Don't move, Bakli!'

The sword lifted, then plunged as he fired, holding the gun steady as it tried to buck and jolt, pouring a stream of searing lead into the gangster's back.

Ravindra's blow never landed.

Instead, bullets ripped into his back, their impact forcing him into a staccato dance of agony. Vikram slithered out of reach, unable to tear his eyes away from the fall of his Enemy, whose swords clattered to the marble and then, with a great crash, fell to his knees, then onto his face. Even as powerful a being as Ravindra could sustain only so much punishment to the body he possessed. He quivered and went still as blood poured over the marble.

Vikram saw the detective inspector, Majid Khan, standing like a statue on the landing, his eyes like moons.

Jaichand, he thought immediately – but he knew he had nothing further to fear from his once-enemy. He gave him a silent salute as he came to his feet, then they both looked up at the wounded Sunita.

She's still alive . . . there's still time . . .

Looking into the smoke-filled room, Vikram could discern nothing, but everything had gone momentarily quiet. 'Amanjit?' he called in the darkness. 'Deepika? Ras?'

Amanjit recognised the man in the red bandana who'd entered by the rear door: Detective Sergeant Tanvir Allam. The policeman had a massive gun in one fist and a police badge in the other. He looked at Amanjit – and his sword – in apparent shock, then down at the girls. He opened his mouth to shout something.

'Help me!' Amanjit called, jabbing a finger at Ras. 'Get her out of this smoke!'

He waited until he was sure the cop wasn't going to shoot him before sheathing his sword and sweeping Deepika into his arms. He hurried for the door. Throwing a look backwards, he saw to his relief that Tanvir was already bending over Ras, and that his gun was holstered. *Good man!*

Amanjit burst from the smoke-filled room into the stairwell and saw Vikram with Detective Inspector Majid Khan. They were both running up the stairs towards Sunita Ashoka. The actress had an arrow in her; she looked to be at death's door.

'Up!' he called to Tanvir, 'up to the roof! We've got a chopper!' He stepped over the massive body lying in the doorway and felt a tremor of excitement run through him. *Surely that was Ravindra lying face-down, his back a mess of bullet holes?* But there was no time to pause: the room behind him had finally caught fire and the plastered walls were beginning to burn. He cradled Deepika protectively as he ran, dashing past Vikram and Majid Khan as they bent over Sunita.

He came out onto the roof and looked about him. Then he sagged, groaning.

He was dimly aware of sirens in the surrounding streets and gunfire in the gardens below, but that wasn't what made him curse and bow his head. The helipad was empty of all but the wreckage of the first craft.

Sunita's pilot had lost his nerve and fled.

Vikram and Majid laid Sunita down on the empty helipad and Vikram stroked her head. 'Chand?' she whispered. 'Chand? It's so dark . . .'

'It's me, Gauran.' He felt tears begin. 'I'm here.'

'Don't let Ghori's men take me, love. Kill me before they take me.'

'No, no, you're going to live.' He wrenched his phone from his pocket and dialled the emergency number. A voice crackled, and he shouted over it, 'Send an ambulance – a woman is hurt badly! I'm at Shiv Bakli's mansion! *Get here!*' He looked back over his shoulder to see Amanjit lowering Deepika to the roof, and then a man in a red bandana following him, bearing Ras. He recognised the detective sergeant – *Tilak of Mandore* – but any relief he felt was overwhelmed by the sight of all three young women so close to death.

Dear Gods! Have I failed them all?

Tanvir was shouting to Amanjit, 'Snake-bite – king cobra! She has to go to hospital!' Majid Khan was staring at Sunita, trying to speak, but his words were being drowned by the commotion. Clearly he now understood some of the damage he'd done so long ago through his stubbornness and jealousy. *Yes, Jaichand: this is the legacy that all such crimes leave . . .*

But the Raja of Kannauj had chosen a new path today, and Vikram respected that.

He felt Sunita stir, and saw her eyes clear. She was staring sideways, at Rasita. 'Is . . . is that *her?*' she gasped. 'Take me to her.'

'I can't move you again, my love,' Vikram whispered. 'The arrow is too deep.' Amanjit heard, though, and he moved Ras closer to the dying actress, as gently as he could. Ras reached for Sunita and took her hand. The two women, the actress and the invalid, hugged each other as their eyes locked. They whispered to each other, then Sunita's eyes lost focus.

And so did Rasita's.

*

'It's not like dying at all . . .' the actress whispered into Rasita's ear. 'I feel like I'm falling into you, like into dark water. It feels like coming home.'

Rasita felt a rush of gentle healing energies flowing into her from Sunita: sharing, joining, soothing. It felt so unfair that she was taking and couldn't give anything in return, except a gift of solace. They both knew the arrow was poisoned, a fatal blow. For Sunita's body, there was no hope.

'I give you my broken pieces, the missing parts that will make us one,' Sunita whispered, lucid in her final moments as Rasita, barely comprehending what was happening, whispered comfort and love.

And then Sunita was gone and Rasita pulled away, her body feeling stronger – *much* stronger, and somehow more *whole*. She imagined she could feel her damaged heart mending itself, and she knew she wasn't imagining feeling her soul swell, as if missing pieces of a puzzle had been found and slotted into place, where they fit perfectly.

Detective Inspector Majid Khan walked away, back into the house, down the blood-slicked stairs to where Shiv Bakli lay. He needed to be alone, to confront himself. The intensity of everything he'd seen play out on the roof above was too much.

He found himself standing over the dead gangster, who was just Shiv Bakli again now: a big man, heavily built and powerful, but no longer the monster he'd been forced to shoot.

A necklace of smoky crystals, with several pieces missing, lay on the floor. He picked the necklace up and pocketed it, then went back to the body and turned it over, looking down into the dead man's face.

So, Shiv Bakli: I outlived you after all, and whatever it was you became. Maybe now I can get my life back, reclaim all the things I lost. Maybe I can learn to be a better man.

He stared down at the vacant face of the gangster and allowed himself a smile. To be free of this overbearing, vicious bully opened up all the possibilities of life once more. It gave him the chance to make amends for all the crimes he'd committed whilst hiding behind his badge.

There was a mirror on the wall. He straightened and glanced into it, flicking a hand to his hair.

And froze as he saw what was staring at him from the glass.

CHAPTER THIRTY-THREE

The Final Arrow

Haryana, 1192

The soldiers came a few hours later and manhandled Chand from his cell, marching him through a maze of marble corridors and ornate gardens – this was evidently some Rajput lord's country house, now temporarily the Mohammedan headquarters as they swept inexorably towards Dilli.

Doors crashed open and they shoved him towards a raised dais. He was dimly aware of many men, soldiers and priests, and before him, a man on a throne. They pushed him to his knees, and when he tried to rise, someone kicked him in the back and he fell on his face. 'Prostrate yourself before his Greatness, dog!' a Turkic soldier hissed in broken Hindi as Chand lay gasping.

'Who is this man, that he interests you so greatly, Mehtan Ali?' asked a richly toned voice from the throne: Muhamed Ghori.

When his vision cleared, Chand looked up and saw a powerfully built man in his early thirties, a warrior in his prime, straight-backed with the majesty of kings sitting lightly on him. He was richly dressed, but simply. His long hair and full beard were combed and gleamed with oil. His spotless white turban was wrapped about a spiked crown. His thin lips were pursed; his fixed eyes showed a single-minded purpose. When he spoke, the entire court went silent, hanging on his every word.

The soldier kicked Chand again. 'Do not look upon the caliph, filth!' he growled, his boot smashing into already broken ribs, and Chand almost blacked out.

'Cease!' Ghori told the man. 'I cannot question a man who cannot speak.' Chand felt the soldier withdraw. He was also suddenly aware that Gauran lay nearby, her head in a pool of her own blood-flecked vomit. Rage kindled in his belly, though he was so weak he could barely move.

'My Lord Caliph, you need not question this man at all. He is only a poet.' The voice was Ravindra's – Mehtan Ali in this life. 'Leave him to me.'

Ghori snorted. 'If he was merely a poet, Mehtan Ali, then you would have no interest in him.'

'He insulted me in parley, that is all.'

'Yet you requested him specifically for that parley, am I not correct?'

Chand heard Mehtan – *Ravindra* – shift uneasily. 'Yes, Lord.'

'Then who is he? And why this girl?'

'He is Chand Bardai, Lord, closest friend of the Chauhan maharaja. The girl is a slave he stole from me.' A note of wheedling entered Ravindra's voice. 'Lord, when I promised you my backing, all I asked was that I be given two prisoners of my choice. These are the two.'

Ghori's reply was haughty. 'This war is fought by the will of God! It is not fought to fulfil the petty aims of priests, however high they have risen! Those I elevate I may also bring low!'

Chand glimpsed his Enemy's discomfort as Ravindra went down on his knees and prostrated himself. 'Master, I overstepped. Forgive me.' Chand heard the suppressed rage in the man's voice. Did Ghori? Ravindra could no doubt have slaughtered half the warriors in this room – but the other half would kill him. Even sorcerers had to bend the knee to secular powers at times.

Chand was aware of a faint stirring, as if a great many here were desirous of seeing 'Mehtan Ali' taken down a peg or two.

Ghori looked down steadily at the huge 'priest'. 'It may please me to do as you ask, however. Your service has been great,' he acknowledged. The caliph shifted his gaze to study Chand again. 'Are you truly Chand Bardai, friend of Prithviraj Chauhan, as claimed?'

'I am, Lord,' Chand replied, staring at a point beneath the caliph's feet.

'Who are you to have earned the enmity of my counsellor Mehtan Ali, poet?'

'My Lord—' Ravindra sounded alarmed.

Chand sensed an opportunity and spoke over his Enemy. 'Lord, he is a sorcerer and a murderer who has lived for centuries. He is no more a Mohammedan than I, but he is steeped in evil and lies.'

The entire court went quiet.

Then Ghori laughed, and his court joined in, though many threw Ravindra speculative looks. Ravindra joined in the mirth uneasily, though his eyes burned into Chand, promising revenge. Finally Ghori signalled for silence. 'You are a poet indeed: a superstitious fantasist. A fitting friend for a dreamer-king like Prithviraj.' He turned to an aide. 'Bring out the Chauhan.'

Chand felt as if his blood had clogged in his body. *Prithvi is here? He's alive?*

He watched as a broken figure shambled out, limping, hunched. He was blindfolded and the guards prodded him along with their spear-butts, stopping him a few feet from Chand and pushing him to his knees.

'Prithvi?' he whispered. *Oh Gods, what game are you playing with us?*

The nearest soldier tore the blindfold from the maharaja's eyes. Not that it allowed him to see: someone had burned out his eyes.

The court erupted with laughter and Chand watched helplessly as his friend cowered from the humiliation and pain. Fury enveloped him, lending him the strength he needed. Whilst everyone in the hall mocked their fallen enemy, he climbed to his feet and embraced his king. 'Prithvi, it's Chand. I'm here.'

His friend went utterly still. 'Chand?'

'Dear, beloved Prithvi. It's me.'

'I prayed that you escaped, but the gods have abandoned us, Chand.'

'Never. Stand, my friend. It is better to die on your feet,' he whispered, then hauled his blinded friend to his feet. He felt a surge of renewed pride, a defiant sense that they had fallen so far now that all that was left was to regain dignity. You couldn't do that on your knees.

The court fell silent at this disrespect, this rebellion, and the guards moved in. Ghori raised a hand. 'Stay!' he told the guardsmen, peering at Chand and his companions with narrowed eyes. 'Let the Chauhan stand.'

Chand acknowledged the leniency with a bow, then turned to Gauran. 'Dear wife, please stand at my side.' He scarcely hoped she would hear and understand, but somehow, his words got through and she moved. He reached down, pulled her upright, and Gauran was suddenly a woman again, despite the filth and disarray. 'Well done, my love.'

She met his eyes and something sparkled dimly there that threatened to break his heart all over again.

I should never have taken you in. I'm so sorry. Unable to look at her again, he turned back to the caliph. 'Caliph Ghori, may I speak?'

He saw Ravindra scowl, but Ghori controlled this court and

the caliph was interested, sensing something mysterious at work here. 'Yes, poet, you may speak.'

Chand looked about him, trying to measure the gathering, to see the differences, the contentions. Soldiers and priests. Old and young. Fanatics and pragmatists. Surely there were factions; there always were – but he had no time. He could only guess at them. There were no friendly eyes, just mockery and hatred. There was no hope. There was no escape. There were only different ways to die.

He found his voice. 'Lord Ghori, I thank you. Yes, I would speak. I would speak of my dearest friend, of the greatest friend a man could ever have: Prithviraj Chauhan. My king. My life. A man who bestrode this world as a giant: a man of great dreams and great accomplishments. A man whose personal prowess in love and war is unmatched, the greatest warrior of this age, the true summit of Rajputana.

'He is the only man to bring defeat upon your mighty self, and he is now brought low by fate and conspiracy, by forces greater than us all.

'My Lord Ghori, it brings you no honour to humiliate and mutilate such a man. Enemy to you he may be, but war is war: it has a beginning and an end. To make war on the defeated is beneath you. An honourable man deserves an honourable death. And this man deserves even more.

'Prithviraj Chauhan was Master of the horse! Master of the blade! Master of men! Master of the council chamber and the bedchamber! He was Master even of *shabd bhedi baan vidya!* He was incomparable.'

He stared about the room defiantly, amazed to see slow, wary gestures of approval, even some accusing stares at Ravindra. Chand knew who had ordered the blinding of the king.

'Well spoken, poet,' Ghori said, after taking the measure of the room. He looked at Chand for a long moment and Chand stared back into those steely eyes and planted a thought there. Ghori stroked his beard, and then asked, just as Chand had wished him to, 'What is this *shabd bhedi baan vidya* you speak of?'

'The art of archery using only sound to guide your aim, Lord.'

Ghori raised an eyebrow. 'You claim he can do this?'

'Lord—' Ravindra tried to put in.

'Silence, Mehtan Ali! I have not commanded you to speak!' Ghori's voice was thunder. He turned back to Chand. 'Well? Can he?'

'Yes, Lord. He can.' He glanced at Prithvi, who had gone totally still. 'He can.'

Can you still do it, Prithvi?

Ghori clapped his hands. 'This I would see.'

The caliph cleared his court, everyone, including Ghori himself, retiring to the balconies overlooking the chamber. Chand heard Mehtan trying to remonstrate and once again being angrily silenced. They left only Prithvi and Chand below. Gauran they took with them, and placed her alone near the northern corner of the balcony, where her stink would not offend her captors' noses. All along the balcony, Turkic archers watched, their own bows strung and ready. There were at least forty of them.

At Chand's instruction, they strung crockery plates in four places about the courtyard. Prithvi was handed a Turkic bow and four blunted arrows. Chand walked Prithvi to the centre of the courtyard and placed the four arrows in a quiver at his feet.

'Behold, Lord Ghori. The king is blind.' He turned Prithvi around and about. 'I spin him, to disorientate. The sun is gone. There is no heat to guide him. Sound alone must direct his aim.'

'Chand, I haven't done this for years,' Prithvi hissed in his ear. 'And I've never hit more than one.'

'Then roll back those years, Brother. Our past is finite and our future almost spent. Let your last shots be how you are remembered. Let them be glorious.'

Prithvi stroked his face. 'Thank you, Chand. For this moment. For Sanyogita. And everything else. You have been true and loyal, when so few others have. You are my one true friend.'

'It has been my privilege to serve you,' he replied, inadequate words when so much had been left unsaid. *For the years I have envied you, resented you, lusted after your wife – please forgive me*, he wished he could say. *And for what I did to Shastri and Darya, may I one day find the courage to confess it, and be forgiven.*

There was no time now for such words. If he was truly to find forgiveness, then that would have to await other days in other lives.

'Let no one speak,' Chand said aloud to the court. 'Let no sound distract him.' He tapped Prithvi on the shoulder. 'Prepare, my king. Prepare.'

'Do not speak, I beg you, my Lord,' he heard Ravindra exhort Ghori. 'He will mark your position.'

'Thank you for revealing your own, Mehtan,' laughed Prithvi, suddenly himself, as if the feel of a bow in his hand had restored him. The caliph's court guffawed as Ravindra flinched.

Chand walked to the first plate. 'Silence!' he called, then he tapped the plate and stepped away.

Prithvi whirled and fired.

The plate shattered and the watching crowds erupted, for to hit even once was a great feat. They reluctantly fell silent again as Ghori raised a hand, leaning forward with his face alight with curiosity. One hit could, after all, be a fluke . . .

Chand picked up the arrow and walked to the next plate. He tapped and moved.

Thwack. Smash!

An excited buzz of noise swirled above. He could see Ravindra scowling, flexing his hands, wondering how to regain control. Bending, Chand picked up the second arrow and walked on, back the other way, to the opposite side. 'Quiet, please, my Lords,' he called, giving Prithvi his clue as to where the next target was. He saw his friend adjust slightly as he nocked the third arrow.

Tap.

The third arrow smashed the third plate, and now the court cheered lustily. The archers above licked their lips in admiration. Ghori was entranced, and Ravindra simmered as Chand walked to the final plate.

Tap. *SMASH!*

All about them, the watching soldiers whistled and stamped, marvelling. The archers rattled their weapons against the balcony, their mouths open. Even Gauran was smiling in a dreamy way, as if this display had somehow penetrated the layers of illusion she had wrapped about herself. He saw her mouth moving and heard her begin to sing softly. He recognised the song, one of his own.

Only Ravindra didn't applaud. He leaned over the railing with fire in his eyes, as if at any moment he would spit venom.

Prithvi bowed to all corners. Chand walked towards him, a smile spread all over his face. 'Well done, my friend. Perfect. Utterly perfect.' He took the bow from his king's hand, blinking away tears. 'Goodbye, my king.'

'Farewell, Chand. Until next time.'

Chand whirled, the first arrow nocked, the ancient words welling from his lips. It had been too long since he'd done this, so mired had he been in the twin drugs of Gauran's soul and composing the *Prithvi-raj Raso*, but the powers he'd let congeal inside him flowed one last time at his call. His first arrow burst into flames as it struck Ravindra in the breast and his chest exploded.

The massive man fell out of sight as people shouted and staggered away.

The second shaft took Gauran in the heart. Her song choked in her throat, her eyes flying wide. *Goodbye, Padma. I couldn't let them have you.* She staggered, clutched the shaft, and fell.

An arrow from above rattled on the stones at his feet and pinged away. His third arrow flew.

With a hoarse cry, a young Turkic nobleman threw himself in front of Ghori. The burning agniyastra tore the youth's chest apart. Chand cursed, nocking his final arrow.

Something slammed into his back, staggering him. Looking up he glimpsed the blur of arrows sleeting down. Three struck Prithvi in thigh, belly and back. The maharaja roared in defiance, spreading wide his arms as a dozen more shots mowed him down. Chand could still hear Gauran's song. The gods were singing it, their terrible eyes burning into him. A shaft slammed into his shoulder and spun him. Another speared his chest, and his breath turned to blood. He coughed once as a hailstorm of shafts struck him, beating him to his knees. His final arrow slipped from hands suddenly gone numb.

As if in a dream, he saw Ravindra reappear at the balcony, his chest rent, his eyes aflame. He howled in hatred, his eyes burning into Chand. Then the arrow-storm struck him too, and he fell, his face an image of shocked fury: unmasked, thwarted.

The blood-slicked floor of the chamber rose and smashed into Chand's face. He turned from Ravindra's burning eyes and gazed at Prithvi's lifeless ones as all light dimmed and went out.

CHAPTER THIRTY-FOUR

Clean-Up Crew

Mumbai, 13 November 2010

Policemen entered the mansion cautiously. It was filled with smoke, and they could see wreckage and corpses all over the garden. Those of Bakli's men still living had fled and an eerie silence now hung about the vast lobby. The shattered body of a woman lay in the middle of the stairwell, an arrow protruding from her eye. They shuddered as one, despite their years of experience.

Slowly they worked their way upwards, movements coordinated as they covered and protected each other, but all was silent and still. At the top of the stairwell, they found Detective Inspector Majid Khan, gazing thoughtfully into a mirror. His right hand held a gun, his left was fingering a necklace, which he stuffed into his pocket. He turned as the first of the squad saw him and raised a finger to his lips. 'Hush!' The inspector pointed upwards. 'They're on the roof.'

The squad closed in, guns swivelling. They took in the half-naked dead man sprawled in the doorway, riddled with bullets. Majid smiled. 'Yes, Shiv Bakli is dead.'

'Then who's up there?'

'Criminals,' the detective replied. 'They've murdered Sunita Ashoka.'

The policemen gaped and glanced at each other. 'Then what are our orders?'

'Capture them. They're armed.' He readied his gun. 'Let's go!'

Vikram knelt over Deepika, monitoring her fluttering pulse. Abruptly he pulled the smoky heart-stone from his pocket and slipped it inside her top, against her heart. 'Live, Darya. *Live!*'

Did he imagine her breath becoming stronger?

Tanvir smoothed his bandana and walked to the door, saying something about finding Majid Khan. *Tilak . . . and Govinda, too*: it was obvious when you knew what to look for. Miraculously, Rasita was sitting up, hugging Amanjit, though her eyes strayed constantly to Vikram, as did his to her.

She's Padma now, whole and complete. Healed, perhaps? What does this mean . . . for her, for me? For us all?

Vikram suddenly remembered Amanjit's kirpan, which he'd jammed into his belt after releasing the spell that had made it temporarily a sword. He tossed it to Amanjit. 'You dropped this, bhai.'

Amanjit caught it wordlessly, and inclined his head in thanks.

Tanvir opened the door and stepped into the stairwell, then in a sudden crackle of gunfire, he spun like a top, roaring in pain, and staggered away from the door. He fell across Deepika, grabbing at her blindly, gritting his teeth against the pain, his shoulder bloodied. Rasita screamed and Amanjit bellowed in alarm. Vikram leaped up and kicked the door shut, but seconds later it exploded in splinters from a hail of bullets.

Then Majid Khan's voice rang out: 'Vikram Khandavani, we are here to arrest you for the murder of Sunita Ashoka. Surrender, or die!'

'Jaichand, you bastard!' Vikram heard himself bellow. Amanjit snarled, gripping his sword, stepping in front of Deepika with hopeless desperation in his eyes.

Harsh laughter echoed. 'They're insane,' Majid Khan told his men. 'Insane criminals. Move in!'

Vikram turned, barely troubling to aim, and fired a shot out towards central Mumbai. The arrow flew – and stopped a foot away from the bow, hovering immobile in the air. 'Amanjit, it's a musafir-astra,' Vikram told him urgently. 'A traveller's arrow; I invented it myself. You just hold on to it – it's like the arrow I used at the Mehrangarh earlier this year, remember? Take Ras and go!'

Amanjit hesitated. 'But Deepika——! And Ras hasn't got the strength to—'

'Ras will be fine, and we'll take care of Deepika! Go, dammit!' Vikram shoved Amanjit at the suspended arrow, then looked at Ras. 'Hold on to him,' he told her, then whispered in her ear. 'We need a rendezvous: first of March, in Udaipur!' That was months away, but he'd need that time for what he had in mind. He almost lost himself in Rasita's eyes: *She's Padma . . . and Sunita . . . and Gauran . . . and yet, she's still Ras . . .*

He groped for words, but she understood. 'I remember everything,' she whispered, her voice awed. 'Every life!' Then she wrapped her arms around her brother as Amanjit grasped the arrow in both hands. With a lurch it moved, following the same trajectory it had been shot, pulling them off their feet. They went slowly at first, then they cleared the roof and soared into the night sky, dangling with legs kicking, desperately hanging on. Within seconds they were lost in the darkness.

Tanvir gaped up at Vikram, one bloody hand holding his shoulder. '*Who are you?*' he whispered. From the stairs came the sound of stealthy movement.

Vikram looked down at the undercover cop, and Deepika

beside him. *There's no time.* He bit his lip. *He's Tilak, and Govinda — I can trust him, but Til always dies earlier than us, life after life . . .* He made up his mind. *I can't stay here.*

'You must get her to hospital, Tilak. You must save her.' Vikram spun and shot another arrow in a different direction, towards the city. It too halted, poised in midair. Tanvir nodded, despite the puzzled look on his face at the name 'Tilak'. He cradled the girl protectively.

A policeman appeared at the door, aiming his gun but not yet firing. Another followed. 'Freeze! Put your hands up! Drop the bow!' Then they saw the arrow, and gaped. Behind them, Majid Khan was framed in the doorway, taking aim.

Vikram put his hands up.

And grasped the arrow.

The cops stared open-mouthed as he lifted away from them. Two shots flew wide: the inspector was the only person firing.

In seconds he was nothing but a black spot far away in the darker sky.

EPILOGUE

Present

Mumbai, November 2010

Tanvir wouldn't let anyone else get near the stricken Deepika Choudhary, despite his own wounds, until the medics arrived. He was sure she would die – but inside her sequinned top there was a pendant of some sort, a gemstone that pulsed to her heartbeat, and if he didn't believe in magic before, he surely did now.

In particular, he kept Majid Khan away. He no longer knew the man. He was someone else, possessed, rabid and very dangerous – but Tanvir refused to cower from him. When their eyes met, he let whatever was lurking inside Majid's head know that if anyone tried to harm the girl, he would die, and there were enough straight cops in their unit close by that Majid backed down.

Somehow, Deepika survived the trip to hospital and the emergency treatments to counter the snake venom. Tanvir stayed with her in the ward all night, allowing a doctor to perform field surgery on his shoulder, removing a bullet and bandaging him up. He'd managed to call a Narcotics Bureau commander he knew to be clean and had Majid Khan suspended on suspicion of corruption. At the moment, the only important thing was to protect the girl, and that meant ensuring Majid couldn't simply walk in here and take over. He didn't quite know why he was doing this, but he didn't question it.

In the morning, Deepika woke him. 'Tilak,' she called him — that strangely antiquated and somehow apt name, the same one Vikram Khandavani had used. 'Tilak, wake up.'

Sunlight was streaming through the windows, and a nurse was putting a tray of food and a newspaper on the table. He pulled the paper open, taking in the lurid headlines.

SWAYAMVARA FARCE TURNS TO TRAGEDY!
VIKRAM MURDERS SUNITA!
SHIV BAKLI DIES IN CARNAGE AT
GANGSTER PALACE!
SUNITA'S KILLER ELUDES POLICE!

Every story for the first twelve pages dealt with the débâcle from every conceivable angle, including kidnapping, drug lords, blood and death. It was the biggest story for years, the reporters drooled. The journalists didn't know whether to mourn or run amok, so they did both. But for all the column inches, there were few solid facts. None mentioned the strange collection of antique and modern weapons at the crime scene. None mentioned Deepika Choudhary. Majid Khan was being trumpeted as a hero, praised for his courage and effectiveness, so presumably his suspension had been kept quiet.

But Sunita's death dominated everything. The country was in shock, and seething with fury. Already three young men who looked a bit like Vikram Khandavani had been lynched in different parts of Mumbai. The nation wept, and swore vengeance.

'It's just like the *Ramayana*, you know,' Deepika told him. 'Rama, Lakshmana and Sita, exiled from Ayodhya.'

Tanvir stared at her. 'The *Ramayana*?'

She went on matter-of-factly, 'We all knew, though we tried to deny it. Vikram, Amanjit and Rasita have fled into exile. It's the *Ramayana*, reaching out, moulding who we are.' She held up a pulsing gemstone in her fist, and sighed. 'Again and again and again.' Then she met his eyes. 'But maybe not for ever.'

Uma lay on the couch where Sunita used to lie and contemplated whether there was any real point in going on. Vishi Ashoka was letting her stay in the apartment, for now at least, but without her Sunni, what was there to live for?

Time and again she relived that awful night: the bizarre madness that had swept over Sunita, her sudden infatuation with Vikram, the two of them running off into the night, leaving the crew to cobble together a farcical finale that in the end had fooled no one. And to what purpose? Vikram had killed her, or so the police said.

Uma had seen enough of the world not to believe what the police – or the media – said. There were too many unanswered questions. How could there possibly be a connection between Shiv Bakli and Sunita and Vikram? Who was this Majid Khan? Why had Sunita died of a *poisoned arrow*? Where were Vikram and Amanjit? And that was just for starters.

Every time she thought of Vikram, she wanted to hate him for stealing Sunita away, but when she remembered his manner, and the way Sunita was with him, she couldn't bring herself to believe he'd killed her. She got no answers from the policemen who questioned her, so contemptuous of a ladyman. None of the Ashoka family really wanted to know her any more, especially when there was a massive fortune to be fought over. Pravit was even claiming Sunita had secretly married him before the finale. The assets were already paralysed, and Sunita's will would certainly be challenged.

Which means everything Sunita left me will come to nothing, and I'll be left to start again.

Tears welled up in her eyes. Then her phone rang: an unknown number. She almost rejected the call, but in the end she answered cautiously, 'Hello?'

A girlish voice spoke, full of suppressed excitement. 'Uma? Is that you?'

Uma sat up, feeling disoriented. 'Uma speaking. Who is this?'

'It's me, Uma. It's Sunni.'

Her heart almost burst – and at the same time, logic told her this couldn't possibly be real.

'Don't believe the lies, Uma,' the voice went on. 'It wasn't me who died. I'm okay – I'm *better* than okay. But I don't look the same any more. I have a new face, and a new name.' The voice slowed, and a more adult inflection entered it. 'I will come back to you: I swear it. We'll be together again.'

Uma felt tears running down her cheeks.

This is insane – just a cruel joke!

But it just might be true . . .

'How will I know you, Sunni?'

'Front page, darling.' The tones were pure Sunita, and that alone convinced Uma that this was no evil prank. 'I'm on the front page, as always. Today's *Hindustan Times*, bottom right.' Something bleeped. 'Sorry, Uma, time's up. They're tracing calls. I have to go.' The connection went dead.

Uma sat up, not knowing what to think. Finally, she went to the newspapers that had been thrown unread across the living room floor and found the front page of the *Hindustan Times*. Sunita's face covered it, apart from the bottom right, a story about 'India's New Most Wanted': pictures of Vikram, and a schoolgirl with an angular Punjabi face and big eyes.

The name beneath the photo said *Rasita Kaur Bajaj*.

Uma sank to the floor and hugged the tiny black and white image to her heart.

EPILOGUE

Past

Prince Kola opened the gates of Dilli to the invader and was allowed by Muhamed Ghori to live out his lifetime as a subservient, powerless vassal. When he died, so did the Chauhamanas line. Dilli became a Muslim prize and the Delhi Sultanate, presaging the Mughal Era, commenced. Muslim rule of North India had begun, and would endure until it was ended by the British, half a millennium later.

Jaichand Rathod of Kannauj gained nothing from his refusal to aid his old rival against the invaders. Ghori turned on him next, routing his army at Chandvar in 1194 and driving him from Kannauj. He fled to the Kumaon Hills in modern Uttarakhand, and his descendants resisted Muslim attacks for many centuries, until they finally gained a favourable peace.

By then Muhamed Ghori was long dead. After the defeat of Prithviraj Chauhan in 1192, he followed up by sacking Ayodhya, the legendary realm of Rama and his line, and occupying Dilli. He never quite subdued the Bengalis, despite victories over Lakshman Sen, the Raja of Bengal. He was assassinated at Jhelum, in modern-day Pakistan in 1206, after putting down a rebellion in the Punjab. He was forty-four years old.

The *Prithvi-raj Raso*, begun by Chand Bardai, was embellished and added to by his son Jalhan, as well as succeeding generations of poets and scholars, layering legend upon legend as it was and passed down through time. Prithviraj Chauhan, the larger-than-life warrior, the romantic and tragic maharaja, remains a hero of India to this day.

Forty-two years after the death of Prithviraj Chauhan, a small, skinny scholar was permitted to peruse the effects of Kamla Bardai on the death of that ancient grand-dame in Pushkar. His name was Kirat, but in his heart he called himself Aramchand. He found the precious book quickly, and kissed the battered cover of the journal of Aram Dhoop fervently. But Padma's heart-stone was gone.

END OF BOOK TWO

The Return of Ravana
continues with
Book 3

'THE EXILE'

Glossary

26/11   On 26 November 2008, a number of coordinated Islamic terrorist attacks took place in Mumbai, India, killing 164 people (including 28 foreign nationals) and wounding more than 300. The best-known incident was when gunmen entered the Taj Palace Hotel and indiscriminately killed guests and staff, before being trapped and killed by the Indian National Security Guard.

agniyastra   A magic fire-arrow; see also 'astra' and 'musafir-astra'.

apsara   A female divine being of Hindu mythology. They are associated with water, and are usually found in the halls of gods, tending fallen heroes.

areca nut   A nut commonly chewed in Asia and parts of east Africa as a mild stimulant. Sometimes known as a betel nut, because it is usually wrapped in betel leaves. Areca nuts are also used in Ayurvedic medicine.

ashram   A place of spiritual hermitage, usually
                associated with yoga, but also with music
                and other studies or arts.

astra   A magic arrow.

asura   A 'demon' of Hindu mythology, usually
                portrayed as being a blend of man and
                beast, often with some magical power.
                Though termed a 'demon', not all are evil.

bhai   Brother (a term used between male sib-
                lings and sometimes by friends).

chai   Indian tea (the drink).

chapatti   Indian flatbread.

daal makhani   Indian curried lentil dish.

dhaba   A small family restaurant/road-house.

dupatta   A woman's long scarf, traditionally used to
                cover the face for modesty and protection
                from the sun.

ghagra   A woman's outfit (in northern India).

gurukul   A residential school, usually with a guru
                (a sage-teacher) living alongside the
                students.

howdah   A carriage carried on top of an elephant.

imam   A spiritual leader in a Muslim community.

jadugara   A wizard.

jauhar   The self-immolation of Rajput queens and
                other female royals when facing defeat at
                the hands of an enemy.

jhuggi   A slum zone in a Hindu city.

ji   A form of address approximately meaning
                'revered one' or 'sir'. It has a connotation
                of holiness.

kirpan	The traditional dagger of a Sikh warrior, one of five articles of faith required to be worn by Sikhs.
kurta	A long, knee-length overshirt.
moksha	The State of Grace that Hindus seek to attain, whereby they become as one with God, leave the cycle of reincarnation and ascend to Paradise.
musafir-astra	A magic arrow known as a 'travelling arrow'.
Namaskar	A greeting (like 'Namaste' but a little more formal).
Nautch-girls	Dancing girls.
NRIs	Non-Resident Indians, ex-pat Indians living overseas.
odhani	A gauzy veil traditionally worn by Indian women.
paan	A concoction of betel nuts, betel leaves and spices, chewed as a mild stimulant by many Indians.
pani	The Hindi word for water.
Partition	The splitting of India into India, West Pakistan and East Pakistan (later Bangladesh), which took place after the Second World War.
punkah-wallah	A servant who wields a large fan to keep their employer cool.
purohit	A Hindu priest; also known as a pandit.
rakshasa	A demon with magical powers. They are not necessarily evil.
sahib	A Hindi form of address equivalent to 'sir'.

sati   The now-illegal practice of burning the widow of a man on his funeral pyre. It is derived from the legends surrounding the god Shiva, and was prevalent in parts of India until the nineteenth century.

talwar   An Indian curved sword.

Acknowledgements

With thanks once more to:

Jo Fletcher for her faith in this series.

To Mike Bryan and Heather Adams for their role in its creation: never let it be said that nothing creative has ever come out of a hospitality tent at the polo in New Delhi!

And of course, thank you to my wonderful wife Kerry for the adventure that is being married. This revision was penned in our new (temporary) home of Bangkok, Thailand, as we begin another posting in foreign climes. But no matter where we go, the best part of the trip is being with you.

Author's Note

Prithviraj Chauhan died in 1192. Sources differ over whether he died in battle or was executed as a prisoner of the Muslim conqueror Muhamed Ghori. What does appear certain is that the version given in the sixteenth-century literary work *Prithvi-raj Raso* is untrue. In that epic poem, he and Chand are given a fantastical but implausible death: the two prisoners trick Ghori into allowing them to compete in an archery contest. Guided by Chand's words, the blinded Prithviraj shoots Ghori dead, and then the two of them are shot down, like Butch Cassidy and the Sundance Kid, in a hail of arrows. Inconveniently, there are reliable records of Ghori surviving well after this 'event' — but it is too good a story to just ignore, so I had to use it somehow!

Chand Bardai himself may not even have existed: he may be nothing but a literary construct — a 'person' created by the later writers of *Prithvi-raj Raso* to give a voice to history. John Keay, in *India: A History,* seems to have thought so. But when looking for a poet-character to represent Aram Dhoop's spirit in this story, Chand was irresistible. As for Sanyogita (or Samyukta, as she is also known), she did indeed commit ritual suicide to avoid falling into the hands of the conqueror.

The numbers of soldiers present on either side at Prithviraj and

Ghori's second battle at Tarain is a matter of conjecture. Most sources put Ghori's forces at about 120,000, but Prithviraj's army has been tallied at anywhere up to 2,000,000, a completely improbable number. The size of classical and mediaeval armies listed in old texts are often impossibly high, hugely exaggerated by time and distance from the actual events. I've gone for a conservative 400,000 for the Rajput forces, which would be more in line with contemporary forces of the age.

I am a New Zealander who had the privilege to live in India between 2007 and 2010. India is an incredible and vibrant country, and *The Return of Ravana* series is a gift in exchange for the joy of having been able to live there for a time. The books in the series are fiction, loosely rooted in myth and history. I hope you enjoy them for what they are: entertainment, and a little insight into the things that I found most striking about a rich and intoxicating country.

I'd like to thank the good people at Penguin India for their faith and guidance in letting this Kiwi write an Indian story in his own way; and Jo Fletcher and Jo Fletcher Books for taking on the task of republishing the series, and revitalising it as we take it to a larger audience.

I'd also like to thank my arbiter on all matters of content and good taste, my wondrous wife Kerry, who, as always, edited and provided the very best in feedback and suggestions. I couldn't do this writing gig without her.

David Hair
India, New Zealand and Bangkok